MINERVA LANE

At Minerva Lane Matthew saw Ruby as far as the backyard gate of number 11.

"I suppose I'd best say goodnight to you out here," he said after he'd kissed her. "I don't think I ought to come in the house, do you." It was a statement more than a question.

Ruby stood on tiptoe with her arms round his neck and hugged him. She loved Matthew so dearly; she wanted to reassure him of that, even though their evening had been ruined. But just as she started to speak, a sudden commotion broke out, sounding like a boy's yells followed by the shout of angry words, coming from the open bedroom window.

"That's Jack having trouble wi' our Joe again," she said, pulling away. "I'll have to go—"

The moment for reassurance was lost. Dragging her shawl from her shoulders she ran inside the yard and shut the gate, leaving Matthew standing in the moonlight. Until a few weeks ago, she would have said, 'That's our Joe in trouble wi' Jack again.'

A subtle difference; and it betrayed how far her loyalties had altered.

*Also by the same author,
and available from Coronet:*

**The Stallion Man
Sisters and Brothers
To Everything a Season
Birds in a Gilded Cage
The Imagination of the Heart
Tiger Lilies
Mirabelle**

About the author

Judith Glover is the author of seven powerful romantic novels including most recently *Tiger Lilies* and *Mirabelle*.

She was born and bred in Wolverhampton and feels a deep affinity for the town's historic character which is reflected in her Black Country novels.

Minerva Lane

Judith Glover

CORONET BOOKS
Hodder and Stoughton

First published in Great Britain in 1993
by Hodder & Stoughton
A division of Hodder Headline PLC

A Coronet paperback

10 9 8 7 6 5 4 3 2 1

ISBN 0 340 60991 5

Typeset by Keyboard Services, Luton, Beds

Printed and bound in Great Britain by
Cox & Wyman Ltd, Reading, Berks

Hodder and Stoughton
A division of Hodder Headline PLC
338 Euston Road
London NW1 3BH

Minerva Lane

The boy lay shuddering in his unconscious state, his pale, pinched face only inches from the boots of the children gathered round him. They stood looking on in fascinated silence until he was quiet at last, and then with the indifference of the very young they left him lying in the grass and went back to playing their interrupted game.

Only one little girl stayed behind, her thumb in her mouth. After a while she crouched beside the boy and started poking at him with a stick; and when he still didn't move she got to her feet and trotted off along the path to an arch leading into a cobblestoned yard stacked with barrels.

From an open door at the other side of the yard sounds of laughter and loud drunken voices spilled into the April evening. Earlier today Lizzie Gallimore had married her lodger, Jack McShane, and many of their neighbours from the closely-knit community of Minerva Lane had packed into the saloon bar of the Harp to help the couple celebrate their wedding.

While the small child stood uncertainly, an older girl came out through the door, glancing back over her shoulder with a smile for someone behind.

The child recognised her. Taking the thumb from her

mouth she piped up, "Ruby – oh, Ruby come quick, your Joe's fell down and he wo' shift!"

The smile vanished from Ruby Gallimore's young, pretty face. "Where is he, Pru?" she asked, instantly anxious.

The little girl turned and pointed.

Taking her by the hand, Ruby hurried with her through the archway back into the garden where the children were running about at their game of tag. Her brother Joe was still where he'd fallen, lying with an arm thrown up to cover his face, his legs pathetically spindly in their polished, too-big boots.

She flung herself on her knees to examine him, her tawny-coloured hair spilling forward in heavy, loose waves. A young man who had followed her out of the yard came and knelt at the boy's other side.

"What's happened here?" he asked her, concerned. "Another of his turns?"

Ruby thrust the hair from her face. "Aye, looks like it, but I think he'll be all right. He hasn't hurt himself." She raised her brother's head, supporting it gently against the small, soft curve of her breast.

"Here, let me take him–" Matthew Dyson eased Joe from her and got up, cradling the limp body in his arms. "He ought to be in bed, it'll be better than here wi' all this racket. The excitement's probably been too much for him, what wi' the wedding and everything."

She nodded. Then, jumping to her feet she said, "I'd best run inside and tell our Mother first. You go on wi' him, Matt, and I'll follow as quick as I can."

Catching up the long skirt of her green plaid dress, the

fifteen-year-old girl darted back into the yard and through the door, to the crowded saloon at the far end of the passage. A setting sun pierced the haze of pipe smoke in the room with shafts of ruddy light that dulled the sallow flare of the gas jets and silhouetted the bonneted heads of the wedding party sitting at a table in the window.

Ruby elbowed her way over. Her mother Lizzie was leaning against the burly shoulder of her bridegroom Jack McShane, both of them flushed with the amount of drink they'd had in celebration. Lizzie's face wore a happily stupid expression, and when Ruby managed to push through to the table she gave the girl an unfocused squint before greeting her with a smile that for a moment lent her fading prettiness something of its former beauty.

"Hallo, here's Ruby! Come to sit wi' your Mam, have you?" she cried, patting the bench. "Come to gi' your new Dad a kiss?"

"Mam, I can't stop," Ruby said urgently. "I'm just off home wi' our Joe – he's been took poorly."

"Eh? Eh, what you say?"

She repeated herself louder.

"Our Joe's took poorly?" Lizzie struggled to collect her fuddled wits. "Oh, he hasn't had one of his faints, has he, Ruby?"

"Now there's no need to worry yourself, Mam. Matthew and me will look after him."

"I'd best come on home." Clutching Jack McShane's arm, Lizzie tried to get up.

"Let the lad be," said Jack, pulling her down again.

"But you heard our Ruby–"

"Let him be, Lizzie! It's your wedding day an' you ain't

3

finished enjoying it yet." Her bridegroom grappled her affectionately, showing the burst seam of his jacket armhole. He was a big man, a furniture remover by trade, with coarsely handsome features dashingly set off by a black moustache and side-whiskers. "Ruby's a capable wench. Her'll take care o' Joe, so stop your fretting."

He winked at his new stepdaughter, and she gave him a brilliant smile in return before pushing her way out again to the door.

Leaving the Harp, Ruby ran down Walsall Street in pursuit of Matthew Dyson and managed to catch up with him and Joe before they reached Minerva Lane. By now the sun had disappeared behind the roofs of tenements and factories and a grape-coloured April dusk was beginning to thicken in the narrow streets.

Minerva Lane lay in one of the poorest areas of Wolverhampton. Bordered on one side by the canal and the railway, and on the other by the Bridge Iron Foundry and the brickworks, it contained a row of shabby terraced cottages at its bottom end which housed a dozen or so families including the Gallimores and the Dysons. Not far away, occupying what had formerly been the municipal workhouse, was Chubb's Lock Manufactory where eighteen-year-old Matthew worked as an apprentice.

He and Ruby Gallimore had been close friends from childhood, attending the same Board School in Walsall Street where young Joe was now a pupil. They had made no secret of their strong attachment and the bond of loyalty they shared. Since turning thirteen Ruby had been employed in domestic service, and in that time there'd been other apprentices and errand boys wanting to walk out with her, but she'd never said yes to any of them – though she teased them a good deal for their boldness.

It was the same tale with Matthew: for him, no other girl in the world could so much as hold a candle to his sweetheart. Being a well set-up, nice-looking young fellow, Matt was just the type to catch the female eye, nor did he drink (his people were strongly Chapel) which favoured him even further, since a man who didn't squander his wages on beer was better capable of providing for a wife and family. Several young women at his workplace had already shown a forward interest in him, but he'd given his heart to the tawny-haired, green-eyed girl from Minerva Lane.

"I'll put the kettle on the hob for a pot of tea for us," Ruby said, pushing open the yard door so that Matthew could carry Joe inside. The boy had started regaining consciousness during the walk back from the Harp and was now in that lethargic, mumbling, drowsy state which always followed a seizure.

After Jack McShane had come to rent the Gallimores' back bedroom six months earlier, Joe's little bed had been brought downstairs to a corner of the kitchen out of the way beside the wooden dresser.

"There, young 'un, now just you settle yourself down for a good nap," Matthew told him, removing the boy's boots and covering him over with the blanket, "and when you wake you'll be feeling right as a trivet again."

Joe murmured something, but his mauve-tinged lids were already fluttering. In another few minutes his breathing had quietened, becoming slow and regular as he fell into a healthy sleep.

Matthew sat at the end of the bed watching Ruby move about the kitchen putting a match to the fire in the black-leaded range, and lighting the single gasolier. This was a much poorer home than his own at the opposite end of the row, the difference showing in its furnishings, not in its standard of cleanliness, for Mrs Gallimore kept the place scrubbed and spotless with her daughter's help. But she'd been a widow these past three years – her husband died in 1882 – and the money she earned serving beer at the Harp was only enough to provide the bare essentials. In Matthew's house the floors were covered with squares of drugget carpet, but the Gallimores had only pegged-rag mats to hide the wooden boards; and at the kitchen window where Agnes Dyson had curtains, Lizzie Gallimore could only afford a piece of ecru netting on a cane.

"It's going to make a lot of difference round the place now your Mam's got a man's wage coming in again," he remarked. "More of a difference than what she's been able to make letting lodgings. Mr McShane's got a good steady job working for that Fred Ingram, the sort of job that pays well an' all."

"Aye, I'm hoping there's better times ahead for us now." Ruby gave him a smile as she went to the dresser for something. "Our Mother's happy at any rate, and that's the main thing. I can't tell you the change it's made in her, having a man round the house to show her a bit of attention. She missed our Dad..."

"I know. I could see it in her face." Matthew glanced again at young Joe, then got to his feet. "Still, she did her best for him, Ruby. If the doctor with all his skill couldn't save your Dad, I don't know what more your mother could have done."

There was silence while they each remembered Charlie Gallimore, one of the cheeriest, most happy-go-lucky of souls, reduced at the end to a wheezing, weakly man aged before his time. The death of this father whom she had so adored and respected had broken the daisy-chain of Ruby's settled, sunny childhood and left a hole in her emotions which was still not repaired.

"God bless him," she said after a moment, "he was a good Dad to me and Joe. And he wouldn't have wanted our Mam living the rest of her life wi'out any husband to look after her. He was never that sort."

"D'you know what I was thinking just now?" Matthew came over to the range where Ruby was stooped down fanning the sticks of kindling into crackling flame. "I was thinking to myself how contented I shall be when you and me have a little place all of our own."

He caught her to him as she straightened, and wrapping his arms round her slender waist went on, "And I can sit down of an evening after work and watch you while you get my supper ready, and maybe read to you from the newspaper. And after supper, in the summertime I'll take you for a stroll down Horseley Fields to show you off, and when winter comes I'll keep you snug by the fire." He pressed his cheek against hers. "Could you fancy that, d'you reckon?"

"Mm, reckon I could. There's one thing you've forgot, though."

"What's that?"

"Before you get me cooking your supper you'll have to wed me first, Matt Dyson."

Laughing, he picked her up and swung her round in a circle. Both of them knew it would be years yet before they could think seriously about marriage – but there was nothing wrong with dreams. Matthew would have completed his apprenticeship at Chubb's manufactory in four years' time when he was twenty-two, and then his wages would increase to something like thirty shillings a week and he could start putting a bit by regularly in savings. He wanted the best start to their life together. A better area than Minerva Lane, somewhere where their children could grow up away from the filth of canal and railway, the dirt-laden fumes of the factories, and the pestilential stench from the abattoir next to the cattle market. Somewhere clean and healthy and wholesome.

He set Ruby back on her feet and kissed her freckled nose. "Oh, I'll wed you, Ruby Gallimore, never you fear!"

Ruby could hear the singing long before the wedding party reached Minerva Lane. After Matthew had gone she'd prepared a bite of supper for herself and Joe; and later, having settled her brother back into bed for the night, she had sat by the fire to pass the time with some mending, engrossed in her thoughts.

The raucous chorus of voices coming along Walsall Street wakened her from a doze. She glanced at the clock on the mantelpiece. It was gone half past ten. Yawning, the girl got up and stretched herself, and went out to the scullery sink to fill the kettle from the pump, hearing the voices turn into the lane and the shouts of goodnight as one by one the little group dispersed along the row. Just as well it was Saturday night – there'd be sore heads in the morning by the sound of things, she thought.

The gate into the backyard clicked. There was a clumsy scrape of boots and some shushing and giggling, and then the door opened and Jack McShane stumbled across the threshold with the new Mrs McShane in his arms. Of the pair of them Lizzie, surprisingly, seemed in much the more sober condition.

"How's our Joe been?" she asked at once, still clinging to Jack's neck as he struggled to shove the door shut. "He's been all right, has he, Ruby?"

"Oh, aye. He's asleep again now. I gave him some bread and dripping for his supper and he wolfed the lot."

"There – wha' did I tell you," said Jack, loosing Lizzie so clumsily she half fell to the floor. "If there'd been anything ailing the lad Ruby would ha' come down the Harp an' said so." He lurched into the kitchen, collapsing in the armchair by the fire. "Dain't I say t' you t' stop your mithering on . . ."

The kettle began singing on the hob and he paused to study it with the elaborate absorption of the very drunk before letting out a sudden happy laugh. "Eh, but we've made a right good night of it, ain't we, Liz. I wo' want t' get married again in any great hurry."

"You wo' be getting married again at all, if I know about it!" Lizzie went over to look at young Joe, sound asleep on his bed in the corner. Bending to brush the thick fringe of hair from his forehead, she said more softly, "We'll shift this bed upstairs tomorrow. He'll have to share the back room wi' you now, our Ruby, and me and Jack use the double bed in the front."

During the months Jack McShane had been their lodger it was Ruby who'd always slept with her mother up there in the front bedroom. When the new arrangements were discussed some weeks ago, the girl had baulked at the fact that once they were wed the cosy warmth of her mother's body in the big brass bedstead was going to be shared and enjoyed by the man who – one way and another – had taken her father's place as well as her own.

Ruby knew what went on in the marriage bed: there was little excuse for ignorance in a district as poor as Horseley Fields where overcrowded conditions bred a lack of privacy which taught children from an early age to accept the facts of life as natural. Somehow, though, she found it difficult to think of her mother and Mr McShane behaving together like that. It seemed . . . shameful to expose their nakedness to one another and do the things that married couples did. Yet it wouldn't be shameful when she and Matt Dyson were married and did it, so where lay the difference?

She thrust the image from her mind, unwilling to dwell on it. "O' course I won't mind sharing the back room wi' Joe," she said lightly, using her apron to lift the steaming kettle from the hob. "I've always liked that bedroom better any way. It's got a view of the cut and the horses towing the boats."

Her mother sat down at the table and eased off her new elastic-sided boots, blowing out her cheeks with the relief of getting out of them at last. "Make haste wi' that pot o' tea, our Ruby, I'm parched!"

"Aye, you can pour us a cup as well," announced Jack,

sitting forward. "I'd best not sup any more ale tonight or I wo' be up t' giving your mother what her's married me for."

"Jack–!" Lizzie shot him a coyly scandalised look. Untying the ribbons of her wedding bonnet, she put the hat aside and went over in her stockinged feet to perch herself on his knee. "You're not to say such things in front of our Ruby. She'll wonder what you mean."

"Her knows what I mean – don't you, sweetheart?" Jack glanced past her to his stepdaughter, and winked.

Ruby felt herself redden. Instead of answering she made a play of busying herself with the teacups at the table, keeping her back to him.

"Now that's made you blush, eh?" he said, pleased with himself. "Don't be bashful, Ruby – gi's a look at your face an' let's see if I've coloured your cheeks for you."

"Leave her be, you're teasing the poor little wench," Lizzie scolded him affectionately, pulling at his side-whiskers. "You know how her hates it."

"Her don't hate it, do you? Her loves a bit o' teasing from her father." Coming from Bilston, he pronounced the word "feyther" in his broad Black Country way of speaking.

"You're not my father," Ruby retorted, sufficiently stung now to turn on him suddenly, setting her hands on her hips. "And I'm not ever going to call you father, either. You'll be Jack to me, just like you've always been."

"That's the spirit!" He grinned back at her, baring his strong teeth under the black moustache. "I like t' see you when your sparks are flying. Any road ... I'm too damn young t' be your father."

"You're thirty-one," reminded Lizzie.

"An' Ruby's fifteen. I can count." Jack pulled his wife

against him and kissed her noisily on the mouth. The fact that he was Lizzie's junior by several years was the cause of a lot of light-hearted banter between the pair of them.

Ruby brought them their tea and left them to get on with it. Usually Jack's teasing never bothered her, and she gave back as good as she got; but that he should refer to himself as her father, even in fun, had flicked her on the raw. He was her mother's husband, and she respected him – admired him in many ways, even thought him handsome; but it was as her mother's husband that she liked him, not as a surrogate father.

The difference mattered very much. And though none of them realised it that first night of Lizzie Gallimore's marriage, in time to come it was to matter considerably more.

2

Over the next few months life at number 11 Minerva Lane gradually adjusted to its new domestic pattern.

In the late spring of that year, 1885, Ruby left her employment as a scullery maid and went to work as under-housemaid to a family in St John's Square for an extra shilling a week. St John's Square was a much better address than her previous place. Though hardly a mile from Horseley Fields, it lay on the other side of Snow Hill and therefore across the social boundary dividing middle-class Wolverhampton from the industrial slums. At the centre of the Square the worthy dignity of its Georgian church set the tone for the respectability of the neighbourhood, a respectability endorsed by the family names of those interred in its high-walled graveyard and the polished brass door-plates on the house frontages bearing the titles of doctors, solicitors, actuaries, and their kind.

Ruby's new employer, Mr Surtees, was chief clerk at the London Provincial Bank in the town. He had three unmarried daughters still at home, very fashionable and popular young ladies who, being much in demand socially, cost him a pretty penny in dressmakers' bills. Every so often the Misses Surtees' unwanted cast-offs were disposed of to the housemaids, as was the practice, so that Ruby's meagre wardrobe (and her mother's) in time acquired several handsome outfits hardly more than a few years out of style.

The girl was happy in her new employment. She liked the family, not least for its benevolence, and was shortly on the best of terms with the other domestic staff. Her happiness was somewhat overshadowed, though, by a shift in the relationships at home.

At first she'd paid no attention when her stepfather began belittling Matthew Dyson, passing it off as just teasing. Whenever Matt called of an evening, for instance, the comment would be, "What, you here again, young shaver? Ain't you got no home to go to?" or if Ruby spoke of Matt affectionately, repeating something clever he had said, Jack McShane would scoff at it and make the lad sound foolish.

After a time she'd found these remarks were starting to grate on her nerves and mentioned the fact to her mother; but Lizzie, like Matthew himself, laughed at her for taking them too seriously. Couldn't she tell it was only Jack's ham-fisted humour? All the same, as the days went by towards summer Ruby noticed Matt was coming to their house less often now, as if he wanted to avoid her stepfather, and this provoked her finally to anger.

"Why do you have to snape him every time you open your mouth?" she demanded of Jack. "He's done nothing to you." And when Jack had responded by shrugging off her quarrel as a joke, she'd persisted – "Don't you like him, is that it?"

"Come on, I've got nothing against him. If the lad don't

14

want to call round here when he knows I'm home, it ain't no skin off my nose."

"But you make him look stupid!"

"Because I pull his leg a bit? What is he, a bloomin' great babby or some'at that has to be coddled?"

For several weeks after, there was a notable coolness on Ruby's side. She answered her stepfather if he spoke to her, but that was all. The ready smile disappeared, replaced by a frosty politeness; and in the evenings, instead of keeping him company till Lizzie came in from work around half past ten, the girl made a point of being with her friends, or else going to bed.

"I don't know . . . things seem different now he's married to our Mother," she complained to Matthew. "The house doesn't feel the same any more with him carrying on the way he's doing."

The two of them were out for a Sunday stroll along the towpath beside the canal, a walk they often took together. The industrial racket of manufactories on the opposite bank was stilled today and the wharves deserted, the reflected sunlight off the water patterning the hulls of barges which lay wallowing sluggishly against their mooring-posts.

"Jack's taken on a big responsibility," Matthew reminded her out of fairness. "Most chaps start their marriages wi' just a missis, but he's got you and young Joe to consider as well as your Mam, so maybe he needs a chance to get himself settled."

"Maybe." Ruby shrugged. "Any way, let's forget him, eh. Let's talk about some'at more interesting." She linked her arm through her sweetheart's, giving him one of her sudden radiant smiles. "D'you know what I was thinking when I woke this morning? I was thinking about the dress I'd like to be wearing when *we* get married. One o' the daughters where I'm working now, Miss Amelia, she's had this cream silk day-dress made for her, and ooh it's *beautiful*, Matt – tiny little bows down the bodice, and the skirts all pleated frills. Cook told me the style was called a princess polonaise."

"You'd knock a few eyes out in Minerva Lane in some'at like that!" Matthew laughed fondly.

"Wouldn't I an' all. If I'm still employed there in four or five years' time I wonder if Miss Amelia might let me have it for our wedding?"

"Here, I'm not having you wed in anybody's hand-me-downs," he reproached her. "We'll only be getting married the once, remember. I'd rather scrimp a bit myself to put the money by and get you a dress some'at like it, if that's what you've set your heart on."

Ruby pressed her cheek against his shoulder. "The only thing my heart's properly set on is you, Matt Dyson – as if you didn't know. It's why I want so much to look my prettiest, so you'll be proud o' me."

"If you was clad in rags, my chick, you'd still be the prettiest wench in the whole wide world as far as I'm concerned." He responded with a kiss, tilting up her face beneath the brim of her flat straw hat. "I only wish we didn't have so many years to wait before I can put that ring on your finger."

"So do I."

"It'll be worth it, though."

He kissed her again, hugging her to him before they

16

walked on slowly, arm-in-arm together, blind to everything but one another.

When they came to the open fields beyond Lanesfield Basin they sat down on the bank by the bridge for a while to rest themselves, watching a solitary horse-drawn narrow-boat sliding out of the shadows of the dripping archway into the sunshine. Two little girls were playing with a litter of kittens on the roof of the gaily-painted cabin, and as the boat drifted smoothly past, one of them held up a kitten and made it wave its paw to Ruby and Matthew.

They waved back, smiling.

"I wonder where that's bound for," Matthew said, shading his eyes with his cap to watch them go. "Aldersley Junction, I expect, to join the Birmingham Canal. Or maybe a bit further on for the Shropshire Union."

He looked round at Ruby. She had picked a bunch of the wild-growing willowherb known as 'codlins and cream' as they'd walked along, and was holding the purple flowers in her lap. Taking one of the stems he twined it into her tawny hair, and charmed by the picture, added another before he leaned across and kissed her nose.

"I hope *we* have a little wench," he said suddenly, just a bit awkwardly. "A little wench the image o' you, chick. If God sees fit to bless our marriage wi' babbies I'll do my best to be a proper good Dad to them."

Ruby was moved to the heart to hear him say a thing like this.

"I mean, how could I be otherwise, the way I feel about their mother," he went on. "Oh Ruby . . . Ruby, I do love you . . . more than words can ever say. I'll never gi' you cause to doubt that."

She touched his face with her fingertips, smiling at his earnest, tender expression, telling herself she must always remember this moment because it was one of the happiest and most beautiful of her life.

"I know, Matt," she whispered. "I know, sweetheart."

Matthew had excused Jack McShane's belittling of him as Jack's need to settle himself into his new role as head of the family. There was more behind the scenes, though, than simply a matter of becoming settled. Jack had known very well the responsibility he was taking on when he'd married Lizzie Gallimore – but he also knew how well he'd be improving his own domestic situation. He was thirty-one and though he hated to admit it, getting past his peak. He had earned a reputation over the years for being a hard-living, hard-drinking man; hard-working as well, but his wages had always been spent as fast as he got them, on beer and on women, with never enough left to save for a place of his own and provide for a wife.

All this had changed for him once he'd met Lizzie. She was a good sort was Lizzie. Not as fresh as Jack liked them, maybe, but he'd never been one to examine the mantelpiece while he was stoking the fire. He knew she could guarantee him a well-fed belly and a warm bed and a paid-up rent book; and to a chap who liked to have his creature comforts these things were more important at the end of a long day's labour than some fancy bit of skirt, and cold lodgings and an empty table.

Also, he did think a lot of Lizzie. She was an easy-natured, loving little woman, grateful for a second chance of marriage, especially to a younger man in good health and regular employment. She'd made herself a lucky catch and she knew it: it showed in her eyes when she looked at him, and in the pride of her smile, and the way she spoke of him. Jack appreciated that.

The only small fly in the ointment was Joe, Lizzie's twelve-year-old son, who'd been used to getting all his mother's attention and expressed resentment of her new husband in a sulky, whining attitude that tried Jack's patience. The lad had suffered from fits since he was little and Lizzie was inclined to molly-coddle him, keeping him tied to her apron strings when he ought to be learning to fend for himself out there in the rough and tumble of the streets. Jack had worked hard to win him over, but it was like trying to get response from a ruddy brick. Nothing he did made a ha'p'orth of difference. Young Joe didn't like him; and the way things were going, Jack didn't much care for young Joe.

Ruby, now – ah, what he thought of Lizzie's daughter Ruby was another story, and he was concerned to think his teasing might have harmed the girl's affection for him. Jack did his best to make amends by shutting his mouth about Matthew Dyson and treating his stepdaughter more tactfully. She wasn't a child, after all. She was turning sixteen and developing into a beautiful, vibrant young creature who needed handling with care if he wanted to stay on good terms.

The strategy worked. Prompted by her mother, Ruby began slowly to respond. Within another few weeks the coolness on her side showed signs of thawing, and though Matthew's name was still seldom mentioned, the breach in their relationship was patched up and she started to share the odd evening now and again after work in her stepfather's company.

Sometimes they'd take Joe to the canal, Ruby keeping herself amused with *The Girl's Own Paper* or old copies of *The Lady* discarded by the Misses Surtees, while Jack half-heartedly did what he could to teach her brother how to fish. At other times, if she wasn't seeing Matthew, the two of them would walk up to the Harp; or a couple of her friends might call round for a chat and they'd sit in the kitchen listening to Jack's stories of his life.

He seemed to have a ready fund of these, embroidered and embellished with re-telling to show him in a flattering light, but mainly true. Like most big men he was proud of his immensely strong physique and enjoyed the riveted awe in the eyes of Ruby and her friends as he bragged to them of his feats, like the time he'd wrestled a full-grown bull to the ground, or the time he'd got his name in the newspapers rescuing a family from a house fire by staving in their front door.

To an impressionable young girl like Ruby, tales such as these were grist to her innocent admiration.

Knowing how fond she was of songbirds, her stepfather bought her a young cock linnet in a pretty gilt cage to hang at her window; and all through the long midsummer evenings until twilight the linnet's song spilled out into the yard, filling the violet shadows with a plaintive sweetness.

Ruby doted on that little yellow bird. It seemed to bring a breath of the country into Minerva Lane, and she *loved* the country. For a child born to the backstreets and the alleys she'd always had an extraordinary passion for getting away from the town. It was a passion that set her at odds with those of her friends with an urban disliking for 'Nature' and fields and horizons; but Ruby preferred to be different. The countryside drew her, she didn't know why; it just did.

Her sixteenth birthday fell midway through August. As a special treat for the occasion, Jack McShane suggested she rearrange her half-day off from work to accompany him on his carrier's wagon to the little Shropshire village of Albrighton. There were some pieces of furniture he'd been contracted to deliver there and it would make a nice ride out for her, he and her mother thought.

"But wouldn't you rather be spending your birthday wi' me?" Matthew demanded when he learned the news. "I was planning on taking you off to the Empire Music Hall that evening as a surprise."

"I'd rather go to Albrighton," Ruby said guilelessly. "I haven't been there before. There might not come another chance. In any case we'd never be back in time for the Empire . . . and Jack did ask me first."

She tried to salve his disappointment with a kiss, but Matthew wasn't to be placated. "You can change your mind, can't you?"

"I don't want to change my mind. What's wrong wi' taking me to the music hall some other night?"

"It won't be your birthday some other night."

"Oh, now you're being awkward! Why don't you come straight out and say you don't wish me going off into the country wi' Jack instead o' you."

"You can go where you like wi' Jack, it's no business o' mine."

Once started, the bickering had continued, flung back and forth as though they were a pair of squabbling children, like children, saying things they didn't mean and afterwards regretted. They hadn't intended hurting one another; but their immature, untried emotions made them over-sensitive, and even when the hasty words had cooled and they'd arranged an alternative evening at the Empire together, there was still a little shadow left where previously there had been none.

Until about four years ago, while Ruby's much-loved Dad had been alive and in good health, the Gallimores used regularly to go on horse-drawn char-à-bang excursions to local rural beauty spots. These outings had been something to look forward to from one year to the next, and when her father's illness put a stop to them young Ruby had been doubly desolate.

Since then, there'd seldom been any further opportunity, so her stepfather's proposal for her birthday treat was received with more enthusiastic eagerness than Jack had been expecting.

They started away from Horseley Fields directly after their midday dinner, as soon as Ruby had changed from her work clothes and given her face a swill. She was sorry her mother couldn't come with them as well, but Lizzie was working an extra shift at the Harp to fill in for someone. Jack had got the wagon ready loaded, the furniture secured with sacks and ropes to stop it shifting; and in honour of this special day he'd gone to more than his normal trouble over his horses, polishing their harness brass and plaiting their manes and tails with coloured ribbon.

Ruby was like a child in her excitement. She had put on one of the Misses Surtees' discarded fashions, in a dark pink poplin with contrasting flounces and a tight-fitting bodice that showed the small swell of her breasts. It was a sophisticated outfit, incongruous on the bench seat of a wagon, but the absurdity was softened by the pleated linen sun-bonnet she wore which lent a sweet naivety to her appearance.

"You look as grand as a royal princess," Jack complimented. "I'm proud to be seen in your company, Ruby, damn' me if I ain't."

The route into Shropshire took them through the suburb of Chapel Ash and out on to the Tettenhall Road; and once past the rock at Tettenhall Green they were into the country. There'd been a shower of rain that morning, just enough to dampen the dusty surface of the road and freshen the air. The canopies of trees above them glistened in the brassy midday sun, and from the fields on either side came an odour of warm, moist earth and ripening vegetation.

After the sour dirtiness of the overcrowded streets they'd left, it smelled like the Garden of Eden.

"You know, sometimes I don't half wish I'd been born a lad," Ruby remarked, shading her eyes with her hand against the day's dazzle.

"That would have been a waste," Jack said drily.

"If I'd been a lad I'd never have stopped in the town. First chance I got I'd have come out here into the country and found myself work on a farm."

"It's bloody hard work on a farm."

"It's hard enough working in service at times!"

Her stepfather turned his head and spat over the footboard. "I had an uncle who farmed, when I was a nipper. After his old woman died he took me on at his place over Himley way. They'd never had sons, only the one daughter, and her wor' a fat lot o' use, being cross-eyed."

"So you grew up on the land?" Ruby's face showed avid interest. "Go on – you never said!"

"Aye, well, maybe I'd soonest not remember. But I'll tell you this, my wench, the land's a cruel hard bugger to them that has to work it. It ain't all summer and sunshine . . . it's ice and frost and pelting rain, the clothes sodden on your back and your belly clemmed wi' hunger."

He spoke with such unexpected bitterness that the girl's joy in this golden day was robbed of a little of its pleasure.

Seeing the tell-tale droop of her mouth, Jack gave her hand a squeeze and pointing ahead with his whip, he went on, "There, look, yonder – see it? That's the Wrekin."

She screwed up her eyes. Away across the rippling, red-poppied fields a hump-backed ridge broke the hazy horizon, the only prominence for miles around. Beyond lay Shrewsbury, and beyond that, the border with Wales.

Ruby's heart lifted again.

In a quarter of an hour they'd come within sight of Albrighton and were soon passing the Hall and then rounding the curve of the lane into the village.

Their destination lay halfway along the High street, at a house opposite the Crown Inn by the green. The owners had only recently moved here and the furniture being carted was part of their household effects. A couple of strong lads were fetched from the Crown to lend a hand unloading the wagon; then Jack drove further on, past the church to Albrighton Pool, to water his horses and give the wagon wheels a soaking to swell out the wood. In weather like this the wheel-rims tended to shrink with the heat and their metal tyres loosened.

Lizzie had packed some refreshments, bottles of beer, and lemonade for Ruby, and anchovy paste sandwiches. They ate them sitting on the grass beside the pool in the shade of a massive old beech, no one else about, and hardly a sound except the snort of the horses and the singing of birds disturbing the stillness of the day.

Ruby took off her bonnet and lay back on the blanket Jack had spread for them. The flickering sunlight shining through the beech leaves patterned her features with reflected luminance, and she half shut her eyes against its glitter.

"It's lovely, in't it, Jack," she murmured dreamily. "I think I could lie here for ever and ever . . ."

He gave a peculiar laugh; and when she twisted her head to squint up at him, she found he was watching her in a way that made her feel, well – suddenly fidgety, that was the only word to describe the sensation. As though her skin was being prickled all over.

"What's the matter?" she asked him hastily, propping herself on her elbows. "What have I said? Why're you looking like that at me?"

"No law against looking, is there?" He tilted his head to gulp from his beer bottle, showing the coarse dark stubble of beard on his throat; then, wiping his wet moustache with the back of his hand, he added, "And you'm a wench worth looking at, don't you know that yet?"

There was something in his eyes and in his voice that Ruby sensed was more than simple teasing. For an instant she felt threatened by it – not frightened exactly, but uneasy; and not knowing what to answer, she turned her face from her stepfather and started picking at the grass, betraying her confusion to him.

He leaned across and brushed back the hair from her cheek.

"Come on, you ain't offended wi' me, are you? I speak as I find, and I'm telling you straight, you'm growing up a regular little beauty."

Ruby could feel herself blush. Nobody had ever called her a beauty before, and to a girl on her sixteenth birthday, at the threshold of womanhood yet still uncertain of her femininity, a compliment like this from a mature, experienced and handsome man was flattery indeed.

"You know you'm beautiful, don't you, eh," he went on in a softer voice. "There's many a lad must have told you so. You don't need me an' all to say it."

She looked at him out of the corner of her eyes; and then, diffidently, with a sudden wary smile that showed her dimples, she answered, "I've been called . . . some agreeable things, aye. Matt Dyson often says I'm pretty."

"Dyson." The way Jack said it made it sound an insult. "What does *he* know. He's still wet behind the ears is that young tripe-hound. We wo' start another row over him, not today, but I ask you, Ruby – what good's a raw green lad like Dyson to you, eh, if he can't do better than *pretty*. Pretty's a word to use for babbies and such, not for a sweetheart as comely and fetching as you!"

It crossed Ruby's mind that her stepfather shouldn't be talking in this fashion, not so familiarly; and as though he'd read her thoughts, Jack lightened the moment, giving her

26

one of his winks. "You mustn't mind me speaking out. It's natural proudness in having a daughter like you."

"I'm not your daughter, though."

"As good as, since I'm married to your mother."

He grinned, but the grin somehow failed to reach his eyes; and after an awkward pause he started to get up, his polished leather gaiters creaking where they rubbed against his boots. Going to his horses in the shallows of the pool he gathered the reins and led the wagon out, then set to putting together the things on the grass.

Ruby watched him, cautiously.

"Up you come–" Reaching down a hand to her, Jack pulled her lightly to her feet; and when she was standing in front of him he didn't release her at once but stood there in the dappled shadows, holding her.

"Afore we go, can I pinch a birthday kiss from you, eh?"

The unexpectedness of the request quite startled her.

Without waiting for any consent her stepfather leaned over and kissed her lightly on the lips, not on the cheek or brow as he did at home. His mouth was warm, and the touch of it sent a little tingle through Ruby's body. She'd been kissed before, and often, by Matthew; but Matthew's kisses had never tasted like this one, and when Jack let go of her she didn't dare look at him.

"By God, you'm growing up quicker than ever I thought," he said in an odd tone of voice, as though he'd surprised himself. "Damn me if you ain't!"

3

Ruby didn't tell her mother about Jack's birthday kiss, nor did she say anything to Matthew. It might have been a bit of harmless fun to Jack, something thoughtlessly indulged in as a moment's whim, but for Ruby that kiss was like some fairytale awakening, turning what had been innocent admiration into equally innocent infatuation.

Before, she had always liked him in an easy-going sort of way (except when he annoyed her). His flattery by Albrighton Pool had ended that, opening her eyes to see him in a different light – not as Jack the lodger, Jack her mother's husband, but Jack the handsome older man who made her feel special and beautiful in a way she couldn't explain, yet instinctively felt wasn't right.

Ruby was naive, but not so much so that she didn't recognise the danger of the situation. In her relationship with Matthew there'd never been this confusion, because she'd always loved Matthew, had grown up loving him, whereas her change of feelings towards Jack McShane had happened swiftly, and quite suddenly. She thought she could control the way she felt about him, keep it hidden, never realising the strength of her own adolescent emotions nor the damage such an attachment could wreak, especially in a girl whose innocent, coltish sexuality was fast maturing.

Her mother might have noticed what was going on; but Lizzie had other problems at the moment. She had been married nearly five months and was starting to find Jack's nightly demands getting too much now. What with the hours she put in at the Harp and the physical effort of running a home, she felt edgy and tired all the while. It wasn't that she didn't *want* to make love, Lord, no – she idolised Jack. It was just that after all day on her feet and five hours serving beer, she'd occasionally welcome a decent good sleep once her head touched the pillow.

Even Jack said how peaky she looked; but it still didn't stop him from wanting his way every night.

"No, chick, please don't–" she'd beg, pushing him off her, "give it a rest just this once, eh."

But arousal made him selfishly demanding; and Ruby, next door on her own sleepless bed, would stare into the darkness and wait for the springs to stop creaking.

There was only one person the girl felt she could open her heart to, one of the other housemaids in service with her at St John's Square. Dorothy Vickers, known as Dorrie, was nineteen, and she and Ruby had become very friendly despite their difference in age. Dorrie was a lively character, nothing much to look at with her snub nose and her wide, ripe mouth; yet there was something about her that drew the men like flies to honey, a gift which didn't necessarily make her popular. Like Ruby, Dorrie had a stepfather; but unlike Ruby's hers was a drunken old brute who'd made her home life such a misery she had left when she was fourteen to 'live in' as a general servant.

Jack McShane was no paragon of virtue, but the more Dorrie went on about her own stepfather the more faultlessly attractive Jack became by contrast. It was all part of the illusion. The stars in Ruby's eyes had blinded her to everything she didn't want to see – her mother's weariness, Jack's nightly selfishness, his cussed attitude towards her brother Joe. She only saw the image her infatuated dreams were fabricating.

"It's been no more than a few months back, as I recall, you dain't have a good word to say for the man," Dorrie observed. "Yet now to hear the way you talk all of a sudden he's the Angel bloomin' Gabriel. What's changed your opinion?"

Swearing her to secrecy Ruby told her, all about Albrighton and how much she'd started liking Jack of late.

"Go on – you ain't stuck on him, are you?"

"Depends on how you mean."

"Well – y'know – fancy him."

"I don't *fancy* him, Dorrie. He's golden to me, that's all."

The two of them had this conversation while giving each other a hand with their housemaids' duties, stripping the bedsheets to air the feather mattresses and change the dirty linen.

"You want to be careful," Dorrie advised her. "You'll come down to earth wi' a bang if your mother finds out he's been turning your head."

"He hasn't been turning my head!"

"Don't sound like it, does it. If I was you I wouldn't give him encouragement. I know from experience, once you let them sort get too familiar you never know where it'll lead."

Dorrie bent and fished out a china chamberpot from under the bed, holding her snub nose as she emptied its contents into the slop bucket.

"You take my advice," she went on, giving the pot a cursory wipe round with a soapy rag before putting it into the cupboard under the washstand, "next time your stepfather starts any sweet-fanny-antics, tell him to flippin' well shove his hook or you'll make sure the neighbours hear about it."

Ruby said nothing. Lifting the bedsheets from the floor she carried them out to the corridor to go into the laundry basket; and when she came back she deliberately changed the subject with a reference to the household's butler.

"By the way, Dorrie, you asked Mr Perryman about having the evening off next Saturday?"

"Not yet I ain't, no."

"Why's that? I thought you were set on coming wi' me and Matthew to the fair?"

Dorrie studied her own reflection in the washstand mirror, straightening the starched, be-ribboned cap on top of her frizzed dark hair. Satisfied, she glanced over her figure and replied, "'Course I want to come wi' you. I'm biding my time, that's all. You know there's to be a dinner party here Wednesday? Well, that means the best brandy coming out, and since Mr Perryman's partial to his little drop I thought I'd wait and catch him in his pantry after, when he's mellow, like."

She smirked at Ruby through the mirror. It was no secret among the domestic staff that Mr Perryman enjoyed sampling the contents of the master's cellar over and above the line of duty.

"Anyway," she went on, turning round, "I'm itching for an introduction to this Matthew Dyson. After all what I've been hearing, I might just fancy the lad myself now you'm so sick of him."

"I'm not sick of him, Dorrie Vickers! Whatever give you that idea?"

"You did, yourself."

"I never."

"Oh, I thought it was Jack McShane you liked smarming round you now." Dorrie's smirk widened to a wicked grin. "Ain't that what you've been telling me this morning?"

Ruby snatched up the bolster pillow and flung it at her. She knew she was having her leg pulled, but sometimes Dorrie's jokes weren't all that funny. "You swore on your oath you'd keep it private, what I told you. Jack's got nothing to do wi' Matthew – nothing, you hear?"

Dorrie picked up the bolster and began waltzing round the room with it clasped in her arms, humming a tune to herself.

"*Dorrie–*!"

"All right, I hear." Tossing the pillow aside on the bed the other became suddenly serious. "You dain't think I meant it, did you, Ruby? Blimey, what d'you take me for – I thought we was pals."

"We won't be pals any more if you don't promise me–"

"I promise, I promise. I won't breathe a word, cross my heart!"

Despite this reassurance, Ruby wasn't certain after whether she'd been wise in trusting Dorrie. The older girl was her friend and confidante; but it only needed something slipping out by accident when they were together on Saturday night to put the fat in the fire. Matthew had been brooding about Jack these last few weeks, annoyed because she'd gone off with him to Albrighton, and Ruby was concerned in case the wrong word was spoken out of place.

She needn't have worried: Dorrie turned up to meet them at the fairground by the market hall with a new admirer in tow and her mind on more exciting things. Where she had met this Frank she didn't say. He had his own scrap-iron business on the Willenhall Road and wasn't short of a bob or two, judging from the open-handed way he spent his money. They'd been into the Tiger pub in North Street earlier and Dorrie was in high spirits, radiating that flirtatious gaiety that made her plainness somehow so bewitching, part of the fascination she seemed to hold for men.

Matthew, who had heard all about her from Ruby, didn't like her. Why, he couldn't say with certainty, except she made him feel uncomfortable. He found he kept wanting to look at her, repelled by her and yet attracted, drawn to the covert appeal of her sexuality even though it roused a strong aversion. When she laughed, it was too loud, her full-lipped mouth wide open so he saw her teeth; and when she glanced at him, the flare of the naphtha flames that lit the booths showed something in her eyes, as though she guessed at his discomfort and was mocking him.

"I can't think what you see to like in her," he said to Ruby as Dorrie soared past in one of the wooden swing-boats, screaming her delight and urging Frank to make the boat go higher still. "To be honest, I don't care for her myself."

"But you've hardly been introduced to her five minutes!"

"That doesn't matter. I can't understand you wanting a person like her for your friend. She isn't your sort."

Ruby pulled herself away from Matthew's hand. "What d'you mean? Isn't my sort?" The criticism stung her.

"She's fast."

"She's *fun*. She makes me laugh. What's wrong wi' that?"

His eyes followed Dorrie. Her skirts had blown up above her shapely calves, and the flesh of her legs gleamed white as the boat swung out of the shadows into the smoky glare and backwards again. "She's fast," he repeated stubbornly, looking away.

"Why, because she enjoys a good time when she's out?"

Vexed now, Ruby began to walk off, and when Matthew came after her she rounded on him, saying angrily, "Dorrie's my friend, Matt, and I won't hear things spoke against her, not even by you. If you don't approve of the company I keep you can always buzz off somewhere else, you know."

"Well – thanks for the advice!"

"Take note of it."

"I will." He caught her by the arm and held her. "What's got into you just lately, Ruby? Ever since your birthday you've been . . . different. What's changed between us?"

She wouldn't meet his gaze, but glanced aside towards the nearest booth. "Nothing's changed. I don't know what you mean."

"I think you do." Taking her chin in his hand he forced

her almost roughly to look round at him. "You're not the same any more, you seem to be hiding secrets from me all the while as if there's some'at going on you're keeping back. It's not to do wi' Jack McShane, by any chance?"

"Let go o' me – you're hurting me." Ruby struggled to release herself but that made Matthew grip her all the tighter, a flush of real anger darkening his strong young features.

"I want to have the truth," he said. "I've got a *right* to know what's happening."

"God's sake, Matthew, what's come over you this evening? First you pick on Dorrie Vickers and now you're dragging in Jack!" Guilt, as well as sudden agitation, lent force to her own rising anger. "Did you ask me to this fair just so's we could have an argument?"

"You know I didn't–"

He let out an oath as a group of rowdy youngsters knocked against them in the alley, barging past towards the skittle tent; and when they'd gone he said impatiently, "I wanted us to have a happy time, enjoy ourselves – and now our night's been blasted spoilt."

"*You* spoilt it!"

"Aye, well, I've got good cause I reckon." Releasing his hold, Matthew shoved his hands into his jacket pockets as though suddenly he couldn't bear the touch of her. "Your stepfather and Dorrie Vickers ought to get together – they'd make a right good pair."

Ruby felt her heart begin to bump. "Oh yes? How's that then?"

But he shook his head. The heat of his temper was starting to drain from him, leaving him miserably bitter. Up till this last month, if anyone had said of her that Ruby was the kind of girl it was easy for someone to influence, he'd have laughed in their faces. She'd always been too open and straightforward, never one for keeping secrets.

If they said it of her now, though, Matthew didn't think he'd laugh so much . . .

Ruby was changing, starting to draw back from him as if there was something, some new part of her life, she didn't want to share with him. It was nothing he could put his finger on, more an intuitive feeling caused by her odd evasions, awkward silences, half-finished sentences. For someone who'd never had an ounce of guile in her, Ruby was behaving out of character, and he could only suppose the root of it lay with her stepfather.

Jack McShane didn't like him, Matthew was well aware of that; the man had made it plain enough. It didn't need words to say he wasn't welcome in their house now Jack was master. So he'd stayed away, thinking maybe if he waited for a while till Jack stopped playing cock o' the roost, the situation might resolve itself.

It hadn't. The one thing Matthew had failed to take into account till recently was that Ruby was beginning to fall under her stepfather's influence, that Jack was using that influence to buy her admiration with his braggart talk and twist her loyalties.

He looked away across the fairground lights; then, letting out his breath on a long, exhausted sigh, he said after a moment, "Tell me the truth. D'you love me enough to want to marry me still? Or d'you feel maybe you'd like a bit o' time to yourself to think about things."

"You mean . . . not see each other?" Ruby stared at him.

"Whatever will help."

The bump of her heart-beat quickened. She couldn't believe he was serious. Clutching his arm she said with a little laugh, "But Matt, I don't want us to be apart. What is it has put such a notion into your head?"

"You have, the way you've been acting."

"There you go again! I'm not acting any different than I always have."

"You're keeping some'at from me," he repeated stubbornly, "and I half suspect Jack McShane's to blame."

Her hand fell to her side. The laughter and excitement of the fairground crowds seemed suddenly like mockery.

"I don't want us to be apart," she said again, more piteously, all her anger gone now, leaving only guilt. "You hurt me to the quick by saying things like that, you do."

"Here, you pair – we thought we'd gone and lost you!" Dorrie Vickers, searching round the fair booths for her friend, arrived just at this moment with Frank in tow. Her face was flushed from the exhilaration of attracting so much masculine attention on the swings, and as Matthew glared round she tossed back her frizzy hair and smiled at him before noticing Ruby's woe-begone expression.

"Come on, cheer up you, misery guts!" she exclaimed. "Frank's going to treat us all to a ride on the horses."

Ruby averted her head. "No, I've had enough o' the fair. I think I'll go home."

"What, already?" Dorrie's eyes slipped back to Matthew. "Oh well, if you ain't enjoying yourself–"

The steam engine driving the merry-go-round increased its clatter, and the rest of her sentence was lost in a sudden swell of organ music drowning her words. Seizing Frank by the sleeve, she mouthed something at Ruby with a sympathetic shrug before dashing away to catch a ride on one of the painted, prancing carousel horses just starting to move.

"Are you staying an' all, Matt?" Ruby asked him tremulously.

"No, I'm coming home wi' you." He tilted her face up to his, kissing the last of her tears and tidying her shawl and bonnet as though she were a little child. "I'm sorry I've upset you, sweetheart . . . truly. We'll try and forget we've had this silly row tonight."

He wished he could forget its cause as well.

With her arm tucked firmly into his, the two of them went by the short cut past St Peter's church towards Queen Square. Away from all the noise and crowds the town felt almost deserted, with not much traffic about the streets for a Saturday night. A harvest moon had risen and was shining behind the gilded onion dome of the Empire Music Hall, flooding the square with a silvery brilliance that lent everything a slightly eerie look. At the far end, imprisoned in the shadows of its railings, the statue of Prince Albert on his horse stared sightlessly away towards the silhouetted roofs of Chapel Ash.

They went past the statue, on down Lichfield Street and into Horseley Fields. It was busier here round the public houses and off-licence shops; even the pawnbroker next to the Star Vaults was still doing business – being Saturday, he had people coming in to redeem their Sunday clothes before pawning them again on Monday morning.

At Minerva Lane Matthew saw Ruby as far as the backyard gate of number 11.

"I suppose I'd best say goodnight to you out here," he said after he'd kissed her. "I don't think I ought to come in the house, do you." It was a statement more than a question.

Ruby stood on tiptoe with her arms round his neck and hugged him. She loved Matthew so dearly; she wanted to reassure him of that, even though their evening had been ruined. But just as she started to speak, a sudden commotion broke out, sounding like a boy's yells followed by the shout of angry words, coming from the open bedroom window.

"That's Jack having trouble wi' our Joe again," she said, pulling away. "I'll have to go–"

The moment for reassurance was lost. Dragging her shawl from her shoulders she ran inside the yard and shut the gate, leaving Matthew standing in the moonlight. Until a few weeks ago, she would have said, 'That's our Joe in trouble wi' Jack again.'

A subtle difference; and it betrayed how far her loyalties had altered.

4

A crack of yellow lamplight showed under the bedroom door as somebody went past. Ruby turned over on her back and listened. From the sound of the heavy tread on the creaking stairboards that was Jack going down into the kitchen.

She half sat up, wondering what time it was. The voices through the wall had seemed to go on most of the night, keeping her from sleep. She guessed it must be after five o'clock because the dark outside the window had the gauzy greyness of approaching dawn and somewhere in the neighbourhood a blackbird had begun its song, hesitant and lonely in the stillness.

Yawning wearily, Ruby threw off her blankets and got up, shivering a little as the chill of the room struck her bed-warm body through the cotton nightgown. Quietly, so as not to disturb the linnet in its shrouded cage nor her brother Joe sleeping near the window, she went to pick up her shawl from the chair where her day clothes were folded, then eased the door open and crept to the top of the stairs.

There wasn't a sound now from her mother's room. For a moment she debated what she should do, go in to Lizzie and see how she was, or go down to Jack.

She went down to Jack.

He was sitting in the pool of lamplight, slumped forward with his elbows on his knees, head in hands, gazing into the dead ashes of the grate. As the stair door closed he looked round; and Ruby saw the tiredness in his face alter to sudden surprise, then something else.

"Oh, I haven't woke you, have I?" he said softly, getting to his feet.

"No, I was half-awake already. I heard somebody come down. I thought it was our Mam." The little lie slipped out so easily. "She's – all right, is she?"

"Aye. Her's sleeping now." Jack's eyes stayed fixed upon his stepdaughter. She was quite unconscious of the effect of her appearance, nothing but her shawl to cover her nightgown, tawny hair tumbled round her shoulders, and her small feet bare. The innocence of her unawakened womanhood made her incredibly desirable at this moment, the more so to Jack McShane because he'd just spent the entire night being denied his satisfaction by his wife.

"We had a bit of an argy-bargy over some'at," he said carefully. "I suppose you could hear it, you and Joe ... what it was about, like."

"No. Joe's been sound asleep all night, and I didn't–" Ruby hesitated. "Well, I wasn't really listening so I don't know what was said."

Another lie. Jack's voice had been raised loud enough to catch his words. It wasn't the first time, either, she had heard him – and always on about the same old thing. He could see for himself how tired her mother was lately. It wasn't fair to bother Lizzie with *that*, not every night.

She knew he was staring at her. He'd pulled on a pair of corduroy trousers before coming down, but that was all; and standing there half-naked there was a primitive power about him so rawly sexual that though she wasn't consciously aware of it, the girl's own sexuality responded. She returned his gaze a moment, then her eyes dropped to his strongly-muscled shoulders contoured by the shadows of the lamp.

A sudden nervousness came over her.

"I'd make us both a pot o' tea," she said, too quickly, "except the fire's gone dead."

"I'll light a fresh 'un in a minute." He didn't move. "D'you ever think about Albrighton, Ruby?"

The question came out of the blue, so entirely unexpected that she was startled into answering at once, "O' course I do!"

"Aye, so do I. You never told Lizzie, did you, about them things I said to you?"

She shook her head.

"There's a clever wench. Shall I whisper you a secret—" Jack leaned across, and beckoning her closer he said quietly, "I enjoyed that little birthday kiss I had off you. In fact I wouldn't mind another like it."

The scene was growing unreal, as though she were caught inside one of her dreams.

"You'd let me, would you?" His eyes were all over her now.

"I don't know . . ." she heard herself stammering awkwardly. "I'm not sure it'd be right."

"Where's the harm, eh?" Her stepfather grinned suddenly. Taking her by the hand he drew her towards him.

Her shawl slipped to the floor, but like a sleepwalker she never noticed.

Putting his mouth against her ear, he whispered, "I like a wench that's game. Shows her's got spirit. And when her's got spirit as well as a face as winsome as yourn, why, then I like her still better."

The tickle of his moustache against her cheek was surprisingly pleasant and Ruby felt herself beginning to tremble.

"You ain't cold, am you, my little beauty? You'm shivering. Dear me, we can't have that, you'll catch your death . . . here, let me warm you, eh."

It *was* a dream. Jack took her in his arms and cuddled her against his hirsute chest, with nothing between their nakedness but the thinness of her cotton nightgown. His skin smelled of sweat and stables, and so strong was the effect on Ruby of his physical virility that the smell made her think of something primitively animal . . . like a picture there'd been in one of her schoolbooks of a man that was half horse.

He hugged her tighter. Only Matthew had ever held her as closely as this before; but Matthew was always so loving and tender, and the strength of his body was nothing like Jack's.

"How about my kiss, now—"

He bent his head and found her lips. That first kiss by Albrighton Pool, so innocently given, had left her in sweet confusion, but this one jolted through her; and when he finally released her Ruby clung on to him, face raised, eyes closed, her limbs turned to jelly.

"You greedy little madam," he laughed softly. "By Christ, you'm made for this, you am."

His hand slid down to cup her small, firm breast, a touch so intimate that it startled her into a gasp of frightened pleasure.

The stair door opened.

"Ruby–" Young Joe appeared from the darkness, rubbing his eyes with his knuckles. "Ruby, what you doing up so early? It in't half past six yet, is it?"

Jack cursed, and thrust her away from him quickly before the boy could register the scene.

"What the hell–" He kept his voice low. "What d'you think you'm playing at – get back to bed!"

"It's all right, Joe." Trying her best to hide her agitation from her brother, Ruby felt herself flushing scarlet with guilty embarrassment at what she'd just been up to in their stepfather's arms. "I . . . I wasn't feeling very well . . . I only come downstairs for a cup o' water."

"Aye, aye that's it." Jack took his cue from her. "Her was feeling a bit giddy, like. In fact her nearly fell as you come in – lucky I cotched hold on her." He managed a wheedling smile for the boy. "No need to worry your Mam when her wakes, lad. You know how her frets, and as you can see, your sister's perked up again now."

Ruby gathered her shawl from the floor. "Come on, Joe–" she held out a still-trembling hand. "Come back to bed for another half-hour while Jack lights the fire."

Her eyes met her stepfather's as she turned on the bottom stair to shut the door. For what seemed an endless moment they looked at one another in the lamplight. It was a wordless exchange, but they both knew what was in the other's mind.

They had just been doing something that was very, very dangerous.

For the next few weeks there was an awkwardness between them. Neither had much to say and they tacitly avoided being alone together in the house. Jack McShane was playing with fire, and he knew it; yet in spite of that awareness his lust for Ruby had been roused, and he saw the situation through a distorting mirror.

The wench seemed game all right. Not like her mother. He was disappointed in Lizzie; he'd thought she was made of keener stuff, and now look at her – six months into their marriage and it was no Jack, not tonight Jack, I'm too tired Jack, like a wilting ruddy wallflower. It wasn't as though she needed to fret about being in the family way: she couldn't have any more kids after Joe, she'd informed him of that at the start.

The way he viewed things, it wasn't doing anybody harm if he treated himself to a kiss and a cuddle from Ruby – but a kiss and a cuddle was all it would be, Jack promised himself. Further than that and he'd be a damn' fool; he'd be risking too much.

As for Ruby herself, she was so infatuated now that if Jack McShane said red was blue she would believe him. She was in love with the *idea* of being in love, with someone who didn't exist except in her dreams, who looked like her stepfather and had his voice and manner but in essence was a fabrication of her own emotions. Just as Jack had his distorting mirror, so did she. Perhaps this was why in her naivety she felt so little guilt towards her mother, especially since Jack had gone out of his way to assure her he was doing nothing *bad* and a little kiss or two couldn't possibly hurt his relationship with Lizzie.

Ruby's only twinge of conscience concerned Matthew; but he and Jack were different men, with different, separate places in her life, and what the eye didn't see she deluded herself the heart would never grieve about.

The middle of October brought a happy event in St John's Square. The oldest of the three Misses Surtees, Louisa, became engaged to the junior partner in the firm of her father's solicitors, a young gentleman of immaculate family background and some fortune. Such was his relief at getting one of his expensive daughters so suitably matched that Mr Surtees gave the domestic staff a bonus with their wage that week and permitted them to drink Miss Louisa's health in a glass of the very best sherry.

Ruby had planned to buy her mother something pretty as a present with her bonus; but she was persuaded instead to spend the half-crown on an evening at the Star Concert Hall with Dorrie Vickers and Dorrie's admirer Frank and a group of his friends. She'd originally been in two minds about going – the Star, in Bilston Street, had a reputation for attracting the type of patron who enjoyed vulgarity dressed up as entertainment (those who wanted a more artistic and better class of music hall went to the Theatre Royal or the Empire) but Dorrie had finally managed to talk her round to it.

The hall was already packed by the time they arrived, and after the freshness of the autumn evening the airless heat inside the place stank overpoweringly of alcohol, stale scent and sweating bodies. Cheaply-painted women sauntered up and down or lounged against the counter at the back, their smiles as hard and hungry as their lamp-blacked eyes as they advertised themselves for business.

This was the first time Ruby had been here. It wasn't the sort of venue to which Matthew ever took her, and once the evening's programme had started she realised why. Sauce was one thing; she didn't mind sauce, it was funny. But smut was quite another, and this *was* smut. The sexually explicit content of the 'turns' brought howls of raucous laughter from an audience which, if anything, grew coarser than the turns themselves as the night wore on and the drunkenness increased.

Seeing Dorrie laughing as loudly as everyone else, Ruby swallowed her embarrassment and tried half-heartedly to join in, even though she couldn't understand the grosser, more suggestive innuendoes. One of Frank's cronies, sporting a rather flash suit and a Pompadour hairstyle, noticed her discomfort. During one of the act changes he moved to sit beside her and ask what was the matter; and when she excused herself by saying she felt hot, he volunteered to nip to the bar and fetch her a glass of something cool to drink.

Whatever was in that glass, it had the effect of making her giggle so much that he fetched her another; and by the end of the evening Ruby was laughing her head off as much as the rest and was obliged to accept the young fellow's arm to steady herself as they jostled their way from the hall.

Once she'd got out into Bilston Street, however, the

rawness of the midnight air in contrast to the heat inside restored her somewhat to her senses.

"Here – Sam Reynolds has just asked me where you live," said Dorrie, indicating the Pompadour. "He's taking you home in a hackney cab, he says."

"I don't want him taking me home–"

"Go on! He's got his eye on you, he has. You want to encourage him, Ruby. Don't you know who his brother is?"

Ruby wasn't interested.

"Him wi' all them butcher's stalls," said Dorrie, not to be put off. "You know him, Jabez Reynolds out the market."

She still wasn't interested.

"They'm rolling in money, the Reynoldses," Dorrie pressed on. "They've got a place the size of a bloomin' great mansion this end o' Tettenhall Road *and* acres o' land in the country, according to Frank. Cor, you'd be daft to turn up your nose at young Sam if he's offering to see you safe home!"

Ruby reconsidered her objection. It was late; she *would* be daft to walk back by herself this time of night, and it was civil of Mr Reynolds to think of her welfare.

If she was troubled that he might try taking advantage of her in the hackney, she judged him wrongly. Away from the rest of his friends Sam Reynolds appeared quite the gentleman; and having helped her from the carriage at the bottom of Minerva Lane, he raised his bowler hat to wish her good night and hoped they'd meet again at some future occasion.

"I'm sorry, by the way," he said, "if I got you a little bit tipsy. I could see you weren't enjoying yourself, so I thought I'd cheer you up. Am I forgiven?"

"I suppose so." Ruby tried to sound annoyed, but couldn't. "What was it you put in my drink?"

"Only gin. Next time, I'll buy you champagne."

She gave him a disbelieving look, then turned away and started to walk down the lane, hearing him say to the hackney driver – "You can take me on to Palmerston Place in the Tettenhall Road. There's an extra five bob if you do it in twenty minutes."

By the time she'd reached the back gate of number 11 the rattle of the horse's hooves had faded out of earshot; but already her mind had forgotten Mr Reynolds and was totally engrossed with Jack McShane. Jack had promised he'd wait up for her. It would be the first time they'd been alone since he had kissed her all those weeks ago, and as Ruby shut the gate she was nervously wondering whether he'd try to kiss her again tonight.

Her stepfather had been drinking; that was the first thing the girl noticed when she went into the kitchen. It was unusual for Jack to drink much in the house, but the evidence was there to see in the empty bottles lined up on the table and another one, half-full, beside his chair.

"And what time d'you call this?" he said without preamble, jerking his head towards the mantel clock. "You said you'd be back afore eleven. I was just about to set off looking for you."

He sounded put out, Ruby thought. "I told you where I'd be – the music hall wi' Dorrie Vickers. You needn't have stayed up waiting if you wanted your bed."

"I *said* I'd wait up, dain't I. I was worried for you." Jack swallowed the rest of the beer and got up to put the bottle with the others. "You dain't come home all by yourself, I hope."

"No, somebody saw me back." She took off her jacket and feathered bonnet and hung them behind the scullery door.

"What somebody?" he asked suspiciously.

"Oh ... a friend of Dorrie's." Coming to the fire, she stretched out her hands to warm them and looked at him uncertainly across her shoulder. "Our Mam's asleep, is she?"

"Aye, sleeping like a ruddy babby. Her was that dead on her feet when her come in I made her go straight up." He gave a mirthless laugh. "Her dain't need telling twice, poor soul."

They continued looking at one another, before Ruby lowered her eyes and glanced again at the fire.

She heard her stepfather moving behind her.

"Will you take a drink wi' me, Ruby?" he said in a softer voice, and as always when he spoke to her like that she felt a catch at her heart. "A glass o' beer to keep me company?"

"Haven't you drunk enough?" She turned and faced him, hoping he'd think the flush in her cheeks was the heat from the flames.

"Never you question the amount o' drink I put away, my wench. That's an error your mother's begun making lately." Jack's voice was quiet still, but the expression in his narrowed eyes warned her that he could become aggressive. "As long as it's me that's paid for the beer, it's me that'll drink it, and if others don't blasted well like it–" He made a gesture.

Ruby bit her lip. She hadn't meant to vex him.

"Ah, what does it matter." Suddenly he was amiable again. "Lizzie can say what her likes. I'm master here now."

He came closer. The girl could smell the drink on his breath but it didn't offend her. She returned the smile he gave, a little awkwardly, and because she wanted to please him she said, "If you're having another one yourself, I'll take a glass wi' you."

"You'm a fast learner. But we both know that already, don't we, sweetheart." He caught her face between his powerful hands and kissed her on the mouth, before releasing her to go into the scullery and open two more bottles, humming to himself in a tuneless, jaunty sort of way.

"What shall we drink to, Ruby?" he said, coming back into the kitchen and giving her the glass he'd poured. "How about you and me and ... our little private business, eh."

"What private business is that?" she asked huskily, her face beginning to burn, knowing full well what he meant.

Jack raised his bottle to his lips and took a swig. Above his head the gas jet dimmed as the pressure dropped, softening the light and sending shadows from the fire flickering across the ceiling. Instead of answering her question he pulled the girl against him, his arm about her waist, and kissed her again.

"Drink up, my beauty," he urged; and she obeyed him, gulping the beer from the glass until she was breathless.

"That's the way, my lovely wench! And another–" He tilted her hand, and when some of the beer ran over her chin he licked it away, sliding his tongue from her jaw to the curve of her throat.

"Now look what you've done–" he said in mock reproach. "You've wet your pretty clothes." Giving her his bottle, he started to undo the tiny jet buttons at the top of her high-necked blouse, his fingers clumsy as they fumbled among the lace frills for the fastenings.

"Come on, drink up," he said again, but now it was with sudden whispered urgency. "Come on, my little chick."

Ruby's hand was trembling so much that the glass rattled against her teeth. She wasn't used to taking alcohol, and already the effect of half a pint of strong ale on top of the gin Sam Reynolds had slipped her was beginning to make her light-headed.

Jack watched her closely, half smiling; and when she'd drained the glass he took it from her and put it on the table with his bottle.

"It looks like a bar-room in here," she said nervously, with a little shivering laugh to cover her apprehension. "What our Mam'll say tomorrow morning–"

"Shut up about your Mam."

He grabbed her in his arms, pressing his body against her and starting to kiss her, not tenderly this time, but hungrily, with passion. Had he not been so inebriated, decency and moral conscience might have prevented Jack from going any further; but the alcohol had fired his lust and he was out of control, with no thought for the dishonour or disgrace that could result from the seduction of his stepdaughter. The primitive urge for sexual gratification had mastered him now, and Ruby was no longer his wife's sixteen-year-old daughter but the compliant female body he needed to assuage his blind desire.

Groping with the rest of her buttons, he pushed his hand inside her bodice and found her naked breast, then bent his head to kiss it, excited even further by her little whimpering moans.

Ruby felt the room begin to sway. She wanted him to stop, and yet she wanted him to go on, intoxicated as much by the feeling he was rousing as by the gin and beer. His hands were hot on her, all over her, stroking and caressing; and when he hoisted up her skirt and touched the soft, bare skin above her stocking garter, the sensation was so wonderful that she groaned aloud with pleasure and he had to silence her again with kisses.

"Don't tell Lizzie," he kept whispering, "for Christ's sake don't tell Lizzie."

All Ruby could remember after that was being on the pegged-rag rug in front of the fire with Jack McShane above her, and the gas jet fading to a little glow of amber light, like a watching eye.

5

It was Lizzie McShane's tragedy that she loved her second husband too blindly to see him for what he really was, self-centred and morally weak, a man who was shrewd but in a cunning way, who used his physical attractiveness and charm to camouflage a vain and shallow nature.

Had she doted on him less, she might have guessed what was going on with him and Ruby; but she didn't guess, and that too was part of her tragedy because it made her an innocent victim in events which were shortly to follow.

Ruby appreciated her mother's devotion to her husband. It didn't matter that there were arguments between the pair of them. Everybody argued when they lived together – it was human nature, and in an area as poor as Horseley Fields people weren't so proud that they pretended otherwise.

The girl loved her mother very much, and she was shamefully aware of how much damage would be caused if Lizzie ever knew what Jack had done to her – done *with* her – on the kitchen floor that night. Even if they kept it to the three of them, think how cruelly hurt her Mam would be; and if by some calamity it got about Minerva Lane – God! how Matthew would despise her; Jack could find himself in trouble with the law for all she knew, and the neighbours would have a field day with the gossip.

Of all these horrors, it was losing Matthew that she feared the most. Ruby never meant to let her stepfather go as far as he had, but at the end she couldn't stop him, couldn't stop herself from letting him, her body saying yes, oh yes, and her mind saying no, oh no; and afterwards she'd gone to bed and wept, mourning her broken innocence, the dream she had betrayed of keeping herself till the day of her marriage to Matthew.

She'd often imagined their wedding night. They would spend it in the country at some pretty little inn close to a river, with a nice view from the window and the scent of roses drifting in to fill their room. Matthew would be very tender. He would lift her in his arms and carry her to their big comfy four-poster bed, and they'd lie there in the moonlight making love together, giving themselves to each other as husband and wife.

Well, there was no roses and no moonlight; just the hard kitchen floor and the gas-meter running out and her stepfather grunting and sweating on top of her. She might as well have been some twopenny drab against an entry wall for all the romance there was in that encounter. Jack McShane had soiled her innocent dreams, cheapened something infinitely precious, and Ruby didn't know how to forgive herself for letting him.

It was after that October night that those who knew her well discerned the change, which had begun some months before, now quickening. The lively, laughing, carefree child-part of her nature seemed to disappear and a more mature, more introspective side to her emerge, as though the natural flowering of her womanhood had suddenly been hastened forward. Outwardly she appeared very much more self-composed; but that composure was a mask which Ruby trained herself to wear both as disguise and as protection against a turmoil of confused and bruised emotions.

Her infatuation had thrived on her fantasy. As the image round which she wove her adolescent daydreams Jack had been her hero. Like the princess in the fairytale, her sexuality had been awakened by his kiss and she had romanticised it as would any naive virgin of sixteen. On the night of her seduction it wasn't merely her young body he had deflowered, it was her innocence, her modesty, her silly, sweet illusions.

Now, Ruby didn't know *how* she felt towards him. She had reached the end of the rainbow only to find a crock of dead, cold ash; and yet she couldn't hate him. She could only hate herself. What was Jack – he was only a man after all, like any other, and whatever the rights and wrongs of their situation, if she had said no to him in the first place he would never have been tempted into doing what he had to the point where he'd lost all self-control.

She could think of several further reasons why she should hate herself. She had deceived Matthew, betrayed her Mam, which was bad enough – but now there was worse, because try as she might she simply hadn't got the will strong enough to resist him to prevent it from happening all over again when Jack demanded it.

He said she was doing her Mam 'a favour' by satisfying him in Lizzie's place; that without so many arguments their home life would be happier for Joe. The girl suppressed her guilt with these excuses, making herself doubly a victim by allowing herself to be forced, believing the lies because she had no other choice if she wanted to silence her conscience.

Then, in the spring of 1886, there came the reckoning.

In common with other females of her social class, once her monthly courses started showing Ruby had to make do for her personal hygiene with cloths from old sheets or towelling rag, boiled clean after use and kept in a drawer in her bedroom.

She'd always been embarrassed about her courses and avoided pegging these cloths out on the communal line for everyone to see, preferring to dry them indoors in front of the fire. There was no need to tell her mother whenever she'd started – the evidence appeared quite regularly there upon the fireguard five days or so in every month; so Lizzie couldn't fail but note their non-appearance at the end of March.

"You're late showing this month, ain't you, chick?" she remarked to Ruby.

"I don't think so, am I?"

"It was Valentine's Day you showed last, if you remember. You was vexed on account of it spoiling your evening wi' Matthew."

"Oh – aye, that's right." Yes, Ruby *did* remember.

"That means you've gone two weeks over."

"I've been late before, Mam. I'll be all right, don't fret!"

"I hope so, chick. You ain't been yourself at all just recently. We'll leave it a few days more, and if you still ain't showed by Sunday I'll dose you wi' castor oil to open your bowels."

What 'opened' one part of the body was generally believed to work as well for another, particularly where there was any stoppage. In Ruby's case, however, the castor oil had no effect beyond its immediate function; but not wanting to have Lizzie worry further, she went through a pretence of starting her monthly course, even to boiling and drying her cloths in the usual manner.

She'd been telling her mother the truth – she *had* been late before now, though never by more than a week at the most; and she wondered whether it wasn't the life (or the lie) she was leading at home, caught between the devil of her stepfather's attentions and the deep blue sea of her own guilty desires, that mightn't account for the change in regularity.

It never occurred to the girl there could be some other reason; not until midway through April when her courses still hadn't shown, and growing a little concerned she confided the fact to Dorrie Vickers.

Their employer Mr Surtees had been entertaining a party of guests the previous evening. The drawing room still smelled heavily of stale cigar smoke when the pair of them went in to clean at eight o'clock next morning; and as Ruby was crossing the room to open the windows she was overtaken by a sudden violent nausea.

"God, it stinks in here," she said, grimacing. "I think I'm going to be ill–"

"Shove your head out the window, quick." Dorrie ran to help her push up the sash. "Take a good gollup of air and you wo' feel so bad."

She did as advised – and promptly parted with her breakfast into the flower-bed.

"You must have ate some'at that's disagreed wi' you," said Dorrie practically, surveying the damage to Mrs Surtees' tulips. "Best sit yourself down, you poor wench, while I fetch you some water."

"No, I'm all right." Ruby stayed where she was, clutching the edge of the window and sucking in deep gulps of air. "It's the smell o' cigars in here that did it . . . I felt my stomach turn . . ." She bent forward to heave again, coughing on the sour taste of bile at the back of her throat.

"You ain't ailing of anything, are you?" Dorrie glanced at her hard as she got on with opening the rest of the windows. "Only you've been looking a bit washed-out this past couple o' weeks, I thought."

Ruby leaned against the wall and wiped her mouth with the bottom of her apron. "I'm late wi' my monthly, that's all," she answered despondently.

"Oh? How late d'you call late?"

"Well . . . the last time I showed was Valentine's Day." Dorrie stopped what she was doing.

"I've kept meaning to ask you," Ruby went on. "I was wondering . . . I was wondering if *you've* ever gone, y'knòw, much over?"

"Not two whole ruddy months I ain't!" The other looked her up and down in a curiously suspicious sort of way. "Here, is this the first time you've been sick, like?"

"Aye. Though I felt proper queasy when I woke on Tuesday. Why – does it mean there's some'at wrong wi' me?"

Dorrie rolled her eyes. "All depends what you've been getting up to."

"How d'you mean? Getting up to what?" Ruby felt her cheeks begin to burn.

"You know what, so you needn't look so innocent. I bet it's Matthew Dyson, ain't it, eh?"

There was a pause while Ruby stared at her. "What's Matthew got to do wi' it?"

"Plenty, from the sound o' things! Don't you know the facts o' life yet, Ruby Gallimore? You should have done the same as I do and made him catch it in his shirt-tail."

However crudely put, she guessed of course what Dorrie meant. But Jack McShane had always taken care to pull away from her at the last minute, so she couldn't *possibly* be in the family way. In fact it wasn't a thought that had even crossed her mind till now . . .

Mistaking her silence for admission, the other continued drily, "You'm a sly one, ain't you. What's this story you've been spinning me about keeping yourself pure till you was married? And that Matthew such a virtuous clean-living Christian, trotting off to chapel every Sunday wi' his Mam and Dad to say his prayers—"

"Oh, shut up will you, Dorrie Vickers!" Ruby glared at her, angrily unhappy. "If you think I've been misbehaving myself wi' Matt and got into trouble, you're wrong 'cos I haven't."

"Two months late and feeling sick? If that ain't getting yourself into trouble then I'm the Queen o' blinkin' Sheba."

Ruby hung her head, wringing her hands in her apron. She wouldn't accept it, she wouldn't; she *couldn't*.

"He always stopped himself in time," she said pathetically, close to tears suddenly. "He always promised it was safe."

She meant Jack; but Dorrie misinterpreted. "Men – they'm all the same inside their trousers, they'll promise a wench the moon on the end of a string. Still, never mind, Ruby," she added, looking on the bright side, "you was going to marry him anyway, so it don't make any difference really."

Lizzie mustn't know. That was the overriding thought in Ruby's mind. Her mother must never find out that Jack was this baby's father.

In May, when three months had passed with no sign of her courses, she was finally forced to acknowledge the fact that he'd got her with child; and the ghastliness of her predicament so appalled her that she even contemplated drowning herself in the canal. Only Dorrie knew about her condition, nobody else. And Dorrie was sworn to absolute secrecy. In her desperation, Ruby had enlisted the older girl's help to try and procure a miscarriage, using the plausible excuse that she and Matthew didn't want a family till he'd finished his apprenticeship at Chubb's.

Dorrie believed her. There was no way on earth Ruby would ever admit it wasn't Matthew but her stepfather who'd lain with her, and now she was having to pay for the wrong she had done. She couldn't wreck her mother's life by owning to the truth; she could only hope and pray her wretched problem was disposed of before it advertised its presence to the world.

She hoped and prayed in vain. When the pennyroyal pills

that Dorrie got her failed to do the trick, Ruby was left with no alternative but go to Jack McShane.

The haulage contractor who employed Jack had his premises in Gordon Street, not far from the General Hospital, in one of a row of houses converted to commercial use. At the side of the house a pair of wooden gates led through an archway into the cobbled stable-yard at the rear, and beyond that to the sheds where the wagons were kept.

The yard was the only place Ruby could think of to speak to her stepfather privately, away from number 11 Minerva Lane, and she'd chosen it knowing he'd be alone here Monday afternoon, her half-day off, because he'd mentioned the fact to her mother the night before.

He was inside one of the stables when she arrived. She could hear him whistling between his teeth as he groomed a horse.

"Hello, Jack," she said. It didn't sound like her voice at all, and she cleared her throat nervously before she called out to him again a little louder.

He came to the stable door and looked through the open square at the top, wiping the sweat from his forehead with the back of his arm.

"Ruby—?" He was surprised to see who it was. "What brings *you* along? Nothing amiss at home, is there?"

She shook her head. All morning she'd been rehearsing what she would say to him; but now the moment had come she was overtaken by a sudden fit of panic and all she could think of was – "Mr Ingram won't be displeased if he finds me here, will he?"

"No, he ain't in the office. He's out wi' a load." Jack reached over to unbolt the bottom door and swing it open. "If this is just a social visit, why don't you come inside – we can have a chat while I'm rubbing down the horse."

Ruby hesitated.

"Come on – I ain't going to bite you!" he said with a laugh. "Mind, I might gi' you a kiss if you ask me."

A kiss was the last thing she wanted from him, now or ever. Nevertheless, rather than stand in the middle of the yard she did as he invited and went into the stable, holding up her skirt to avoid the stale-soaked straw that had been cleared away from the stalls. Out of the brightness of the pleasant afternoon the building was cool and full of shadow, its dimness irradiated by shafts of dusty sunlight which filtered down between the rafters, and underlying the warmly acrid reek of horses was an aroma of hay and mildewed leather.

"Well, my beauty–" Jack made to put his arm round the girl, but she pushed him off and went to stand at the other side of the stall, setting a barrier between them.

"I haven't come here for any o' that," she said awkwardly, avoiding his eye. "I – I've come to tell you some'at."

He looked at her hard for a moment before he carried on rubbing down the big bay Shire that stood quietly nuzzling inside its bag of fodder.

"Couldn't it have waited till I was home this evening?" he asked across the animal's shoulder.

"No it's . . . personal. I didn't want to say anything in the house for fear you got angry and started raising your voice."

"Why, have you been getting up to some'at to make me angry?"

Ruby looked at her feet, then out through the cob-webbed window.

"Let's hear you!" he prompted her, sensing something amiss from her show of reluctance.

She drew a deep breath and held it for a second while she steeled herself; then, squeezing her eyes tight, she blurted out – "I'm expecting, Jack. I'm carrying your babby and I don't know what to do about it."

There was a terrible silence. She opened her eyes again. Her stepfather was staring at her over the back of the horse, and the expression she saw stamped across his features made her recoil.

"Don't look at me like that," she whimpered, putting her arms round herself in a childlike gesture of self-protection. "It in't my fault if I've gone and fallen pregnant–"

"Whose bloody fault is it, then!" His voice, like his face, had a sudden frightening coldness. "You ain't holding me to blame, by Christ you ain't."

"But there hasn't been anyone else, there's only been you."

Another man might have been swayed by the pathos of the young girl's situation, but Jack McShane thought only of himself. Throwing aside the rag he'd been using, he came out of the stall. "What about Matthew Dyson, eh? I bet you've hoiked up your skirts for him a few times."

"I've never! I swear it! You're the only one that's ever laid a hand on me."

"It was more than a hand, as I recall," he told her coarsely.

"And now I'm in the family way because of it . . ." Ruby's throat was clogged with sudden tears. "God, what am I going to do?"

Jack's eyes ran over her. "You don't look in the family way to me," he said; and then, remembering something – "You ain't even late wi' your monthlies, you silly young bitch."

The contemptuous way he said that stung her. "I'm three months late, if you want to know," she flung back. "I've been pretending for our Mam's sake – it'd kill her if ever she knew what you've been doing wi' me on our kitchen hearth. And I've started being sick of a morning, an' all. Does that satisfy you?"

He cursed obscenely. "I've always been damn' careful whenever I've — you," he said, using a term no man would address to a woman he respected. "If you'm knocked up, my wench, that's your bloody bad luck, not mine."

No apology, no sympathy; just an attitude that made Ruby feel so cheapened, so degraded, that any affection she might still have had for him was killed stone dead.

Swallowing her tears, she raised her chin defiantly to brave him. "When I think how I've let you take me in, believing every lying word you've said to me–! I might have guessed you'd only be concerned to save your own hide. But we're both in this together, Jack McShane. I don't want to have a babby any more than you, so what're you going to do to help me – tell me that?"

"Have you tried getting shot o' the perishin' thing?"

"Aye. I've tried pennyroyal pills and jumping down the stairs, but nothing's worked."

He cursed again. Swinging away, he walked to the open

stable door and stared outside, chewing his moustache; then after some moments, turning back to her, he said in an ugly tone, "If you ever let on to your mother – God help me, I'll swing for you, Ruby. You hear? If you drop me in it, I'll break your blasted neck."

He meant it as well. He'd got his feet too comfortably under Lizzie's table to have his whole domestic life put into jeopardy. Lizzie didn't love him so devotedly that she wouldn't throw him out with his bags on to the street if she learned he'd been amusing himself with her daughter.

"What on earth I ever saw to like in you–" Ruby looked at him disgustedly. "Going behind our poor Mam's back is some'at I'll regret to the end o' my days – and no, I won't tell her it was you, Jack, because I'm too ashamed. It would break her heart and finish her, it would."

"I'm glad you'm seeing sense at least–"

"It in't sense! If I had any sense I'd never have let you touch me in the first place!"

She was bitterly angry now. Coming from behind the stall she shoved her way past him towards the stable door, pausing on the threshold to turn back and face him.

"This is yourn as well as mine," she said, holding the flat of her hand against her belly. "*You* put it there. *You* better think of some way to help me get rid of it."

6

The Sunday midday meal was, as always, a muted affair at number 3 Minerva Lane, the Dysons' house. Sundays were generally muted altogether, being the Sabbath, and idle talk, like idle tasks, was discouraged. Agnes and Eli Dyson were strict in the observance of their religious duties: with Matthew their son they attended the Methodist New Connexion Chapel in Horseley Fields morning as well as evening, and passed the rest of the day piously and quietly, reading Scripture and preparing the coming week's class-meetings for Christian Fellowship which Eli Dyson as a lay preacher helped to organise.

"I'm going out for a while this afternoon," Matthew told his mother as he helped her clear away the dinner things from the table. "I told Ruby's Mam I'd take Ruby a bit of a walk around West Park."

Agnes Dyson, a small, neat, upright woman with grey hair pulled severely from her face into a bun, made no response other than to glance at her son with a tightening of the mouth. She had always been critical of the closeness between him and Ruby Gallimore, preferring he would choose his company from among the respectable young women of their chapel; but since Ruby was the one he'd set his heart and mind on having, she suffered herself to bear her cross in silence. Ruby was a decent enough girl; but the mother – the mother worked as a barmaid in a public house, and that to Agnes Dyson was quite as bad as working in one of the Biblical slime-pits of Siddim.

"Mind you're back in good time for chapel," said Eli Dyson, looking at Matthew over his steel-rimmed reading spectacles. "I don't want you coming in late, d'you hear. It's Jeremiah Henty from Bilston preaching this evening."

"I'll be back in time." His son carried the plates into the scullery and put them in the brownstone sink, his mind preoccupied with other thoughts than chapel duty. He'd seen nothing at all of Ruby for the past six days while she'd been ill off work in bed – her stepfather wouldn't allow him, nor would he have the doctor to her, telling Matthew she was only sick from eating tainted meat.

With the weather as warm as it was for the time of year, meat exposed all day on butchers' slabs went 'off' quite quickly, becoming fly-blown if it wasn't swabbed with vinegar. The effects from eating it were often very serious and Matthew had felt worried that she hadn't been examined by the doctor. Six days was a long time to be ill with stomach-poisoning.

Ducking to glance at himself in the piece of mirror set above the sink, he ran his fingers through his thick dark hair and straightened his necktie.

"Right, I'll be off then," he called to his parents.

"Tea's on the table at five o'clock sharp, Matthew," his mother reminded him, raising her voice as he went out the door.

He tapped on the window to show her he'd heard; then pausing to put on his cap in the yard he walked along the alley towards Ruby's, nodding good afternoon to two of the neighbours as they went past.

His sweetheart was waiting for him by her gate. Her sickness had so altered her appearance that the change in her quite shook him for a moment when he saw her. Her young face which had always been so round and pretty had a pale, pinched look as though the flesh had shrunk on it, and her eyes were ringed with bruise-like shadows. Even her hands when Matthew caught and held them felt like fragile little bird-bones. She had made an effort to dress herself attractively in a soft green outfit trimmed with mauve, and matching ribbons on the hat; but Matthew never noticed.

"I know. There's no need to say anything," Ruby told him sadly as he made to speak. "I look like a warmed-up corpse, don't I, Matt. But I'm feeling ever so much better now . . ." Her voice trailed off.

"Are you certain you're strong enough to go out this afternoon, my love?" he asked her, desperately concerned to see how ill she'd been.

"Aye. The little stroll will do me good." She took his arm. "In any case, I'm starting back to work tomorrow."

"Does your mother think you ought to?" He matched his pace to hers, shortening his stride as they came out of Minerva Lane and into Horseley Fields.

Ruby didn't answer the question directly. "I'll lose my employment if I have any more time away. Mam went to see Mr Perryman – y'know, the butler – yesterday morning, and he told her he'd arrange for me to do light duties just for a bit till I'm properly back on my feet."

"I called round your house every night to ask how you were—"

"I know. I heard your voice. I wanted to talk to you out o' the window only *he* wouldn't let me." Ruby gave that *he* a peculiar emphasis, uttering the word with such contempt that something obviously had soured her previous high opinion of her stepfather.

"No, I wasn't even invited through the door," said Matthew. "Not that I was much surprised, seeing how he's never made me welcome since your mother's marriage. What did surprise me though, I must admit, was that he wouldn't get the doctor in to you, nor let your mother send for medicine."

"Oh, he wouldn't want no doctor treating me—" Ruby started bitterly; and then, changing the subject with an odd abruptness, "D'you mind if we don't go as far as West Park, Matt? I don't feel up to walking all that way."

"Of course I don't mind! I didn't intend to make you walk there – we were going to take the omnibus from Princes Square."

"I tell you where I'd like to go instead." The girl indicated one of the narrow terraced streets off to their left. "If we cut down here through Shakespeare Street we can have a wander round in Boney Park."

Boney Park was the local gallows-humour name for St George's churchyard, one of the oldest and largest of the town's burial grounds, an area of overgrown paths and tombs and trees which was popular as a rendezvous with courting couples.

Reaching it, they entered through one of the side-gates in the high stone wall and walked along until they found a secluded little spot where dog roses and ivy twined about the railings of a lichened table-tomb. It was very peaceful here, with that atmosphere of tranquillity which seems to haunt all churchyards. The grass was strewn with drifts of fallen hawthorn blossom, and from the trees around the throaty cooing of ring-doves hushed the occasional noise of horse traffic.

Ruby closed her eyes and stood drinking in the peace for a moment or two before she sat down with her back against the railings and pulled off her hat.

Matthew sprawled full length beside her. Propping himself on an elbow and reaching across to take her small, thin hand, he said, suddenly remembering, "By the way, I saw that friend o' yours, that Dorrie Vickers, in the street on Wednesday. I wondered if she'd called to visit you."

For some reason, he thought, this comment seemed to agitate Ruby because she gave him the strangest look and asked quickly, "She didn't see *you*, did she, Matt?"

"Well . . . no. At least, I think not. She didn't speak at any rate."

As though his answer had relieved her, she heaved a little sigh and then said, "Aye, she came to visit on her evening off. She brought me a bunch o' flowers and some copies o' *Peg's Own Paper*."

"How did she get on wi' your stepfather – was he all right wi' her?"

"How d'you mean, all right?"

"I mean was he polite, or did he try and turn her from the door like me."

"Oh, he was polite."

Ruby bent her head and played with Matthew's fingers in a distracted manner. "You remember what you said when you met her at the fair that once, how her and Jack McShane 'd make two for a pair?"

"That was the sentiment, yes."

"Well, you weren't wrong. She hadn't been in the house above half an hour and he was smarming round her as though she was–" She stopped, and after a second glanced away, biting her lip.

"I wish that woman wasn't such a friend of yours," said Matthew quietly. "You've changed completely in the time you've known her. I've told you this before, my love, but during this last year or so, d'you know I've hardly recognised you sometimes. First I thought it must be Jack McShane who'd made you so – well, *giddy*, if you like. But then you started acting secretive, going out at night with Dorrie Vickers and her crowd instead o' meeting me. And since October ... to be honest, you haven't been the wench I love, you've seemed more like a total stranger."

"Everybody changes, Matthew. Some of us not for the better, I'm afraid."

Ruby looked back at him, and in her eyes he read an expression of such frightening emptiness that he sat up to face her, taking her other hand to draw her closer. "What is it, sweetheart? I can feel there's some'at troubling you. Won't you tell me what it is so I can help you?"

"Nobody can help me any more. I wish he'd killed me, do you know that? I wish he'd killed me wi' his filthy powders." She turned her head away again abruptly.

"Ruby–?" Matthew grasped her tighter; and when she tried to pull from him he rose to his knees on the grass and stared at her, mystified by this behaviour. "D'you mean your stepfather? Mr McShane's been giving you powders, is that what you're saying?"

She nodded dumbly.

"He's been dosing you wi' some'at for your stomach upset?"

"It wasn't no stomach upset. I only wish to God it had been."

There was a pause. And then, suddenly out of the blue, she went on in a low voice that was vibrant with emotion, "He's ruined me, Matt. I'm no good to you any more. He's ruined me, so it's best we finish things atween us . . . here and now. It's why I'm seeing you today . . . so I can tell you. Find yourself another sweetheart, somebody respectable that won't ashame you."

For a minute he thought she must be pulling his leg, that this was a joke, a childish, bizarre sort of joke. He even started to laugh – till he saw her face.

"I'm pregnant by Jack McShane," Ruby said; and Matthew felt as though a sledge-hammer had slammed into him, shattering his world into fragments. "Them powders he's been giving me, they were supposed to make me miscarry. But they didn't. They only made me ill. That's why he wouldn't have the doctor in to me."

As long as he lived, he would never forget how she'd looked as she made that confession. And when, disbelieving – wounded – furious – he demanded to know what in God's name had been going on, she told him everything, speaking quietly and tonelessly, relating the facts without sparing either the guilt or the deceit of the role she herself had played in her seduction.

Matthew heard her out to the end in livid silence, gripped by an anger so violent that by the time she finished he was visibly shaking with it. Not anger against Ruby – for her he felt a savage, outraged pity – but against the man who had used her naive innocence so selfishly, so casually, and fouled his own domestic nest not only with adultery but with incest.

"Our Mother mustn't ever know." Like a litany, Ruby kept repeating that throughout her wretched story.

"She'll *have* to know!" Matthew cried finally. "How long d'you think you can go on protecting McShane? How long, eh? Another month to six weeks and your mother will *see* that you're pregnant. For God's sake, what will you tell her? Who will you name as the father?"

"She mustn't find out–" For the first time, the self-control disintegrated and Ruby gave way to helpless tears. Burying her face in her hands she started weeping uncontrollably, and it was several minutes before she'd recovered enough for her plea to make any sense through the noise of her sobs.

"I know I haven't no right to ask you . . . not after what I've gone and done across you . . . but please, you must swear to me on your honour you'll never breathe a word o' what I've told you ... not a word. Please, Matt ... *please* promise me."

Horrified as he was by her appalling plight, his hurt and anger were still master of him. "I'll breathe more than a word to McShane, I can promise you *that*. I'll knock him from here into kingdom come soon as ever I lay my hands on the bastard." And it was a measure of the strength of his emotions that Matthew Dyson used such a pejorative expression.

"Oh no, Matt, you mustn't – he'll kill you!" Ruby burst into fresh sobs. "I'm not worth it. Forget about me ... find yourself a wench that's decent! ... I'm just rubbish, I am."

"You're what *he's* made you! Why in God's name couldn't you have come to me for help when all this business started? *Why*? Did you fear I'd blame you? If anybody has to take the blame it's *him*. He led you into doing wrong. *He* was the one who encouraged you, turning your head with his attentions when he surely knew how trustful and naive you were. Poor chick, he took advantage of you, played on your affection for him, had his bit of fun wi' you – aye, and his pound of flesh as well! And now that the Devil's handed him the bill McShane won't pay it, will he?" Matthew's voice was raw with bitterness. "You can't let him escape scot-free to spare your Mam a broken heart. She's bound to find out one way or another."

"Not from you she in't – *please*, Matthew!"

He flung himself away across the grass as though he couldn't bear to listen to her.

"I'm not protecting Jack McShane," Ruby went on

desperately, fighting to control her grief and speak coherently. "I hate him far more now than I admired him, so I do. He's ruined my life—"

"He's ruined mine, as well!"

"But I in't going to break up the home. Much as I hate him, I in't doing that."

"What choice do you have – you're expecting his child in November."

"I do have a choice. It in't much, but it's better than nothing. I'm running away, Matt. I'm packing my bags and I'm running away. I've thought it all out."

He stared at her over his shoulder. "But – where will you run?"

"I'll go to a place where nobody knows me, like Birmingham. They've got institutes there for wenches in trouble like me. And when . . . when the bab's born I can have it adopted, and then I can go back in service again. I think that's the best thing . . . don't you?"

That Sunday evening Matthew Dyson didn't go to chapel with his parents to hear Jeremiah Henty of Bilston preach. He went in search of Jack McShane instead, and tracked him down to the canal behind Minerva Lane where Jack was sitting by the road bridge, fishing.

"I want a word with you," he said without preamble, walking up to stand behind the older man. "I think you know what it's about, as well."

Jack took his time with the bait he was attaching to his hook; then slowly looking round, he answered curtly, "If you'm addressing me, young 'un, you'll kindly remember your manners and gi' me a name."

"Oh, I'll give you a name right enough. How about seducer, or adulterer – or maybe lecher fits the bill more neatly."

Jack's face, always a good colour, flushed dark red. Laying aside his rod on the bank he rose to his feet and measured Matthew with his eye in an unpleasant fashion. "Now you look here a minute, Dyson–?"

"No, *you* look here, *Mr* McShane. I take a very poor view of you forcing your incestuous attentions upon Ruby and indecently abusing her."

"You what–?"

"You heard. She's your stepdaughter, for God's sake. She's an innocent young wench who's half your age. She's the wench *I* love and intended to marry. D'you know what I think about you? I'd like to see you flogged at the end of a rope till your ribs are laid bare – and I'd do it myself!"

Jack's look narrowed. The muscle in his jaw began to work. "Right, have you said your piece now? Because if you have, I suggest you clear off out of here afore I lose my patience wi' you."

"I'm not clearing off anywhere till you've told me what you mean to do for Ruby and the child she's carrying. You've disgraced her – aye, her *and* her mother, with your tom-cat antics–" Matthew's tone betrayed his furious anger. He'd somehow managed to control himself all afternoon, but now the self-restraint had snapped completely. "And if you think I'm going to let you walk away from your responsibilities, McShane, you'd better think again, I'm warning you!"

The other started rolling up his shirt-sleeves.

Though probably not quite as tall, he was thicker-set and heavier as well as stronger-muscled than the nineteen-year-old facing him.

"And *I'm* warning *you*," he said in a voice that was all the more menacing for being quiet, "you threaten me just one more time and I'll rearrange your blasted features for you. I'm not carrying no can for Ruby Gallimore, whatever tale the hussy's been and blabbed. If her's in the family way, more like it's you what's knocked her up, not me – her's hot-arsed enough for both of us and half the bloody street besides, I shouldn't wonder."

A red haze seemed to swim in front of Matthew's eyes. He heard himself shout out – and then a sudden violent pain stabbed through his fist and Jack McShane was teetering away from him, blood oozing from the corner of his mouth.

This was the first time he had ever struck a living thing in anger, but by God the blow had been deserved.

Jack wiped his chin and looked at the blood on his hand. "That wasn't very clever of you, was it," he said viciously. "I think you need a lesson teaching, young 'un."

He came dancing towards Matthew with his fists bunched, in the stance of a bare-knuckle fighter, and lashed out a punch that the younger man managed to dodge as it shot past his ear. Caught off balance for a second, he didn't see Jack's other fist until he felt it thud against his ribs. Letting out a grunt of pain he ducked and swung a wild punch in return, catching his opponent with a left hand to the stomach.

Winded, Jack clutched at him, and as they strained together on the towpath, wrestling with one another chest to chest, he butted Matthew hard in the face with his forehead.

For a moment Matthew saw stars. Then the blood gushed from his nose and he staggered away, Jack coming after him throwing a punch at his chin which he fended blindly aside on his forearm.

A woman screamed; but neither man noticed. Panting, they faced up to one another.

"That's enough for starters," Jack said hoarsely. "Now let's see the stuff you'm made of, shall we, Dyson?"

"Aye – come on, I'm waiting for you." The other raised his fists defiantly and stood his ground, prepared to give a good account of himself.

"*Matthew*–!" The woman screamed again, this time distracting him for just an instant; and as he turned his head, Jack was on him with a blow that took him square on the side of the jaw.

Matthew went reeling backwards, semi-stunned. He caught his heel in a tussock of grass at the edge of the towpath and lost his balance, his hands meeting nothing but air as they grabbed for support. Arms cartwheeling, he tried to recover himself – then with an almighty splash he was in the canal.

Fortunately the water at this point was no more than chest-deep and he floundered to his feet, coughing and spluttering, the shock of the immersion clearing his wits a bit. There were people leaning from the bridge to watch the fight, and others had appeared along the towpath –

among them his mother and father with Lizzie McShane, and running behind her, young Ruby.

"*Matthew–*" his mother screeched a third time. "Save him – oh, somebody save my poor son!"

Jack had no intention of saving anything other than his own skin; but actions seemed to tell a different story. Jumping into the water he seized Matthew by the jacket collar and gave him a punch in the eye before losing his footing. The Dysons, thinking he was rescuing their boy, shouted encouragement; but their shouts quickly turned to alarm again when they saw Matthew raise his clenched fist and start striking at Jack in return.

The blows were delivered with the strength of desperation and caught the other in the mouth with force enough to split his lip and knock a couple of teeth out.

"You—" Jack spat blood and swore at him obscenely; and that was the last thing Matthew registered before the world exploded and turned inky-black.

Mayhem erupted on the towpath.

Ruby went off into sobbing hysterics and clung to her mother, who was standing wringing her hands and crying to Jack to leave off. Mr Dyson, seeing his son knocked completely insensible, was preparing to take off his waistcoat and jump in to help him; while Agnes Dyson, horrified by such a shocking spectacle, appealed alternately to the Almighty and the neighbours gathered round her to tell her what this wickedness was all about.

"I'll tell you what it's about, Missus–" Jack hauled the unconscious Matthew up by the armpits. "I've been giving the young bugger a damn' good hiding, that's what. He's gone and put our Ruby in the family way–"

He raised his voice for everyone to hear.

"So unless he wants my horse-whip taking to him, he'd better do the decent thing and marry her!"

7

Matthew could have called Jack's bluff; but it would mean a public slanging match with Ruby in the middle, her shame exposed and he himself seen as accuser. In a situation like this there were never any victors, only victims. She wouldn't be the first young wench in the history of Minerva Lane who'd had to hasten into marriage; by keeping silent, neither admitting nor denying being the father of her child, Matthew hoped to shield her from the muck-raking of vicious gossip and let the mischief die a natural death.

What were the alternatives? Call Jack McShane a liar and brand *him* the father? They'd all be losers then. Let Ruby run away as she had threatened? Had Matthew loved her any less it would have seemed the obvious solution; but because he thought the world of her, because in spite of everything he knew he'd always stand by her, he couldn't, *wouldn't*, let her bear the burden all alone.

They would have married any way, when both were older. It was the argument he used against his parents to defend himself when, shocked and bitterly ashamed, they'd turned on him in private.

If they'd but known the facts, Agnes and Eli Dyson

might possibly have seen their son's dilemma and whilst not sympathising, at least in Christian charity might have accepted his decision. It would have meant the truth becoming public knowledge though, so Matthew kept his silence and said nothing; and for this he had to suffer their continual reproaches, had to watch them forced to share in his opprobrium at chapel meeting, had to bite his tongue when sanctimonious comforters blamed Ruby's moral laxity for leading him astray into temptation.

Brought up as he'd been to know his Scripture, Matthew was familiar with the passage from Isaiah: 'He was oppressed and he was afflicted, yet he opened not his mouth: he is brought as a lamb to the slaughter, and as a sheep before the shearers is dumb, so he openeth not his mouth.'

God knew the truth of his position. God alone should judge. From this he drew the strength to follow his decision through, and marry Ruby. It was a strength demanding sacrifice however, and in time to come its cost would prove very dear.

It was about a week after the brawl with Jack McShane that Matthew called round during his dinner hour to see Lizzie at number 11.

He found her busy making pastry for a rabbit pie, with young Joe helping at the table.

"Why – hello, Matthew!" she exclaimed, taken by surprise to see who it was putting his head round the door.

He took off his cap. "Can I have a word wi' you, Mrs McShane?"

"Of course. Come inside and sit yourself down, don't stand on the step."

She glanced quickly at his face in the sunlight streaming through the kitchen window. It still bore the punishment of her husband's fists, one eye badly swollen and contusions on the cheekbones and the jaw, the bruised flesh turning an unsightly purplish-yellow.

"Is that what Jack done to you?" Joe chipped in as she started to say something else. "Crikey, he din' half give it you! It's worse'n what you done to him–"

"Hush, Joe, that's enough."

The young lad took no notice. Coming round the table he gawped up at Matthew. "Here, is it true what Bertie Phillips said at school, our Ruby's having a babby and you'm the dad?"

"Joe – I said that's enough." Lizzie caught him by the shoulder and propelled him in front of her through the scullery door. "Outside in the yard and play for a bit till I call you back in."

"But Mam–"

"*Out*," she repeated more firmly, "or you'll stop in your bed the rest o' the day. Now do as you're told."

Shutting the door on his protests, she turned to give Matthew an embarrassed smile. "I'm sorry about that. He'd be at lessons only he had another of his turns this morning."

"I can see you're busy so I won't keep you long," the young man answered. "I wanted to speak to you in private, that's why I've called round this dinner-time."

"I'm ever so glad you have." Lizzie brushed a whisp of frizzed hair from her forehead, leaving a smear of flour.

"I know Jack thought he was doing right, but he shouldn't have knocked you about like he did. He's a good man really, Matthew. A good husband . . . I wouldn't be wi'out him. But he's got a terrible temper on him at times. You'll have to forgive him."

"Well, that's between him and me, Mrs McShane. It's Ruby I've come about."

She nodded. "Aye, I thought it must be." Taking up her rolling-pin she started again on the pastry as though she needed to be occupied, working it back and forth on the table top in short, quick strokes.

"I love Ruby very much," Matthew said awkwardly. "There's never been any other wench that's appealed to me, only her."

"I know that, son." Lizzie glanced at him over her shoulder.

"We'd planned on getting married once I'd finished my apprenticeship . . . when we'd got a bit of money set aside." Twisting his cap round and round in his hands he watched the strong, thin arms shaping out the pastry. "What I'm here to ask you, Mrs McShane . . . I know Ruby won't be seventeen till August, and I've still got another few years before I'm a qualified locksmith, but the way things are . . . I want us to be married soon as ever we can."

"I'm pleased to hear you say it, Matthew." She flicked some water from a cup across the floured surface. "I wish you hadn't jumped the gun, but these mistakes do happen." It had nearly happened to Lizzie herself with Charlie Gallimore. Thank God in her case she hadn't fallen pregnant till after the wedding else her Dad would have killed her. "Have you spoke to them at Chubb's about you getting married?"

"Aye. The Gaffer's not best pleased, but I've explained the circumstances."

Under the regulations controlling indentured apprentices marriage was not forbidden, although it was heavily frowned upon. An apprentice couldn't normally be dismissed for misconducting himself unless the misconduct was of a grossly serious nature; and as Matthew's 'gaffer' or manager at Chubb's had pointed out, a little sarcastically, putting a wench in the family way might be immoral but it was hardly a hanging offence.

"How'm you going to support her, have you considered?" Lizzie reached across the table for a basin. "She wo' be stopping at St John's Square once the babby's showing, and there's few places as employ married housemaids."

"I expect we'll manage somehow," he answered, not very hopefully. On the money he was earning at the moment it would be hard going to make ends meet without Ruby's wages.

"You know *I'll* help you both as much as I can, son, but it wo' be a lot I'm afraid."

She came by him to get to the meat-safe, lifting the window net to check on young Joe; and returning with a plate of jointed rabbit, she went on, "Sit yourself down, why don't you? I'll make us a pot o' tea when I've finished this pie."

"No . . . I'm all right standing, Mrs McShane, I mustn't stop long on account of the time."

Matthew glanced at the mantelpiece clock, then his eye

inadvertently dropped to the cheerfully coloured pegged rug that covered the hearth. For a moment he had the vision of Ruby lying there half-naked being mauled by her stepfather, and he had to turn away before Lizzie should notice the hard emotion in his face.

"There's always good jobs going in the market," she was saying now. "I'm sure our Ruby could find herself work on one o' the stalls for a bit, and I'd let you have space here till you'd fixed yourselves up wi' some'at."

"What – lodgings, d'you mean?"

"Aye, lodgings. You've got to live somewhere!"

The notion of living at number 11 made Matthew's gorge rise. "It's kind of you ... thank you. We've got accommodation though. My parents have agreed we live wi' them." That was a lie; nothing of the sort had been agreed yet, but he would rather have slept homeless in the gutter than share a roof with Jack McShane. "There's plenty of room round at our house so it'll be less ... inconvenient."

Lizzie seasoned the rabbit and added some thyme. "I dare say you're right. And Ruby wouldn't want to stop here anyway. I don't know what's got into her just lately – she can hardly manage a civil word to Jack, and he's no better either, the way he keeps avoiding her. They used to be such pals an' all," she added sadly.

Matthew made no answer. He wondered what Lizzie would say if he told her the truth; and knew that he couldn't. Life in Minerva Lane hadn't treated the poor woman very kindly, yet not once had he ever heard her protest or bewail her hard lot. When Charlie Gallimore fell ill and lost his job she'd nursed him day and night until he died, then scrimped and scraped to keep the family together, always cheerful and bright and uncomplaining, taking in lodgers, working at the Harp, neglecting her health for the sake of her home and her children.

The hardship had taken its toll. She was how old now–? Matthew stopped to think. Thirty-five or so, and looked ten years older. Her face in profile was so much like Ruby's they could pass for sisters: the same small nose and chin and pretty neck, the tawny hair worn fastened in a bun. Yet as soon as she turned her head the likeness vanished and she was a thin little middle-aged woman with gentle eyes whose weariness was etched in every feature.

Only a brute would deliberately add to her trials.

"Have you set a date yet?" Lizzie was asking him. "It'll be the chapel I suppose, not church?"

"The wedding, you mean?"

"Aye, the wedding, what else!" She smiled at his slowness, and her smile dispelled the cruel lines from her face. "We've never been much for religion in this house, so chapel or church it wo' matter to us either way."

"Chapel," said Matthew. "Otherwise my parents 'll be–" he was about to say offended, but they were grievously offended as it was. "It's what they'll wish," he finished lamely.

"And the day? Best not leave it too late, else you'll have it coinciding wi' the christening." It was meant as a joke.

"Well, I'll have to consult wi' Ruby about that," he said, his eyes drawn back towards the hearth again. "I wanted to know I'd got your permission before I – proposed to her, like."

Lizzie threw up her hands. "You're a caution and no mistake, Matthew!"

Coming over to him she raised herself to kiss his cheek affectionately, careful of the bruises. "You've got my permission, chick, o' course you have. I'll tell you this – I've always believed things happen as they're meant to, and even though I wish you'd made a better start, I'm proud to have you for a son-in-law."

It was harder convincing Ruby she must wed him. She was pitifully grateful, but racked with guilt that she'd be dragging him down and ruining his life as she'd ruined her own.

"No, I can't let you do this for me, Matt," she'd wept in his arms. "I *won't* let you do it. It's asking too much."

He was stubborn though: no matter what the argument she raised he had an answer. Even if she ran away he'd only follow her and bring her back. Their love was strong. Whatever trouble might beset them, they'd see it through together, and survive.

'Things happen as they're meant to . . .'

They were married on the last Saturday in June at the New Connexion Chapel in Horseley Fields. The minister was quite aware of the young couple's circumstances, but being a fair-minded man he took the view that matrimony was better late than never at all, and in a brief address reminded all those present that the Good God ever loved the sinner however much He might detest the sin.

As chapel chastisement went, it was very mild.

Ruby had refused point-blank to be given away by Jack McShane. Only she and Matthew – and Jack himself, of course – knew why, and there was some nudging in the back rows of the pews when she appeared on the arm of Eddie

Gallimore, her father's younger brother, who kept a barber's shop at Cradley Heath. All Minerva Lane knew there was bad blood between Jack and Matthew Dyson, though everyone agreed that Jack had been within his rights to give the lad a damn' good hiding. That was the way these things were done, and family honour demanded it.

Even so, when Lizzie McShane turned up at her daughter's wedding without her husband, it fuelled the gossip.

While Jack was getting blind drunk in the Harp, the wedding party adjourned to the Temperance Hotel a short way along Horseley Fields. The choice of venue had been dictated by Matthew's parents who would no more have entered a public house than sup with the Devil, and the chill sobriety of the place added to the staid formality of the celebration.

Dorrie Vickers, who'd attended Ruby as her bridesmaid, thought it was more like a funeral than a wedding. She'd been looking forward to champagne and port, not a cup of stewed tea; and as soon as she could see a chance she excused herself to go to the closet, and slipped to the New Inn a few doors away where several strong ales got rid of the taste in her mouth.

On her return she went back to sit with Ruby, ignoring Mrs Dyson's suspicious sniffs; and in a jollier mood now, began talking about the evening she'd spent with 'her' Frank at the Empire last Friday.

"Laugh? You should ha' seen us, Ruby! I swear I nearly bust my corsets at some o' the turns. There was one of 'em had this great big–" giggling, Dorrie leaned over to whisper, "and you wouldn't credit the antics he got up to, I

thought he'd do himself a bloomin' mischief! Ooh, here –
and d'you know who was asking after you?"

She paused and shot a furtive glance at Matthew,
immersed in conversation with Eddie Gallimore; then in a
lower voice went on, "D'you remember Sam Reynolds?
You met him that one time all of us went to the Concert
Hall in Bilston Street."

It was an evening Ruby recalled only too painfully, since
it had ended in the arms of Jack McShane.

"Wasn't Sam Reynolds the one who saw me home?" she
said after a moment.

"You've got him! He wasn't half knocked sideways when
I told him you was getting wed. He'd taken quite a shine to
you apparently."

Ruby twisted the cheap brass ring Matthew had just
placed upon her finger as a makeshift wedding-band till he
could buy a gold one.

"Didn't you tell me Sam Reynolds's brother had stalls in
the market?" she asked suddenly.

Dorrie nodded, smiling with false brightness at Mrs
Dyson who was eyeing her gaudy outfit in a withering manner. Old cat, she thought. "Jabez Reynolds the butcher,
that's right. Here – now *he'd* maybe gi' you work if Sam put
in a word for you!"

"Aye, that's what I was thinking . . ." Ruby looked
pensive. There'd been a conference between Matthew and
his parents, and her mother and herself, about how the
young couple were going to manage once Ruby had worked
out her notice at St John's Square. In view of the past
kindness of her employer Mr Surtees and his family, she'd
hoped to receive a little something as a parting bonus; but

when Perryman the butler informed them of the reason for her leaving, a frosty note of moral disapproval had stiffened their benevolence and she was lucky even to get so much as a reference.

"D'you think Sam Reynolds *would* put in a word?" she wondered. "Our Mam was saying about getting work in the market, but I don't know it'd be that easy . . . not in my condition."

Dorrie pressed her hand. Despite her rough exterior she was genuinely fond of Ruby in a pitying sort of way.

"I'll see what I can wangle for you," she promised, catching Matthew's eye as he turned towards his new young wife and giving him a little wink from force of habit. "Just leave everything to me, all right?"

The pale, cool softness of the midsummer moon spilled across the bedroom floor and touched the single deep red rose which Matthew had picked earlier. In the warmth of the air its petals had unfolded, and several lay fallen on the gleaming polished surface of the chest of drawers, like crimson teardrops.

Moonlight and roses . . . they made a mockery of Ruby's dreams, for it could hardly be called idyllically romantic to start her married life in the antiseptic cleanliness of number 3 Minerva Lane and listen, not to nightingales, but her husband's parents praying in the room next door.

"Are they doing that on purpose?" she complained, turning from the window towards Matthew waiting naked in the shadows on the bed. "Or have we got to stick it *every* night?"

He didn't answer. From the moment they'd arrived here

from the Temperance Hotel he'd felt embarrassed – not only by his parents' disapproval of his bride but the awkwardness of married sexual intimacy. This was his wedding night; Ruby and he had wanted privacy. Yet since eight o'clock they'd been sitting downstairs in the parlour engaged in stilted conversation like a pair of strangers in a doctor's waiting-room, watching the fingers of the wall-clock creep slowly, oh so slowly, towards bedtime.

It was almost a relief when Matthew's father enlivened the evening by reading aloud a chapter from the Bible; at least it had given them something else to think about.

Now here they were, the two of them alone at last together in the room they were to share as man and wife – *his* room, the room he'd had since childhood, where he'd grown into a youth and spent the past few years dreaming – fantasizing – of this very moment. It was a room where 'sin' had always been forbidden. No one else had come in here except his mother; small wonder the sight of Ruby seemed unreal to him.

Unreal, and also deeply troubling.

Matthew was a young man, with a young man's normal, healthy sexual appetite, and Ruby was his wife; yet when she had undressed herself just now he felt no physical desire for her. Love, yes, and tenderness; but not the strong arousal he'd expected.

Modestly, she had blown out the lamp and used the moonlight for illumination while she took off her outer clothes and hung them up. He'd watched in silence, his mouth going dry and his heart beating loud as a drum, his eyes on the curve of her shoulder and breast as she moved past the window.

Then she'd half turned, her silhouette betraying the slight distortion of her abdomen from pregnancy – and the thought of the child in her womb had killed all desire.

"Sweetheart – d'you hear what I said?" Ruby came towards him slowly, almost shyly, her arms crossed on her small, sweet breasts to cover them. "Do your Mam and Dad pray *every* night?"

"Not usually."

"Thank God for that!"

She touched his cheek, stroking the backs of her fingers up and down its faint stubble. "Are you glad we've got married?"

"Aye." Matthew turned her hand over to kiss the palm, then pulled her down to sit beside him on the bed, folding her in his embrace. "Of course I'm glad."

"I wish we didn't have to whisper. Will they hear us, d'you think?"

"I never hear *them*."

She giggled nervously against his shoulder. "I shouldn't think they've ever done it but the once. P'raps that's what they're praying for, for strength." Raising her head she looked into his face, the glimmer of the moonlight in her eyes. "Shall we go under the covers now? I'm getting chilled wi' nothing on."

This wasn't what Matthew had hoped for on his wedding night. He felt humiliated by his lack of sexual response to Ruby's closeness, but the image of her with Jack McShane kept intruding into his mind, and stupidly he said, "Aye, let's get into bed. I expect you're tired and want to sleep."

"No . . . I don't want to sleep yet awhile."

There was puzzlement in her answer; and when they

were lying down in each other's arms, the springs protesting at their double weight, she went on softly, "I'm all yours now, Matthew . . . *properly* yours, I mean. Don't be afraid you'll hurt me. You won't hurt me. You're my husband and I love you . . . I'll do anything to please you, sweetheart."

She began covering his face with little kisses, then took his hand and cupped it round her breast. Matthew felt his body quicken into physical excitement. He pressed her leg between his thighs and hugged himself against her, for a moment overmastered by arousal.

Then his fumbling fingers touched the place enclosing McShane's child, and he flung himself away from her, unmanned again.

"What is it?" she asked urgently. "What is it, Matthew? Don't you want me?"

"Aye, I want you." He stared at the darkened ceiling.

She raised herself to look at him and leaned across to kiss his mouth, but he turned his head aside in misery.

"Ruby . . . I can't," he said, ashamed.

"Yes you can!" Her hand slipped over his taut, flat belly to the cause of his shame and awkwardly started caressing him.

"I *can't*. Not with the babby in you."

"Mam said it wouldn't harm the babby," Ruby said, still trying to arouse him.

He caught her hand and pulled it from him. How could he explain to her, when he hardly understood himself? It wasn't just the child, it was – oh, it was this room, and his parents next door, and McShane and the whole situation.

"Amen," he heard his mother say distinctly.

"You do love me, don't you, Matthew?"

"I love you, Ruby Dyson." He rolled over and took her in his arms, stroking back the hair that swathed her face.

"Ruby Dyson." She repeated the new name dully, disappointed, feeling that she'd already failed to be a proper wife. "When will I be *Mrs* Dyson, though."

"How d'you mean?"

"Is it going to be like this atween us right until the babby's born? Sleeping together like ... brother and sister?"

He didn't answer her. He didn't know.

8

The retail market hall in front of St Peter's church at the heart of the town was one of those enormous temple-like edifices so beloved of mid-century Victorian architects. From the outside it looked heavy and ugly with its blind arcaded walls and Grecian-pillared entrance; but within, the huge glass roof and ornate cast-iron columns produced a pleasing contrast of airiness and space and light.

From morning until early evening the scene here was a melée of activity, with traders bawling out their wares and customers crowding the aisles in search of any bargains. Everything was displayed in random order – florists beside haberdashers, greengrocers next to confectioners – all except the fishmongers and butchers, whose white-tiled stalls were in a section of the hall where the raw smells from their marble slabs caused least offence.

Ruby had been in the market many a time with her mother. The reason she'd come by herself today was to seek an interview with Jabez Reynolds, whom she knew of course by name, though not by sight (Lizzie generally bought their meat from rival Whitehouse's).

Presuming the butcher to be the middle-aged man in boater and striped apron who was standing by the stall, she approached him nervously.

"Excuse me . . . Mr Reynolds?"

"What can I do for you, cock?" he said, not hearing her properly because of the shouts of the fishmonger opposite.

"I've come about a job—" Should she call him 'sir' she wondered? "A pal o' mine, Dorrie Vickers, she knows your brother Sam, and it was him as said that I should come and see you."

The man looked at her mystified.

"Sam Reynolds . . . your brother," she reminded him a little awkwardly. Dorrie had kept her promise about mentioning to Sam she was looking for employment; and at the start of the week he'd sent back word to tell her there might be a job on the stall if she applied.

"Sam Reynolds ain't my brother, cock!" the man said, starting to laugh. "If it's the Gaffer you'm wanting, he's most likely round at the Vaults."

Ruby flushed in confusion. "Oh, I'm sorry . . . I've made a mistake. What does Mr Reynolds look like so's I'll know him?"

"Big chap. Clipped moustache. You can't miss him, he always wears a flower in his buttonhole."

She gave an embarrassed nod of thanks and hurried away. Would Mr Reynolds object if she went round to the Vaults to speak to him? Or should she wait and hope to catch him later? In two minds what to do, she sat in the sun in St Peter's churchyard for half an hour, glad of an excuse to be away from Minerva Lane and the sour, oppressive atmosphere of her in-laws.

She and Matthew had been married less than three weeks – *three weeks* – and already the strain of living in that funeral parlour of a house was making her wish they'd never gone and got married at all. She'd be driven mad unless she found a job to take her out of the place.

Suddenly resolute, the girl stood up and walked from the churchyard down into busy Queen Square.

The Vaults was a public house fronting the Empire Music Hall, and one of the oldest licensed premises still doing business in the town. After the glaring brightness of the July day the saloon interior felt cool and dark, and it took a couple of seconds before her eyes adjusted to the jaundiced yellow lighting of the gas-globes. Used as she was to frequenting public houses, it was disconcerting to discover herself the only female among the dozen or so customers; and hoping she wouldn't be taken for a woman off the streets she went up to the counter.

"I'm looking for Mr Jabez Reynolds," she informed the barman. "Could you tell me whether he's here, please?"

The barman carried on drying a glass while taking stock of her appearance, then satisfied she seemed respectable, jerked his head in the direction of a gentleman sitting alone at a table in the corner.

Screwing up her courage, Ruby walked across.

The master butcher had his back to her, and as she approached she was surprised to note that he was dressed like a person of some quality. He was engrossed in a trade journal, holding it slantwise to catch the light from the window; and when she spoke his name he didn't break off immediately but finished reading the last few sentences.

"Now then, young lady–" he said briskly when he'd done, glancing up, "how can I be of assistance to you?"

She seated herself opposite, noticing the red carnation he was sporting. "I've come about enquiring after a job, sir.

I'm Ruby Dyson... *Mrs* Ruby Dyson. I believe your brother Sam has mentioned me?"

Before he answered Mr Reynolds subjected her to a thorough scrutiny, taking in the small, enchanting features, the neatness of her hair and dress, the work-roughened hands clasping a pair of new cotton gloves. He also observed the anxiety of her manner, and the fact that she was some months pregnant.

"Aye, I believe young Sam *has* mentioned you," he said at length in a rather kinder tone. "Let me get you some refreshment now you've gone to all your trouble finding me. I was about to have another myself–" he indicated the empty whisky glass in front of him. "Then we'll have a little chat about this job."

"Thank you, Mr Reynolds ... that's ever so nice of you, but I don't really want anything."

"You're sure?"

She nodded.

Excusing himself, he pushed back his chair and went to the bar. On his feet he was taller than she'd imagined, and his dark worsted suit was beautifully tailored to fit his long limbs. He was also a good few years younger than she'd supposed him, despite the grey flecks in his hair and moustache; and his face had a maturity and strength of character which made him better-looking than his brother.

She saw him saying something to the barman, and then shake his head.

"First of all–" He came back with a refreshed glass and sat down again. "First of all, my dear, how old are you?"

"I'll be seventeen next month, sir."

Pathetically young to be married; but the Criminal Law

Amendment Act passed only this last year had set the age of consent at sixteen, so her status was legally in order.

Jabez Reynolds rolled a sip of single malt appreciatively round his tongue and swallowed it, without taking his eyes off the girl. "And what was your previous employment?"

"Under-housemaid, sir. With a family in St John's Square. I've brought my reference–" She reached into her woolwork reticule and produced an envelope, placing it on the table between them. "I hope you'll find it's satisfactory."

He left the envelope where it was for the moment, to ask, "Have you ever had experience of shop work, dealing with the general public, anything of that sort?"

Ruby wished he'd stop looking at her quite so hard; it was beginning to make her self-conscious. "I've sometimes lent a hand behind the counter at the Harp, sir. That's the pub in Walsall Street where our Mother works. And when I was smaller I used to help on Saturdays in Beresford's in Mary Ann Street – Beresford's the grocery shop, I mean – weighing out the sugar and the flour. Oh, and yes, I know how to skin and gut rabbits, sir, and draw poultry," she added, trying to remember all the details she'd rehearsed to tell him.

Mr Reynolds smiled. "A young lady of some versatility, in other words." The smile reached his eyes, which were of a steely blue, surrounding them with crinkles and removing all the severity from his face. "And your husband, my dear – how does he make his livelihood?"

"He's an apprentice locksmith at Chubb's."

The candid way she answered his questions impressed him. Taking up her reference now, he unsealed it and enjoyed another mouthful of whisky while he perused its contents. As testimonials went, what Mr Surtees had written about his former housemaid was brief and to the point; and in the circumstances fair enough, thought Jabez Reynolds.

"So–" He refolded the page and handed it back in its envelope. "You ceased employment with this family on account of your condition."

"Yes, sir."

"And may I enquire when the baby will be born?"

"In November." Ruby put the reference away again inside her reticule. "I went to see the doctor this last week, and he said I'm very healthy and there in't no reason why I shouldn't work. Not lugging heavy coal-sacks, mind–" encouraged by his smile she braved a touch of humour "but anything that didn't cause discomfort."

"Good!" Taking an engraved gold hunter from his waistcoat pocket Mr Reynolds opened its case to glance at the time; then replacing it he said, "I hope your condition hasn't made you tickle-stomached, Mrs Dyson?"

"Tickle-stomached, sir?"

"If I offer you employment on one of my stalls you'll be doing things like plucking and drawing and gutting, and that isn't dainty work, you'll understand. I can't employ people who faint or feel ill, I'm afraid."

"Oh, I'm over my morning sickness, I can stand the sight o' blood, sir!" Ruby leaned towards him, hands clasped together, hope as well as earnestness in her expression. "I'm a good hard worker, Mr Reynolds – reliable an' all – and if I didn't think the job 'd suit me I'd never have presumed to trouble you."

He smiled at her again. "Very well, I'll try you out, my dear, and see how you get on."

Swallowing the remains of his whisky, the master butcher rose to his feet to close their interview.

"Eight o'clock sharp in the market next Monday. Oh, and your wages – I'll start you off at seven shillings a week, all found."

It was something of a minor triumph for Ruby to go back to number 3 Minerva Lane and see the expression on Agnes Dyson's face when she told her mother-in-law the news. At least she could hold up her head again instead of being made to feel she was living off their blasted charity like some indigent pauper.

She wouldn't have minded their attitude so much if they were short of a penny themselves, but the Dysons were probably better off than many of their neighbours, having only the one grown son and being so abstemious in their habits – and this on a salary of almost two hundred pounds a year that Mr Dyson earned as a clerk with the London and North Western Railway Company.

She hated Agnes Dyson's tight-lipped disapproval, her cold politeness, her way of looking down her nose at everything that Ruby said or did; and she hated the joyless Christianity, the praying and the Bible-reading, the whole hypocritical humbug of professing to love God while practising intolerance and censure.

In the opinion of her parents-in-law – an opinion they took no pains to hide – Ruby had tempted their dear boy off the straight and narrow path into wickedness. It went without saying that they didn't consider her good enough for him, that it was a *great* disappointment, a *mortifying* shame he'd had to marry her.

Still, the Good Lord moved in a mysterious way and they must resign themselves to make the best of it . . .

Ruby wondered sometimes if they guessed that she and Matthew led an almost sexless life, that they slept together passionless as children, that their marriage hadn't yet been fully consummated. The pair of them were intimate, but only to a point. Night after night he would try to make love, and fail. It was always the same; the child inside her body was a barrier between them and Matthew couldn't – not wouldn't, *couldn't* – physically possess her.

Even though she now utterly loathed her stepfather and went out of her way to avoid him, Ruby's memories of lovemaking with Jack McShane rose up to mock her with the pleasure she had previously experienced. However cheap and sordid that had been, her frustration at not having the same pleasure with her husband put a strain upon their fledgling marriage. Matthew was a virgin. He knew the mechanics of intercourse but not the art of gratifying his partner; and Ruby was too inhibited by the next-door presence of his parents to gain much satisfaction from his fumbling efforts.

"Things'll be better once the babby's born," was the excuse they used to comfort one another; and if either had their doubts of that, they never shared them.

All in all, it was not the happiest of beginnings to a marriage. This job of Ruby's in the market was a lifeline for her, since it took her from the house all day and gave her back a little pride in helping Matthew with their board and lodging. Her mother, God bless her, had offered to give a shilling a week, which Ruby refused. If anyone should be making a contribution, by rights it ought to be Jack McShane; but she would sooner have slit her own throat than take money from that devil, and he had never proposed it of course, being rather too worried it might beg some questions.

Her trial week on the market stall proved satisfactory. As Mr Reynolds had warned, it wasn't the daintiest of work – particularly not for a pregnant woman – but neither was it arduous, and Ruby found she was well able to cope. She had a compassionate nature, but she wasn't squeamish. She'd seen gorier sights on the streets of Horseley Fields from fights and factory accidents and brutal cruelty, and her background had to some extent inured her to such things.

One other young woman shared her work with her, a twenty-year-old named Martha Becket with whom she soon fell in. Martha was a friendly and confiding type of person, with silvery-fair hair which helped to soften rather plain, pointed features. She had been brought up at Dunstall Old Hall, where her parents – both now dead – had been in service many years, and her unassumed refinement and the way she spoke seemed oddly out of place in her present employment.

"Well you see, I would have gone into service myself," she told Ruby, "since that's what I'm bred to. I thought of becoming a cook, as my grandmother was – she cooked for the Wightwicks, you know – but the chances of being engaged by the *right* kind of family are so few and far between in Wolverhampton."

By this, Ruby presumed she meant the Manders and the

Levesons and Giffards, who with the Wightwicks were the cream of the established local gentry. It still did not make clear, though, how she had come to be working in the market.

"I enjoy the preparation of food," Martha explained to her. "A good cook should be familiar with every process if she wishes to be truly competent, and since meat is so important a part of the diet I decided I should set myself to learn about it. My father was a relative by marriage of Mrs Jabez Reynolds's, and therefore it seemed by far the most sensible course that I apply to Mr Reynolds for employment."

Her genteel manner of speech, so incongruously out of keeping with the mottled arms and blood-smeared apron, fascinated Ruby.

"What's Mrs Reynolds like?" she wanted to know, cumbrously getting up from the stool where she'd been skinning a rabbit, and hanging the naked carcase on a hook.

Martha pondered a moment. "Not a lady *exactly*, though almost, being one of the Fowlers of Bilston. In her youth she was considered a most handsome woman, particularly on horseback ... then alas, she contracted a wasting disease of the limbs and for the past half-dozen years it has forced her to keep to her bed. A very sad story, for her husband quite doted upon her, you know."

"And have they got any children?"

"Unfortunately not. Nor likely to have any now, I suppose. Mrs Reynolds resides at their place in the country near Brewood."

Ruby considered this gratuitous piece of information.

She was coming to like her new employer Jabez Reynolds, and anything to do with him interested her.

"So ... Mr Reynolds is living apart from his wife?" she ventured to ask. "There's only him and his brother on the Tettenhall Road, while his Missis has got their other house all to herself?"

"Oh, they don't live *apart* – well, not as the word implies. Mrs Reynolds requires the country air for her condition, that's the reason *I* have heard." Martha finished the plucking of a brace of pigeons, tying their legs together with a twist of raffia. "Mr Reynolds is most solicitous about her health. He's had no end of doctors to examine the poor woman – specialists from London and the like – and every year he takes her abroad to one of the spa towns hoping for a cure."

Brushing the pinkish-grey feathers from her apron, she interrupted herself to attend to serving a customer; then coming back to Ruby she went on, "I've always felt about Mr Reynolds that he exhibits a great depth of pity towards those who suffer want or sickness. He's the benefactor of any number of charitable institutions, why, he's even endowed the General Hospital with a bursary. You ought to count yourself most fortunate, my dear, that someone in your delicate condition has such a benevolent employer."

Ruby hadn't a notion what endowing bursaries entailed, nor did she like to show her ignorance by asking, but she was aware already of Mr Reynolds's kindness, having heard several others speaking highly of him. Indeed, as the summer months waned into early autumn and her body thickened out with pregnancy, he made it his concern to see she was eating sufficiently well by giving her free gifts of meat; and in her seventh month, when walking any distance made her tired, more often than not at the end of the day he'd make sure that someone drove her home to Horseley Fields.

Jabez Reynolds was kind; but he wasn't soft. On the contrary, he'd made his reputation by his firmness and determination, and guarded his position as a master butcher jealously. His grandfather, after whom he was named, had founded the family business at the beginning of the century, handing it on to son and then to grandson, and with each new generation it had prospered and expanded. In return for his benevolence Jabez Reynolds expected top-class work, for top-class service; and once Ruby's condition made her less than adequately efficient she was laid off from employment.

"I'm sorry we've got to lose you," he told her on her last day at the market in October, "you've been an excellent employee, and the customers will miss you. Perhaps a little later on – in the New Year, shall we say – you'd consider coming back again part-time?"

"Indeed I would, sir," Ruby answered very readily.

"Well, you have my word a job will still be open for you."

During those final tedious weeks of pregnancy Ruby frequently wished she had run away to Birmingham as she'd intended, instead of letting Matthew marry her. He was a good and decent lad (*too* good and decent sometimes) and he'd done a noble and unselfish thing by salvaging her threadbare honour – but at what cost to them both!

They loved one another dearly, nothing could alter that.

Nothing could alter either, though, the fact that lodging with his parents was causing them terrible tension in their relationship. It was like living in a strait-jacket: no freedom to move, to laugh, to be themselves, no privacy of any kind, not even to be lovers.

She resented it – God, how she resented it! And once she'd been delivered, she'd be trapped inside this house with the child and Agnes Dyson as her gaolers.

May heaven forgive her, Ruby thought, but she didn't want the babby. It was Jack McShane's, a cuckoo in her body. Her one abiding horror was that it would resemble its real father. True, Matthew was dark-haired, but not as dark as Jack, and she had heard that an infant's paternity could be identified the moment of its birth.

She was dreading her delivery, the more so for this awful fear, this sword of Damocles. Matthew especially had gone to so much sacrifice and effort to prevent her mother finding out the truth – was that to be for nothing now? Would the guilt of her misdoing be stamped upon her babby's innocent features, to condemn her in the eyes of all she loved?

The thought tormented her.

In the event, Ruby had had no need to worry – not for that. After an agonisingly protracted labour she was finally delivered of a daughter, the very image of herself, a tiny silent little thing that only lived eleven hours.

9

"If you want my opinion, it's the kindest thing that could've happened," Dorrie Vickers said, trying on Ruby's best straw hat and admiring her reflection in the washstand mirror. "They'm nothing but a screamin' nuisance, babbies."

Had she not been so preoccupied with looking at herself she might have caught the misery that passed across the pale, drawn face as Ruby turned her head against the pillows.

"You'm well off out of it I say," she chatted on, removing the hat and licking her fingers to smooth down the frizz of her fringe. "Poor wench, the only pity is you had to suffer all them hours o' mortal pain for nothing. I felt for you, I really did."

Perhaps my babby would have lived if I hadn't been so long in labour, Ruby thought. She was such a little, helpless scrap of life. Her head was no bigger than the palm of my hand when I held her. She hadn't got the strength, that's what the doctor said; the life just ... faded out of her.

"We had her baptised, you know," she said aloud in a toneless, weary voice. "The babby, I mean. Mr Dyson went and fetched the minister to come and do it."

Dorrie glanced away from the mirror, pausing a moment in her primping. "Oh?"

"Aye. I had her named Elizabeth, after our Mother."

Elizabeth Dyson. Every time I whisper her name in my heart I feel she's still close to me.

"I wish you could've seen her, Dorrie. She was so ... perfect. Not a blemish on her."

"P'raps you hadn't ought to talk about it, eh," Dorrie advised uncomfortably, coming to sit at the end of the bed. "Look, you'm making yourself cry again. I don't know why you'm taking it so badly, Ruby – often enough I heard you say you wished yourself well rid of it."

"Aye, and this is how I'm served for being so wicked." The tears brimmed over, spilling down her cheeks, and she dashed them away with the back of her hand. "I *did* wish I was rid of her. I took them pills you got for me and–" she was about to say her stepfather's disgusting, filthy powders, but she had never told Dorrie about those. "And other stuff."

If my babby had been a little lad would I have felt this wretched, Ruby asked herself. If she'd looked like Jack McShane would I be grieving like I am for her? I only know the minute I set eyes on her I loved her and I wanted her that much I could hardly believe she was mine ... so maybe I never will know the answer.

"Well, just try looking on the bright side, Ruby, eh? When you and Matt have got yourselves better sorted out and settled, you can always have another one," said Dorrie, turning practical again. "You've made a bad start, that's all. You ain't the first 'un by a long chalk that's had this happen to her."

She got up from the bed again and began wandering round the room, picking things up and examining them. "Here, I know what I've forgot to tell you–" she went on suddenly, trying to lighten the gloom of her visit, "you remember that Frank Poulton I've been walking out with?"

Aye, Ruby remembered.

"Twelve bloomin' months of my life I've chucked away on him, waiting for him to do the decent. I got fed up wi' it I can tell you! So I said to him the other week – ever so tactful, like – Frank, I said, have you thought about us getting married? And d'you know what he answered me?" Dorrie rolled her large brown eyes in indignation. "'You don't chase after the omnibus once you've caught it' – them were his very words, cheeky perishin' blighter."

Ruby wiped her nose on her nightgown sleeve. "I hope you gave him back as good as you got."

"I did an' all. I told him where he could go and part his hair in future." There was a sidelong little smirk. "And just to show him there's better fish in the sea, I've started walking out wi' one of his pals – I bet you can't guess who it is."

A shake of the head. "No, who?"

"Go on, think of a name. You only know the one."

"Not – Sam Reynolds?"

"Sam Reynolds." Dorrie looked hugely pleased with herself. "Quite a prize catch, eh? Although when I say we'm walking out, it's more like ... stopping in, if you know what I mean." She winked. "I meet him on my half-day off and we generally has a drink in the Bodega before we toddle along to this little house he rents off Chapel Ash."

Now Ruby's interest was completely captured. "But I thought Sam lived at his brother's on the Tettenhall Road – what's it called, Palmerston Place?"

"Aye, he does. But it ain't exactly *private*, is it, Ruby. And let's be honest, I ain't the type for swanning about in drawing rooms wi' my nose cocked up and talking all lah-di-dah."

"Don't be daft, Dorrie, the Reynoldses in't lah-di-dah, they're Trade."

"They may be Trade but they'm *wealthy*, that's the point, and Jabez Reynolds wouldn't thank Sam for bringing a wench like me into his house unless it was by the servants' entrance. Mind you–" Dorrie came back to sit at the end of the bed again, "*he's* got no room to talk. There's been some funny goings-on concerning *him* from what I hear."

"How d'you mean? What sort o' goings-on?"

Dorrie pursed her lips as if she knew something she wasn't telling; and then putting her hand to her mouth and starting to snigger, she said, "Your Mr Jabez Reynolds has been a naughty lad by all accounts. He's keeping some young woman on the sly, and every so often he gives the domestic staff an evening off and has her round at the house."

"So ... what if he does?" said Ruby on a curiously defensive note. "His wife's an invalid and he's a man still in his prime. I wouldn't expect him to live like a blinkin' hermit!"

Dorrie shrugged. "I only thought you'd be interested, that's all, seeing as how you've been working for him. This 'un he's got now, her ain't the first 'un either," she couldn't resist adding. "His last 'un was a singer off the Halls. Still, if you don't want to hear about it . . ."

A couple of days after Dorrie's visit, Jabez Reynolds himself called at Minerva Lane to enquire after Ruby. She was downstairs by this time, still pale and rather weak but not as deeply despondent as she'd been. Mr Reynolds had business at the cattle market in the neighbourhood, and having learned the sad news from Martha Becket, being so near he thought he'd take the opportunity to see how she was bearing up.

It was young Joe Gallimore, Ruby's brother, who answered the front door to him. Joe had just this minute popped round from number 11 while Agnes Dyson was out of the way at one of her Methodist meetings. Now almost fourteen, he'd grown into a wiry, thin-faced lad, still undersized for his age, and since leaving school had been employed on a casual basis as an errand boy, being unable to get more regular work because of his 'turns'.

His eyes widened when he saw the figure in caped overcoat and bowler hat on the doorstep, and the spanking-smart Lawton gig behind at the kerb.

"I wonder if I have the right address?" said Jabez Reynolds. "I'm looking for a Mrs Dyson. Does she live here?"

"Who is it, Joe?" Ruby called out from the kitchen, answering his question.

"Tell her it's Mr Reynolds, will you, son?"

Joe obliged.

"Lord above – we'd best ask him into the parlour!" Ruby exclaimed as soon as she knew their visitor's identity.

119

"We can't leave him standing there in the street." She threw a flustered look at herself in the chiffonier mirror, hastily neatening her appearance before following her brother along the passage.

"Mr Reynolds! Would you care to come inside, sir?" she invited, pulling back the door. "Our Joe 'll hold your horse for you, won't you, Joe." Should she offer him a cup of tea or something? "I'm sorry if it in't very warm in here but the parlour fire's never lit excepting Sundays."

Jabez Reynolds took off his bowler and looked round the spartan, spick-and-span cleanliness of the room into which she showed him. "I hope this isn't any inconvenience," he said. "I've merely called in passing to enquire how you are and . . . offer my condolences."

"Thank you, sir. That's very good of you. Won't you – won't you sit down for just a minute now you're here?"

"Aye, but it *will* have to be a minute, I'm afraid. I mustn't stop." He seated himself on the hard black horse-hair sofa and waited till Ruby had taken a chair before he continued, "I wondered, is there anything I can do . . . any way I can be of assistance? If there is, I hope you wouldn't hesitate to ask, my dear. I'd be only too happy to help however I could."

She glanced at him; then smiled and shook her head. In the steely sheen of the November light reflected through the window, her features had the sculpted quality of alabaster, the paleness of her skin emphasising the violet shadows underneath her eyes. She looked older; and yet the spattering of freckles and the ribbons in her hair gave her a pitifully childlike vulnerability.

Jabez Reynolds felt his heart go out to her. "I'm sure

your husband must be proving a great comfort and support at such a tragic time."

"He is, sir," she responded awkwardly.

That wasn't quite the truth. Matthew was trying as best he could to be supportive, but the suffering of childbirth was a woman's lot and only her mother had been there to share it with her till the last few hours. Rather than listen to her screams that night Matthew had gone from the house; and now he seemed to be turning his own uselessness against himself, setting yet one more barrier between them.

"But it's different for men," she heard herself go on, "they don't know what it's like . . . the pain . . . and then the grieving, when a babby dies."

"I think you're wrong, Ruby." Jabez Reynolds looked away towards the empty grate. "*I* know. My wife lost our child in very similar circumstances. A son, it was. And I'm not ashamed to say I wept for days . . . aye, and still mourn him even after all these years."

It must have cost him pride to admit a thing as personal as that, she thought, touched that he should want to share it with her. Since hearing about the state of affairs at Palmerston Place from her friend Dorrie Vickers, Ruby's awe of Mr Reynolds had begun to moderate. Her respect for him, and her admiration, still remained as warm; but she was starting to see him now as a man – an attractive, successful and powerful man – whose needs were as basic as anyone else's. Who could blame him if he kept some woman 'on the sly' as Dorrie put it? He was in the prime of life; his wife was ailing. Surely to God he was only doing what half the married men in Wolverhampton did – if not in fact, then in imagination.

"I didn't realise you'd lost a son," she said. "That must have been very hard for you . . . and for Mrs Reynolds."

"Aye, well–" Taking his bowler from the sofa Jabez Reynolds got to his feet again. "I *can* understand, you see, my dear."

Ruby nodded, and as their glances met for a moment she felt suddenly very close to him because of the experience of suffering that both of them had had to bear.

She showed him to the door.

"You must take good care of yourself now," he said, feeling inside his coat pocket for a shilling to give young Joe for watching the horse. "Mind you get your proper rest, build up your strength again. I want to see the roses back in those pretty cheeks, d'you hear?"

Matthew thought it generous of Mr Reynolds to send them such a handsome piece of beef subsequent to calling upon Ruby. He wondered though whether the generosity was being a fraction overdone when the following week there came an invitation to spend Sunday afternoon at Bishops Aston, the master butcher's country house and farm.

"Why is he taking such a confounded interest in you, Ruby?" he said truculently. "Gentlemen in his position don't normally go sending letters to employees offering to entertain them!"

"That in't what the invitation says." Ruby took it from his hand to read it out. "In the first place it's addressed to *you*, 'Dear Mr Dyson'–"

"I know who it's addressed to." Matthew snatched it back again.

"And in the second place–" she made a grab for it but he held it out of reach above his head, "it refers to my health and the benefit it'll do me to get out for an afternoon in the country air. He in't offering to entertain *me*. All he's doing is showing *us* a bit o' kindness – and if you don't want to come wi' me, Matt, I'll bloomin' well go by myself!"

Her obvious annoyance silenced him; but it was with something of an ill grace that he accepted Mr Reynolds's well-meaning invitation.

There was a pony trap waiting for them at the railway halt at Four Ashes, a little rural hamlet a mile or so from Brewood. The day was overcast, with a watery sun trying to pierce the sullen web of cloud, and during the drive through leaf-deep, rutted lanes to Bishops Aston, Matthew seemed morose as though the weather had depressed his spirits. It irritated Ruby that he couldn't show more interest in their outing, or share her enthusiasm for the lovely brooding views of field and woodland back-lit by a lambent pewter light from the horizon.

Useless to ask him what was the matter. Lately he'd been acting out of sorts, growing edgy and withdrawing into silences she couldn't penetrate. Today he hadn't been to chapel either. "Maybe I'll go tonight," he'd told his mother, "and then again, maybe I won't. Depends what time we're home," which hadn't gone down very well.

"See that place there–" The fellow driving the trap turned to indicate a brick-and-timber house set back beside the lane. "That's Boscobel is that. 'Tis where King Charles hid in the oak tree. And over yonder–" he waved his whip towards a clump of trees some distance off "–that there's White Ladies priory where the King took refuge wi' the Penderels."

Ruby examined the house and view with avid curiosity. She knew the tale of King Charles in the oak from school, where they'd celebrated Oak Apple Day each twenty-ninth of May by wearing leaves pinned to their hats. "Who were the Penderels?" she enquired.

"Them were the folk who had White Ladies at that time," explained the driver, twisting in his seat again to answer her. " 'Tweren't a priory then, o' course, that part were ruins and 'twere just the house. My mother were descended from the family," he added with a simple touch of pride. "Her grandfer were the–"

"How much further is it still to Bishops Aston?" Matthew cut in testily. "I don't want my wife taking cold, she's not very strong at the moment."

" 'Tis only another half-mile," the man responded, seeming not to mind the interruption. "There's a blanket underneath the seat if her do need 'un."

Rounding the corner they reached the brow of a hill, and after descending a little way he pointed out a farmhouse coming into view between the trees. Like Boscobel, it was built of brick with timber framing, and had a walled orchard and gardens on two sides. Closer to the lane, the barn and out-buildings stood separated from the house by a laurel drive which curved towards its entrance.

Jabez Reynolds had been out all morning with his stockman taking a look at the store-cattle being fattened for their winter slaughter. He came down the steps on hearing the crunch of the pony trap over the gravel, and though he had changed from his farming corduroys into something more suitably Sunday, his face still showed a healthy glow and he smelled of the open fields and the earth and fresh air.

He treated Matthew, whom he hadn't met before, most civilly; and after the usual courtesies took them in the trap himself round the estate, explaining something of its management in layman's terms. Bishops Aston was both arable and livestock: as well as the herd of beef which supplied Mr Reynolds's market stalls, the land was used for barley and mangel-wurzels whose by-products of tops and leaves and barley straw went into the cattle's feed – what his farm bailiff, he said, called grist for the growing of profit.

Much of this talk went over Ruby's head, but she was happy to enjoy the tour and see the sights. Loving the country as much as she did, it was glorious to feel the cold, clean wind against her skin and watch the rooks flocking home to their nests in the gaunt-branched elms as the afternoon faded away into sombre sunset.

They were at the house again before it grew quite dark. The oil lamps had been lit indoors and the windows shone with a welcoming golden warmth across the yard. Much to Ruby's disappointment, it turned out that Mrs Reynolds was unable to receive them: she had been unwell all yesterday, her husband told them in apology, and he didn't wish her disturbed. She tired very easily. One of the reasons she preferred living here at Bishops Aston was the peace and isolation and the privacy from constant visitors. He hoped his guests would understand.

Tea was served in the farmhouse kitchen, a long, low-ceilinged room with a good fire blazing in the open hearth and smoked hams hanging from the rafters. Jabez Reynolds didn't join them – he'd be eating later with his wife – and Ruby and Matthew found themselves with Mrs Reynolds's housekeeper-companion, a stout little bustling woman in black bombazine who showed great interest in the two of them.

Matthew hardly had a word to say to her. All afternoon he'd been practically monosyllabic, speaking only when the conversation warranted, and although he hadn't meant to be unmannerly he'd made himself look ignorant and boorishly behaved in Ruby's eyes. At a loss to understand her husband's attitude, she nursed her mortification in angry silence on their journey back to the railway halt at Four Ashes; but once the trap had departed and they were left alone on the deserted platform, she could contain herself no longer and turned upon him sharply saying, "Well I hope you're pleased wi' yourself, Matthew. You've managed to show me up and no mistake. We won't get asked back *there* again."

"We shouldn't have been asked at all in my opinion," he responded. "I don't see the point in being trundled about the countryside for no reason other than blasted charity."

"It wasn't charity."

"What else d'you call it, then?"

"I'd call it kindness o' nature – aye, and sympathy, some'at *you* used to have till you showed me different."

"When have I never showed you sympathy?" In the gleam of the single gas lamp lighting the platform she caught a flush of sudden hurt in his expression. "That's a cruel and untrue thing to say. I don't deserve it."

Had she not been in such a taking, Ruby might have

126

regretted her hasty words and left matters there; but she didn't. "Well, I haven't noticed you putting yourself out to offer me much comfort. You know how distressed I've been about . . . about losing the babby. I wonder sometimes if it in't a crime to grieve for her, the way you've acted."

"Here we go again–" Matthew blew out his cheeks on a breath of exasperation. "I'm *sorry* about the babby, Ruby. How many times do I have to tell you that? I'm sorry! But all the being sorry in the world won't alter things and bring her back again. What's the use of harping on about it all the while? It's finished. Done with. How can the two of us build a future for ourselves if you won't let go of the past?"

"I can't just forget her, Matthew! I can't just wipe her from my life and forget I ever gave birth to her!"

"I'm not asking you to do that. I simply wish you'd stop blaming yourself for what happened as though it was a punishment or some'at."

"But it *was* a punishment. Can't you see? I never wanted her while I was carrying her – neither did you, and that's why you don't feel any sympathy. It was a convenient riddance for some'at that got in the way." Ruby's chin began to tremble, her anger further fuelled now by distress.

"I'm not going to argue with you," Matthew said in some disgust. "We've had this out a dozen times before. If the babby had lived I'd have done my best to be a proper father to it, and I can't say fairer than that."

"Maybe not. But you haven't no compassion for the loss I felt, and Mr Reynolds had – *he* understood."

"Mr Reynolds–! I'm just about sick of Mr Jabez Reynolds. To hear the way you talk of him he's Father Christmas and the Angel Gabriel rolled into one!"

"That's right, Matthew. Make a mockery of him. It says a lot for your character that you'll eat his meat and accept his hospitality and yet haven't a decent name to give to him."

"He can keep his meat and his blasted hospitality." Thrusting his hands in his pockets, Matthew walked a short way up the platform to compose himself. In the stillness the eerie moan of the wind could be heard as it flapped the dog-eared edges of the railway timetable pasted on the fence behind them. The moon was rising, frosting the tracks and telegraph wires with a silvery shimmer that matched the brilliance of tears in Ruby's eyes.

"He's a good, considerate man," she said, defensively.

"And why shouldn't he be? We're the deserving poor, me and you, and men like Mr Reynolds can afford the luxury of patronising us because he's wealthy."

"What if he is – it in't a bloomin' crime!"

"It is to those of us with any pride."

"Oh, so that's what's been bothering you, is it. That's why you've had a face on you all afternoon. He's damaging your *pride* wi' his generosity."

"No, Ruby. He's damaging my marriage." Matthew came slowly back towards her. "And let me tell you some'at else before you interrupt – ever since you went to work for Jabez Reynolds I've noticed you've started shutting me out, just like you did when you fancied yourself wi' Jack McShane. It strikes me I'm being used as a convenience – the damn' silly fool who loves you enough to put up with it all while you're mooning around after older men – and you can hold your tongue and listen while I finish–" he went on, raising his voice against her violent protest. "I *care* what happens to our marriage. I want it to be a good one. I know we've got our problems, but for God's sake, Ruby, stop making me feel such a failure as a husband!"

10

"He loves you, my chick. You mustn't blame him if he's seeming jealous." Lizzie McShane wearily hoisted her laden shopping bags and followed her daughter across the street. As usual of a Saturday evening they'd met each other in the market hall, where Ruby was working again, and made the journey home together to Minerva Lane. "Pay no heed to him. Least said soonest mended, is my advice."

Ruby trudged on ahead through the gaslight-shadowed snow that clogged the pavements. "I wouldn't mind so much, our Mam," she said over her shoulder, "if Matthew had some *cause* for jealousy. But he imagines things. Look at the way he sulked over Mr Reynolds. He kept that up for a whole blinkin' week."

"It was only resentment. He told me that himself."

"What's he got to be resentful of?" Ruby waited for her mother to catch up. "He's like a dog wi' a bone the way he worries over every little thing. Drives me mad, it does."

"You'd be better off, the pair o' you, living somewhere on your own," said Lizzie, changing bags from one hand to the other to relieve their weight.

"Aye, we both know that!"

"You can come back home, you know. I'd let you have the front downstairs. We could always put a bed in there."

"No, Mam." Ruby turned and started walking on again. "I'd never share a roof wi' Jack McShane, nor Matthew wouldn't either."

"All on account o' that one silly fight? Jack only did what he thought the lad deserved. You know what he's like. Don't you think it's time you buried the hatchet, chick?"

Ruby pretended she hadn't heard.

"There's lodgings off Union Mill Street coming vacant in a week or two," she said, stepping into the snow-choked gutter to make room for an old woman shuffling towards them. "Mr Evans told me at the corner shop. The rent's not much. Matt said he'd go and see the landlord dinnertime tomorrow."

"Whereabouts off Union Mill Street?"

"Somewhere near the gasworks. I suppose that's why it's cheap."

They emerged from Lichfield Street and crossed Five Ways to get to Horseley Fields opposite. The main roads here were smudged with dirty streaks from ash thrown down to stop the horses slipping on the treacherous surface; and an ice-honed wind knifing its way round the corners carried the sooty smell of smoke from innumerable chimneys.

"I hope you'll take some note o' what I said," Lizzie began again once they were safely across the busy junction. "You'll have to learn to cultivate a deaf ear for a bit, my wench. It's one o' the secrets of a happy marriage."

"Deaf ear to what, Mam?"

"Matthew and his grumbling. Men are funny creatures. They wo' come out and tell us straight what's making them ill-humoured. They like to sulk about it first. I'll tell you some'at else you need to do, an' all – that's turn a blind eye." Lizzie paused to swop her bags round once more, putting them down in the snow for a minute to give her thin shoulders a rest.

Perhaps it was bad conscience, but Ruby thought she caught some subtle emphasis in this advice, and before she could stop herself she'd asked guiltily – "*You* never had to turn a blind eye, did you, Mam?"

"Oh, many a time." Her mother gave her a weary smile as she took up her shopping again. "Jack don't think I know about his boozing. But I do. I look away, that's all, my chick. He wo' drink any the less for me belly-aching about it, so what's the point of argument?"

"I wish Matthew would enjoy a drink!" said Ruby, her conscience easing again.

"Never you wish that on him – you're better off wi'out a drunken husband."

"I don't want him a *drunkard*, but a glass of ale might do him good. He's got no recreation, that's his trouble."

"He's too firmly tied to his mother's apron strings, you mean," said Lizzie darkly.

"Aye, well ... that's why I'm hoping we'll get these lodgings. If it's only a couple o' rooms, at least we'll have more blessed privacy, then maybe we can start to have a marriage."

Gas Yard had taken its unlovely name from the works built in the vicinity when Wolverhampton first began using gas for lighting in 1821. It contained two dozen or so terraced dwellings crowded round a narrow cobbled courtyard illuminated by a single wall-lamp, and on a winter's afternoon with the soft dusk shrouding it in greyness it had a murky, melancholy atmosphere.

Matthew and Ruby Dyson came to live here at the end of January, seven months after their wedding, renting a couple of upstairs rooms from an Irishman called Michael Byrne. The pleasure of having somewhere of their own, however mean or ill-furnished, initially compensated for the inconvenience of sharing a privy with four other families, and their landlord's kitchen for cooking on a dirty iron gas stove.

Ruby did all she could to make the lodgings more cosy. Having given the place a thorough good scrubbing, she sewed new curtains from the pretty material of two old dresses (gone at the armholes) once adorning the Misses Surtees of St John's Square. The lumpy, sagging bed was covered with a patchworked counterpane; bowls of newly-opened snowdrops added brightness to the rooms; and her yellow cock linnet (which Joe had been looking after because Agnes Dyson didn't care for birds) made number 5 Gas Yard a deal more cheery with its sweet, enchanting song.

Matthew's parents came to call on them just once, using as excuse their fear that their son might be unwell since he hadn't attended chapel for that morning's service. It was Matthew's own decision not to go – he'd wanted the Sunday free to distemper the walls – but Ruby could tell from Mrs Dyson's rancid attitude that they held *her* to blame for this neglect of his religious duties.

"I can't imagine," said Agnes Dyson, "what on earth made Matthew want to leave a nice, clean house to live in such a slum as this," looking about her in dismissive fashion at the threadbare homeliness of the couple's living-room. "It isn't healthy."

"No more unhealthy than Minerva Lane," said Ruby very coolly.

"Nonsense, you've got damp in here–" her mother-in-law's glance swept the patches of brown discolouration scabbing the ceiling. "And cockroaches, I shouldn't wonder."

"The damp won't show once Matthew's whitewashed over it, and I went round the place wi' Keating's Powder the minute we moved in. Anything else?"

"The smell from the gasworks isn't very pleasant," Matthew's father complained, short-sightedly peering from the window towards the gaunt silhouette of the chimney stack which overshadowed the yard.

Ruby's irritation rose a notch. "Smells never did harm to anybody yet. If they had, the canal stink in your house would've killed us off."

Agnes Dyson sniffed. It was the sort of sniff that managed to express dislike, disdain and disapproval all in one. "*Smells* can affect my son's stomach. Remember that, my girl. He wasn't brought up to live amongst squalor and dirt."

"We're making the place as decent as we can, Mother," Matthew chipped in, seeing the warning flash of Ruby's eye. "We've only been here a couple of weeks. We can't do a lot when the pair of us are out at work."

"Why you had to move at all stumps me," his father

grumbled. "What was wrong with the home *we* gave you, son? It's wounded your poor mother to the heart, it has, the uncharitable way you pair have treated her, turning your noses up at everything she's tried to do. I mean to say—"

"Dad, we've had this out already," Matthew interrupted him. "I'm sorry if Mother feels hurt, but Ruby and me – well, you can understand we needed somewhere of our own. The accommodation's hardly the grandest in town, I agree, but it suits us for what we want at the moment."

It was unfortunate timing that their landlord, Michael Byrne, who was downstairs enjoying his usual bottle, chose this very second to add to the noise in the yard with a maudlin rendition of 'O Erin My Country'.

Agnes Dyson sniffed again. "And what do you do for your meals, may I ask?" she demanded of Ruby. "How do you manage to feed you both in this hovel?"

"There's a gas stove below in Mr Byrne's kitchen, and we've the fire-grate for toasting bread and suchlike. Don't fret yourself, Mrs Dyson. Your son won't starve, not while he's wedded to me."

"It's a pity he's wedded to you at all, if you want my opinion."

"When I want your opinion I'll ask for it, thank you."

Older and younger woman glared at one another.

"Then you shall hear it against your will, my girl," Mrs Dyson told her harshly. "May the Lord forgive me, but I've held my peace quite long enough. I raised my son to be a Christian, to conduct his life in a respectable and decent fashion, and I rue the day he married a creature as wanton and godless as you."

Ruby set her fists upon her hips. "Aye, you spiteful old

biddy, and I held *my* peace so long as I was lodged beneath your roof – but if you've come here looking for a quarrel then I'll give you one!"

"Don't you dare to address Matthew's mother in that tone," Mr Dyson came in very sharply.

"I'll address Matthew's mother how I like–"

"Ruby, come on, I think we've all said enough," Matthew himself intervened, trying to placate her by going and putting an arm round her shoulder.

She shook him off. "Seven months I've had to choke on their blasted charity, made to feel like some worthless bit o' gutter rubbish. Seven months I've suffered being sneered at and preached at and prayed over–"

"You should be grateful we gave you house-room, you wicked baggage," said Agnes Dyson, her thin nose pinched with indignation.

"*Grateful–?* For crying out loud, I'm Matthew's lawful wedded wife, not a lump o' ruddy dogsmeat! Why shouldn't you give me house-room – I worked to pay you for it, didn't I?"

"Ruby, I said that's *enough*," repeated Matthew. "Leave it now!"

"Aye, that's right – you take *her* side," she threw at him bitterly. "I might've guessed it's your mother you'd support, not me!"

"I think it's time we left, my dear," said Mr Dyson, taking his wife by the arm. "This is becoming unpleasant."

Ruby marched over to the door and flung it open. "So kind of you both to call," she said with heavy sarcasm. "I'd have introduced you to the landlord, but from the sound of it he in't receiving visitors this afternoon."

"We shall see you in chapel next Sunday, Matthew?" Agnes Dyson turned towards her son.

"Aye." He looked down at his boots; and then shame-facedly said, "Aye," again and nodded.

"Your father and I will pray for you."

Drawing herself up, her small, stiff figure tight with dignity, she moved ahead of her husband to the door. As she went past Ruby she eyed the girl in withering contempt, observing coldly, "The worst day's work my son ever did was ensnaring himself with you."

Little by little the bickering between the pair of them became more frequent; and as winter gave place to springtime in Gas Yard, the hairline cracks in their relationship insidiously started multiplying and widening.

Love by itself was no longer enough to bridge the problems of their struggling marriage.

They argued about silly, petty, niggling things. On Matthew's twentieth birthday at the end of March the little celebration was entirely spoilt by a difference over his moustache, which suited him very handsomely now it was grown. He was proud of that moustache; but Ruby was too disturbingly reminded of her stepfather's, and insisted he must shave it off.

Matthew had refused.

A week or so later he made some mild complaint about the reek of meat that seemed to cling to Ruby's clothes, suggesting she left the market stall and got herself a job again in sweeter-smelling service as a housemaid.

This time it was Ruby who refused.

And in between these different stupid arguments ran the

constant thread of dispute over Dorrie Vickers, and Ruby's hostility to Matthew's parents, and her admiration for Jabez Reynolds; and most damaging of all, dissatisfaction with their sexual love.

It was late one evening in April; Ruby had gone out by herself for a drink in the town with Dorrie and some of her crowd. As she turned into the yard entrance St James's clock had just finished striking eleven, and in the sudden stillness the clatter of her boots across the cobbles sent an echo round the walls.

There was a full moon shining behind the chimneys, throwing their outline against the opposite roofs like stumps of teeth. Here and there the dull orange glow of oil lamps shone amongst the shadows from the rectangles of windows; a child wailed thinly; somewhere in the neighbourhood a cat began a tremulous, eerie yowl.

Ruby paused for a moment by the door of number 5 to search out her key, then let herself in, calling goodnight to the landlord as she went up the stairs. The fire in the living-room had burned low, just a few coals still smouldering red, and when she poked them a shower of little sparks flew up the chimney, winked against the soot, and died away.

"Is that you, Ruby?" Matthew's voice came from the other room.

"Aye."

She took off her shawl and flat straw bonnet and hung them behind the door; and after covering her linnet in its gilded cage beside the window, went into the bedroom.

Matthew was in bed, propped against the pillows with his

hands behind his head. The lamp on the dealwood chest of drawers half-shadowed his face, and for an instant it might have been Jack McShane lying there, the same dark tousled hair and full moustache, the same strong-muscled shoulders.

More sharply than she'd intended she said, "I thought you'd be asleep by now."

"I was listening out for you."

In a minute he's going to ask me why I'm late, Ruby told herself.

"You're very late coming in. Where've you been?"

She shrugged, and started unbuttoning her pleated linen blouse. "Round and about. Sam Reynolds bought us supper at the pie stall outside the Seven Stars."

"I wouldn't have minded a pie to eat myself. I'm blasted hungry."

"Didn't you fry that bit of ham I left?"

"Aye." Matthew sounded put out. "But one of the eggs I had with it was addled and I had to chuck the lot away. I couldn't eat it."

"You should've gone down to your mother's then," she said over her shoulder, draping her blouse on the back of the chair. "If you're hungry it's your own daft fault."

"If I'd gone down my mother's she would only have started on again about you swanning off to pubs, and leaving me wi'out a decent meal inside me. Between the pair of you, I don't know which way I'm meant to be facing half the time!"

"And *I* don't know why you couldn't have come out wi' Dorrie and me, like I wanted you to – there was nothing to stop you."

"Except for the company. I was going to offer to take you somewhere myself, but no, your mind was set on gallivanting round the town with *her* lot."

Matthew looked at his young wife's shapely back, turned stubbornly towards him; and after several moments when it was clear she wasn't giving an answer, he went on in a more conciliatory way, "Tell you what, Ruby. I've been thinking. I'll make a bargain wi' you. If you agree to give up Dorrie Vickers, I'll shave off my moustache. How's that."

"Give up Dorrie–?" Ruby turned to stare at him. "In exchange for your *moustache*? Is this what you've been doing to pass the time, dreaming up some'at as crackbrained and barmy as–" She gave a little laugh of disbelief.

"I'm serious about it," Matthew insisted. "I know you think I'm being unreasonable, but see yourself as others see you, sweetheart! There's names for wenches like that Dorrie Vickers – d'you want to find yourself tarred wi' the selfsame brush?"

"I don't know what you mean." She stepped out of her skirt and flannel petticoat. With nothing on but stays and drawers she went past him to the washstand. "She likes a bit o' fun, that's all. She likes enjoying herself."

"The fellows like enjoying her as well, from what I hear."

"Then tell them to whistle another tune. If she's getting her pleasure in bed wi' a man, good luck to her I say."

That comment flicked Matthew on the raw. Since moving to live in Gas Yard, their lovemaking had progressed to consummation; but it was over so quickly for him every time that Ruby was frustrated of her own fulfilment, and his inexperienced efforts to give her satisfaction made things worse instead of better.

He threw off the bedclothes and stood up, his naked body burnished by the lamplight.

"What the devil has got into you of late?" he asked angrily. "You're beginning to sound a right little shrew, d'you know that. I tell you, Ruby, I'm starting to ask myself why I ever bothered to marry you!"

The words hung in the air between them like an opened wound; and the only sound in the sudden silence was the dribble of waterdrops from Ruby's fingers.

Slowly, she straightened and looked at her husband. "So it's come to this at last," she said after a moment, no emotion in her voice. "Aye, I wondered how long it would be. What do they say – marry in haste and repent at leisure? You're repenting are you, Matthew?"

He glanced away, unable to meet her eyes. "I don't know."

"Well, I do. We started off this marriage on the wrong foot altogether. Perhaps we need a bit o' time apart to get us right again."

11

If Agnes Dyson had hoped Matthew would return to live at home, her hopes were dashed. Instead of drawing him back into the nest again, it seemed as though Ruby's departure was the stimulus which finally spurred him into severing his mother's apron strings and stepping from the shadow of her strong, repressive influence.

Her mothering was turning into smothering, he told her bluntly. He respected her and loved her – his father too – but he was not a child any longer to be cossetted, instructed and directed, spoon-fed on religion, feather-bedded from the knocks of life. He was twenty years of age, a grown man, and old enough to claim his independence.

It was Ruby, in her absence, who had to take the brunt of the Dysons' anger, the usual list of criticisms raked up yet again and added to with rancorous interest now she'd left their son. What damned her in their eyes the more was that she'd held her wedding vows so lightly. Marriage was for *life*, not months; not something to be thrown aside the minute it had lost its usefulness. The wench had married to cover up her shame; and now there was no babby to encumber her, quite obviously she wished herself unmarried to live singly again.

Matthew let his parents have their say. He had agreed to

this separation from Ruby in the hope that being apart, the wounds of their relationship would heal, the damage be repaired, the quarrels ended. He tried to view their situation sensibly. He tried to put himself in Ruby's shoes and ask himself how *he* would feel if such and such a thing were said or done. Yet no amount of commonsense or reasoning could fill the void or stop the aching wretchedness once she was gone.

They had thought their love was strong enough to conquer mountains ... and it had stumbled on molehills.

After she moved out of their lodgings at the end of April, Matthew made the decision to stay on in Gas Yard and not reverse the clock by going back to live at home. *This* was his home now, not Minerva Lane, he told his parents. He'd take his evening meals with them, but that was all. He needed to stand on his own two feet, lead his own life; and the only way to do it was by slackening the ties that bound him to his childhood.

Joe Gallimore pulled a scrap of paper from his jacket pocket and squinted at it yet again, deciphering his sister's hasty scribble. *The White Hart, Worcester Street*. He raised his head to read the lettering on the side wall of the public house, mouthing it silently and slowly as he spelled it out.

Aye, this was it, the White Hart Inn, just like she'd said. So if he cut off here – stepping from the kerb to look down winding, cobbled Brickhill Lane – he'd find their Ruby's lodgings on the right somewhere. What number did she put? Another squint at the paper. Thirty-four.

He'd never been in Brickhill Lane before. His errands

and deliveries kept him to the Horseley Fields area, and he wasn't a lad for roaming very far. Setting his cap straight on his lank brown hair he started down the lane, past narrow little gardens full of springtime blossom and brick paths leading to the doors of cottages. This was a part of Georgian Wolverhampton as yet untouched by redevelopment, and though the countryside had receded a hundred years ago and factories now encroached upon it, something of its olden rural atmosphere still lingered in these pretty cottage gardens.

Ruby had taken a room with Martha Becket, her friend from the market, who lived here with an aged aunt. Their home was at the bottom of the lane, behind a hawthorn hedge; and the almond scent of the creamy flowers drifting on the warm, damp breeze stayed with Joe all the way up from the gate. There was a face looking out from an upper window, a pale oval shadow behind the glass; and then the sound of someone running down the stairs, the door flung open, and Ruby there on the step, laughing, crying, "Joe!" and holding out her arms to hug him to her.

He pulled off his cap and wiped his boots selfconsciously before letting his sister take him past the narrow dog-leg staircase into the parlour, a rose-papered room with a deep bow window overlooking the garden and as quaintly pretty as something out of a doll's house.

"Joe–" she said again, giving him another hug and kissing him. "Oh, it's lovely to see you, our chick! You had no bother finding the address?"

He shook his head, still gazing round him at the room, the china ornaments, the sepia-brown photographs, overawed by so much daintiness.

"Crikey, it in't half different from your other place," he said with feeling. "Here, is that a *real* ship in that bottle?" going across for a closer look, not daring to touch.

Ruby watched his young, thin face, so like their father's; not handsome or even good-looking, but with the same open, honest simplicity as Charlie Gallimore's. For a moment it hurt her to look at her brother, as though the ghost of childhood past were resurrected in that likeness; and then, noticing something as he turned and the light from the window caught his features, she asked with sudden quick concern, "What've you done to get such a bruise, Joe? You haven't banged your head falling over, have you?"

He didn't meet her eye but glanced away again towards the model ship. "Aye, that's right, I fell over ... had one o' my turns and clouted myself on a cupboard or some'at."

It could be the truth – he knocked himself quite often in these fits of his – but there was something evasive in the way he answered that made Ruby go across and catch his face between her hands, peering at the bruise which marked his cheekbone.

"If that was a cupboard you'd have broke the skin," she said suspiciously. "It was somebody's fist did that to you."

She pulled her brother with her to the window-seat, shooing away the tortoiseshell cat washing itself on the cushions, sitting him down at her side in the soft May sunlight. "Who was it, Joe? You been in a fight wi' one of your pals?"

He put his hand to the bruise and fingered it, his cuff fallen back to show the raw-boned adolescent thinness of his wrist. "It wan't no fight. He gi' me a good hiding 'cos I had a turn and knocked his glass o' beer off the table."

No need to ask who *he* was. Ruby knew.

"He gi' you a good hiding because–" The image flashed across her mind of her brother, semi-conscious and defenceless in the drowsy state which always followed his attacks, being dragged about and punched by Jack McShane. Her nostrils whitened.

"God, I wish I'd caught him at it. I'd have taken the carving-knife to him, I would!"

"He was drunk," said Joe, as if that excused their stepfather's brutality.

"Drunk or not, it makes no difference. Was our Mother there to see him strike you?"

"She was working up the road–" he meant the Harp. "Jack said he'd clout me twice as hard if I went and told her."

Ruby took him in her arms, holding him protectively as though he were a little child in need of comfort. "If it happens again you're to come and tell *me*, you hear! Blasted bully . . . I'm not frightened of him. I won't have him knocking you about, I won't, he's done damage enough as it is to our family."

"I wish I could leave him and live wi' you." Her brother's voice was muffled in her shoulder. "But I've got to take care of our Mam . . . help her round the house and gi' her a hand wi' the coal and that. She in't much good at lugging things no more." The way he said this, so seriously, made Ruby want to weep.

"You're a good lad."

She kissed him, then released him and stood up, looking out of the window at the garden aglow with cottage flowers, so neat and Sunday-peaceful that to live here was like being in heaven after the poverty and dirt of Horseley Fields.

"Who's this house belong to?" Joe glanced about the room again, studying the sepia photographs with curiosity.

"Martha's auntie. Mrs Finch."

"Is she out the back? Can I ask her who that soldier is?" pointing to the studio portrait of a Sergeant of Horse Artillery.

"No, she in't here, chick. She's got a poorly leg and they've had to send her to the General Hospital. Martha's there to visit her this afternoon."

Ruby glanced down at her brother again, smoothing his hair. "Joe . . . has our Mam mentioned anything about . . . y'know, me and Matthew?"

The day she'd left the yard, she'd gone to number 11 Minerva Lane to tell her mother what had happened and explain about the separation. Lizzie had been saddened; saddened and deeply reproachful. 'The bigger the break, the worse the join' had been her parting words, and they had stayed in Ruby's mind.

"Has she seen him at all, d'you know?"

"Aye. He come round our house this last week," Joe replied, more interested in the cat which had leaped up again to join him on the window seat.

"How did he seem? Was he all right? What did he say?" The questions betrayed anxiety as well as a hint of guilt.

"He seemed all right to me. Said he was stopping in Gas

148

Yard, but eating his dinners at his mother's 'cos he in't much cop at cooking for himself." Joe looked up at his sister. "Here, in't this a nice little cat, Ruby. Look, it's letting me stroke it. What's its name?"

"Tibb," she answered distractedly; and then – "Well, if his mother's taking care of his wants, he doesn't need *me*!"

The guilt was absolved; the anxiety replaced by resolution.

She held out her hand. "Come on, Joe, leave the puss alone. Let's go into the kitchen, shall we. I've done you your favourite figgy pudding for tea."

Martha Becket's aunt came out of hospital, the phlebitis which had swollen up one leg like a balloon successfully responding to the doctors' treatment. She was the dearest old lady Ruby had ever met, very small and stout like Queen Victoria, immaculately clean, and much devoted to the memory of her late employer to whom she'd worked as cook for over thirty years. On his death he'd left her an annuity sufficient to keep her comfortable in Brickhill Lane for the rest of her days.

When Ruby had first confided in Martha about leaving Gas Yard because of difficulties in her marriage, Martha had had no hesitation in inviting her to come and stay at Auntie Ellen's cottage for a while. The two young women shared the dormer bedroom at the front, and it was in this intimate surrounding that their acquaintance had soon blossomed into warmest friendship.

Dorrie Vickers resented Martha for 'stealing' Ruby. She began poking fun at the other's affected way of speaking, mimicking her short, quick hen-like gait, and making spiteful observations about her lack of gentlemen admirers. The jealousy (for jealousy it was) provoked Ruby into taking sides, which led to words, which led in turn to coolness in each other's company.

"I suppose *I* ain't good enough for you now you've started swanning round wi' Lady Muck," Dorrie said nastily, the last occasion they had been together. "I suppose you'd rather be out wi' that stuck-up madam than consorting wi' common types like me. So much for the old pals act! Let me tell you some'at, Ruby Dyson – next time you wants helping out of a corner you can flippin' well whistle!"

Ruby had seen nothing of her since, so she didn't know Sam Reynolds had thrown Dorrie over for another girl; not until she had the news from Jabez Reynolds.

For the past three weeks – about as long as Ruby and Matthew had been living separately – Mr Reynolds had been abroad in Marienbad, where he'd taken his wife for the curative properties of the mineral springs. On the Sunday following their return he was in Brickhill Lane calling on old Mrs Finch, a distant relative of his wife's by marriage, to enquire after her health; and in the course of conversation had learned the identity of the young woman she'd recently taken in to lodge with her.

Just as he was leaving, he encountered Ruby coming down the lane. She was not in the rosiest of humours, having spent a wretched hour with Matthew which had left her feeling miserable and angry. She was so absorbed in herself that she failed to note the driver of the gig until he spoke to her; and the tell-tale flush of temper that still stained her cheek crimsoned to embarrassment.

"Mr Reynolds–! Oh, I'm ever so sorry, I didn't intend to ignore you!"

She halted against the railings, looking up at him, startled by the unexpected meeting; and because he'd been away and she had missed him, she said naively, "It's nice to have you home", and blushed again.

He couldn't resist a smile at her confusion. "I'm glad you're pleased to see me, Ruby. For a minute I thought you meant to walk straight by without acknowledgment. I wondered what I'd done."

"To tell the truth, I never even noticed you, I was in that much of a silly huff."

"Oh? Somebody's upset you, have they?" Mr Reynolds checked the horse.

"Haven't they, an' all!" She reminded herself she was speaking to her employer, not a workmate or a friend, and concerned lest he should think her too familiar, went on, "Aye, somebody *has* upset me, sir. I've had a squabble wi' my husband ... Matthew. I expect you might remember him."

"Indeed. But I understand the two of you are not together any more?"

There was a pause. "Who's told you about that, sir?"

"Mrs Finch. I've been to call on her this afternoon. She intimated something of your circumstances."

Ruby knew of the kin relationship between the Reynoldses and Martha's Auntie Ellen, so a social visit was explained. But that she herself had been a topic of their conversation made her feel uncomfortable.

"Oh – please, you mustn't suppose we discussed your personal business," Jabez Reynolds hastened to assure her, noting her reaction. "I'd no idea the paying guest was you till Mrs Finch made mention of her niece's friend being one of my employees."

He checked his horse from walking on again; then, glancing up and down the lane, he said – "Look, it isn't very private talking to you here. Perhaps you'd like to join me in a drive somewhere for half an hour?"

"A drive – ? What – wi' *you*, sir?"

"Certainly. Why not? I don't think anybody's going to mind, we shan't be long."

He reached across the driver's seat to take her hand, the heavy gold swag of his watch-chain falling sideways as he pulled her up to sit beside him. As always, he was very handsomely attired, even to the grey felt bowler and the flower in his buttonhole; and the fact that she herself looked what she was, a working girl in shawl and skirt and plain white blouse, made Ruby feel doubly embarrassed to accept his invitation.

"I'm not properly dressed for your company, Mr Reynolds," she said awkwardly, glancing over her shoulder in case Martha or Mrs Finch were watching from the cottage window.

"Let me be the judge of that, my dear." He clicked his tongue to the horse and flicked the reins, turning the gig round in the lane in the direction of Merridale. "Do you think I would invite you if I thought you weren't present-able enough?"

They came up to the junction and he manoeuvred them skilfully into the flow of Sunday traffic, needing his attention for the road for several minutes before he addressed her again.

"I expect you're surprised I should take such an interest in you, aren't you?"

The directness of the question startled her, since that was exactly what she'd just been thinking to herself. "I suppose I am, sir, aye."

"You wonder at my reason, even though you're one of my employees."

She hesitated. "Well, sir, I know your kind concern for anyone in trouble, or anyone that suffers wi' their health and suchlike."

Her answer pleased him. "Then you won't object if I ask you about yourself . . . your marriage. You wouldn't be unwilling? Or does that depend on what I wish to know?"

What *did* he wish to know – and why? Did one of the wealthiest tradesmen of the town make a habit of driving about the streets questioning young women on the state of their most intimate affairs, she wondered.

"You don't answer me," he said, when she stayed silent.

"I don't know *what* to answer, sir, that's why."

"You must trust me with your confidence. I want to be of help to you, my dear." He glanced at her as if wishing to gauge her reaction, and then, encouraging her with a sympathetic smile – "Tell me why you've left your husband."

She fixed her eyes upon the road, the trees, the houses, people on the pavements. "We argue all the while . . ."

And once she'd started talking she found it was easy to continue, because of the emotion still inside her from the quarrel she'd just had with Matthew. Some things she avoided touching on, like Jack McShane, and the sexual frustrations of her marriage. Other things she spoke of frankly – not complaining, or self-pitying, but with total honesty, even to blaming herself where none of the blame was due.

The only time Jabez Reynolds interrupted was towards the end, to comment when she mentioned Dorrie Vickers.

"Ah yes, I've heard of Dorothy Vickers from my brother Sam," he said.

"That's right, she's ... an acquaintance."

"*Former* acquaintance. She expected he would marry her, I gather, and Sam felt he must decline her. From all events, Miss Vickers was not amused to meet him with some new young lady–" He steered the gig out to overtake a landaulet beside the road. "She's fortunate not to be facing a serious charge of assault."

"Lord above, what happened?" Ruby stared at him.

"Miss Vickers threw a housebrick. In the street, of course. It missed and broke somebody's window – for which my brother, as a sort of farewell gesture, paid the damage."

Perhaps it was a reaction to the tension of relating her own troubles, but Ruby found the idea of Dorrie, furious with disappointment, lobbing a brick at the Pompadour-quiffed Sam absurdly funny.

She tried to restrain her amusement, but the image dimpled the sides of her mouth into smiles and then into laughing out loud, and she had to cover her face with her hands until she'd controlled herself. Her laughter was infectious. Jabez Reynolds started laughing too; and in the middle of their merriment they looked at one another, the kind of look which passes between man and woman in a mutual recognition of attraction.

The amusement suddenly faded, and they were serious again.

By this time they had passed through Merridale and Bradmore into the countryside at Lower Penn, and as they turned at a crossroad to begin the journey back, Mr Reynolds reined in the horse, bringing the gig to a halt beside a field gate.

"Ruby–" He shifted on the seat, putting one arm along its back as though he would touch her. The afternoon had started turning overcast and the daylight had a pearly quality which reflected the clearness of her skin and eyes and gave a soft sheen to her tawny hair.

He looked at her, as though he'd never seen her properly before. "Ruby . . . do you love your husband still?"

"O' course I do!"

"Then why don't you go back to him and live with him."

She had asked herself this very thing today, arguing with Matthew at their lodgings in Gas Yard. "I suppose – I suppose it's because I in't *in* love wi' him. Oh, that must sound bad, I know, after all Matt's gone and done for me. You can't imagine, sir, how good he's been. But if I was – *in* love wi' him, I mean – things would be so different. I'd stop in of an evening when he wanted. I'd try and get on wi' his mother and his father. I'd even go to chapel–"

She had to glance away, finding her employer's gaze disturbing her. "Maybe that's the trouble when you've *always* loved somebody," she went on. "It's like a part of you. It in't some'at new, exciting, not like meeting for the first time when you're old enough . . . growed up enough . . . to fall in love. I can't explain."

"I won't embarrass you by asking why you married,"

Jabez Reynolds said after a moment. "How old were you? Sixteen? That's far too young." His arm edged closer, his fingers touched her shoulder, brushed her neck. "You've had no life at all, my dear. What a waste for a girl as beautiful as you, to throw herself away on—"

Ruby sensed what he was going to say. She looked back at him, and again there was that too-lingering glance between them.

"I in't throwing myself away, sir." She could feel the warmth of his hand through the thin stuff of her blouse, his fingertips stroking her skin. She wanted to say 'Matthew's all the world to me' but her throat closed on the words.

"Do you know what would give me greatest pleasure," Mr Reynolds said softly. "To make you happy, Ruby. To look after you for just a while. I wonder ... would you let me?"

12

There had been a time, years before, when Edith Reynolds had been the prettiest young woman of her social set, as well as the most eligible. Her father owned a chain-making factory at Bilston and could afford to put his daughter through a private education and bring her up to be a lady. Amongst the aristocracy of Trade, her marriage to Jabez Reynolds in 1869 was considered an excellently suited match – iron marrying into meat, two of the great commercial pillars of the Victorian Age.

Jabez brought his bride to live in Wolverhampton, at Palmerston Place, the elegant town house his own father made over to them. Here Edith could indulge herself to her heart's content in her favourite pastime, becoming noted for her fearless horsemanship, both in her handling of a buggy which she drove at breakneck speed, and riding to hounds with the Albrighton Hunt across the county border in the neighbourhood of Bishops Aston.

In 1871 Edith suffered the first of several miscarriages, followed by the birth of a longed-for son and heir in 1876. The child, alas, did not survive a month. His death was a double tragedy, because there would be no more children from the marriage: within a short time Edith's health began to give concern, and after months of various unsuccessful treatments she was diagnosed as suffering from a disorder which caused wastage of the muscles. Its name was *myasthenia gravis* – 'creeping paralysis' – a chronic disease mainly affecting younger people, more so females in the prime of womanhood, as Edith Reynolds was.

What was particularly distressing was that she must give up her beloved hunting once her strength began to weaken, and exchange the dashing buggy for a staid carriage. She chafed against the debility of her illness, having no patience with the doctors who came and looked at her and went away again advising her to rest – always to rest. "I'll rest enough when I am dead!" she screamed at them. "Oh God, I want to *live!*"

Drink became a refuge for her. At first it was only to relieve her muscular discomfort that she took to drinking in the afternoons, and to while away the tedium of lying on a chaise longue doing nothing, *resting*. But then it became a mental anaesthesia that blotted out reality and helped her to stop hating her useless, feeble body and the narrowing restrictions of her life.

She had always been the sort of young woman whom other women envied; a young woman at home in masculine company where her strongly sexual personality shone at its best. As her illness progressed and her drinking bouts became more frequent, her female friends began to fall away and her circle of admirers dwindled to a few well-seasoned topers who liked to come and drink with her.

It was inevitable that as she changed, her marriage likewise underwent an alteration. The sexual relationship had been a good one for the first six years or so; but after the death of their infant son Edith and Jabez Reynolds seemed to drift apart, at a time when they needed to be drawing closer, and once the wastage of her muscles made intercourse unsatisfactory and further pregnancies unthinkable, the physical side of the marriage had ceased entirely.

Edith was no fool. She realised her husband, not being a saint, would need to turn to other women. She merely asked that he should be discreet and choose his partners well away from home, and elsewhere than her former social circle. This he did. By 1885 when her drinking was becoming an addiction which no one – and certainly not her family or her doctors – could break her of because she *craved* for alcohol as comfort and as consolation, it was decided that a change of habitat was necessary, even beneficial.

Edith herself wished to remove to Bishops Aston, the Reynolds's rural property which she'd always preferred to Palmerston Place. Here she had the privacy she wanted, watching the changing seasons of the countryside while her beauty wasted and withered away: a small happiness for one who once had had so much to live for, but she seemed content. And there was a housekeeper and a personal staff, discreet and loyal, to see she didn't drink herself to death.

Once a year her husband took her abroad, hoping against hope still to find a cure for the disease in Marienbad or Spa or Baden-Baden. Because he loved her, Jabez Reynolds never gave up hope; but neither did he give up his relationships with other, younger women. When first he'd encountered Ruby Dyson, the interest had been purely altruistic even though Mr Reynolds had not failed to note the promise of her quite enchanting beauty. Once Ruby's situation changed, however, so did his considerations. She was alone, she was desirable, and he knew that she was attracted to him.

That she was also still a married woman acted as a necessary safeguard against false illusions.

"I don't know what's got into our Ruby, really I don't," her mother said wearily. "Where did I go wrong wi' her, I ask myself. Why wo' she heed a single word I tell her, Jack."

Jack McShane glanced up from the sports page of the *Wolverhampton Chronicle*. "It's her life, Lizzie. If her wants to make a hash of it, that's her look-out not yourn."

"I've tried my best wi' her, God knows. I mean, it was bad enough her having to get married in a hurry—"

"You dain't think any the worse of her, as I recall."

"I never did, it's true. There's many a one done that before. But walking out on Matthew – and for what?" Seated opposite her husband at the gaslit table, Lizzie shook her head over the mending she was finishing. "I begged and pleaded wi' her – chick, I said, I don't know what you think you'm playing at and I can't agree wi' what you'm doing—"

"I know. You've told me."

"Aye. And then I said to her I said, but if you need a place to come and stop there's always one wi' Jack and me. But would she listen?"

"Ah, leave her to it, Lizzie. Her's a headstrong little madam."

"I'm still her mother, in't I, though. I can't help myself but fret for her."

"You'll fret yourself into an early grave, my wench."

Giving her a look, he turned again to reading about Wolverhampton Wanderers football team.

"It was losing the babby . . . that's what altered her."

"Mebbe."

"She's never been the same. And yet d'you know I was surprised how bad she took it afterward, considering she never seemed much interested before the little mite was born."

Jack made no answer to that. No one had been better pleased than he when Ruby's infant daughter failed to live. The last thing he wanted in Minerva Lane was some blasted nipper growing up the spit of him, particularly when its mother was his own young stepdaughter. Sometimes he'd wondered if those powders he'd dosed her with had harmed the growing babby and made it such a weakly, feeble thing; but he didn't intend to lose his sleep about it.

"I suppose it's useless asking *you* to try and have a word wi' her?" Lizzie said again unhappily, folding up her bit of mending ready for the iron.

"Me—? I'm keeping out of it! It's her husband's place to tell her what her ought to do, not mine."

"He says he wants her back again."

"Then let him do some'at his ruddy self instead o' making you traipse to and fro as if you was his errand lad." Jack shook his paper angrily to turn the page. "I'm getting fed up to the back teeth wi' Ruby and her problems lately. As if we ain't got enough of our own to worrit us! There's young Joe can't hold a job above a week, expecting me to keep him – and you fading away to a wraith before my eyes wi' your fretting and your maundering."

"Oh, I'm sorry, love, I didn't mean to vex you–"

Lizzie reached across the table to him. "I know you try and do your best for us. I wish things didn't have to be so awkward..." Her voice trailed off and she gave him an appeasing smile, cajoling him into a better humour.

Jack grunted. Throwing the paper aside he got up to take his tobacco jar from the mantelpiece and light his pipe.

"I wouldn't have said anything about it, only ... only Ruby called round here this morning," Lizzie began again after a moment, hesitantly watching his expression. "She's moving out o' Brickhill Lane and going somewhere else to live. She wouldn't tell me where. Oh Jack, I'm worried ... I think she's keeping some'at from me."

He made a noise that might have been a laugh except it had no humour. "Her's always keeping some'at from you."

"She seemed ... well, all excited, like. And she's handing in her job wi' Reynoldses she told me."

"To do what?" The pipe clenched between his teeth, he searched along the shelf for his box of Vestas. "Go back in service again, I suppose."

"I wondered that myself."

"What else would her do for blasted work? It's all her knows."

The anxious lines on Lizzie's thin-drawn face began to clear. "You'm right, she's found her a position living in somewhere as housemaid, aye. That's put my mind at rest, you saying that."

Getting from her chair she went and hugged her husband's brawny arm, telling him gratefully, "You'm a blessing to me, you am, Jack! I don't know where I'd be wi'out you, love, I really don't."

* * *

Matthew as well had learned Ruby was moving out of Brickhill Lane; and being no wiser than Lizzie what her plans involved, he could only share the guess that his young wife meant to return to employment in domestic service. The secrecy upset him. He thought perhaps she was trying to pass herself off as a single woman again to make it easier to come by live-in work.

By now, he'd abandoned any hope of an early reconciliation and was sinking into a moody, downcast state of mind. Much to his parents' concern he had also given up going to chapel recently, saying it was a waste of time appealing to a God who never answered him. When the minister called, offering to pray and give him counsel to help him through this crisis in his faith, Matthew declined. 'Ask, and it shall be given you,' said Scripture. 'Knock, and it shall be opened unto you.'

Well, he had asked for Ruby to come back. She hadn't. It seemed to him, he told the minister, he must be knocking in vain – and at the wrong blasted door.

His mates at Chubb's Lock Manufactory, where he'd always been popular among the young apprentices, commiserated with Matthew's situation although his constant moroseness was starting to try the patience of a few of them. He ought to get out of an evening and enjoy himself, they said. He ought to find himself a little lady-friend who'd cheer him up. His missis would soon come running if she heard he was making eyes at somebody else.

Matthew didn't want 'a little lady-friend'. He only wanted Ruby; only wanted life to be the way they'd dreamed and planned between the pair of them before it all turned sour.

Judith Glover

He was coming back from work one evening when he did
something that would have shocked his mother into fits if
she had known. He went into a public house.

Although his parents were rabidly teetotal, Matthew had
occasionally – out of curiosity, no more – drunk a glass or
two of ale with his mates. The sensation hadn't been
unpleasant. This evening he felt so depressed he couldn't
bear to face the empty lodgings in Gas Yard, sitting on his
own till bedtime with nothing to do but pick at the scab of
his misery until he'd made it bleed afresh.

The day had been one of those long, hot, lovely ones of
early August, warm enough even at half past six for boys to
be splashing naked in the canal by Lock Street bridge.
Matthew paused to watch them, envying their merry-
hearted spirits; and as he turned to continue on his way he
thought suddenly – blow it, I'll go and have an ale, that's
what I'll do.

There was a public house in nearby Broad Street, the
Eclipse, where some of Chubb's apprentices went for a
drink after work – a friendly, ordinary sort of place with
low ceilings and smoke-yellowed walls and sawdust on
the floor. Finding the saloon bar almost empty, Matthew
tried the public bar next door and espied a couple of
chaps he knew sitting by the window with a blonde-
haired girl he vaguely recognised from the factory's
machine shop.

"God blimey, look who's just walked in!" one of them
exclaimed. "You're a stranger, in't you, Matthew! Come
and join us – what you drinking, mate, I'll stand you one."

"That's decent of you. I'll have a pint o' mild, please,
George."

164

While the other went over to the counter, he drew up a stool and sat himself beside the girl, and smiled at her. "Hello," he said.

She returned the smile. She had a heart-shaped face, like a kitten's, with wide blue eyes and a little tip-tilted nose; pert more than pretty, but certainly attractive and worth the second look he gave her.

"Sorry – I don't think I know your name." He had to raise his voice against the noise from a neighbouring table.

"Thompson," she informed him. "Gatty Thompson."

"Gatty? That's a rum 'un, isn't it?" Matthew glanced across at the second lad and winked, already beginning to feel a bit more cheerful.

"It's Gertrude, really. But everybody calls me Gatty." She dimpled again. "I know what *your* name is. I know where you used to live an' all."

"You do?"

"Aye."

"Somebody's mentioned me at Chubb's, I suppose."

"That 'd be telling."

"You wants to watch her, mate," said George, returning with his pint. "She's a proper little sauce-pot. In't you – eh?" He pretended to tweak the girl's nose as he went to sit down.

"Oh, leave off, George – you're always pawing at me!" Good-humouredly she jerked her head away. "You know I hate it."

"Garn, you love it." He grinned at her; then raised his thumb in response to Matthew's thanks and said, "Good cheer", before taking a pull at his own glass of ale.

"I thought you lot didn't come in public houses," Gatty

remarked a little while later in the conversation, looking at Matthew over the rim of whatever it was she was drinking. "You're Methodist, in't you. New Connexion Chapel – that right?"

He responded to her look in puzzlement. "You're very well informed."

"Her's pulling your leg, that's all, mate," came in Stephen, the other apprentice at the table. "There used to be this wench what shared her workbench–"

"Oi, it's my story, *I'll* tell him!" Gatty pressed her hand over Stephen's mouth to silence him, and turning back to Matthew – "Maria Rowley. D'you remember her? Fat podgy thing wi' ginger hair. Left the factory nigh on a year ago."

He tried to think. Aye, there *had* been a girl with ginger hair, a bit on the large side, who'd worked in the machine shop. He took a drink of his ale, savouring the clean, cold, sweetly bitter taste against his tongue; then said, "I didn't even know she'd gone."

"Shows how much you've missed her, eh," laughed Gatty. "You're a heartless bad 'un, Matthew Dyson, no mistake – and to think the poor wench nearly chucked herself in the cut on your account!"

When he looked taken aback she went on, "Don't say you never noticed? She ate her heart out over you for months, Maria did. Talk about in love – you was the chicken's blinkin' elbows, you was! *I* should know, I had to stick it all day long like an hurdy-gurdy – drove me daft, it did. She could even tell us what you'd ate at brew-up time."

"Aye, we dain't half used to twit her," Stephen added to this friendly ribbing. "Her brother was a pal o' mine. He said her had a neckerchief o' yourn her used to sleep with tucked beneath her pillow."

"I remember losing that neckerchief." It had been a paisley-patterned one, a birthday gift to Matthew from his grandma years before, and he'd worn it till it almost frayed apart. "D'you know, I often wondered what had happened to it."

"I used to say to her," said Gatty, emptying her glass and licking her lips in a most delightful way, "it won't do you any good, Maria, I used to say, 'cos Matt's already spoke for. And when you went and got *married*–" She rolled her eyes. "Crikey, never mind hysterics, she was going to jump in the cut and drown herself and all the rest of it–"

"But she didn't, I hope!"

"O' course she din't. Even a wench like her has got more sense. The last thing I heard o' Maria she was walking out wi' some lad off the railways."

"And they all lived happy ever afterwards," said George. "Come on, Matt, sup up – these glasses are standing empty."

Matthew downed the rest of his ale. "Here, let me pay for the next round. What are you drinking, Gatty?"

"Another gin and lemon, please."

"And Stephen–?" glancing across.

Stephen shook his head. "Ta, mate, but I best be pushing along. The old 'oman 'll have my food on the table."

"How about you, George?"

"Mine's a pale ale."

As he got to his feet George handed him the empties,

observing with a touch of pawky humour, "You drunk that first 'un pretty quick for a teetotaller."

"I needed it."

Smiling, Matthew went across the busy public bar, nodding to several other chaps he recognised. The leg-pulling over Maria Rowley had lifted his mood, and the companionship and the pleasant effect of a pint of beer inside him made him glad he'd thought to call in here this evening. It was better than Gas Yard, feeling miserable and lonely, any rate.

While he waited to be served he thought about Maria. There'd always been one or two girls at Chubb's who wouldn't have said no to going out with him, but he'd never had eyes or thoughts for any of them but Ruby. Ruby had been the love of his life, his whole horizon. Some would say he'd been a blasted fool to stay so true; perhaps they had a point . . .

Balancing the two full glasses and Gatty's 'short' he made his way back to their table, calling cheerio to Stephen as the other lad departed through the door.

"I was just this minute saying to George," Gatty remarked after he'd sat down again, "as how you can't be having much of a jolly time these days – y'know, the way things are at home, I mean. It'd do you good to enjoy yourself like this more often."

"I was thinking the same myself."

"Well, if ever you're looking for friendly company–" she gave him another of her dimpled smiles, and her kittenish face wore a mischievous expression as she reached to touch her glass to his. "I'm generally here of an evening after work if you wants to have a little chat. You won't forget?"

An agreeable euphoria seemed to settle warmly over Matthew.

"I won't forget," he said.

13

There had been a thunderstorm, but it had passed over now and the sky was clearing, pouring out a soft, pure light over the countryside. The scene was like a freshly-varnished landscape painting, everything picked out in sharpest detail – the lustrous emerald enamelling of leaves, the diamond shimmer of raindrops on the thatch of cottages, the beaten bronze of the cornfields. The ruts in the lane were filled with puddles mirroring the sky, through which the pony trap splashed and lurched, shivering their reflection into muddy ripples and making Ruby hold on tightly to the seat rail.

While the storm was at its height, she and Jabez Reynolds had taken shelter at a coaching inn, the Bradford Arms, further back on the brow of the hill along the main road. She had wondered why Mr Reynolds preferred to seek the overhang of a roof in the stable yard, and not go inside the inn where they'd be comfortable and dry; but she didn't like to ask, and presumed he must be anxious to press on to Ivetsey Bank as soon as the rain had eased.

When he'd proposed to her recently that she leave her job on his market stall and lodge in a cottage at Ivetsey Bank on the edge of his estate, Ruby hadn't hesitated very long about accepting. Her only qualm concerned her mother, that Lizzie might be even greater upset if she knew she was moving to live away in the country, and would try to dissuade her from going. It was better, perhaps, to say nothing for the moment than to cause her Mam that extra bit of worry on top of all the rest.

The girl was sorry to be leaving Mrs Finch and Martha, but it had always been understood that her lodging with them was only a temporary measure until she'd found somewhere; and now here she was, with her box of belongings strapped behind and her linnet in its covered cage held on her lap, being driven down a twisting high-banked lane towards her new employment.

"Not far now," said Jabez Reynolds suddenly, breaking the silence which had fallen between them since turning off the road. "There's a water splash at the bottom of this next dip, then we're there."

He glanced at Ruby, his eyes lingering over her pretty face in a look that was half-smile, half-serious; then he turned his attention back to handling the trap round a steep little bend which took them down towards a shallow ford running across the lane. On its further side there was a rise, and when the lane levelled out again Ruby found they were almost at the gate of a cottage standing behind the hedge in a garden bordered by lavender and sweetbriar bushes.

"Oh – is this it, sir?" she asked, craning her neck for a better look and thinking there wouldn't be much work to do in a place so small.

"Aye, Ruby, this is it." Jabez Reynolds brought the trap to a halt on the daisy-dotted verge in front of the gate, and got down to secure the pony's reins before coming round to help her dismount. "Do you like it?"

Her enchanted expression was answer enough. Holding her bird-cage, she stood beside him in the lane drinking in the scene with a delighted childlike disbelief, her eyes going from the cottage to the view beyond it of the undulating Shropshire countryside stretching away beneath an ivory sky towards the distant Clee Hills.

"It's ... beautiful," she said after a moment, almost breathlessly. "*Beautiful*, Mr Reynolds."

"I'm so glad you're pleased, my dear."

Pushing back the wicket gate he ushered her along the path past a grey-lichened apple tree heavy with ripening fruit, to the cottage porch, where he produced a latch-key.

"How long has the place been empty?" she enquired, itching to see inside. Although her employer had never exactly said as much, Ruby had taken it for granted that her new job was to be as live-in caretaker looking after the property and keeping it cleaned and aired ready for its next occupation.

"It hasn't been empty all that long–" Mr Reynolds opened the door and stood aside to let her enter first. "A month or so, I don't remember now. The previous tenant didn't care for the isolated situation ... too lonely or something."

Ruby hardly heard him. She had stepped into a low-beamed room furnished with a sofa, an occasional table, and several spoon-back chairs upholstered in Berlin wool-work. A long-case clock stood at the bottom of the stairs, and an upright piano with brass candlesticks and mother-of-pearl inlay occupied the wall opposite. A door on the left led into the little kitchen with its black-leaded range and brownstone sink; and upstairs–

173

"Can I go and see upstairs, Mr Reynolds?" she asked excitedly, putting the linnet's cage aside on a chair.

"Of course. And while you're doing that I'll bring in your box."

"Oh no, sir, really – I can see to the box myself!" she said as he moved back to the door, not liking the idea of him doing her fetching for her.

"It's no trouble, my dear." Again there was that look, half-smile, half-serious. "You go along and I'll follow. I'd like to be sure everything meets with your approval before we . . . how shall I say, discuss terms."

Ruby hesitated a moment, torn between duty and training and her eagerness to see over the rest of the place. Eagerness won. Holding the hem of her striped skirt she ran up the stairs and found herself on a narrow landing with a door at either side into the bedrooms. One room, that on the right, contained a brass bedstead with its mattress rolled back showing the bare springs, and in the corner a washstand with blue-and-white china basin and ewer. The other appeared to be used as a dressing-room, being furnished with a small wardrobe, chest of drawers, and a table fitted with a toilet mirror. Both rooms were lit by low dormer windows set in the slope of the roof, and had been prettily decorated with a frieze of rose-patterned paper round the walls.

Allowing curiosity to get the better of her, Ruby peered inside the wardrobe. Its emptiness exuded a faint smell of scent, like violets; and as she went to close the door again she noticed a single white silk stocking lying in a corner. The chest of drawers likewise yielded clues that the cottage's previous occupant had been a young woman:

there were a number of corrugated hairpins, an empty bottle of Nisbett's Damask Rose Drops for colouring the cheeks, and the whalebone rib from a pair of corsets.

Hearing Jabez Reynolds at the foot of the stairs she hastily shut the drawers and stepped out into the doorway, standing aside to let him come past with her box.

For want of something else to say, she asked with just a touch of awkwardness, "You wouldn't happen to know where the sheets and things are kept, sir? Only there in't no clothes for the bed in there."

He set down the box by the chest, and went across for a cursory glance into the other room; and she heard him let out a sound of annoyance when he saw the unmade state of the bed.

"Damn it, that was supposed to have been seen to yesterday! A woman at the top of the lane who does the laundering – she was asked to wash all the linen and have the blankets ready aired to make the bed up before we arrived."

"Maybe she left the things down in the kitchen," Ruby suggested. "Shall I go and look, sir?"

"Aye, if you will. I'm sorry, my dear . . . this isn't quite what I envisaged," Mr Reynolds told her, seeming mighty put out, she thought, over what was really no more than a trivial omission. But then, he was the type who liked everything done to the letter, and a request from someone as up in the world as him should be treated as an order and properly attended to.

Sure enough, when she went down there on the kitchen table was a large, heavy bundle of bed linen and blankets wrapped inside a patchwork counterpane.

"It's all right, sir. It's here–" Ruby called out, reaching for the knotted ends to drag the lot towards her and twisting round to hoist the weight across her slender shoulders.

She was struggling to get it balanced on her back when Jabez Reynolds followed her downstairs. "Come on – you can't do that," he said, coming through the door and making to take the bundle from her. "Let me have it."

"No, I can manage. You carried my box."

The line of reasoning caused him some amusement. "And because I fetched a box, I must now stand by and watch you take your turn straining to lug that great load up the stairs all by yourself?"

She let the bedclothes drop back on the table. "You're my employer–"

"And that precludes me from lending you assistance, does it?"

"Well . . . it in't hardly your job to do *my* job for me, is it, sir," she answered frankly. "I mean, you're paying me to do this work."

The amused look faded, and he was serious again. Taking hold of her by the hand he said, "Perhaps you don't quite understand your situation, Ruby."

"Aye, sir, 'course I do," she said, thinking by 'situation' he meant her employment here. "You're engaging me to be like a sort o' housekeeper, in't you?"

He stared down into her face, seeing the open, trustful naivety of her expression, almost childlike except for the way she looked back at him, with that slight widening of the eyes which betrays a woman's feelings and which Jabez Reynolds found so appealingly attractive, particularly when combined with such enchanting features.

"I think . . . we should have a little talk, my dear," he said, drawing her closer and placing his arm round her waist. "Let's go and stroll in the garden, shall we."

Ruby wasn't to know that he found the cottage, with its recent memories of the last pretty young charmer to occupy it, more of a distraction than he'd allowed for. He needed to be outside, in the sweet fresh air, where the echo of argument and recrimination wouldn't mar their first pleasurable moment of intimacy together.

The way he held her, with his arm round her – not a casually patronising gesture but something much more affectionate – threw Ruby into confusion. It was the sort of thing she'd sometimes dreamed of Mr Reynolds doing, but never in a million years had she ever thought such daydreams could be realised. Even after that drive they'd taken together the other week from Brickhill Lane, when he'd made the suggestion about looking after her, even then she had assumed he was only trying to be kind.

From their very first meeting in the Empire Vaults – how long ago, over a year now, surely – she had admired Jabez Reynolds and known herself physically drawn to him. The fact that he was *who* he was, successful, wealthy, one of the foremost businessmen in Wolverhampton, was attraction enough in itself; but harnessed to the appeal of his mature good looks, and the aura of power he seemed always to carry about him – all this upon a girl as impressionable as Ruby had a devastating effect, the more so now she found herself alone with him and in such intimate contact.

"Aye, I – I'd like a walk in the garden," she heard herself stammering. "I haven't seen round the back except out the window."

He gave her waist a squeeze, and taking her by the hand again, unlatched the kitchen door. It opened directly on to a stone terrace, with a tarred water butt against the wall for catching rainwater from the eaves, and a path leading off to a beehive-shaped privy next to the wood-shed.

The garden was mostly laid to grass, with beds of sweet william and pinks and the old-fashioned rose bushes known as 'Maiden's Blush', as well as several fruit trees whose branches were now beginning to bow under the weight of russets and purple-skinned damsons. At the further end the ground sloped towards the stream which the trap had crossed back at the ford in the lane, and in the stillness of the summer's afternoon the murmurous sound of its water purling among the stones carried to them clearly.

For Ruby, so much beauty was all part of the wonder she had fallen into. She allowed herself to be seated on the still-damp grass and waited in trembling silence for Jabez Reynolds to speak, her eyes fixed not on the lovely scene around but on his face.

"Do you remember I told you I wanted to make you happy?" he began after a moment. "And that I wanted to take care of you?"

"Aye ... I remember," she whispered.

"I haven't brought you here to be housekeeper, Ruby. This cottage is yours to live in – not as a lodging or a place of service, but as your home for as long as you want it. And I shall visit you from time to time not as your master or employer, but as a friend calling upon a young woman whom he happens to admire especially. A friend ... who wishes more than friendship. Do you understand what I'm saying, my dear?"

She felt her cheeks start burning as the implication of his words sank in. "Mrs Finch said—"

"I know what Mrs Finch said." He smiled. Raising his hand he traced the blushing contour of her face with his fingers. "Ellen Finch and Martha were only repeating what I led them to believe, that you were coming here to work as a domestic. A man in my position doesn't advertise his private life."

Ruby dropped her gaze and in her agitation began playing with her brass wedding-ring.

"I'm sorry if I seem to be guilty of deception," he went on, "but I'm sure you can appreciate why I needed to be careful, Ruby. It would never have done for you to go about telling people you were being set up in your own little place as Jabez Reynolds's—" he hesitated to use the term which a man of the world would apply to a girl who provided him with her sexual favours – "as Jabez Reynolds's young lady friend. And besides . . . perhaps you might not have wanted to come, my dear."

She glanced up at him again, nervously. "I'm a married woman, sir."

"Only in name."

"I – I don't know as it's right."

"You're not afraid, surely? You know I'll always treat you with consideration."

"But what would our Mam say – and Matthew? Dear God, what would *he* say?"

Mr Reynolds took her restless hands and stilled them. "He'll say nothing if he doesn't know, and neither will your mother. In any case, why should you care now you've left him? If your husband's good opinion matters so much to you, perhaps we should forget all this and you go back to your lodging in Gas Yard. Is that what you'd prefer to do now, Ruby?"

She looked at the hands holding hers, work-hardened and strong, and at the heavy gold signet ring on the little finger. Then her eyes moved slowly upward over the spotless shirt cuffs, the immaculate reefer jacket sporting its trademark buttonhole, the loose-knotted tie, to his face with its lean, firm lines of seasoned manhood – and of all the things to think about at such a crucial moment, it occurred to her that though she'd hated facial hair on Matthew because of its association with her stepfather, on Jabez Reynolds the close-clipped greying moustache was like a symbol of authority that handsomely became his features.

Experience had already taught her the devastating effect of falling for an older man's attraction and succumbing to her own physical desires. For that reason alone she ought to refuse his offer. But then she thought about her young brother Joe. Maybe – maybe if she did as Mr Reynolds wished and pleased him, it would be helping Joe, for surely the master butcher would then be willing to find her brother some sort of decent employment.

"Well–?" he prompted. "Have you decided? Do you wish to stay, or shall I return you to your husband."

"What about *Mrs* Reynolds, though? She's only living a couple o' miles away – won't she be bound to find out all about me?" Without realising, Ruby had answered his question.

"Who needs to know you're here? I hope I can trust us both to be discreet."

"But I can't stay invisible, can I? I mean, I'll have to go up into Ivetsey Bank to buy myself food—"

"Not at all. The laundering woman I mentioned, she'll see to your requirements for you. I pay her to keep a still tongue in her head."

Freeing Ruby's hands, Mr Reynolds gently tilted her chin so that she was forced to look him directly in the face. "I'll be honest with you, my dear. Since my wife became . . . indisposed, I have had recourse to a few sweet, obliging creatures like yourself, and brought them here. It's a common enough arrangement and I hope you won't think any the worse of me for it. I may be wealthy and influential and successful . . . but I have a man's ordinary needs, and I'll confess that often I am very, very lonely."

"I know you've had other women," Ruby blurted out before she could stop herself. "Dorrie Vickers let drop about you entertaining them at Palmerston Place. Your brother told her so."

"Damn him, he'll say too much one of these days." The moment of intimacy was broken. Jabez Reynolds's expression tightened into anger, and releasing her he turned away, then after a second got to his feet, irritably brushing bits of damp grass from his trousers.

Thinking he meant to walk off and leave her there, Ruby bit her lip for blabbing things without first thinking. Of course he'd take offence, having his private affairs discussed behind his back – and now most likely he was telling himself she wasn't to be trusted with his confidence.

"I'm sorry . . ." she said humbly. "I should've known better than to mention a matter like that, sir. It in't any o' my business."

"Actually," he answered over his shoulder, "I'm glad you know. It saves deceit. I suppose you'd like me to take you back to Wolverhampton now."

She followed slowly to her feet and stood looking miserably at the view which only a little while ago had held her completely enraptured. Above the murmur of the stream a thrush was singing, and the light breeze carried the bleating of sheep on some distant hill pasture.

"You don't want me to stay?" she said again at last, unable any longer to bear his silence.

He took a moment; then turning back to her, replied, "It's what *you* want, Ruby. I won't place any conditions on you, beyond that of circumspection. If you decide to remain here you're free to do so for whatever length of time you wish. It's up to you, my dear."

She thought about Joe again. "I . . . I'd like to stay, Mr Reynolds."

All the severity in his face melted away into a look so suddenly, nakedly hungry that Ruby felt her heart leap in response to him. He came and drew her into his arms and held her, crushing her against the rose in his lapel, and before he kissed her for the first time she heard his whisper – "Thank you."

14

Surely she had lost her husband for ever now. Even if they smoothed out all their problems Matthew would never want to have her back again, Ruby was convinced, so she might as well burn her bridges and make this new life into something worth the while. Their marriage was beset with troubles anyway, and as for her respectability – she'd forfeited that, and decency, the night she'd let her stepfather debauch her.

What was there left to lose . . . except maybe her shabby, outworn sentimental loyalties.

After that first time in the garden in the damp grass underneath the trees when he'd been like a starved man frantic to sate his famished appetite, Jabez Reynolds proved himself a versatile and considerate lover, and far more skilful than Jack McShane had ever been. With Jack, sexual intercourse was always a grabbing, pawing, grunting, sweating copulation carried out with one eye on the door for fear of being discovered. With Mr Reynolds it was a most gloriously satisfying exploration of pleasure, languorously, tantalisingly enjoyed in the rumpled comfort of a sun-warmed bed, with the soft champagne glow of the summer's afternoon slowly deepening to shadow.

He never stayed the night. He'd never shared a bed to sleep with any woman but his wife. It was one of his rules. And he didn't visit Ruby at the cottage every day but only Mondays, Tuesdays, Thursdays (early closing day) and occasionally Sunday evening. For the rest of the time she was happy to amuse herself playing at being the lady of leisure, not getting up till ten or eleven o'clock, doing a bit of housework or tending the garden, going for walks across the countryside, picking out tunes on the piano, writing circumspectly to her mother ... not lies exactly, but trying to spare her mother from hurt by juggling with the truth to make it sound as if she was working here as maid.

Several times a week in Mr Reynolds's absence Ruby received her only other visitor, the laundering woman, Mrs Skinner, who brought along her provisions. Mrs Skinner was married to a cowman two miles up the lane at Woodhouse Farm and reminded Ruby a little of Agnes Dyson, Matthew's mother, with her sharp observant eyes and purse-lipped mouth; only in Mrs Skinner's case the shape of the mouth was due to a lack of teeth rather than severity of character.

Neither of them ever mentioned Mr Reynolds except indirectly and only when it became necessary; otherwise their conversation was dictated by the continuing fine weather, Mrs Skinner's domestic trivia, or Ruby's requirements, paid for out of the money Jabez Reynolds left her weekly for the purpose. Sometimes she would catch Mrs Skinner regarding her with a certain pitying, enquiring look, and would feel tempted to ask her what the other 'sweet obliging creatures' had been like. She resisted, having no real wish to have a face or name that would put flesh upon the existence of her predecessors at the cottage.

Now that she was what the world would call Jabez Reynolds's kept woman (though she preferred to think of herself as his 'darling girl', the endearment he used in lovemaking) Ruby was able to give full rein to the strength of attraction which she felt for him; an attraction she knew now had been there from the very start hidden beneath her love for Matthew – not just admiration and respect but something deeper, like the early intoxicated rapture of her feelings towards Jack McShane before infatuation withered into disgust.

In moments of reflection she asked herself whether the failure of her marriage hadn't been in part due to this underlying attachment. Maybe she would have been less readily dissatisfied, more willing to make allowance, to be patient and considerate, less selfish, if only there hadn't been this romantic yearning filling up her daydreams and providing the excitement which her marriage seemed to lack.

Such fits of introspection didn't last. Ruby believed herself in love with Jabez Reynolds, even though what she was really in love with was the aphrodisiac of wealth and power which men such as he represented.

Mr Reynolds himself never spoke of love. Ruby charmed him – he found the appearance of reserve in such a pretty female, with the hint of darker passions underneath her outward modesty, more exciting than blatant sexuality – but it was his wife he loved. Like most men, he was capable of a sincere and caring devotion to one particular woman, whilst entertaining feelings of carnal attraction for any number of others, and he thought nothing unnatural in doing so. He found Ruby an apt and eager pupil in what was to him an arrangement of convenience for them both; and because he wished to keep her happy he responded to her lovingness with real affection, even though he kept her under no illusion that their relationship would ever lead to anything more permanent.

As a treat and change of scene for her, once a week he would take the girl to Shrewsbury or Ludlow or Bridgnorth, and while he attended to business in the livestock markets, Ruby passed the hours looking round these lovely Shropshire towns. Shrewsbury she liked especially, because it was bigger and had emporia to wander through, and because she was so charmed by the curious names – Dogpole, Murivance, Shoplatch – of its medieval streets, and its liquorice-striped black-timbered buildings leaning like old gossips overhead.

These weekly trips became part of the excitement life now held for her; and if she thought at all of Matthew or Minerva Lane, the prick of conscience didn't hurt enough to cause regret.

In fulfilment of a promise made to find her brother Joe employment, Jabez Reynolds had now begun paying the lad to do the gardening for Mrs Finch in Brickhill Lane. This was just the sort of work that Joe was suited to, and the old lady – knowing about his fits – would be sure to treat him with the greatest kindness. Joe could turn his hand to any little job, but regular paid work was hard to come by for a lad like him, since people in their ignorance thought his disability affected his mentality and were reluctant to engage him.

His employment was another reason for Ruby to feel beholden; and as is the way with gratitude, it influenced and strengthened her devotion towards Jabez Reynolds.

Autumn drew on, and the views from the cottage at Ivetsey Bank slowly changed. The golden fields of August were shorn of their harvests and left stubbly and bare. The lush green of the summer woods blazed into glorious flame and burned against the misty hills, then dropped their leaves in heaps of withered sunsets on the earth. A quiet melancholy seemed to settle over the countryside. In a morning Ruby would wake to find the garden wet with dew and every bush spangled with shimmering cobwebs, and a coolness freshened the air as though the dying breath of the year were being exhaled in readiness for winter's hibernation.

The afternoons began to shorten. The oil lamps were lit at six o'clock now, filling the shadowy rooms with the warmth of their glow. It was cosy sitting by the open fire; yet Ruby found the solitude becoming oppressive, the stillness of the place *too* still. She didn't notice it with Jabez Reynolds there, but once he'd gone and she was left alone again, the cottage felt less friendly than it had in summer.

The truth was she was growing homesick for the streets of Wolverhampton, homesick for the gas-lit tenements, the crowded pubs, the noise, the smells . . . and more than all this, homesick for her mother. It was nothing unusual for girls in domestic service in the country not to see their families all that often, on account of distance, so Lizzie herself would not be worried on that score. Even so, three months was over-long without a visit.

"What will you tell your mother if my name crops up?"

said Jabez Reynolds when he took Ruby to Four Ashes halt to catch the early train. "Remember, dear, we have an agreement. I must rely on you to be discreet."

"I know – and I will," she assured him.

He didn't wait to see her on the train but drove away through the clearing morning mist, leaving her to wait there on the platform where once she'd stood with Matthew, arguing because of Mr Reynolds. It was incredible, she reflected, how her life had gone round full circle.

Having written in advance telling Lizzie to expect her at Minerva Lane, and knowing how houseproud her mother always was, the state of number 11 came as something of a shock when Ruby saw it. Normally the back step would have been scrubbed, the floor tiles washed, the windows cleaned. Instead, everything looked dusty and untidy, as though no one had done any housework for the last few weeks. There was a pile of soiled washing in the scullery, just chucked down on the floor and left to lie there; crumbs and all sorts underneath the table, and ring-marks on the dresser's varnished surface where Jack had stood his empty beer bottles.

But far more upsetting even than this was the change in her mother's appearance. Lizzie McShane had never carried much weight on her bones, but she'd got to look gaunt and suddenly *old*, Ruby thought, and there was a purplish tinge to her lips that the girl didn't like.

"Oh, Mam–" she cried, throwing herself into her mother's arms, almost frightened to hug her too tightly for fear she would bruise. "Oh, Mam, what's happened here – you look so bad! Have you been ill? Why din't you say in your letters so as I'd know?"

"I dain't want you worried over nothing, chick," said Lizzie. "I'm better now. And our Joe's been doing what he could round the place, bless his heart."

"But couldn't one o' the neighbours come in to gi' you some help?"

"Your stepfather dain't want me asking them. You know how he is – he never likes to feel beholden."

"He'd rather have you kill yourself–" Ruby glanced about the kitchen angrily, chiding herself for neglecting her mother this long. Living at Ivetsey Bank had served to open her eyes to the shabby poverty that Lizzie lived in – not poverty of purse, so much as poverty of pleasures and possessions. "I hope he had the sense to fetch the doctor in to look at you?"

Her mother gave her a kiss and drew away. "I'll put the kettle on–" she started; and when Ruby interrupted her for an answer, she said with a little tired smile, "No, he dain't. There's nothing much a doctor can do for me, our chick. My heart's wore out, that's all. Now let's forget it. Come and sit you down and tell me all what you've been doing wi' yourself these past few months. There's so many things I've been meaning to ask – and now blowed if I can remember half o' them!"

The girl felt an uncomfortably sharp guilt about the story she'd been rehearsing, the pretence of being in service to some 'dear old lady' in the country. Writing letters from the cottage had seemed easy – but now, face to face with Lizzie, her nerve was beginning to fail her. She had never been a liar, let alone a plausible one; and what sort of daughter could look her sick, frail mother in the eye and spin a total fabrication of the truth? She had promised Mr Reynolds to be discreet, but if she tried inventing facts she'd betray herself the minute she opened her mouth – and Lizzie would know it.

"We'll talk about everything later, Mam," she said, going to take off her short-waisted jacket, "when I've cleaned up the mess in this kitchen and put the place straight again."

"Oh, but Ruby–"

"Oh but Ruby nothing. You don't think I intend leaving you to manage it all by yourself, do you? Our Joe can take that washing down the Chinese laundry in the barrow – and if Jack McShane says anything, you tell him from me he can ruddy well jump in the cut!"

Lizzie made a funny choking sound. She turned away, putting a hand to her mouth, her body shaking; then suddenly she broke down into tears. Her distress was so naked that Ruby went to her and held her, rocking her backwards and forwards in her arms, her own eyes filling with emotion. "Don't, Mam, don't . . ." she said into her mother's hair.

"My chick, I've missed you so. You've felt that far away from me," Lizzie gasped after a moment, making an effort to compose herself. "I wish you'd stopped wi' Matthew . . . I wish it hadn't all gone wrong between you."

"But I've tried to explain–"

"Jack says he's seen him drinking in a public house wi' some young wench from Chubb's . . . laughing and joking together, he says." She burst into pitiful sobs again, leaning her face against her daughter's shoulder. "That I should live to see this day . . . my own child parted from her husband, and him turning to other females for his consolation."

Ruby's expression hardened. "Jack's always had it in for me and Matthew. He'd tell you a story like that just to make mischief."

"No, I heard the same from Mrs Moss at number 8. Her'd seen him in the street wi' his arm wrapped round some wench's waist, her told me."

A quick, raw stab of jealousy pierced Ruby. It had never crossed her mind Matt might decide to go and take up with anybody else.

Yet, why not? Sauce for the goose was sauce for the gander. What right did she have to be so resentful that he was only doing the same as herself? It didn't make sense it should suddenly feel like betrayal.

"Why not go back to him, chick, before you lose him altogether," Lizzie pleaded, using the edge of her pinny to wipe her eyes. "It ain't too late, I know the lad still loves you."

"I can't," Ruby said shortly.

"Then shall *I* ask him?"

"No. Please, Mam, no . . ." She moved away, unbuttoning her cuffs and rolling up her sleeves, busying herself to calm her agitation.

"You'm a stubborn wench, our Ruby. If only you'd heeded what I said to you the time you married." Her mother started following her round, picking things up and putting them down in a distracted, aimless manner. "Don't let your pride stand in the way of happiness. You had a rough beginning, aye I know that, but where there's a will there'll always be a remedy–"

"Put the kettle on the hob, Mam, will you," the girl interrupted her. "I'll make a start of the floor in here and then I'll go and scrub the step to clean that muck off."

Seeing she might as well change the subject as waste her breath, Lizzie opened a drawer in the dresser to pass her daughter a pinny before attending to the kettle. "It's young Joe knocking the mud off his boots has made so much mess," she said, her voice still shivery with tears. "He carries half o' Mrs Finch's garden home wi' him."

"Oh, but he's happy wi' his work there, in't he?" Ruby tied the pinafore round herself, and taking up the pegged-rag rugs went out to shake them in the yard.

When she came back she carried on, deliberately casual, "I meant to ask – has Joe mentioned anything about Jabez Reynolds lately?"

"Mr Reynolds? No. Not since he put your stepfather's back up."

"Who did? How d'you mean?"

"Our Joe did. Well, you know how it is – maybe the lad had too much to say in praise o' the gentleman. Anyhow, Jack thought he was a-doing it on purpose to annoy him and forbade him to speak the name again."

Ruby raised her eyes in disbelief. "God's sake – how d'you stomach living wi' a man like that!"

"I love him," Lizzie said quickly and defensively. "And when a woman loves her husband she has to accept he's master in the house. A lesson you could learn yourself, my wench."

"Thank you, I've already been learned enough lessons by Jack McShane–"

The girl stopped herself short there, biting her lip before

something was let slip she might regret; and going to the cupboard to get the mop and bucket she went on across her shoulder, "I wish I could still like him, Mam, for your sake, but I don't and neither does our Joe. He's not what I would call a decent father."

"You say that, and yet I mind a time you could hardly bear him out o' your sight! He always tried his best. If he's harsh on Joe it's for the lad's own good," said Lizzie, still defensive.

"Forbidding him to speak o' Mr Reynolds? I ask you now, what good is that? Jabez Reynolds has offered more kindness to my brother – aye *and* me – these past few months than Jack could show us in a thousand years."

She came by towards the range to fill the bucket from the singing kettle, aware of her mother's eyes fixed attentively on her.

"So it *was* Mr Reynolds as found you the job at Ivetsey Bank," Lizzie said after a moment. "I thought to myself I saw his hand in it somewhere, the sudden way you went and cleared off, only I mentioned nothing in case I was mistaken." She saw Ruby's face flush red and knew it wasn't only the heat from the fire. "This old lady you say you'm working for – she wouldn't be *another* relation o' the Reynoldses, by any chance? Like Mrs Finch?"

Ruby took her time about responding, giving her attention to the task of adding soda to the water and hefting the bucket to the floor before she straightened herself and turned towards her mother.

"There's some'at ... I want to tell you," she said awkwardly, "about Ivetsey Bank."

"Aye, I guessed there might be."

Lizzie sat down, as though preparing herself to hear the worst, Ruby thought. Now it was the moment for confession she didn't know where to start, or what to say; and felt almost relieved when her mother began for her – "You must think I'm blind as well as daft, my wench. Them letters you've been writing ... between the lines I could sense there was some'at being kept back from me. You never gave no name to your employer, nor you never said what she was like to work for as a mistress – the sort o' thing I might expect to read. It was always airy-fairy vagaries on about the weather and the country and the walks you'd took." The whitened knuckles of the work-rough hands clenched in her lap showed Lizzie's perturbation. "It ain't nothing you'm ashamed to tell me, is it, chick?"

Again, Ruby didn't answer her immediately, and the silence seemed to sag between them.

"It *is* to do wi' Mr Reynolds, ain't it," her mother prompted finally.

A reluctant nod.

"He's paying your wages, is he?"

"I suppose ... in a manner o' speaking, aye, he is."

Lizzie examined her. "Come on, Ruby, what have you been up to. Spit it out. Your Dad always said to tell the truth and shame the Devil."

"I never meant to tell you lies, our Mam, I didn't want you worrying, that's all," the girl said, hanging her head, not looking at her. "After what happened the last time I didn't want you thinking–" She caught herself again. "I mean, I'm not all bad ... but supposing you turned round and told me I'd disgraced you and you didn't want no more to do wi' me?"

"And why should I say a thing like that? You'm my own flesh and blood."

Ruby made a little helpless gesture. "Because Jabez Reynolds is *keeping* me. There in't anyone employing me at Ivetsey Bank . . . I'm my own mistress in the place."

Later, recalling she had said that, she realised its incongruity, since she was Mr Reynolds's mistress not her own. But the way she'd phrased things hardly mattered; the secret was out at last, and her mother was sitting – speechless – staring at her as though she'd been struck in the face.

"Don't look at me like that – don't, Mam!" Ruby cried. "It in't wrong. I did it to help our Joe!"

"God almighty . . ." Lizzie struggled to gather herself together. Her colour had gone a dreadful putty grey. "And you think that excuses everything."

"Maybe it doesn't, but I wanted to be honest wi' you–" In her agitation Ruby seized up the mop and started swabbing round the kitchen floor. "If only you knew how much he's done for me, how much he's given me."

"Aye, at the price of your family's self-respect."

"What self-respect? Our Joe wouldn't care, he's grateful enough for the work Mr Reynolds has found him. And I don't give a cuss about Jack McShane, he can go to hell."

She left off mopping. A terrifying thought that moment occurred to her. "Oh, but you won't tell him, will you–? He might go down the market hall and start shouting his mouth off and cause a lot o' trouble. I wouldn't put anything past a man as low as him. Don't tell him, Mam!"

Lizzie got up from the table, one hand pressed to her

breast as though her heart were paining her. "It'd serve that Jabez Reynolds right, taking advantage o' you . . . a young married wench . . ." She couldn't seem to get the words out properly and her voice sounded curiously fluffy. "Man of his position . . . serve him right if his customers found out what he'd been up to."

"*Please*, Mam – don't tell Jack," Ruby repeated, pleading, too blinded by the urgency of that concern to heed her mother's strained manner. "There's nobody else must ever know. I've only confided in you because I couldn't bear to carry on deceiving you."

"And what about Matthew – what about deceiving *him*?"

"Matt's made his own arrangements by the sound o' things." She started on her work again, banging the mophead into the table legs in the vehemence with which she set about it. "In any case he in't supporting me, I don't need his permission for the kind o' life I live."

Lizzie cast her a look, not so much of anger as aggrieved reproach. "Our Ruby, you'm a self-willed little madam . . . you mark my words, you'm riding headlong for a fall the way you'm carrying on. One o' these days–"

She sagged back into the chair, wincing in pain, still clutching at her breast. Her daughter, with her back turned to her, didn't notice. "One o' these days you'll be out on the streets wi' no bread in your belly and selling yourself," she finished.

Ruby got on with the kitchen floor in awkward, sullen silence. It was only after she'd carried the bucket into the scullery to empty it and rinse the mop and put them in the yard to dry that she responded, coming back, "Don't worry, I can look out for myself, our Mam. I'm turned eighteen. I'm old enough to know my mind and what I want."

Her mother, having managed to rally herself, was on her feet again. "What *you* want is someone to gi' you a blasted good hiding and knock some sense in your head," she answered over her shoulder; and then turning in time to catch her daughter's misery, her eyes softened. "Oh, I don't want a quarrel, our Ruby. You've lost your name, maybe you've lost your husband, but there's one thing sure – you ain't lost your mother. I'll always stand by you."

She reached her arms out to the girl.

"We'll say no more, eh. Whatever you've done, I forgive you because I love you . . . never you forget that, chick."

It was a savage irony that Ruby had kept secret from her mother the relationship she'd shared with Jack McShane; and now she and her mother were keeping a parallel secret from Jack. Lizzie never breathed a word to him about the girl's entanglement with Jabez Reynolds. Much as she idolised her husband her daughter was right, he *would* have caused trouble; and then Ruby's disgrace would have been all round Minerva Lane . . . another juicy bit of gossip for the neighbours to exchange across their back-yard fences.

The secret weighed heavily on Lizzie. It was one more thing to fret about on top of all the rest – Jack's boozing, the aggression between him and Joe, her own ill-health. The doctor had warned her if she didn't take it easy she was likely to drop dead at any minute; but having time off would cost her the bit of pin-money from her job at the Harp.

All these worries . . . life was one long problem. In the

early hours of a dark, cold morning in November, Lizzie went down to the kitchen for some bicarbonate of soda for her heart-burn. She didn't return. When Jack McShane got out of bed at half past six he found her lying on the hearth as though she'd curled herself up like a child to go to sleep.

When he shook her there was no response. Her troubles were ended.

15

The weather was kind – kinder in any event than life had been – for Lizzie. Her coffin was carried to the graveyard beneath a sky of soft pearled blue from which the wintry sunlight fell like a blessing upon her final journey homeward. She had a good following to see her buried, not only her immediate family and neighbours from Minerva Lane, but some who had known her only as barmaid at the Harp, or as a regular customer; and others who'd not known her at all but were here to show respect as friends of Ruby.

The first tidings the girl had received of her mother's death was from young Joe, in a message sent post haste to Ivetsey Bank. 'Our mams dead Ruby come home quick,' it read. That was all. Nothing else.

'Our mams dead . . .'

The intervening days had passed like some terrible dream from which Ruby could neither awaken nor escape, a disbelieving stupefaction filled with grief so numbing that it robbed her of her wits. She found herself installed at Brickhill Lane and couldn't remember how she'd come there from the cottage; she was in her mother's bedroom, howling, sobbing, somebody – was it Matthew? – holding her, the hot tears wetting Lizzie's cold, calm face, so peaceful and so beautiful in death; she was in St James's church-yard, weeping quietly now, her brother with her, uncle Eddie Gallimore from Cradley Heath, family she'd last seen on her wedding day a year and a half ago.

The graveside service brought her to her senses. Instead of the hysteria she'd dreaded, Ruby felt herself becoming strangely calm as though the tears she'd wept these days and nights had somehow dulled the rawness of her heart-break, smoothed the jagged edges of its pain. Through the veil of black crepe concealing her swollen features she was able to look at Lizzie's coffin and feel a certain assurance. It was only a tired and worn-out body they were burying, a shell; not her mother's love, not a lifetime's memories, not the enduring image locked like a precious treasure in her mind.

As she watched the coffin being lowered slowly into its earthen resting-place she was aware of someone's hand taking her by the elbow to steady her, and thought it must be Joe. The shock of their mother's death had brought out a sudden and unrealised strength in her young brother's character. He too had done his share of weeping, but for all that he was not yet quite fifteen Joe had been the one to do the comforting throughout, not Ruby.

When she turned, though, she saw it wasn't her brother standing there beside her. It was Matthew.

"It's almost over now," he said, speaking to her quietly and gently. "Bear up just a while longer if you can."

There was a look of such tender concern in his eyes that the pain in Ruby's throat swelled up again bringing with it fresh hot tears that dripped down her face and soaked into the veil; and suddenly she felt herself longing for him to take her in his arms and hold her close and safe against him, her need desperate for the solace of his love, his strength, his reassurance.

Then the curate, Mr Roe, was asking her to follow Joe forward to the grave's edge, and to cast some earth upon her mother's coffin as a last respect.

With Matthew still supporting her Ruby knelt to take a handful of the gritty soil and threw it down, hearing the dull noise as it struck the deal-wood lid. The sound brought back the memory of standing in this self-same spot five years ago in 1882, the day they'd buried her father Charlie Gallimore: then it had been her mother who'd performed this final leave-taking; and now another circle had been closed and it was Lizzie herself lying down there with him, reunited . . .

Ruby turned her face into Matthew's shoulder. There were awkward murmurs of sympathy and condolence as one by one the rest of the mourners filed past to add their own token of earth, each handful hitting the lid like the thud of a nail. She didn't want to look at them. Especially she didn't want to see her hated stepfather baring his grief, however genuine, over her mother's grave and have to go through the motions of sharing it with him for decency's sake. Jack McShane had taken Lizzie's death as he'd taken her life, with *Self* uppermost in his considerations: disconsolate, yes, but in a peevish sort of way as though he blamed her for dying and causing him the inconvenience of losing her.

The curate came across from Joe for a quiet word, and Ruby thanked him for his services. After he'd gone again, taking off his purple stole as he walked away to speak to the gravediggers leaning on their shovels, she said, "I couldn't have got through this wi'out you, Matthew . . . people being so nice and kind about our Mam . . . I'm all right as long as nobody talks to me, but the minute they start showing sympathy . . ." She shook her head, unable to go on, biting her lip to stop its trembling.

He put his arms round her and held her. "You know I want to do all I can for you, sweetheart – whatever will help. I've taken this almost as bad as you and Joe. She was a good woman, was your Mam . . . I loved her an' all."

"Aye."

"There's many will miss her." He felt a shudder go through Ruby's body and wisely refrained from saying more, but pressed her against him while she wept afresh, giving her the comfort of his silence.

Above them hung the autumn-bared branches of a willow, its few remaining yellowed leaves fluttering down into the open grave. Matthew watched them, while his thoughts went this way and that; and then his eye was distracted by something else and the feelings of love and sadness and remorse, and pain, were overtaken by irritation as the figure he'd just noticed detach itself from Jack McShane started moving in their direction.

He hadn't seen Dorrie Vickers in a long time, but the sight of her face with its ugly too-big mouth and sly, sexually inviting look, aroused all its old abhorrence in him. For a split second he was reminded in some manner of Gatty Thompson, the girl from Chubb's he'd been knocking about with now for a couple of months, and the recognition jarred unpleasantly.

"Ruby, it's me . . . it's Dorrie." The over-painted figure picked a way across the grave clods, wearing an expression of sorrowful concern to match her tone. "I'm ever so sorry about your Mam. Poor wench, your luck don't get no better, does it."

"Aye. Thank you." Matthew cut her short.

"Oh ... I ain't interrupting nothing, am I?" she said, switching quickly to apologetic innocence. "Don't let me butt in. I only wanted a minute to pay my condolences and ask Ruby how her's bearing up, seeing as how I ain't had the chance to speak to her since all this happened."

Ruby released herself reluctantly from Matthew's arms and took out a sodden handkerchief to blow her nose. "I in't too bad, thanks, Dorrie," she answered in a little whisper.

"That's the ticket. Chin up, eh. I was only just saying to Jack – to Mr McShane – good job you've got your husband to console you." Dorrie's eyes flicked back to Matthew. "Your Mam'd have been real pleased to know her'd brought you pair together again. It's what her wanted, ain't it."

There was an awkward silence.

"Funny thing, I'd never have knowed her'd died if I hadn't chanced to bump into your stepfather last Monday night in Dudley Street," Dorrie went on, as though impervious to the tension she was creating. "And o' course, I ain't seen you lately to tell you *my* news, have I, Ruby – about Perryman the butler getting me dismissed from St John's Square?"

Ruby sniffed and shook her head, glancing up at Matthew, wishing Dorrie would go away and leave them alone.

"Miserable old perisher – he thought it was me as went

and told the Master he'd been drinking the best brandy and fiddling the pantry book to make it look as though–"

"If you don't mind," Matthew interrupted again, very tersely, "you can see how much Ruby's distressed. Can't you leave her in peace?"

"Well pardon me, I'm sure I never meant to go upsetting her!" said Dorrie, bridling with indignation. "I was doing no more than trying to cheer the poor wench up a bit. I'll take myself elsewhere if I'm not welcome."

"I'd be obliged."

"I thought her'd want to know what's been happening, that's all, seeing as I troubled myself to come to the funeral. Though I might've guessed the way the wind was a-blowing when I saw that po-faced Martha Becket here today."

"Martha came as a friend," Ruby reproached tearfully.

"So did I! Small shrift I get for it an' all." Dorrie exchanged hostile looks with Matthew as she turned on her heel to walk away; then thinking of a parting shot she paused and tossed back spitefully, "I'll say this much for Jack McShane, after all the bad I've heard folk speak of him, he's treated *me* most civil and considerate."

"Like attracted to like, I dare say," commented Matthew as she moved out of earshot. "I saw those two over-close together before she came over and wondered what was going on between them. I didn't know they were acquainted."

Ruby blew her nose again and wiped her eyes, adjusting the covering of black veil. That little scene with Dorrie Vickers had shattered the intimate closeness she'd felt with Matthew, bringing her back to the reality of their relationship.

"Jack's met her at Minerva Lane," she said, making an effort to compose herself and trying to push from her mind the memory of Dorrie calling on her there to commiserate on the death of her newborn daughter. It seemed almost too cruel that Ruby had lost that precious little mite almost a year to the day that her Mam – after whom the babby had been named – had been taken from her likewise, and she flinched from dwelling on the reminder for fear it would pile fresh grief upon what she was suffering now.

"I suppose," said Matthew, changing the subject abruptly and thrusting his hands in his pockets as though to keep himself from the temptation of touching her again, "I suppose your new employers have given you a couple o' days off, have they?"

How was she to answer? Jabez Reynolds knew, of course, about her sudden bereavement, but Ruby's overwhelming, terrible despair had wiped clean out of her mind anything he might have said on the subject of her returning to Ivetsey Bank.

"Aye," she responded after a moment, hating herself for the lie.

"And in the meantime, I take it you're stopping at Brickhill Lane?"

"Aye."

Matthew looked down at his boots, scuffing the leaves. "I'd like to come and see you there, Ruby–" There was a pause while he hunted round for the words, his young, strong face furrowing with the awkwardness of his predicament. "Only there's some'at going on . . . some'at I ought to get out o' the way before we have a proper talk. I'd rather not say too much for the present. It's . . . well, it's a personal sort o' matter."

Ruby's instincts told her he was referring to his relationship with the girl from Chubb's, but she held herself back from asking. Just as Jabez Reynolds was *her* affair, her secret, so this was his; and though she had been jealous and resentful when she'd learned about it from her mother, Lizzie's death had afterwards sapped her of every emotion except grief. It wasn't until today, until just now when Matthew held her, that she'd felt something being rekindled in her heart . . . a spark of feeling which had only ever been damped down, but not stubbed out.

She looked at her husband as though seeing him properly for the first time in a long, long while; not even minding the moustache any more because it suited him so very handsomely. And then, remembering that the grave-diggers were still waiting to complete their work, she cast a final sorrowing glance in farewell to her mother and moved away, walking down the path to rejoin the rest of the mourners.

"I have every sympathy with you, my dear," said Jabez Reynolds, trying to keep the irritation from his voice, "and I am exercising the utmost patience. But you must appreciate that this continuing dejectedness helps neither yourself nor our relationship. For three weeks now, each time I've been here I've found you wallowing in misery – yes, *wallowing*," he repeated as Ruby gave a little cry of protest, "and quite frankly it makes me disinclined to share your company."

"I'm sorry if I can't seem to amuse you," she responded,

getting up from beside the open fire where she'd been kneeling and pulling her wrapper round her half-clothed body. "The way you're going on at me, anybody 'd think my poor Mam went and died on a purpose to deprive you of your entertainment–"

"Don't be childish. Your mother's death was most unfortunate, and I hope I've sufficiently expressed my regret – but I repeat, it's been three weeks since you returned here to Ivetsey Bank, and not once have you permitted me to touch you or in any other physical way console you."

"I can't just put on an act!" Ruby crossed her arms over her breast and hugged herself as though in self-defence, her tawny hair falling forward half-hiding her face. This was the first disagreement she had had with Mr Reynolds, and it all started when he'd arrived a few hours earlier this afternoon obviously in a mood for making love to her. He'd been very good about restraining himself on previous visits, respecting her reluctance to recommence their sexual frolics so soon after her mother's funeral; but a man with such strong priapic appetites couldn't be expected to abstain indefinitely, and today he'd made his wishes very plain. Not to put too fine a gloss on it, he considered it time she began to justify her keep again.

"I don't wish you to put on any act," he told her, reaching from the sofa to refill his glass with a measure of malt whisky from a bottle on the side-table. "That would be an insult to the pair of us. All I'm asking, Ruby, is that you try and damn' well cheer up a bit."

"Don't you think I *want* to!" She turned towards him, flinging out her hands in a gesture of appeal, the wrapper falling open again exposing the tantalising beauty of her figure clad in nothing more than lace-trimmed whalebone corsets and a pair of white silk drawers. Mr Reynolds himself had divested her of the rest of her clothing in anticipation of their lovemaking before her lack of responsiveness had caused him to accuse her – thoughtlessly – of 'being like a corpse' in bed, thus precipitating their disagreement.

The red flush of a winter sunset streaming in at the latticed windows warmed her naked skin to a golden peach and gave a glow to the tawny richness of her hair. "It don't help that I'm left here so much by myself," she went on despondently, unaware of how desirable a picture she was making.

"Aye, I suppose there's that to it." Jabez Reynolds put his glass aside and got to his feet, moving across to her. "You've got too much time on your hands with nothing to do but brood about what's happened, that's the trouble. Misery feeds on its own company."

He reached to stroke the back of his fingers over the smooth, bare swell of her breasts, his hunger for her becoming aroused once more by the temptation of her semi-nakedness. "Please . . . don't deny me, Ruby," he said more softly. "Won't you let me try and help you to forget, even if it's only for an hour or two?"

She flinched away from his touch as though it burned her. "I can't. I'm sorry." She wished she could tell him the truth, that it wasn't simply the memory of her mother – the grief that had become her daily bread – that was holding her back from wanting sexual intimacy. It was Matthew.

Ever since the funeral, Ruby's feelings for her young

husband had confused her. What was worse, she couldn't seem to rid herself of a sort of rankling anger against this other wench from Chubb's whom he'd been seeing. However hard she tried to push it from her mind, the image of Matthew touching and kissing this somebody else refused to go away and stop tormenting her. Even if he intended breaking it off as he'd seemed to suggest, that still didn't alter the fact that he had shared himself, his company, his laughter, his enjoyment – aye, just as Ruby had shared hers with Jabez Reynolds, conscience taunted her – and the seed of jealousy which had withered in her mourning for her mother had suddenly sprung new life and grown during these past miserable lonely weeks at Ivetsey Bank.

She could no more enjoy making love with Mr Reynolds now than fly in the moon.

"You're being a very stubborn young woman, my dear." Seeing his cajolery and sympathy were nothing but a waste of time he turned away from her, needing to employ iron self-discipline to check his resentment at having his sexual advances rejected yet again. "I don't intend pursuing any further argument. I'm simply looking at the situation from the most expedient point of view."

Taking up his whisky from the table where he'd left it, he finished the contents off in a single gulp and stood rolling the empty glass between his palms while he stared out through the window at the dying sunset. Several tense minutes had passed before he went on again, abruptly, "I think you ought to leave this place, Ruby. Move back to Wolverhampton. In the circumstances it's probably the wisest course."

She read a finality in those words that left her silent. She had never expected their affair would come to an end in quite such a cursory fashion – as though she were a servant being dismissed from her employment. Yet wasn't that exactly the role she had played in this relationship? And if she were being honest, Ruby asked herself, wouldn't she much rather have it finish like this, while she still respected Mr Reynolds, than have it become something shamefully ugly and distasteful?

She had believed herself to be in love with him, and for that reason – as much as for her brother Joe's sake – she had let herself be kept here; but all of a sudden she was starting to appreciate how romantically naive she'd been. Mr Reynolds had never loved her in return. He'd always made it absolutely clear that his wife's position in his life was unassailable, and that Ruby was but the latest of his transient diversions, one more pretty plaything in a long line of young women with whom he could enjoy his relaxation.

He'd only ever lent himself; he never gave.

With the bewildering recent changes in her own emotions the rose-coloured blinkers had been torn away and she was finally starting to see her situation with Jabez Reynolds precisely for what it was: the casual amour of a wealthy man with a working-class wench.

"If you're worried what's now to become of you," he said, misinterpreting her silence and taking it for distress, "please be assured that I'm not about to put you on the street. I'm a fair man. As long as you remain under my protection I'll take every care of you."

Ruby examined the tall, straight, immaculately-attired

back still turned on her. "A minute ago you were saying you wanted shot of me out of here, that I should take myself off back to Wolverhampton."

"You misunderstood me, perhaps. The countryside's a lonely place in winter, especially for a wench in your low state. I own a property in Waterloo Road you can move to, where I shall still visit – although of course our little arrangement will need to be modified in the interests of circumspection. Waterloo Road is in the centre of town, after all."

He half moved from the window to look at her, his handsome face severe, his tone more briskly businesslike.

"You'll be happier there, my dear. Aye – and I dare say so shall I be."

16

The girl returned Joe's smile in a friendly manner as they passed each other on the street corner. She had honey-coloured curls beneath her tam o'shanter, framing a face so pretty that the lad looked round for a second appreciative, lingering glance after she'd gone by. He was beginning to notice girls much more often of late. Particularly he was noticing the bits of them that rounded out their bodices and bustles, the bits he and his mates used to snigger about at school and make rude drawings of. And he'd taken to daydreaming about them while he was doing his work in the garden at Brickhill Lane, wondering what it would feel like to kiss a wench on the lips, and other things.

In a few days' time, on the ninth of February, Joe Gallimore would be fifteen years old. He was never going to be tall; but his frame was growing stronger with all the physical work he was doing and he'd lost that gangling, awkward, out-at-elbow look and was starting to acquire in its place a certain sturdiness that made up for his lack of height. He was glad to be growing up, glad to be escaping from the shadow of a weakly childhood. Already he'd had his first taste of ale, and he was longing impatiently to take the milestone step of shaving off the faint, dark fuzz of hair appearing on his upper lip – only he daren't use an open razor for fear of cutting himself in one of his fits and was therefore saving up his halfpennies to buy one of those new-fangled safety razors.

Out of the wages Joe was earning these days from Mrs Finch for gardening and odd-jobbing, all but a shilling a week was taken off him by his stepfather Jack McShane as rent for his bed and board at Minerva Lane. The arrangement had worked well enough while his mother had been alive to cook him a proper evening meal; but things were different now, and if Ellen Finch out of kindness of heart hadn't fed Joe every day at her own table, the lad would have been hard stretched to buy himself adequate food as well as find his other few expenses.

He threw a last final look over his shoulder at the retreating figure of the girl, then pushed on through the thickening winter dusk towards Minerva Lane. There was a time when his feet would have quickened into a run at this point and he'd arrive home coughing and breathless to the welcome haven of the kitchen and his Mam's affectionate fussing. There was nothing to run home for now, though. No place called home to run to. Since Lizzie's death all the happiness and warmth and feeling of love had gone out of number 11, as though the heart had been removed from the place, leaving the house a shell that only held memories.

Yet even memories were precious; and however bleakly empty and awful those four walls felt without his mother's presence they were still the strongest link Joe had with her, and he'd every intention of carrying on living there.

The dusk had thickened to darkness by the time he reached the back gate. He noticed the gas jet in the kitchen had been lit – he could see its yellow light shining between the slats into the alley – and he thought at once that his stepfather was back before him, which was unusual this early in the evening. Stopping to peer through the net at the window before he opened the scullery door, the lad could see Jack had company – a female – sitting at the hearthside with her legs thrust out towards the fire and a glass of ale in her hand. It must be one of the neighbours, though he didn't think he recognised her.

He deliberately let the door bang shut behind him to announce his arrival, and took off his cap and muffler, hanging them on a nail in the scullery. As soon as he entered the kitchen he saw at once he'd been mistaken, for the woman turning in her seat to gawk at him wasn't a neighbour. It was that friend of their Ruby's, the one who'd worked in service in St John's Square. The one who'd been tagging around after Jack McShane at the funeral.

"What's *she* doing here?" he said truculently, directing his question at his stepfather lounging in the chair opposite with his boots up on the fender.

"You keep a civil tongue in your head. The young lady's here by my invitation," Jack responded, equally truculent. "Now mind your blasted manners and bid her good evening."

Joe glanced at the gaudy cuckoo which had roosted in their domestic nest. She was got up in an orange and green striped outfit and with her black frizzed hair and her rouged red cheeks she looked a proper tart, he thought.

"'Evening," he muttered with as little grace as he could manage. Blowed if he was going to be polite to a creature like *her*!

Dorrie Vickers pulled an exaggeratedly pained expression. "Not very friendly, are you?"

He didn't answer.

This appeared to vex her further. "You'll have to learn to change your tune if we'm to get on, otherwise it's going to make things awkward. Ain't it, Jack?" She raised her glass of ale to her lips, glancing over the rim at Jack McShane.

"Aye," he said, "that's right. You'll watch the way you speak to Miss Vickers, you hear me? Because if you don't, my lad, you'll find yourself out on your ruddy backside, I'm warning you."

"Why – she in't stopping here, is she?" Joe asked, growing suddenly suspicious.

Dorrie emptied her glass. "I suppose you'd best tell him, Jack. He's got a right to know, don't you think, seeing as how our little arrangement involves him an' all."

"What's she on about?" Joe stared from one to the other. "What arrangement's this, then?"

His stepfather took his boots from the fender and sat up, leaning forward for the poker to prod at the coals in the grate. "Her's moving in to live," he stated briefly, not meeting Joe's eye. "I fetched all her tranklements across from Raby Street this afternoon."

It took a few seconds to absorb the implications of this piece of information. And then as the shock of it dawned on the young lad's face Jack began again in a blustering, bullying manner, "Now I don't want any argument about it. If you don't like the way things are, you can bugger off somewhere else and find you lodging – I won't stand for trouble, you hear!"

"She's got no right to move in. This is our Mam's house."

"It's *my* name on the rent book now your mother's dead, which makes it *my* house, so *I'm* the one to say who'll live here. Best you understand that clearly, lad. It cuts both ways."

"All right, but where's she going to sleep? She in't having my room!"

If Dorrie hadn't been half-drunk from celebrating the turn-up in her circumstances, she might have thought twice about answering that one for herself. But in the state she was in, she didn't care – she'd got what she wanted, her feet tucked snug and secure under Jack McShane's table. Number 11 Minerva Lane wasn't no Buckingham Palace, but God knows it was an improvement on that single filthy, squalid room in Raby Street where she'd been forced to lodge since getting dismissed from service in St John's Square.

"I ain't dossing down on the flippin' floor, if that's what you think. I'll be sharing a bed wi' your stepfather," she informed Joe, touching her fingers to her frizzy hair and giving him a sidelong sarcastic little smirk. "He wants a bit o' company to help keep him warm at night. It's lonely for him now your mother's gone."

It was as much as Joe could do not to strike the smirk from her grinning red mouth. Heatedly he said, "Couldn't you have waited a decent time, the pair o' you. Our Mam's not even been dead three months–"

"Cut that out," Jack told him, throwing the poker aside in the hearth and rising to his feet. "I've told you already, if the situation don't meet wi' your approval you can pack your stuff and bugger off out of it. You'm nothing but a

217

bloody nuisance round the place as it is. Christ knows why *I* should be saddled wi' you now your mother ain't alive to namby-pamby you."

He came across and thrust his face into Joe's, causing the lad to back away a step. "Why don't you go and lodge wi' that sister o' yourn. Or that old woman you'm working for in Brickhill Lane – aye, why not her, seeing as how you'm practically living at her house anyway."

"I'm stopping here," Joe answered stubbornly. "This was my home long before you ever showed up on the scene. Why should I be the one that has to get out just because you've fancied setting yourself up wi' some painted trollop–"

Jack clouted him open-handed round the side of the head, a blow that made his ears ring. "Any more o' that sort o' talk and you'll get what's damn' well coming, now I'm warning you."

"I should flippin' well think so an' all!" Dorrie chimed in, flaring up in drunken indignation and making an unsteady attempt to get to her feet. "Painted trollop indeed – I'll painted trollop him, I will!"

Holding on to the chair arm she aimed a swipe of her own at Joe which missed him by a yard as she lost her balance and fell inelegantly back into her seat, knocking the dregs of her ale across the hearth.

"I'm stopping here," the lad repeated, retreating behind the kitchen table out of Jack's reach, wary of his step-father's brutal temper. "I've a good mind to go and tell the landlord what you're doing – *he* won't have any truck wi' her if she in't paying rent. He'll have her out as fast as she come in, he will."

The ringing in his ears changed pitch, and at the same time the light from the overhead gas mantle seemed suddenly to blur into a halo. Jack shouted something at him, but the words reached Joe in a tinny-sounding echo and he felt the kitchen tilting and slipping away.

His eyes began to roll. Oh God, he thought, I'm going, I'm going . . . and then the familiar blackness came rushing in to engulf him.

"What the hell's wrong wi' him?" Dorrie let out a squeal of alarm as the lad fell to the floor unconscious and started writhing about in convulsions, drumming his heels and banging himself into the legs of the table. "Do some'at quick, Jack – he's choking himself!"

"I wish he bloody well would," Jack said grimly, going round to the arching, shuddering body. "He's having another of his fits, that's all it is. It ain't anything that'll kill him–"

He knelt down and grasped Joe's head, searching for something to insert between the lad's teeth to keep him from biting his tongue.

Dorrie turned her face away. "Ooh, it's horrible. How often does he throw a turn like that?"

"More than enough times for my blasted liking." Reaching up to take a spoon from the table Jack wrapped its handle in his neckerchief to make a gag. "But no need to fret yourself, sweetheart, I'm finished playing nursemaid to him. Whether the young perisher likes it or not, he's getting turfed out o' this house – and he ain't coming back."

Gatty Thompson yawned and stretched herself luxuriously before she rolled over to cuddle against Matthew's warm, strong, naked body. Now that she'd taught him all she knew about making love he was proving himself a most satisfying and able sexual partner; and to a girl like Gatty, whose lusty appetite had led her into no end of amorous adventures, it was a matter of no small pride that her own personal skills had turned the clumsy and inexperienced Matthew into such an excitingly proficient lover.

She was glad he hadn't done anything so foolish as to lose his heart to her. It took all the fun out of a relationship when men started to get emotional, wanting to tie her down to a serious commitment and spoiling the enjoyment with their jealousy and their possessiveness. One of the things she liked best about Matthew was that he never wished to talk about his feelings. He never said much about anything, come to that; which made a change from all those others who'd bored her to tears by falling in love with her. There was nothing more tedious than to have a straightforward sexual flirtation ruined by a lot of moonstruck sentiment; and the reason this present affair had lasted months instead of weeks was that it was purely and entirely on the level.

They had a drink together; they went to bed together; they enjoyed each other. Beyond that they led completely separate lives.

Yawning again, the girl propped herself on an elbow, pushing the tangled mess of fair hair from her eyes. Matthew lay on his back with his hands behind his head, staring up at the pattern of damp patches on the ceiling. The February daylight was beginning to fade in the room and in the grey quietness the chime of bells ringing for Evensong carried across Gas Yard on a mournfully sonorous note.

"How late is it?" she asked him drowsily.

He didn't move. "Must be nearly half past six."

She fell back again among the rumpled pillows and lay still for another few minutes; then she said with a sly little smile, "I've enjoyed myself this afternoon. You get better every time, d'you know that ... mmm, better and better and better. It's like they say, I suppose, about practice making perfect."

"And I'm getting plenty of practice," Matthew replied sardonically, looking at a damp stain near the chimney breast which in the half-light had taken on the outline of a bowl of flowers.

"I don't hear you complaining, though," she started teasing him, slipping a hand beneath the sheets to the thick springing diamond of hair on his taut, flat belly. "You took to it like a bloomin' duck to water once I'd showed you what to do, you greedy lad."

He caught her hand and held it still. "Aye, well – I hadn't had the experience, I'll admit, but I've made up for it since. Ignorance isn't always bliss, as I've discovered from knowing you these last few months."

Gatty laughed at that, pleased by what she regarded as a compliment to her own sexual expertise, her face more kittenish than ever as she showed her small white teeth. "And blimey, you *were* ignorant, I'm telling you! No wonder your Missis got so fed up she went and walked out on you, the miserable time you must've been giving the wench–"

"That's some'at I don't want to talk about." Matthew sat up abruptly, throwing back the sheets and reaching for his trousers from the end rail. He hated it when Gatty

221

mentioned Ruby in their bed-talk; it forced him to realise how this relationship had cheapened everything he once had cared so deeply for – his principles, his faith, his marriage vows.

Oh, he liked the wench well enough; but he wished to God he had the strength of mind to give her up instead of degrading himself by carrying on as they were, simply *using* each other for sexual relief. Many a time he'd rehearsed in his head how he was going to tell her he wanted to end things between them; but pure physical desire, and loneliness, had weakened his resolve on each occasion and she only had to smile into his eyes and lick her lips to excite his lust for her. He was like a fish on a line, hooked by his own masculinity. Gatty had taught him all the tricks she knew to give him – and herself – endless exhaustive satisfaction, and if he'd been any other sort of chap Matthew would be counting himself damn' lucky to spend his Sunday afternoons in bed with her.

The only problem was, he didn't love her. He loved Ruby.

When Ruby had moved away to work in the country at Ivetsey Bank last summer he'd believed she had done so deliberately, so as to put the barrier of distance between the two of them. Then when her mother died, when the shock and the distress had robbed her of her senses for a time, in her grief it had been *him* she'd turned to, and Matthew had been glad to comfort and support her in her hour of need, hoping it might bring them together again. After Lizzie's funeral he'd fully intended ending his affair with Gatty Thompson and making an honest breast of things to Ruby; yet when he'd tried to visit her in Brickhill

Lane he learned she'd already left there and returned to Ivetsey Bank.

At the New Year, there'd arrived a letter from her. It was so stiltedly worded and formal in its language it was like a child's school exercise and plainly had been rewritten several times before she posted it, as though she'd been over-anxious about its content. She was no longer at Ivetsey Bank, she said; she'd decided to come back again to Wolverhampton and was presently lodging on Waterloo Road 'where it would be very agreeable if you would care to let me know when you can come to visit me'.

Matthew's hopes of repairing his marriage from the rubble of its broken dreams had been revived; and too impatient to waste time on a reply, he'd gone round to the address she gave immediately after work that same evening. It was in a terrace of large, stone-fronted, shabbily elegant houses with a sign in one of its downstairs windows advertising 'Rooms to Let'.

As he went to mount the flight of steps the front door had opened and a man – a gentleman – emerged, wearing a heavy caped overcoat and bowler hat. Matthew stood aside to allow him to come down; but apparently failing to notice him there on the pavement the other had paused and half-turned back to speak to somebody behind in the hallway.

"I may not call upon you again before a week on Tuesday," Matthew heard him say – and then a voice, a woman's voice, replied, "In that case I'll expect you when I see you."

It was Ruby who'd just spoken, he would swear to it. And the man was Mr Jabez Reynolds.

As the master butcher began descending the steps Matthew moved quickly into the shadows beyond the light of the street gas-lamp, not wanting himself recognised, and waited till the other had gone by him. What the devil was Mr Reynolds doing here at Ruby's lodging? It was no chance visit, that much was plain from the few words they'd exchanged just now. 'I may not call upon you again before a week on Tuesday...' And her response, so casually offhand, without even the courtesy of a 'sir' to soften it.

His reaction was to go inside and seek the explanation from Ruby herself; but then a sudden fierce pride had held him back. If Jabez Reynolds was still dispensing his damnable interfering charity it would be no reconciliation if another argument broke out between the two of them because of it. Maybe he was letting resentment get the better of judgement, but Matthew had been so keyed up with impatience to see his wife again that the brief scene he'd just witnessed was like a bucket of cold water in his face. God knows she'd hurt him more than enough when she walked out of their marriage. He didn't want her to hurt him again like that.

He swung on his heel away from the house – and then seeing someone going in the place next door, on an angry impulse had hailed them to enquire who was the landlord of the property.

His suspicions were confirmed when he was told that it was Mr Reynolds the butcher from out the market.

The bells for Evensong had ceased now. Picking up his shirt from the floor at Gatty's side of the bed, Matthew leaned across her and lit a Vesta to the oil lamp on the deal-wood cupboard. The wick sputtered a little before its blue flame steadied and started burning evenly, shedding a warm, soft glow into the darkened room.

"You're very tetchy on the subject of your wife, in't you," Gatty said coolly, put out that he'd spoken quite so sharply to her. "If you feel that strong about her still, maybe you ought to be asking yourself a few serious questions."

"I told you, it's some'at I don't want to talk about." He deliberately kept his back to her while he fastened the shirt buttons and tucked the tails inside his trousers, his shadow cast in jumps against the ceiling.

"Please yourself. It's no skin off my flippin' nose," she retaliated, hunting around under the sheets for her pair of drawers. "I in't all that interested any way. Only I get the feeling sometimes that it's *her* you're with, not me, when we're in bed together, and I've got my pride."

"What pride?"

This indifference stung her even further. "There's many another fish in the sea apart from you."

"Aye?"

"Aye. I could name you a dozen more lads who're itching for me to tip 'em the wink."

"Maybe you shouldn't keep them waiting, then. You've always boasted how you like variety–" Matthew threw her a glance as he bent to look for his boots, "especially between the bedsheets."

"And you wouldn't care, I suppose," she goaded him.

This time he didn't bother to respond, because the truth was – no, he really *didn't* care. Not about Gatty Thompson. Only about his faithless wife.

17

The relationship between Ruby and Jabez Reynolds had not been resumed once she moved from Ivetsey Bank to live in Waterloo Road. She saw him only on those occasions when he visited the house for other reasons, when it was obvious from the formality of his manner that their intimacy had reached an end; and though nothing as such was ever discussed, it was implicitly understood that the reward for Ruby's silence was free lodging here – at least, until she'd found employment and was able to support herself again.

This question of employment presented something of a problem. Naturally enough in the circumstances Mr Reynolds didn't intend having her back to work on his market stall; and while she could have taken a job in domestic service passing as a single woman, her awakened loyalty to Matthew made Ruby shy away from disavowing her marriage.

That left only one other type of work of which she'd had experience and offered her accommodation: serving in a public house, as her mother had done.

Before committing herself in this direction, she made up her mind she ought to discuss things with Matthew first and ask his advice. It would give her the excuse to let him know her whereabouts, as well as the chance of seeing him again, and an entire afternoon had been zealously spent composing a letter inviting him to call and visit her.

For a week she had sat in her lodgings waiting, watching from her window for the postman, expecting every day to hear from him. But when a second week dragged by without any answer from her husband, Ruby's hopes had turned to ashes and her happiness to disappointed tears.

"He in't bothering wi' us," she whispered to her linnet, "he's ignoring us. Serves us right for being such a bad 'un, eh birdie."

That pretty little yellow bird was the repository for so many of her confidences recently. There'd been times since her mother's death when it seemed the only true pal she had in all the world (an irony, considering it was originally bought as a present from Jack McShane). Here at Waterloo Road, as at Ivetsey Bank, the linnet brightened the endless days with its sweet song, and in the sleepless nights its presence was some consolation for her loneliness.

For she *was* lonely here. Despite receiving visits from her old friends from Minerva Lane and close companions like Martha Becket, solitude was now a way of life.

Whether Martha had ever suspected that her relationship with Jabez Reynolds was anything other than what it appeared on the surface Ruby had no idea, and most certainly never discussed – along with her curiously old-fashioned refinements and her servant-class gentility, Martha would have considered it a gross impertinence to broach a matter so personal unless she were invited. Since Ruby had, however, opened her heart fully on the subject of Matthew, her friend felt no such similar constraint; in fact was urging her to swallow her pride and write to him a second time.

"For all we know your first letter may have gone astray," she observed, "the post isn't always as reliable as one might wish for."

"It in't the fault o' the post. I know the reason for his silence," Ruby told her, hunching herself miserably on the narrow bedstead, the only place to sit in the one-room lodgings apart from a chair which Martha occupied, wedged in between the mean little grate and the crockery cupboard. "Why should he want me while he's still got this other for company?"

"The young woman from Chubb's? Oh, but didn't Matthew lead you to believe their acquaintance was finished now?"

"He hinted as much at Mam's funeral, aye. He could've changed his mind though. That day he called round at your Auntie Ellen's – who's to say but he hadn't come to tell me that he'd chosen her in place o' me?"

"Stuff!" Martha answered roundly, setting her teacup on the floor. "Would he have behaved himself in such an anxious manner when he found you gone? He appeared really quite distraught, I can assure you."

"If he was so distraught, then why have I heard nothing from him."

"Because, my dear, he may have thought it was you yourself who wished for the separation, departing so soon after your poor dear mother's burial. Although of course I did explain to him–"

"Explain what?" Ruby prompted her, a shade too anxiously.

"Why, that we cannot pick and choose the terms of our employment. A week was more than generous leave of absence when two days or three is the usual practice in domestic service. Matthew appreciated that."

"He left no message for me, though."

"And with good reason," Martha argued sensibly, "for what would have been the point? By then you had returned to Ivetsey Bank. A message would be no more likely to reach you through me than if he had troubled to send you one directly."

Pulling her shawl round her shoulders, Ruby got up from the bed and stood framed in the soft spring sunlight at the window, gazing down into the street below. After a moment she said on a note of stubborn hurt, "I love him . . . but I in't getting down on my knees to grovel after him."

"Then perhaps you don't love him enough, my dear."

"I do – oh, I do! I wish to God I could put back the clock and have these last twelve months all over again. The silly, stupid arguments I used to pick wi' him–" She turned from the window to look at her friend. "Our Mam was right. She always told me how selfish and wilful I was. I had to have everything *my* way, and blow the feelings o' them around me. No consideration, that's my trouble, I can hear Mam saying it now . . . aye, and she had good cause an' all."

"You're too harsh on yourself," Martha interjected sympathetically.

"Why not when it's true. If I hadn't been so blinkin' headstrong I'd have listened to Matthew instead o' defying him, going against him. It makes me that angry when I think how wrong I was, how right *he* was. Take Dorrie Vickers–!"

Some weeks past, young Joe had called round here to let Ruby know what was going on at home between their stepfather and Dorrie. Ruby couldn't believe her ears when she'd heard it. Dorrie Vickers – with *Jack McShane*? It didn't bear thinking about, that pair lying together in her mother's bed, in her mother's house, drinking and carrying on and doing with each other the things Ruby still remembered to her shame Jack had done with her once on a time.

"Serves me right for not paying proper heed to Matthew's judgement," she went on, contemptuous of herself. "He never cared for Dorrie from the start. He didn't trust her."

"No more did I," said Martha with a sniff. "A sly, conniving, *cheap* little madam if ever there was one."

"And to think how I stuck up for her! She was everything I liked and admired and wanted to be – *her*, that thing! I wouldn't hear Matthew say one word against her." Ruby's mouth drooped. Turning away to gaze through the window again, she added almost as though to herself, "How mistaken I was."

"You shouldn't reproach yourself, my dear. The Miss Vickers of this world have a brash appeal that in some ways is attractive, but self-centredness betrays them in the end. Whatever feelings of friendship you entertained, you must judge her by her morals and her callous attitude towards your brother."

Aye, Martha was right. Dorrie had shown herself in her true colours, taking up with Jack McShane with Mam scarcely cold in her grave, installing herself at Minerva Lane as bold as you please. Young Joe had been very bitter against her. She was for ever egging Jack on to get shot of him out of the house, he'd revealed; but at least Joe had the landlord on his side and he wasn't prepared to go without showing a fight. Ruby would gladly have taken her brother to lodge with her here, but Mr Reynolds had refused when she'd suggested it.

"It's a pity we haven't a room for your brother at Brickhill Lane," Martha went on as if reading her thoughts. "Aunt Ellen is so very fond of him, she regards him almost as a member of the family. But there's only the two bedrooms as you know, dear, and we could hardly invite him to live in the garden shed!"

It was meant as a jest to lighten the conversation, but looking across her shoulder Ruby answered in all earnestness, "Even a shed would be better than how he lives now, treated worse than a dog, shoved here, pushed there, threatened wi' the buckle-end of his stepfather's belt if he so much as dares speak to him – and as for that Dorrie the way she nags and carries on, Joe says it's a wonder her tongue don't catch alight."

"He'd be wise to find himself lodgings elsewhere."

"He won't though, Martha, that's the trouble. It in't just him being stubborn . . . it's these fits he has an' all. He can't be alone in a place he in't familiar with."

Ruby turned away again, leaning her forehead against the window-pane, a sigh of despair forming a mist on the glass.

"Oh, I don't know. I wish I knew what to do for the best . . . not only for Joe, but for Matthew and me. It's all such a ravelment."

* * *

The Saturday evening following, Ruby received an unexpected caller. She'd spent the day enquiring round the town after employment as a bar-room maid; but of the dozen or so public houses she had asked at, only one had offered accommodation with the work – a dark, evil-smelling cubby-hole a step up from the cellar.

She'd come back to her lodgings feeling too dispirited to cook herself a proper evening meal. Instead she went round to the pie shop on the corner; and having lit a small fire in her room she was just sitting down to eat when she heard a sound at her door of the handle being tried.

"Who's there?" she called. "Is it you, Mrs Wilson?" thinking it must be the woman lodging on the floor above who sometimes came to borrow from her.

The door was tried again. Ruby went across and turned the key to unlock it – a precaution she took since the main door of the property was unsecured except at night-time when the street lamp was put out.

"You've got a visitor to see you," said a man's voice; and for one split second a thrill of joy went through her at the thought it might be Matthew here at last. She pulled open the door. Leaning against the jamb cradling a bottle in his arm, bowler hat tilted forward over his eyes at a rakish angle, stood a figure she failed to recognise for a moment till he spoke again.

"You remember me, don't you, Ruby? It's been a long while, eh." It was Sam Reynolds, Jabez's brother.

Without waiting for her invitation Sam came past into the room and took off his bowler, tossing it aside on the bed. He was still sporting the Pompadour quiff she recalled from those times she'd met him in the company of Dorrie

Vickers, before he and Dorrie had split up. Staring Ruby up and down, he grinned at her before casting a quick glance round him at the meagre furnishings and the room's threadbare look of secondhand economy that went with cheaper lodging-houses.

"You're a bit cramped in here, Ruby, aren't you?" he observed. "Couldn't Jabez find you anything better than this little mousehole?"

"It does me well enough." She returned his glance with a frown of curiosity. "Why, has your brother sent you round about the accommodation or some'at?"

"What d'you take me for, his dun? No, I heard you were all on your ownsome now, so I thought maybe you'd care for a bit of company to cheer you."

Sam took a step over to the table where the mutton pie she'd got for her meal congealed on its plate in a little pool of gravy. "I see I've timed my arrival to a nicety," he said with a laugh, putting down the bottle he'd been carrying. "This'll help you enjoy the taste of your supper. You surely didn't suppose I'd gone and forgotten, eh."

"Forgotten what?" asked Ruby, beginning to feel uneasy and wishing she could think of some excuse to make him leave. He smelled as though he'd been drinking.

"My promise to you, Ruby! Don't you recall? That night I saw you home in the hackney cab? I said I'd buy you champagne – and I'm a chappie who keeps his promises to wenches."

"There in't any reason I should've remembered a detail like that. Like you said, it's a long while ago."

"And life hasn't been without its distractions, from all I hear."

He smirked at her in a way she didn't care for. "Oh? What's this you've been hearing, then?"

"Come, dear Ruby, there's no need to be coy with *me*. Jabez is my brother, after all—"

"I know who your brother is, Mr Reynolds," she interrupted him shortly. "It's nice o' you to think to call, but as you can see I wasn't expecting company and I've other things to do this evening."

He looked at the cold mutton pie. "Tell you what — let's have some of this excellent champagne, eh, and we'll discuss a little proposition I want to make you."

"No, if you don't mind I'd be happier if you took your leave. I – I might be having a visit from my husband." The wish that were true made her snatch at the lie.

"Your husband hasn't been near you since you've lodged here," Sam told her amiably, peeling the lead foil from the neck of the champagne bottle, "so I think that'd be stretching coincidence a bit too far, don't you?"

Colour flooded Ruby's face. "How do *you* know he in't been near me – that's none o' your business! Or have you been having me spied on or some'at?"

"Jabez likes to know who comes and goes, and the tenant on the ground floor has a busy little pair of ears. Except for your young brother, the only visitors you've entertained have all been ladies – I use the term loosely, of course."

"I've entertained *your* brother, don't forget—" In her anger it was said before she could stop herself. "Did your snoop tell you that an' all, I wonder?"

There was a little pop as the cork was eased and a frothy dribble of bubbles ran down to wet the table.

"Glasses are where – here?" Sam jerked his head

towards the cupboard; and when Ruby didn't answer him he went and opened it himself, hunting round the shelves before making do with a couple of water tumblers.

"As far as my 'snoop' is concerned," he said, still amiable, half-filling each glass and offering one across to her, "Jabez calls on you as landlord of these lodgings and for no other reason. You wouldn't deny that? He doesn't visit you for other purposes ... at least, not any longer. And no one will believe you if you choose to tell 'em otherwise."

"Oh, and what d'you suppose there is to tell?" She ignored the champagne and stared at him defiantly, daring him to answer, wondering how much he knew already.

Pursing his lips he looked up at the ceiling, the jaundice-yellow light from the gasolier giving a bilious hue to his complexion and clashing with the mustard checks of his too-loud suit. "You might p'raps mention ... Ivetsey Bank."

"You know about Ivetsey Bank–?"

"About everything, Ruby."

"But how? He made me swear to keep it private." Her tone betrayed her sudden dismay and embarrassment. "He said I'd got to be discreet and never tell nobody we'd been ... together. Well, *he* in't been very discreet from the sound of it, blabbing the whole thing to you and who else!"

"What an unkind word to use of Jabez – *blabbing*." Sam removed his gaze from the ceiling, appearing even more amused.

"It's an unkind thing he's been and done across me." Anger mastering her again, she set her fists on her hips. "I hope you enjoyed having your snigger, the pair o' you ... I hope you thought it fun to talk about me as if I was a flippin' trollop or some'at."

"Whoa, hold your horses. My God, he never said you'd got a temper!" The amusement turned to admiration. Taking a leather brandy flask from inside his jacket Sam added some of the contents to his champagne and swallowed a mouthful. "We never discussed you, Ruby dear – not that way, at least. The fact of the matter is, I know all about my brother's peccadilloes and the use he has for the cottage at Ivetsey Bank. And I know that your affair with him is finished. No, hear me out–" he said as she interrupted, "I'm coming to the proposition I mentioned. That first night we met, at the Star Concert Hall – see, I even remember its name – I took quite a fancy to you, but I didn't bother pursuing it when I learned from Dorrie Vickers you were spoken for. I've never forgotten you, though. It pleased me to do you a small service by having a word with my brother on your behalf about work in the market." He paused for another mouthful, eyeing her over the rim of the glass.

"That was only because Dorrie asked you," Ruby said aggressively.

"You owe me the favour, even so. Look – have a drink of champagne, for heaven's sake, and let's sit down!"

"I'm sorry, I'd rather stand. I hope you're leaving in a minute."

"I'll leave when I'm ready, and you'd be well advised to show more friendliness. I can do you a lot of other favours if you start being nice to me. You see–" moving from the table Sam reached suddenly across to take her by the hand and pull her to him, "brother Jabez has made me a present of you, Ruby dear. He's passed you on. It's me who's going to be your protector now."

She gaped at him, too stunned for a moment even to speak, incredulous; and seizing advantage he pulled her closer still and started pawing at her in a way she found utterly loathsome, trying to kiss her face and her neck, his breath reeking of alcohol.

"Leave off you – you–" she struggled furiously to push him away, "or help me God, if you don't, I'll scream the house down!"

"I wouldn't advise it." Grinning, he pinioned her arms against her sides and fastened his lips on to hers, sucking at her greedily, the taste of his saliva in her mouth. Impeded by her skirts Ruby began kicking at his shins; but this only seemed to encourage Sam the more and lifting her he shoved her backwards on to the bed, half falling on top of her.

"I've got a cosy little place in Chapel Ash where I can set you up ... all the clothes you can wear ... think of it, Ruby."

"Get *off* me!"

"You're ginger right enough–" He fastened on her mouth again, grasping her outstretched wrists above her head, his body holding her down. "I like a wench who's hot for a rough and tumble. Are you angry with me, Ruby ... really angry? If I pull your drawers off will you scratch my face? Mmm, I'd rather enjoy that ..." all this in a friendly, conversational tone which she found even more obscene than his molestation.

Arching her back and fighting to throw him off-balance, Ruby managed to drag her head to one side. The scream for help was muffled by the pillows but it served its purpose, for Sam promptly loosed one wrist to clamp his hand across her mouth, not so amused now, saying urgently, "For God's sake, woman, what's the matter with you? Be sensible, I'm not going to hurt you!"

That was as far as he got. Ruby fastened her teeth into the fleshy base of his thumb, and with a shout of pain he rolled away from her, stumbling to his feet, shaking his bitten hand in agony.

"You little bitch—"

Opening her mouth she let out another scream, piercingly shrill this time.

"All right – all right – I'll leave you alone, I'm going!"

Snatching his hat from the end of the bed he straightened his clothes and opened the door. "But I'll be back. You haven't seen the last of me, don't think you have—"

"*Get out!*" Ruby made a lunge for the table, and grabbing the champagne bottle flung it with all her force at the closing door. There was the sound of Sam's retreat along the landing.

For a moment she stood shuddering with anger and revulsion; then throwing herself across the bed again she fell into a torrent of passionate weeping.

18

Ruby quitted Waterloo Road in the middle of March that year, 1888, to take up work at the Old Still public house in King Street. The parting from Jabez Reynolds had been a horrible embarrasment for both of them. He was on the point of going abroad with his wife on a visit to Evian, and was livid with anger that his brother's crass behaviour might have affected his plans, vehemently denying Sam's allegations, which he dismissed as 'dangerous nonsense'.

Ruby was making too much of the incident, he said. Was it likely he would carelessly discuss the details of their love-affair – he, who guarded his privacy so jealously? Her name might have been mentioned, yes, but not in that connection; and as to Sam's remark about her being 'passed on' to him, Mr Reynolds could only suppose it was drunkenness talking – drunkenness or downright mischief, since his brother found amusement in such stupid capers.

Ruby was made to feel she'd become a hindrance, an annoyance. Far from sharing her distress at the way she'd been insulted, Jabez Reynolds had seemed anxious to diminish it. He was gentleman enough, however, to offer a sincere apology for his brother's behaviour; and before he left for Evian he troubled himself to see she had a reference to help her in her efforts to find live-in work.

For that at least, she thought, she should be grateful. But it was a cold and comfortless goodbye.

The Old Still where she'd succeeded in getting a job was a family-run establishment patronised by clerks and shopkeepers, and as a public house it struck her as rather more respectable than many of its fellows. It occupied the site of a distillery from which it took its name, pre-dating the building of King Street in the reign of George the Second, and the panelled, oak-beamed rooms and narrow stone-flagged passageways were redolent with the atmosphere of an earlier age.

Whatever malevolent star had been dogging her life for the past couple of years, its influence appeared to be relenting: Ruby had fallen on her feet getting work in such agreeable surroundings. She had a tiny attic room all to herself overlooking the cobbled yard at the rear where the landlady, Emma Tranter, grew tubs of herbs and flowers according to season and kept a coop of Leghorn chickens. Emma was an excellent sort, a tall, stout, dark-haired woman always dressed in black with a clean white apron crisp with starch and an amethyst brooch at her throat. She was warm-natured without being soft, and if she mothered her customers as though they were family it was often with a dose of brimstone and treacle for their own good.

Where Emma was large, her husband Fred Tranter was short, but as solidly built as one of his own Banks's barrels and seldom without his brindled bull terrier Cato beside him. Ruby had less to do with Fred – her work kept her mainly to the kitchen and the public saloon – but she could hear his laughter bellying from the tap-room on the other side of the passage, and the piping of the penny whistle he played after enjoying a pint or two at the cribbage board with his cronies amongst the sawdust and the reek of shag tobacco.

There were two daughters, both of them with youngsters, and a son as yet unmarried who was serving with the Army out in India. A collodion print of him in uniform had pride of place on the bar shelf of the saloon between sepia studio portraits of the grandchildren and picture-postcards sent from seaside places.

There was also a niece, Queenie, just turned sixteen, who helped about the place, and a lad who worked in the tap-room, and a cellarman. They all seemed very helpful and agreeable, showing her what she had to do, where everything was kept, and so forth; and after the first week's strangeness in unfamiliar surroundings Ruby found herself feeling less unhappy and far less lonely than for a long, long time.

The Tranters knew she had a husband from her reference, which had named her in her married title. She was worried they might count this fact against her, and when Emma enquired to know whether Mr Dyson was still living, she had been totally honest about her situation.

"He's not likely to start coming round here making trouble for you, is he?" had been Emma's only question; and when Ruby reassured her she had said, "Well, your marriage is your own concern, my lamb. As long as it doesn't interfere wi' your work for me, I'm happy to employ you for a couple o' months on trial and see how you fare at the job."

Ruby liked the Old Still; and the Old Still seemed to like her. After the isolation of Ivetsey Bank and the depressing lodgings on Waterloo Road, it was as though her life were taking on warmth and colour and even some value again. She applied herself diligently to being pleasant, and discovered after a week or two that smiles and laughter came to her quite readily without being forced, that she was singing as she went about her work – something she hadn't done for ages now – that she woke of a morning looking forward to the day instead of dreading it. Customers began to ask after her once they'd got to know her face behind the counter (a welcome sign in a public house, where a friendly, pretty, sympathetic barmaid was always good for business); and if at first Ruby made mistakes, someone was generally around to set her right with a word of kindness and encouragement.

The only dark cloud in her brightening life was the anguish eating into her still for Matthew. In spite of what she'd said to Martha Becket recently, she wasn't so proud that she'd let her husband's silence keep her from getting in touch with him again. It wasn't pride now holding her back, it was something else: she was suddenly ashamed to face him, ashamed of herself and what she'd done, ashamed of confession. Since the links with Jabez Reynolds had at last been severed she'd naively hoped that would make everything all right again, that the past could be pushed into a corner and forgotten.

But it wasn't so. The past had become a pitfall for the future.

It was Matthew's twenty-first birthday at the end of March. Ruby was anxious to buy him a present to mark his coming of age, something special as a token, and send it to him with a little message. After a lot of deliberation she'd chosen him a white silk scarf with tasselled fringes, a highly impractical gift for a working man, but it looked so smart on the dummy in the window of Hyam's in Dudley Street and it was something he could wear for best of a Sunday, she thought.

The message enclosed with the ribbon-tied packet said simply, 'Best wishes for your birthday, Matt, I love you', and gave her new address. She had intended leaving it outside the door of their old lodgings at number 5 Gas Yard, where he'd find it after work; but on second thoughts, worried somebody else might see the present there and be tempted to take it, Ruby had entrusted it instead to the landlord Michael Byrne downstairs, asking him to see that Matthew got it safely when he came in from Chubb's that night.

"I'll do that for you, sure," Mr Byrne promised, putting it aside. "I'll have it in my hand for him the minute I hear his step at the door, so I will."

"You won't forget?"

"Have I not said?"

It was a simple thing to expect the landlord to remember, and she'd had no reason whatever to doubt his word.

The present was still there, undelivered, in Mr Byrne's ill-lit kitchen, underneath some dirty washing and a copy of the *Sporting Life*, when young Joe Gallimore came round to Matthew's lodgings a week later.

Matthew hadn't long been in from work and was swilling himself at the washstand basin before going out again to spend the evening at his parents', a duty he'd neglected during the time of his affair with Gatty Thompson.

That was all over and finished with now – it hadn't taken Gatty long to find herself somebody new for consolation – and his existence had returned to a more sober and celibate routine which somehow he preferred. It made himself far easier to live with.

The familiar sudden creak of the top step out on the landing halted the tune he'd been humming. Using the towel round his neck to dry his head, he went just as he was with his trouser braces hanging down, across the room to the other door, expecting to find the insurance man who called each week to collect his penny premium.

It wasn't the insurance man. In fact, for a moment Matthew failed to identify the slight, bent-over figure hunched there in the stairhead shadows until the face was raised to him, and in the bruised and bloodied features he recognised with a shock it was his brother-in-law, Joe Gallimore.

"What the–"

"Let me in will you, for pity's sake," Joe said with a groan, clutching himself round the ribs. "I'm just about done in–"

Matthew caught him as he stumbled into his arms, and half carried him, half dragged him inside the room.

"Take it easy now . . . that's right, that's it, lad . . . let's sit you down and see what damage there is." He lowered Joe into a chair beside the empty hearth and went and got an oil lamp, setting it on the table while he examined the youngster's injuries. Most of the blood seemed to be from a gash at the top of his head in the hairline, but his nose had been bleeding as well, and he had a split bottom lip that was swollen and caked with a darkening crust.

"How in God's name have you managed to go and do this to yourself?" he wanted to know, concerned at the state of him. "You look as though you've walked slap in the path of an omnibus!" It wasn't the result of one of Joe's turns, Matthew would bet on it – somebody's fists had been the cause of this mess, he could tell from the bruising.

Joe eased himself back awkwardly, still nursing his ribs. "It was him ... Jack McShane ..." He winced at the sting from his split lip.

"McShane–? I might've guessed!"

Matthew let out an oath of angry disgust. "Nobody else but him would pick on a lad half his size and gi' him such a bloody hiding. Well, the police are going to hear about it this time–" It wasn't the first occasion he'd seen evidence of the treatment young Joe had had to suffer from his stepfather, but it had never been as vicious a beating as this. He remembered the fight he'd had with McShane himself, over Ruby, remembered the force of the blows from those bone-solid knuckles.

His face darkened. He swung away, meaning to fetch the basin he'd been using, and cleanse Joe's wounds; but the lad caught him weakly by the arm and said with a desperate pleading urgency, "Don't get the police, Matt. It was me as started it ... I hit him wi' a bottle."

"I don't give a damn who started it, Joe. McShane's a grown man, he should know his own strength. Another leathering like this 'un, and next time he might find himself in the cells for more than assault."

"There in't going to be a next time." Joe's hand fell back, and his body seemed to sag like a punctured sack of sawdust, hopeless, defeated, the stuffing literally knocked out of him. "I thought I could stick up for m'self against him and that Dorrie Vickers. I went and told the landlord she'd moved in to live wi' us . . . he said he'd have her evicted."

Matthew knew about the situation in Minerva Lane from his mother, who – hardly surprising – viewed the domestic arrangement at number 11 as a scandalous disgrace and had already complained to the landlord, Hodgetts, herself. Only a creature as brazen-faced as Dorrie Vickers would have stepped into a dead woman's shoes the way that one had done, flaunting herself in front of the neighbours with Jack McShane and drunk most evenings, the pair of them, according to Agnes Dyson.

"Aye, but *is* he having her evicted?" Matthew said, disgusted still, fetching the wash basin in from the other room and kneeling to put it down by the chair. Taking the towel from his neck he wrung it out in the tepid water to use as a swab. "She's been there all of a month and there's no sign of the baggage shifting herself."

"She's agreed to pay him full rent, that's why. Y'know what he's like, he never argues wi' money does Hodgetts." Joe flinched as the towel touched the bruise-proud skin on his face. "I trusted him, Matt . . . I thought I'd got him on my side."

"Is that what gave you the courage to pick up a bottle and clout Jack McShane?"

"No."

"What, then?"

"It was some'at Jack said about our Ruby. About her . . . going wi' other men afore she married you. I called him a liar, and he laughed at me and said . . . said he knew better."

Matthew paused; then wringing out the towel again he held it to the gash still oozing a trickle of blood at Joe's hairline. "Did he explain what he meant by that, or was he maybe trying a shot in the dark to find out if you knew anything," he said harshly.

"I don't know, that's when I hit him. Why?" The young lad shifted in discomfort, trying to look at his brother-in-law from under the towel. "None o' what he said was true, was it? How could it be? Our Ruby never went wi' any other chaps – no, never. The only one she ever had a fancy for apart from you was Jack himself, until she turned against him."

"Hold your head still," Matthew told him with sudden unnecessary roughness, "I can't see what I'm doing. I only thought – well, maybe somebody might have let fall mention o' some'at now your mother's dead, that's all."

"Mention o' what, Matt?"

"I've said too much already. Leave it."

"But I want to know!" Joe caught his hand and gripped it. "I in't a kid any more to hide things from, I'm fifteen now, I'm a working man. If this is about our Mam or our Ruby I've got a right to be told. Was it anything to do wi' Ruby getting herself in the family way?"

"Look, I've spoken out of turn where I shouldn't have ... I'm sorry. If you want the truth, go to Waterloo Road and ask your sister."

Matthew got from his knees and put the basin of stained water on the table. Lizzie McShane was dead and beyond any hurt. Why shouldn't Joe know his stepfather had seduced Ruby and given her a child – there was bad feeling enough there already. Ruby herself might not see it that way though, and he deeply regretted the moment of thoughtlessness which had led him to say what he had just now.

"Let's have your jacket off, shall we," he said in a kindlier manner. "I'll find a bit of old sheet to bind your ribs before I take you round the doctor's, ask him to have a look at you."

"Ruby in't at Waterloo Road," Joe persisted, refusing to leave the subject alone, worrying at it. "She moved from there the middle o' last month – I thought you knew?"

"Why should I know anything. She hasn't been in touch wi' me to tell me."

"But she wrote and sent you a letter."

"That was January. Here – hold the towel to your head a minute while I empty this basin out in the slops."

Matthew had to turn away in case his face betrayed him, trying to keep the tension from his voice, the ache of stubborn pride starting its twisting round his heart again, familiar companion of his days and nights since Ruby left him. "I suppose Mr Reynolds has found her a new situation, has he?"

"No. She's been and got herself a job as bar-room maid at the Old Still pub in King Street," Joe informed him. "I think she was glad to get shot o' Mr Reynolds, for all the kindness he's been doing her. There was some'at going on there that I never understood ... she wouldn't tell me anything, she just seemed down in the mouth all the time, and if I asked her she'd say it was the weather or the lodgings or some'at."

The lad waited for his brother-in-law to return from the other room. "Was it to do wi' what Jack said about her, d'you reckon, Matt – them lies about her knocking about all over the place wi' other men?"

"I don't know. I said to leave it, didn't I. Where's Ruby living now she's got this bar-room work?"

"Over the pub. Why didn't you ever go and see her at Waterloo Road? She grieved her heart out on account o' you because she got no answer to that letter."

"She didn't need me. Not while she had a gentleman as well-heeled and influential as Jabez Reynolds to play benefactor to her." Matthew lifted the towel away from Joe's wound and examined it carefully by the lamplight. Only the slightest tremor of his square, strong hand revealed he wasn't entirely master of his emotions. "You'll need a stitch or two in that ... What makes you suppose Ruby's been grieving for me, then? Does she talk about me ever?"

"Now and again, aye."

"And – what sort o' thing does she say?" He tried to keep his voice even, not daring to let himself believe there might be something – anything – his fragile hopes could cling to, giving his concentration to easing Joe forward and helping him off with his jacket. The shirt underneath had been partly ripped from its buttons and he could see a darkening area of bruising where Jack McShane's punches had marked the lad round the ribs.

"She says–" Joe's face screwed up with the painful effort of raising his arms "–she says she was wrong to fall out wi' you ... the arguments there was and such ... she wishes she could make it up."

"Ruby says that?"

A nod, and another grimace as the shirt came off.

"She wishes she could make things up between us?"

"Aye."

"Then why didn't she remember my birthday if she was all that eager," Matthew said with a sudden bitter change of feeling, throwing jacket and shirt aside on the chair opposite. "Wishing is one thing – doing is another. I thought at least she could've sent me a line o' greeting or some'at to show she hadn't forgotten I'd turned twenty-one."

The bubble of hope burst itself on the needle-sharp memory of the hurt he'd felt when Ruby failed even to acknowledge his coming of age, as though she'd turned her back on every thought of him. His fellow apprentices at Chubb's had clubbed together to mark the traditional rites of passage with a special celebration, but Ruby's silence had completely overshadowed the occasion when one word from her would have made it into something far more enjoyable. Perhaps she was paying him out for that business of the letter, Matthew thought.

"But she didn't forget it was your birthday, Matt," Joe said in a puzzled tone. "When I went to see her at the pub last Friday week she told me herself she was buying some'at for you."

"If she did I never saw it. Any road, it doesn't matter, lad ... getting you to the doctor is more important for the minute, then I'm bringing you back here and you can lodge wi' me the night."

So he'd been wrong. Ruby *had* remembered. She wouldn't have told her brother she was getting him a present if she wasn't. Matthew wondered what had become of it; maybe she'd changed her mind. Either way he was the loser. One thing was sure though – it was time this damn' blasted situation was sorted out for good and all. He'd had enough of it.

19

There was no sound in the attic room now Ruby was finished. The curtain at her open casement moved a little in the morning breeze, letting in the noises of the Sunday world outside; but within the room lay an almost tangible stillness.

She studied her brother hunched on the end of the bed, his face hid in his hands, and pitied him with all her heart for what he must be feeling at the moment, questioning herself whether in fact she'd done right to tell him. She hadn't wanted to. What good could come of it? But Joe had got this bee in his head from something Matthew had apparently said; he'd kept on and on at her about it until in the end she'd been forced to confess the whole wretched story, for the sake of clearing Matthew's name in her brother's eyes by revealing the true identity of the man who'd made her pregnant.

Ruby had found it one of the hardest things she'd ever had to do, telling Joe about their stepfather, hearing her voice as though it was a stranger talking; explaining the bald facts, with no excuses for herself, and no emotion. Joe didn't want to believe at first – *wouldn't* believe her. After that he had broken down and wept, cursing uselessly and helplessly between his angry tears, swearing he'd stick a knife in Jack for what he'd gone and done across her and their Mam.

And now he was drained, huddled on the bed bereft like a child, all the heat of his revenge gone out of him into miserable silence, just a young lad powerless to redress the wrong of what had happened.

"Promise me you won't speak o' this to anybody else," Ruby repeated, not able to bear the stillness of the room any longer. "You'll only be raking up trouble, and knowing Jack he's bound to deny it. I know how bad you feel about it, Joe, but *promise* me you won't say anything!"

He made no answer.

"If ever the neighbours get to hear, it's our Mam they'll think the worse of," Ruby persisted. "They'll be saying she must have known what was going on wi' Jack and me and did nothing to stop it – that she was frightened o' losing him or some'at. You know how gossip spreads. They'll have a field day."

She moved over to sit next to her brother, stroking his hair. The week-old bruises on his face had faded from livid to purplish-yellow now, and she thought if Minerva Lane wanted something to gossip about then surely this and Dorrie Vickers was already enough against Jack McShane without Joe adding further ammunition.

"I wish Matthew hadn't mentioned anything," she said regretfully. "It's all in the past and I never wanted you to know."

"You should've told our Mam what he was doing to you." Joe pushed her away and got up as though he couldn't bear the touch of her. "Filthy devil, she'd have kicked him out the house she would. You should have told her, Ruby!"

"But she *worshipped* him, and I couldn't bear to hurt her. Joe ... please try and understand, why can't you. Think what it would've done to Mam if she'd found out."

"A fat lot you cared. If you didn't want Jack interfering wi' you why did you show him so much encouragement."

The pain and contempt in her brother's voice cut Ruby to the quick. "He led me on and I fancied myself in love wi' him, that's why. I was only fifteen, same age as you are. I thought I knew it all and I didn't, I knew nothing, I was just a silly innocent who'd had her head turned by an older man."

"Until he got you pregnant. That brought you to your senses quick enough."

"Aye ... it did."

Joe went and leaned his elbows on the casement ledge, looking down into the yard where Emma Tranter's chickens were making a throaty contented clucking on the sun-warmed perches of their coop. In one of the neighbouring streets someone was playing a barrel-organ and the sound of its tinkling echoes above the occasional passing traffic held a gaiety that seemed to mock the young lad's bitterness.

"I'm glad the babby died," he said after a moment abruptly, almost aggressively.

"No, don't say a thing like that, you mustn't!" his sister cried out in quick hurt. "It wasn't my poor little babby's fault who its father was – it never asked to be brought into the world, and Matthew would've stood by us–"

"Aye, he's more than you deserve, is Matthew."

"I know he is – oh, don't you think I know he is! I'd gi' my right hand just to make things up wi' him and have him take me back ... but he in't been near me." Her voice broke a little and she had to avert her head, pressing her hand to her mouth to stifle her sudden anguish. She had set so much store on Matthew's birthday present as a peace-offering, and yet still she'd had neither word nor sight of him.

"I thought at least he'd like the gift I left him for his twenty-first," she went on in a note of despair, getting off the bed, not noticing the way her brother turned to look at her. "A line or two o' thanks wouldn't have cost much even if he didn't care for what I'd gone and bought for him."

"But you didn't send him any flippin' present," Joe retorted. "He told me so himself."

"You mean – you mean he never got it?" Ruby stared at him. "I left it wi' the landlord at the lodgings, Mr Byrne – aye, and he swore blind he'd gi' it Matthew the minute he come through the door from work!" Despair became vexation that after all her care and trouble the gift had never even been delivered, and she'd been waiting, hoping, over a fortnight all for nothing. No wonder Matthew hadn't been near to thank her – dear God, and who could blame him, she thought angrily.

"If you wanted some'at taking why didn't you give it me to do?" said Joe.

"Why didn't I! I can see now what must've happened – Mr Byrne put the present by, then went and forgot all about it. Drunk again I suppose, blinkin' old fool. Oh, Joe–"

Ruby went to her brother at the casement and wrapped

her arms round him, hiding her face against his shoulder. "Oh, Joe, we mustn't quarrel. Tell me why do I make such a bodge of everything – when am I going to learn."

"Aye, you made a right bodge o' things wi' that Jack, and look where it got you." But he softened the words with a clumsy little hug; and then raising her chin he said, "*I* in't ever going to let you down."

"I know that, chick."

"So if there's any more bother, our Ruby, leave it to me to sort out for you, eh."

She thought he was referring to her and Matthew. She was wrong. Young Joe was thinking of their stepfather.

"Steady there, Bill – hold it while I lift it from this end," Jack McShane shouted, taking the strain of a heavy chiffonier in the back of the haulage wagon and struggling to manhandle it towards the tailboard.

"No, we can't do it like that," Bill shouted back from under the tarpaulin. "The bugger's jammed too tight against this wardrobe – ease up a bit and I'll have a go at shifting it from my end."

Jack lowered the piece of furniture to the wagon floor again, catching his head a nasty crack in the process and cursing ferociously, to the entertainment of a gang of children standing in the roadway watching them unload. He cursed a second time, beneath his breath. He could have done without this ruddy job this morning after the amount of drink he'd poured inside himself last night and stopping up till three o'clock, forgetting he had to be out of the house again by seven.

"Hey – mister!" one of the children called to him. "D'you

know your horses are unhitched? Gi' us a tanner to hold 'em for you?"

"I've warned you already, clear off out of it–" He jumped down from the tailboard, aiming a cuff at the nearest lad and sending the rest scattering in squeals of mock alarm along the cobbles. "Go on – clear off back to your mothers, or I'll take my hand to the lot o' you!"

Checking to see the two cart-horses were still securely tethered to the lamp-post, their heads down in their feed bags, Jack clambered back into the wagon damning and blasting the world to perdition, and took another hold of the chiffonier.

"You got it free yet, Bill?" he shouted to his mate.

"Hang on a minute." There was a scrape and a couple of hefty bumps. "Aye, gi' it a try now – I reckon that's shifted it. Mind out for the cupboard handles–"

That lad out there just now had reminded Jack of his stepson Joe and the reason he'd gone on the binge last night hoping the beer would drown his problems. Thank God Dorrie was out of the house. She'd gone to spend a couple of days with her mother who'd been taken bad with an attack of milk leg after being delivered of her fourteenth child. He wouldn't have wanted Dorrie to hear what that ruddy young half-wit Joe had had to say, opening his mouth about matters Jack had hoped he wouldn't know of, and threatening to go and tell the neighbours. It wasn't the neighbours so much Jack cared about; but Dorrie might not like it. And he didn't want to lose her.

"Left hand up a bit, Bill–"

He took the weight of the chiffonier again, the muscles of his burly shoulders straining against the frayed seams of his waistcoat, and backed his way slowly down the tail-board. Bill appeared from the tarpaulin with the other end, shuffling forward in quick little steps, grunting. He was an older man than Jack, running to fat and not as strong in the arm as once he'd been.

The gang of children had regrouped again, like flies; and the same young lad started jeering and poking fun at the hauliers' efforts until one of the mothers, watching from her next-door window, came out to drag him inside by his ear with a clout round the head for his cheek.

"Behopes that'll learn the rest o' you little perishers!" Jack said, grimly satisfied. He'd felt like giving his stepson a damn' good leathering last night, except he knew he couldn't trust his temper. He'd done too much damage the other time, God knows – even Dorrie had had a go at him for that, telling him the neighbours would be having the Cruelty Man round after him. She'd witnessed violence enough at home from her own stepfather, she said; there must be other ways of showing Joe the door than using him like a ruddy lump of dogsmeat.

Jack was learning a few things about Dorrie since they'd started living together. Besides the powerful sexual magnetism which had first attracted him, and her artful teasing nature, and her sudden bursts of firework fury turning her into something wild and beautiful, he had discovered another side to her; a damaged side. Her stepfather had been a nasty piece of villainy by all accounts.

"I hope this bugger's going in the front parlour," Bill complained, dropping his end of the chiffonier to the kerb and wiping the sweat from his eyes with the back of his sleeve. Giving a jerk of the head towards the open door of the house where they were delivering, he went on, "If ever her wants it upstairs her can ruddy well lug it herself 'cause her wo' get me twisting my tripes humping it there for her."

"You'm getting slack, mate," Jack told him testily. "Any case it'd go straight through the floorboards, thing this dratted weight." He bent to his task again, waiting for Bill to lift before he edged backwards across the pavement and up the scrubbed-white step, the strenuous exertion turning the thumping ache in his head from last evening into piercing hot screws of pain.

The chiffonier's elderly owner was standing just behind in the hall passage, getting in the way as they always did, thinking if they didn't keep their eyes on you every single blasted minute the job wouldn't get done properly.

"Where d'you want this putting, Missis?" he called across his shoulder.

"Oh, I think in here against the parlour wall, if you don't mind."

Thank Christ for that!

"Go careful with it, won't you, my man. It belonged to my dear late husband, you know, and I wouldn't want it scratched or marked."

Jack compressed his lips on his response and angled the piece of furniture in through the doorway. What was it young Joe had said last night that had riled so much? Something else about Dorrie. Oh aye – he'd said maybe she wouldn't care at all for Minerva Lane if she was to find out Jack had given their Ruby a bastard daughter.

That had struck home hard it had. Harder than the other things the lad had the nerve to threaten, about how he'd say nothing so long as Dorrie was asked to pack her bags and go, and Jack started treating him fairer. Oh, he'd treat him fair all right – treat him to something he didn't expect, cocky young whelp.

Jack hauled the chiffonier the length of the hallway, ruckling the carpet runner into concertina folds. It was all that cussed Ruby's fault for opening her mouth and blabbing to her brother, instead of staying mut and saying nothing. Well, he'd pay *her* out as well, he swore he would; teach the pair a lesson that it didn't do to cross a man like him.

"You'm acting very civil to Joe lately, ain't you. What's come over you of a sudden?" said Dorrie Vickers, examining her reflection. Behind her Jack McShane lay sprawled across the bed naked except for his unbuttoned shirt, the muscles of his thick, hard body contoured by the glow of lamplight. "Had a change of heart or some'at, have you?"

Jack responded with a grunt, his eyes never leaving her, watching the way she played with her hair and twisted herself to view the effect in the mirror.

"Only he's seemed quite chirpy since I got back from our mother's," she went on, "and I notice he's even bought himself another cap to wear. He ain't in love is he?"

It wasn't a part of Jack's ploy to let Dorrie know *he'd* given Joe the money for the cap. "He's seeing some'at of a wench, aye," he said, as if indifferently. "Her name's Queenie. Helps out at the pub where Ruby's working."

"Is that where he is again tonight?"

Another grunt.

"It's going to cost him a bob or two, ain't it, if he's

starting courting–" Dorrie leaned forward and pouted her carmined lips in a kiss to her reflection, then pleased with the image smiled at herself in an arch sort of way before looking at Jack through the mirror. "And he ain't earning much at Brickhill Lane from the gardening and bits o' jobs he does that Mrs Finch."

"Aye, so he's been complaining. He reckons the old woman's a proper pinch-fist. Got more money than her'll ever need, he says. Tranklements and suchlike cluttering the place – not rubbish neither, her's even got some solid silver candlesticks, he tells me."

"He seems to be telling you a lot considering you flippin' well half-killed him laying into him the other week."

"I've been trying to make it up to the lad," Jack said glibly, propping himself on his elbows to get a better view of Dorrie's rounded, dimpled buttocks showing provocatively beneath her corsets as she bent and started rolling down her garters. "I've been a bit too blasted hard on him just lately."

"You be careful what you'm doing being so chummy, or he'll want to stay and we'm *never* going to be shot of him. Any case, I thought he was planning to lodge wi' that husband o' Ruby's? There's plenty more room for him there." Dorrie straightened herself and put a foot up on the bed-rail to peel down her black lisle stocking. "He talked o' nothing else for over a week, then it all went quiet and I ain't heard a word more said about it."

"Because he ain't got no money for lodgings. It's why he's so bitter against that old woman – *her's* got plenty and yet her wo' give him a penny-piece more than what her's paying him now, he says."

"If I was him I'd pinch her blinkin' silver candlesticks!" The other foot went up.

Jack smiled. "Why don't you suggest that to him, eh," he said, and his mouth had an almost sinister twist to it under the thick dark moustache. Then his mood changed and he made a sudden, playful lunge across the bed, catching Dorrie by the ankle, causing her to squeal and grab out at the bed-rail for support.

"Come here, let me take your stocking off, and — Joe Gallimore." He used the obscenity quite casually, knowing Dorrie didn't object to it, one of the things he liked about their love-making.

Pulling her over the rail into his arms he held her imprisoned on top of him, kissing the swell of her breasts and teasing the warm deep cleavage with his tongue until her squeals turned into a purr of pleasure. Then as his own arousal grew demanding, he rolled over so he had her pinned beneath him on the rumpled bedclothes, and straddled her with his muscular thighs, his shadow from the oil lamp rearing huge and powerful across the room.

"You wo' leave me, Dorrie, will you," he said unexpectedly, almost urgently, staring down at her, the eternal question of a lover in need of reassurance. Of all the wenches he had ever had Jack wanted this one more than any, not only in his bed but in his life; and the thought that he could lose her was torture to him. He'd been watching young Joe like a hawk these past few days, pretending to be friendly and show him a bit of goodwill, all the time waiting for the lad to open his mouth about that blasted affair with Ruby, dreading it might cost him this woman here in his arms . . . this woman he loved.

It was a desperate situation which demanded desperate measures. Joe had him over a barrel, and Jack was prepared to use any weapon – lies, cunning, violence, *anything* – to rid himself of the threat his stepson represented to his future and his happiness with Dorrie.

20

"I've said it to you once and I say it again – it was the worst day's work you ever did, letting yourself be tricked into marriage wi' that Gallimore wench," Agnes Dyson railed at her son. "I warned you'd live to rue the day and the good Lord has proved me right."

"I don't think the Lord much concerns himself in my affairs," Matthew answered a little wearily, pushing his dinner plate away.

"And now from all I hear she's earning a living as bar-room maid in a public house. What sort of respectable work is that for a woman! I'm ashamed to show myself I am, when I think what the neighbours must be saying about us, decent chapel-goers like your father and me with a daughter-in-law selling beer and strong liquor in one of those temples of the Devil. I can only be thankful our minister doesn't know about it." Mrs Dyson's thin face had two round red spots of indignation painted on its cheek-bones.

"There in't a great deal he could do if he did. It's hardly a hanging offence, selling beer."

"It was disgrace enough that you had to be married in such an indecent haste," she carried on harshly, ignoring that remark. "We've always held her to blame for that, your father and me–"

"*Please*, Mother, don't start again," Matthew interrupted, his irritation boiling over. "Every time I've been here for my dinner lately all I hear is the same damn' blasted thing, and to tell the truth I'm just about sick and fed up of it."

"You'll mind your mouth how you speak under this roof, Matthew – I won't have profanity! That's another thing your father and me have noticed since you let yourself fall by the wayside and stopped attending chapel."

He spread his hands. "I'm sorry. I didn't mean to cause offence. But I wish you could stop pulling Ruby to pieces. You're only setting yourself against us, Mother. It was because you disliked her so much after we first got wed that she felt she didn't want to live here, and it's then everything started to go amiss between us."

"The baggage walked out and left you – you can't lay *that* at my door."

His mother removed the plate in front of him and went into the scullery, and he could hear her scraping the chop bones into the bucket kept behind a piece of curtain under the sink.

"And neither can you blame your father or me for these last twelve months she's been living apart from you," she added returning to the kitchen.

"I'm not putting the blame on anybody except myself," said Matthew. "If I hadn't been such a poor sort of husband I know I'd still have a wife and a marriage. Aye, and if I'd been less than a dutiful son to you I'd have done some'at about it by now, an' all."

Only a few days ago there had been an acrimonious

confrontation here in the kitchen at number 3 when he'd told his parents he was going to see Ruby with the intention of asking her to come back to him. All the old prejudices had been given an airing, all the old hypocrisies trotted out with a leavening of Scripture to give weight and justification to his mother's argument. Ruby was 'a stone of stumbling and a rock of offence' (quoting Isaiah); she had forfeited the name of wife by abandoning Matthew; he should set his face against her and remember that 'a virtuous woman is a crown to her husband, but she that maketh ashamed is as rottenness in his bones' (Proverbs).

In the end, mindful that as their only son he still had a duty towards his parents, he had complied with his father's insistence that he sleep on his decision; and having slept on it was twice as determined as before to repair his marriage and heal the breach of the past.

"I know your heart is hardened against it, Mother," he went on, getting up from the table, "but Ruby's my wife, I love her still whatever she's done and I mean to have her back wi' me if she's agreeable."

Agnes Dyson's lips set into a bloodless line. "You're a bigger fool than I took you for," she said acidly. "She'll come back as long as it suits her, aye, but I tell you this much – don't think for a minute you'll keep her, because you won't, my lad."

"I'm prepared to take my chance."

"Then she'll be the ruination of you. It's but a short step from serving in a public house to a life of vice and disease in the gutter, which is where she's bound, you mark my words – I can see it coming. She's a bad lot."

Matthew went and fetched his cap and scarf from the peg behind the staircase door. "Maybe you'll say a prayer for us both, if you will," he answered levelly, refusing to let his mother's vindictiveness goad him into another argument. "You've always held prayer to be a powerful persuader."

"You think I don't go down on my knees and pray enough as it is! I've offered you up to the Lord's keeping every hour of your life since you were born—"

"And in the Lord's eyes Ruby and me are one flesh, so whatever you plead for me you plead for her an' all."

Mrs Dyson was too rigidly entrenched in her Christianity to deny that; but she tried to skirt it with the pious response, "Then I'm doing no more than obeying His will since the Gospel enjoins us to pray for those who despitefully use us."

"It also enjoins us to forgive one another." Matthew started doing up the buttons of his jacket. "I don't understand why you and Dad can't bring yourselves to tolerate what can't be changed, and try to help instead of hindering. Maybe if you set a more charitable example I might be persuaded to come back to chapel – and bring Ruby wi' me if she's willing. Though whether she'd be welcome is another matter."

His mother made to answer; but then paused. One of the worst hurts the Dysons had had to endure from their son's marriage was his lapse from his religious observances; and for the salvation (as she saw it) of his soul, Agnes Dyson came as near to changing her tune in this next moment as distaste for her daughter-in-law would let her.

"The door to grace is always open. If Ruby's prepared to

make the effort and amend her sinful ways, no doubt the congregation would be of a mind to accept her. But from the way she's carrying on she has a long mile yet to go towards repentance!"

"Well . . . I'm off to see her now, maybe I'll pass on what you've said."

There was a hint of sardonic inflection in Matthew's reply. He was glad when he'd made his goodbyes and was gone from the house. Much as he respected his mother, he found it very hard at times to love her.

Setting his cap on his head and knotting his new silk scarf, the young man started away through the deepening violet of the April dusk along Minerva Lane in the direction of Horseley Fields. As he passed the door of number 11 he glanced at the windows with a thought for young Joe Gallimore, but the curtains were still undrawn and the only light came from the reflection of the street lamp opposite, shining dully against the greasy dirt of the panes.

In Horseley Fields the pubs were already beginning to fill, and he noted the usual Saturday night queue outside the pawnbroker's being entertained by a local eccentric known as Singing Margaret, a pitiable old woman whose sole companion was her mangy donkey. Matthew crossed the street to put a couple of coppers in her box, wishing he could afford more, then turned down the alley into Pipers Row which would bring him out by a short cut into the town centre.

By the time he reached his destination in King Street he was starting to sweat with nerves. So much depended on this evening. Tucked inside his pocket-book was Ruby's little birthday message sent with the scarf he was wearing, and delivered by his landlord only days ago amid abject maudlin apologies for the oversight.

'Best wishes for your birthday, Matt. I love you.'

I love you. The words were etched upon his heart. He took them as a token that all was going to be well again, because as long as Ruby truly loved him Matthew felt he yet had something, some hope, to build on for their future.

At the entrance to the Old Still public house he paused, and with a quickening of the pulse collected himself a moment before pushing open the door and going inside. After the cool of the evening streets the stone-flagged passage greeted him with a pleasant warmth scented by the smells of woodsmoke and malt and pipe tobacco, and coming from somewhere he could hear the trickling notes of a penny whistle above the background swell of conversation.

A girl came out of the saloon bar carrying a tray of dirty glasses, pushing the door ajar with a thrust of her hip and shutting it with her foot, all in one smoothly dextrous movement. She had pretty-coloured hair which looked almost apricot in the flare of the gas-jet on the passage wall, and a spattering of freckles across her snub nose.

"Excuse me –" Matthew put out a hand to attract her attention as she moved away, "can you tell me if there's a Ruby Dyson working behind the counter in there?"

"Ruby – aye, she's this minute popped out the back for some'at. Will I tell her you'd like a word?"

"No, no," he said hastily, "I only wanted to be sure I'd find her. I'll speak to her when she's serving."

The girl gave him a look and an obliging smile and went about her business, the glasses on the tray chinking together and her boot-heels clicking on the flags.

Matthew entered the door she'd just come through. At one end of the half-filled saloon there was a fire burning in a deep-set hearth, framed on either side its ingle by a pair of wooden settles, and round the walls hung oleograph prints of hunting scenes and dogs and jolly squires. The room exuded a welcoming homeliness and he felt at once easier that Ruby was working in a decent place and not in some disreputable pot-house.

Making his way across to the counter he asked for a pint of Banks's bitter and was served by a tall, handsome-looking woman dressed in black whom he took to be the landlord's wife. She addressed him very civilly, remarking on the lighter evenings before resuming conversation with her customers along the bar, leaving Matthew to carry his drink to a vacant table at the ingleside where he could watch for Ruby without being overseen.

In his anticipation he felt as nervily excited as a child. He had planned and dreamed and rehearsed this moment over and over again in his mind for so long now.

And then she came in – and it was suddenly as though the miracle of love were happening to him as never before, that he was seeing her for the first time, as a woman, in every detail clearly. She had taken to wearing her hair in a different style, pinned up on top of her head into a chignon, with ringlets curling over her ears which prettily showed off her slender neck. Her features seemed not so much thinner

273

and finer, he thought, the cheekbones more pronounced, the chin less round, giving a mature and lovely definement to her face. The change in her since last they'd spoken together five months ago was such that Matthew couldn't tear his eyes from her.

She ducked below the bar flap, answering something in response to one of the other customers, laughing; and he realised that part of the alteration was that she looked so happily contented and relaxed. Then somebody at one of the busy tables called across to her, raising their glass, and as Ruby acknowledged the pleasantry her glance strayed round the rest of the saloon.

For a second her eyes passed over Matthew without apparent recognition; and then she gave a start, the colour coming and going in her face as she stared between the shifting heads down the room at him.

Should he go to the bar and speak to her, or should he sit here and wait for her to come . . . he didn't know. Time had frozen into stillness. He had given no thought to anything beyond this moment.

It was Ruby who responded first. With a brief word to the landlady, she ducked again beneath the flap and made her way towards the hearth in a deliberate manner as though her errand were to mend the fire, all the time gazing at her husband in disbelieving wonderment.

"Matthew–" she said a little breathlessly when she drew near enough.

His throat was so tight he had to clear it before he could answer.

"Hello, Ruby."

"I thought I was seeing a ghost." She gave him a timorous

half-smile as she knelt to act out her charade of tending the coals; but after a moment she quickly had to turn her head away, betraying herself with the tell-tale sudden brightness of welling tears.

"Are you pleased I've come to find you?" he asked unsteadily.

The fire's glow rimmed her lovely profile, and only the dimpling quiver of her chin showed how hard she was having to struggle to govern her feelings.

"Aye," she said in almost a whisper, "aye, Matthew, I'm pleased."

"Can you sit wi' me and talk for a minute?"

There was a hurried glance across her shoulder towards the bar, and a shake of the head. Taking the coal tongs from the andiron she started making up the fire, and he saw the sparkle of a single teardrop fall from her lashes.

"Where, then?" he pressed. "Give me a time – a rendezvous – and I'll be there. Ruby, there's so much I want you to know, so much that needs to be discussed–" He would have reached out to touch her if he'd dared, but a crowded saloon was hardly the place and he was conscious of compromising her situation.

She sat back on her heels, wiping her cheek with the flat of her hand, and after a little hesitation answered, "I'm free in the morning. Shall I meet you in Boney Park . . . eleven o'clock?"

"Eleven o'clock. Aye, that'll do perfect. I'll wait for you by the gate off St George's Parade."

"You *will* be there – promise? You won't let me down?"

There was such wistful appeal in the way she said that, and such pleading in the look she turned upon him as she rose again to her feet that it was as much as Matthew could do to sit and endure the casual interest paid by those around and have to act as if this was only chit-chat.

He started to reply.

"Ruby! Everything all right there?" the landlady shouted across, interrupting. "If you've seen to that fire can you come and attend to these orders for me?"

"Aye, Mrs Tranter, just on my way," she called at once; then lowering her voice – "When you've finished your pint, let me draw you another. It won't look so awkward if we're talking at the counter."

Matthew watched her move from him, admiring the cheerfulness resumed for her customers as though nothing at all untoward had taken place; and when his glass was empty he forced himself to wait a decent interval before following, trying for all the world not to look like a man at the extremes of an intense emotion.

"So he got round in the finish to giving you your birthday present – better late than never, I suppose!" Ruby said afterwards with a sort of feverishly eager brightness, snatching conversation between serving. "I can't tell you how vexed I was when I found out old Byrne hadn't done what I'd asked him – after I'd gone to all the effort making sure you'd get it on the day, an' all."

"You should've gi' it me yourself, saved so much misunderstanding." Matthew retied his silk birthday scarf which they'd both just been admiring and cast a glance along the counter, where Emma Tranter was keeping a suspicious watch on him. When Ruby had explained a little earlier about him being her husband the reaction he'd received was far from cordial; but if the landlady of the Old

Still was expecting trouble, her vigilance behind the bar was wasted.

"Oh, but I *did* want to come and see you, Matt, believe me I did," Ruby assured him earnestly, signalling good-night to a couple of departing customers, "only when I never got any answer to the letter I sent you at the New Year, I wasn't certain if I should in case you might – well, y'know, not want me to."

"What happened over your letter is some'at we'll have to thrash out tomorrow when we meet, that and a few dozen other matters. There's a lot needs clearing up between us, Ruby ... a lot o' bad judgment and silly mistakes we've both made, maybe me more than you, I don't know."

For a moment the sparkle of vivacity died in her eyes, replaced by a shadowed, melancholy look as if she'd been reminded of something she'd rather forget. Then, brightening again, she gave him a nervily radiant smile.

"What made you come in here tonight to see me?"

"My mother," Matthew said, attempting a joke to lighten things. "No, I'm only pulling your leg, chick – I'd have come a damn' sight faster if it hadn't been for Mother and Dad chucking spanners in the works, creating merry hell about having a barmaid in the family. I know I shouldn't judge them, they're entitled to hold their own opinion–"

"And they *are* your parents, Matthew. You'll never have any other once they're gone."

"Aye, so I keep on reminding myself."

"What prompted you to come, then?"

"That's another thing we'll add to the list to talk about tomorrow. Joe had a bit to do wi' it though, letting me know you'd shifted out o' that lodging house in Waterloo Road. Thank God he did an' all, I'd never have known where to find you otherwise–"

Just at this point Ruby was called away to serve somebody else who had come up to the counter, and while she was gone Matthew was drawn into conversation with the pretty-haired girl he'd encountered earlier in the passage.

"I'm told you're Ruby's young husband," the girl remarked in a friendly manner.

"That's right, I am."

"Aye, she's talked about you. You in't been married very long, have you."

"Two years come June."

"That all? Well I hope you in't going to make no embarrassment for her–" there was a teasing little wink and a toss of the head towards Emma Tranter. "Auntie's been wondering whether she ought to fetch my uncle Fred out the tap-room. We're all family here at the Old Still, y'know, but Ruby's treated extra special, like, being such a favourite."

"I'm very pleased to hear it. She's special to me an' all."

"Oh – I see our Queenie's gone and introduced herself," Ruby chipped in coming back, with another nervous, over-bright smile for Matthew that wrenched at his heart. "Has she told you she's started walking out wi' Joe? I can't get over it! It doesn't seem above five minutes since I was wiping his runny nose for him yet here he is now, all growed up wi' a wench on his arm and plastering his hair down wi' macassar."

The animated way in which the words spilled out

betrayed what a state of inner agitation she was in; and Matthew had to take a hold of himself not to leap across the counter and pull her into his arms to reassure her. Tomorrow seemed a thousand hours away.

Instead he took a drink of the beer he was holding, answering, "I admire Joe's taste. He's picked the best o' the bunch, like I did," his eyes never leaving Ruby's face.

"Ooh, hark at him, he's a one for the flattery, in't he!" Queenie giggled, prinking herself and looking childishly pleased.

"No, it's truth. Flattery's for them that's insincere and want some'at."

"Is that a fact."

"Aye. And I'll tell you some'at else an' all – love's a precious rare commodity. It's like good health, you don't realise the value of it till you've lost it. Joe Gallimore's a sound lad, Queenie. You hold on to him."

As he meant to hold on to Ruby, he thought desperately, if she would let him. If she would forgive him. If she'd agree to take him back after what he had done against her with another woman.

Matthew was more deeply in love with his wife than he'd ever imagined or even thought possible. Seeing her again this evening, it was as if he'd been living only a half-life all these months, shutting and bolting his heart to keep it from breaking, fooling himself he could manage without her.

He couldn't. Not now. His feelings for Ruby were the strongest things within him, he had realised, conquering that stupid, stubborn pride which had kept him so long apart from her. But his happiness contained one fatal flaw.

How was he going to confess to her about Gatty Thompson and clear his conscience of the wrong he'd done their marriage?

21

It had been earlier on in the day, that same Saturday Matthew was at the Old Still to see Ruby, that Jack McShane slipped away from the haulage premises in Gordon Street to carry out an enterprise which, if it was successful, would relieve him of the problem of his stepson.

He went to considerable trouble that no one should witness him leaving the haulage yard. Instead of using the entrance by the stables, where he was supposed to be giving the horses their weekly 'drench' of resin and crushed soda, he took an unfrequented alley which ran along the rear of the wall on to waste ground and then past a building site.

Emerging into Steelhouse Lane he set off in a southerly direction through a maze of narrow terraced backstreets avoiding the town centre, and when he reached the road to Penn, crossed over it and started working his way north again to bring himself by an indirect route into the lower end of Brickhill Lane.

There was method in the planning of this round-the-houses journey: by going so much out of his way Jack ran far less risk of bumping into anyone he knew or who might recognise him.

At the junction of the lane a large horse-chestnut tree leaned across a crumbling stone wall, its branches sweeping down to form a pale green canopy of newly-opened leaves. For a good five minutes he stood here in its shelter observing the row of cottages further along, alert for any signs of movement at the windows, checking through his mind the separate details of what he was about to do.

He'd already ascertained that Joe Gallimore would be busy down the bottom of Mrs Finch's garden all this afternoon putting in sweet-pea sticks and planting rows of seed potatoes; that the niece, Martha Becket, was never home from the market hall before evening; and that (most crucial to his plan) the old woman herself would be out of the cottage. She had a bedridden neighbour somewhere up the lane and always went to visit of a Saturday to sit with them – a fact young Joe himself had told him, unsuspecting, after Jack had loosened his stepson's throat and lowered his guard with a couple of ales.

Waiting till the lane was clear of passers-by and traffic, he emerged from his shelter pulling his broad-brimmed hat down over his eyes, and strolled in an unhurried manner across to the gate of Ellen Finch's cottage. If by some ill chance anyone along the row came out to challenge him Jack had his answer ready: he would pretend to be enquiring after such-and-such and seemed to have the wrong address. It always worked.

Once he was in the garden and safely concealed by the thickness of a hawthorn hedge he was up the path to the door in a trice and with another look round him, trying the handle. No one secured their houses in the daytime, not in an area as quiet and respectable as this.

Closing the door again, softly, he stood still for several moments holding his breath, ears pricked for any sound of movement. He could hear Joe working outside in the back garden, whistling, the ring of his spade striking a stone as he dug; but here indoors there was nothing except the ponderous tick of the long-case clock at the foot of the stairs just in front of him.

Cautiously, every nerve on the alert, Jack crept towards the parlour door and listened again. Stillness. Nothing there. Aye, good. He edged inside the room, hurriedly scanning the portraits on the rose-patterned walls, the shelves of pretty ornaments, the doll's house daintiness of frills and lace and crochet-covered surfaces; and then finding what he'd come for, a glass-fronted cabinet whose contents caught the reflection of the window's light in a silvery grey gleam.

Steady now, cock, he told himself. Take it quiet now. Go on over, turn the knob. Ah damn it, the bloody thing's locked! You'll have to smash the glass to get it open. Use some'at – an ornament – aye, wrap it in this cap o' Joe's, that'll fix the bugger's hash for him.

He pulled out of his pocket the cloth cap his stepson always wore before he'd given him the money for a new one recently. Jack had been very clever, very cunning, keeping it by him to leave here as incriminating evidence. When Mrs Finch discovered her silver candlesticks were missing it was Joe who'd cop the blame, that was the plan; he was the only one with opportunity as well as an apparent motive. Aye, Jack had been clever right enough. He'd got it all worked out what lies he'd tell the police when they came asking, how the lad had been cussing the old woman for her stinginess, and griping about being strapped for the readies to treat his sweetheart. They'd give him five years for the

theft, at least. That should shut his face for him. Pay him
back for crossing Jack McShane, that would.

He smiled, grimly. Taking a shepherdess figurine from
the mantelpiece and wrapping it round with the cap he
smashed it against the cabinet front, splintering the
Georgian glass into jagged slivers; then reached inside for
the catch and opened the door.

Along with a fluted silver teaset and a small canteen of
hallmarked cutlery there were two pairs of candlesticks,
just as his stepson had described. Solid an' all, judging by
the weight of them. He took them from the shelf, hefting
one in his hand—

Christ, what was that? That noise? It sounded like a
floorboard creaking!

Jack leapt to his feet, grinding splints of broken glass into
the carpet, his heart hammering, eyes staring towards the
source of the sound. Somebody was out there. Somebody
was coming. He could hear them shuffling down the
passage, hear them breathing, hear a tap like a stick against
the skirting.

God alive, it must be the old woman!

Cursing obscenely to himself he looked round wildly for
somewhere he could hide. Too late. She was at the
doorway. She had seen him.

As though it were in slow motion he saw the expression
alter on her face, the faded, milk-blue eyes begin to widen,
the puckered mouth fall open in a gape of terrified surprise,
the hand dark-veined and mottled clutch at her throat.

She would know him now, he thought. Damn her, damn
her.

"What are you doing here? What do you want?" Ellen

Finch cried in a frightened voice; and time picked up its pace again and started moving faster.

She turned away from him into the passage. "Help! Thief – help!" The heavy silver candlestick was still gripped in Jack's hand. When he struck her she began to scream, a thin, piercing, old-woman scream, and tried to beat him off with her cane and her strengthless fists.

He struck her again, and again, in a panic that he couldn't make her stop that blasted screeching, his blows raining down on her head, her arms, her shoulders.

She fell to the floor and suddenly everything went quiet; quiet except for the shudder of his own breathing. He straddled the crumpled body, hand raised ready to strike again, the red mist slowly clearing from his brain, his wits returning. A crooked trickle of blood oozed from the snow-white plaits of hair; her eyelids quivered. There was no other movement.

You've killed her, Jack, oh Christ, you've killed her. What am you going to do, what am you going to do – think, *think*!

His thoughts flew every way. Glancing frantically round the room he saw Joe's cap amongst the shattered glass.

That's it. Blame the lad – aye, blame the lad. It was robbery, and now it's murder. Who's to know, Jack. Nobody's seen you, you'm too clever. Get the cap . . . that's right. Wipe the candlestick on it, there has to be blood . . . that's it, good! Now drop it here by the old biddy's hand, make it look as if her grabbed at it. Don't rush. Take things steady. Aye, that'll do . . .

He stepped over the body into the passage and listened intently. Sounds of hammering carried from the garden where Joe was knocking in his sweet-pea sticks, still whistling. Poor young bugger, Jack thought without pity, you wo' be happy for much longer, cock; but he felt no remorse at what he'd done, only a harsh relief that the lad hadn't heard Ellen Finch screaming.

Opening the front door an inch or so, he peered outside. A trap went bowling past. He waited another few moments till the noise of its iron tyres receded before he risked a second look; then shutting the door he went at a crouch along the hawthorn hedge and through the gate. Two women were standing a good way further up, their backs turned to him, talking. He took a chance, resisting the urge to bolt, forcing himself to walk at a natural pace in the opposite direction down the lane.

A few dozen yards round the corner in Merridale Street there was a drinking trough for horses. Jack paused here and rinsed the blood off his hands; then setting a faster speed, he made off by the roundabout route he'd come through the warren of back streets, his only concern to provide himself now with a cast-iron alibi.

Joe Gallimore stowed his tools away inside the shed, flexing the slight ache from his shoulders, pleased with the work he'd managed to get done this afternoon. The daylight was starting to fade, filling the garden with soft, pale, muted colour, and in the west behind the darkening silhouettes of trees the April sky had turned a lovely duck-egg green with the approaching sunset.

He wondered why Mrs Finch hadn't called him for his bite of tea yet, but she'd probably been putting her feet up and taking a rest. Generally of a Saturday she visited a neighbour in the lane, only today she hadn't been feeling too grand with her legs, she said, they were playing her up some'at dreadful.

He cleaned the soil from his boots with a stick, his thoughts half drifting off again into the reverie that had kept him company while he'd been gardening, dreaming of Queenie Tranter and what they'd be doing together tonight and how much he loved her. Joe still couldn't believe he was walking out with a wench of his own, still had to pinch himself every time she let him kiss her. She was the prettiest, softest, sweetest little thing in all the world, was Queenie; aye, the queen of his heart – she liked him telling her flowery things like that, it made her giggle.

With a catch of joy he lifted his young face to the sky and closed his eyes, for an instant suddenly happier than he could ever remember. His luck had changed at last. Even the situation at home with his stepfather was easier to bear of late, with fewer hard words and fewer blows and a little more kindness.

Aye, his fortunes were taking a turn for the better, thought Joe.

There was no light showing in the cottage windows and the kitchen was in semi-darkness when he went in, which struck him at once as being out of the usual: Mrs Finch always had a fire lit in the range by now and a meat pie or whatever in the oven for the evening meal. She wouldn't have gone out surely, not with her legs as they were. And any case, Martha would be home from work in another half an hour.

"Hello?" he called out. "Hello, Mrs Finch? Are you there?"

No answer, not a sound. Maybe she was fast asleep upstairs.

He took off his boots and left them by the outer door, and went in his stockinged feet into the passage. The shadows were thicker here, but there was just enough glow from the sunset slanting through the fanlight to see his way to the staircase.

"Are you up there, Mrs Finch?"

Still silence.

This is blinkin' odd, he told himself after he'd stood and listened for several minutes, not liking to go up into the bedrooms and yet wondering if perhaps he ought to.

He tried again – "Hello?" – much louder.

The old lady's cat ran crying past him from the stairs and made him jump.

As he turned and glanced down the passage after it, he noticed there was something showing just inside the parlour doorway. In the thin grey light it looked like a sack on the floor. The lad went towards it. And then with a sudden thrill of shock he realised what it was slumped there.

"Mrs Finch–! Oh God, what's happened – have you hurt yourself?"

Going on his knees he tried to turn the old lady over, thinking she'd taken a tumble and knocked herself cold. She couldn't walk without her stick, her legs were always paining her with the phlebitis and they sometimes let her down: he'd seen it happen once or twice before while he'd been working for her.

She was lying very still. That scared him. There was blood on his hand, blood all over the carpet by her head, sticky and dark in the half-light. She must have caught herself a right old clout when she fell – aye, broke some'at an' all, he thought, there was bits of glass on the floor and some ornament in smithereens, and one of her silver candlesticks from the cabinet here by her hand. And some'at else . . . a rag was it? No, a cloth cap, all smeared and bloody. Peculiar, that . . . what did she want wi' a cloth cap in the parlour?

A feeling that something wasn't quite right started coiling itself into a knot inside Joe's stomach. The smell of blood, a raw, sweet, sickly smell, became suddenly nauseous and made him want to gag. Seizing Ellen Finch's shoulder he began to shake her, her head lolling backwards and forwards like a broken doll's, her white plaits stained.

"Wake up – wake up, why won't you? Please, Mrs Finch–!"

A sound like a little sigh escaped her parted lips, but that was all. He touched her face. She was only slightly warm. He ought to fetch help – aye, that's it, run round the neighbour's tell 'em what's happened. But the cap drew his eyes again like a fascination, and the knot tightened into an inexplicable horror as he suddenly recognised it now as being his own, his old one, the cap he'd always worn before Jack treated him with money for another.

The room shivered in front of him as though he were looking through water; he felt dislocated from the scene, floating away inside his head, his heart-beat drumming. The smell of blood grew stronger in his nostrils, blood-flowers opening their petals in a suffocating odour of decay . . . and he was falling . . . falling into them.

* * *

When Joe opened his eyes again he seemed to be lying on something flat and hard that gripped his limbs and jolted him awkwardly up and down. He guessed from how he was feeling that he must have had another of his fits and been unconscious, but he couldn't remember anything. He never did. After these turns his mind went totally blank for a bit.

He was in some kind of vehicle; he could tell that by the way it lurched and the clop of horse-hooves over cobbles and the noises of a busy street outside the dark tarpaulin walls enclosing him.

A voice spoke near his head.

"Here, Sergeant – I think the blighter's coming to," it said; and a second voice, a deeper voice, replied – "Best check his straps then, see they'm still secure. We don't want him trying any more blasted tricks."

He felt somebody tug at whatever was restraining him, and saw above him in the shifting glimmer of street-lights the unmistakable outline of a policeman's helmet.

"What's happening?" he tried to ask, but his words were slurred and nobody answered him.

Confused, and beginning to feel frightened now, the lad started wrenching at his bonds to free himself; only to get an immediate clip round the head from a leather-gloved hand and be told, "Damn you, lie still there."

"But ... where am I? Where are you taking me?" He struggled to make himself more coherent, his fear and confusion giving way to sudden panic at his helplessness.

"You'm going to the central police station, Red Lion Street."

"The station –? What for? What's going on? What have I done?"

"What have I done. D'you hear that, Sergeant? Ruddy amazing, in't it, how they always ask the same blinkin' question after we've cotched 'em red-handed at the scene o' the perishin' crime. What's the betting he'll be telling us next he don't remember a ruddy thing."

What crime? In God's name why wouldn't they say why they were holding him?

"But I *can't* remember anything – I suffer wi' fits–"

"Don't they all, lad, don't they all. Very convenient, is fits," said the deeper voice, the Sergeant's. "If I earned promotion for every time I've heard that 'un offered in court as excuse, I'd be ruddy Chief Constable."

The police van swayed as it turned past the Town Hall into Red Lion Street.

"Right, let's have you on your feet now–"

The straps securing Joe were slackened off and a pair of handcuffs fitted to his wrists. He stood up very unsteadily, staggering a little with the effort of keeping his balance, wondering why they'd taken away his boots from him and why, if they thought he was lying about himself, they'd gone to all the bother of restraining him.

And then, like the distorted reflection of a broken mirror, his memory began returning in a series of disjointed images. Brickhill Lane . . . he was looking for something . . . no food in the oven . . . no lamps lit, everything silent . . . the parlour . . . his cap on the floor. Glass! Blood! The old lady.

Oh God! the old lady–

Joe's panic started swelling into outright terror.

"Watch him, Constable! Grab hold on him!"

The van pulled to a stop. Its back flap was thrown open, revealing the high, cruel-spiked walls of a gas-lit yard. Still struggling, he was bundled down to the ground and half dragged, half carried across into the station, protesting his innocence and crying out for someone to believe him.

22

Ruby had never felt so excitedly happy yet anxious and nervous as she did that Sunday morning. She had been awake long before dawn, lying in bed in her tiny attic room at the Old Still watching the faint, grey, glassy shadow of her casement window growing lighter as the sun rose, impatiently counting the hours till the rendezvous at Boney Park with Matthew.

Last night seemed like an incredible dream. She could hardly convince herself he had come at last to find her after all these dreary, fretful months; hardly believe how tender yet how mature he'd seemed to be. The wonderful lad she had loved and married, then foolishly let go, had become an even more wonderful man in her absence; but it had taken their separation to make her fully realise the quality of what she'd almost thrown away in exchange for her wantonly naive involvement with Jabez Reynolds.

She was still in her room and getting ready to go out, trying the arrangement of her hair in different styles, when her humming was interrupted by the noise of someone running up the narrow wooden staircase and her name being called – not once, but several times, and urgently.

The door burst open. It was Queenie Tranter.

"Oh, Ruby, you've got to come below at once—" the girl cried out, white-faced, "there's a policeman here to see you about Joe!"

Ruby's hands flew to her breast. "What's happened to him? There in't been more trouble at home, has there?"

"I don't know, but they said it was serious. Oh, come quick—"

Snatching her shawl from the chair, Ruby dashed ahead down the three flights of stairs. God, what if Joe had had another fight with Jack McShane? That was her first thought; followed at once by a worse fear, that her brother had suffered a fit in the street and a vehicle had run him over. She'd always been afraid of that after seeing it happen to somebody else.

Emma Tranter had shown the policeman through to the empty saloon bar. He was standing by the counter, a burly, red-faced constable with a bristle moustache and close-cropped hair whose intimidating presence was softened by the kindness of his manner when he spoke to Ruby.

"Mrs Dyson? I regret I've got to trouble you of a Sunday morning. Are you the sister of a lad named Joseph Gallimore?"

"I'm his sister, aye. What's this about? Is he hurt? Is he in hospital?" she asked in considerable agitation.

"He's not hurt, ma'am, no, but I'm afraid it ain't good news for you. Your brother's being held at Red Lion Street station charged wi' a criminal offence."

There was an appalled silence. Then young Queenie gave a little gasp and burst into tears, burying her face in her hands against her aunt Emma's bosom.

Ruby had gone as white as a sheet. "There must be some

mistake," she said, shaken. "Our Joe's a decent lad. He'd never do anything as 'd break the law."

"Ma'am, I'm sorry–"

"Look here, what are you saying he's supposed to have done?" demanded Emma Tranter, most indignant. In the time they had known him, she and her husband Fred had formed a good opinion of young Joe – and as publicans they took a pride in their judgment of character.

The constable picked up his helmet from the counter. "It ain't for me to tell you that, ma'am. My duty this morning is to advise Mrs Dyson of her brother's situation and take her down the station if she wants to see him."

"O' course I want to see him!" Ruby cried; and turning to Emma, "I don't know what on earth they think he's been up to, Mrs Tranter, but Joe's never been in trouble in his life, I swear he hasn't."

"I'm sure of it, my lamb. What a pity Fred's in Brummagem today – he'd make quick work o' clearing up this nonsense, that he would. He'd go and sort it out wi' the Inspector–" Emma directed a glare at the constable, "who as it happens is one of our best customers."

The constable seemed unimpressed.

Depositing Queenie in a chair, the landlady removed her apron. "I'll come wi' you down the station, Ruby. Poor wench, you can't go by yourself. You run along upstairs and get your hat while I go and roust young Albert out the cellar and let him know what's going on. Queenie! Wipe your eyes, chick. If we ain't come back by dinner-time there's a bit o' cold beef and pickle in the–"

"But I want to come an' all," wailed Queenie.

For a moment her brother's plight had driven all other

thought from Ruby's mind. Now she clapped a sudden hand to her head. "Oh good God, I was forgetting about Matthew! I'm meant to be meeting him at eleven. What shall I do? How can I let him know I won't be there?"

"Queenie'll take a message," Emma said, practically. "Give her some'at useful to occupy her while we're gone."

"Aye ... I suppose that's best. You remember what Matthew looks like, don't you, Queenie. You were talking to him at the bar last night."

The young girl sniffed and gulped and nodded.

"He'll be waiting outside Boney Park – the gate off St George's Parade. Tell him what's happened and ask him to come down the police station, fast as he can."

Ruby could have sat and wept when she returned up to her room to fetch her things. All the brimming hope and eager, anxious happiness the morning promised her on waking had gone flat, and the face in the mirror that had smiled at her so short a time ago seemed like a stranger's now.

She pinned on her hat and went downstairs again. The constable was waiting for them in the passage. Outside in King Street there were one or two who recognised Mrs Tranter and stopped and turned to gawk as they got into the covered police van, no doubt wondering what was going on; but in the station yard in Red Lion Street no one was around to watch except a couple of gaunt-ribbed dogs tied to a chain in the wall on their way to the pound.

"If you'll follow me this way–"

The two women were conducted through the entrance

door along a corridor that smelled of sweat and leather and carbolic, and into the duty room to have their particulars noted in the register.

Here they were handed over to the care of a Sergeant Darke.

"Well now, Mrs Dyson," the Sergeant said to Ruby, indicating them both to be seated and putting on a pair of steel-framed reading spectacles to consult the charge sheet on the desk in front of him, "well now, this is a serious business and no mistake. I don't like seeing a young chap of previous unblemished character go off the rails so suddenly and violently."

"For pity's sake, what's my brother accused of doing?" Ruby appealed to him, too anguished to feel intimidated either by his manner or the grey-walled forbidding atmosphere of her surroundings.

"Aye, what's the lad done?" echoed Emma. "If you want a testimonial for him, Sergeant, you only needs apply to my husband Fred Tranter at the Old Still pub in King Street, and he'll gi' you as good a reference–"

Sergeant Darke cleared his throat loudly. Looking at Ruby over the top of his spectacles, and with an occasional glance again at the sheet, he said, "Your brother, Mrs Dyson, is charged that on the twenty-eighth of April – that is to say, yesterday – at his place of employment in Brickhill Lane in the district of St Mark's, he committed a grave assault upon one Ellen Finch in the pursuance of a felony, to wit, robbery, and that–" Here he paused a little impatiently.

"Come, come, you'll allow me to finish the charge, ma'am, if you please," as Ruby interrupted him in horrified disbelief "–and that as a result of being detained at the scene of the aforementioned offence he was cautioned and brought to this station for further questioning. And may I add," the Sergeant concluded, laying aside the sheet and removing his spectacles, "that young Joseph Gallimore is extremely fortunate not to be facing an even graver indictment."

"No – I can't believe it!" Ruby cried again. "I *won't* believe it. You've made some terrible mistake."

"I must remind you, Mrs Dyson, that your brother was detained at the scene of the crime."

"If you mean the cottage in Brickhill Lane, o' course he'd be at the scene. He works for Mrs Finch, he does her gardening and odd jobs for her. But robbing her ... attacking her? A kindly old woman like that? Not Joe – no, never!"

"I'm afraid the evidence speaks for itself. Your brother was discovered not only on the premises but inside the very room in which this unfortunate lady was rendered unconscious. The person who found them both – a niece, I believe it was – summoned immediate assistance, which gives us several witnesses who'll testify to seeing Mr Gallimore in close proximity to the victim."

"But he was maybe only trying to *help* her," Ruby protested.

"With a bloodstained silver candlestick?" the Sergeant responded sarcastically. "And no boots on his feet, the better to creep up and surprise her? Hardly likely, Mrs Dyson."

Emma Tranter stirred. "Surely the lad's given some explanation of himself. What does he say?"

"He claims he can't remember. It appears he most conveniently suffered some sort of seizure–"

"He *does* suffer wi' seizures," Ruby interrupted, angry and disgusted by the Sergeant's attitude. "And our doctor will tell you that, an' all. He's had them ever since he was a babby. It's disturbance or sudden fright as brings them on–"

"Or violence? The police surgeon who examined him here at the station last night reported that your brother seemed very agitated, ma'am. Is he normally agitated after one of these attacks of his?"

She could have lied and answered yes, except the truth was quite the opposite; Joe was nearly always drowsy. Instead she responded heatedly, defensively, "If he was agitated is it any wonder, coming out of a fit to find himself arrested on suspect o' being a thief and worse? God alive, he thought the world o' Mrs Finch. He would never have laid a finger on her, never – not her nor anybody else. He in't that sort, he hasn't got it in him, please believe me!"

Giving Ruby's hand a squeeze of comfort, Emma Tranter put in an observation of her own. "It's plain to me the police haven't got round to asking the old lady any questions yet, otherwise they'd know for sure it wasn't Joe. In't that right, officer?"

Sergeant Darke pushed back his chair from the desk and got up, straightening his tunic.

"Naturally, as soon as the General Hospital allows it, we will be questioning her, aye, but for the present I understand she's still very badly concussed. Now, Mrs Dyson, if you want to see your brother for a few minutes–"

he moved round behind her to open the duty room door "–I'll have somebody take you downstairs. Not you, ma'am–" as Emma made to rise as well. "This isn't a social visit. Relatives only."

Emma muttered something, fortunately inaudible, and sat herself down on her chair again to wait.

Outside, Ruby was handed into the charge of another officer and escorted down a flight of poorly-lit stone steps to a lower corridor. Here the smell of carbolic and sweat was stronger, and naked gas-flares threw a sinister wavering shadow along the windowless walls, adding to the depressing atmosphere.

The officer produced a set of keys on a ring at his belt and unlocked a door at the far end; and a faint noise Ruby had been aware of all the time she was upstairs suddenly swelled to a wretched snivelling wail.

"Shut that racket, Dwyer," the officer ordered, going to the nearest cell and banging on its bars, "or you'll be on bread and water."

"Is he ill?" asked Ruby.

"Repenting of the drink, ma'am."

She was taken past an adjoining cell to the one containing her brother; and as soon as he heard her voice Joe leapt up from the narrow bunk where he'd been sitting with his head sunk in his hands, and came and clung to the window bars of his door.

"Ruby – Ruby, thank God!" he cried a little wildly, craning to see her. "Do some'at – they won't believe me! Do some'at and get me out of here!"

She did her best to reassure him. "Don't worry, Joe. It's all right, chick. There's been a terrible mistake–"

"I keep telling them, I found her like that when I went in the cottage. She'd fallen down and banged her head—"

"I know, pet, I know."

"But I can't remember anything after. The police are saying I did it, but I didn't, Ruby, I didn't, I didn't. Why should I want to harm Mrs Finch?"

There was such confusion and fear and desperation in that cry that Ruby ached to take her brother in her arms and hold him safe. Turning to the officer she begged, "Can't you unlock the door and let me inside wi' him? Just for a minute?"

"Sorry. Against the regulations, ma'am."

Damn the regulations! She put her hands up to the bars. Twining her fingers round Joe's, she said urgently, "Listen, tell me what happened, as much as you *can* remember. There has to be some'at – anything. What was the time you went in the cottage?"

"About seven. Aye, that's right, the sun was setting. I'd been doing the gardening, planting seed potatoes—"

"Did anybody see you in the garden who'd confirm that?"

"Maybe. I don't know. Any road, it was getting past dinner, so I thought I ought to go indoors and gi' her a shout in case she'd nodded off or some'at. Ruby – Ruby, she was lying in the parlour wi' her head all bloody – and there was my cap, my old cap—" The lad sounded dazed.

"What about your cap, chick?"

"It shouldn't have been there. How did it get there?"

Ruby couldn't make any sense of this. "But didn't you have it wi' you?"

"No! That's what I don't understand. They're saying I

must've dropped it after I attacked her – but how could I? I wasn't wearing it yesterday. I was wearing that other, the new 'un Jack bought me." His voice rose again towards panic. "I never touched her, Ruby. I swear to God I never laid a hand on her. She was lying there when I went in ... just lying there ... all bloody."

The officer took a turn round the cell room, dispassionately inspecting the other prisoner, Dwyer, whose noise had quietened to a sobbing moan.

Joe's eyes strained to follow him. "After that ... after I'd found her, all I know is Martha was shaking me and shouting, and faces gawping down at me ... and then the police van."

Surely it wouldn't have been Martha who had called the police? One of the neighbours, more likely. Martha *knew* Joe, she knew his character, knew he wasn't capable of striking down an old, defenceless woman.

"Everything's going to be all right, chick," Ruby reassured her brother with vehement conviction. "Matthew and me, we'll have you out of here as quick as we can. Try not to work yourself into too much of a state – soon as Mrs Finch wakes up in the hospital the police are going to ask her questions, and the minute they know the truth they'll let you go."

St George's church clock was striking midday. Matthew counted off the sonorous chimes, trying desperately to convince himself Ruby had said to meet her here at twelve, and not eleven.

The morning service was just finishing, and to get rid of the ache in his legs from standing still so long, he walked a little way into the churchyard to watch the congregation emerging from the porch, wishing he could as easily be rid of the ache in his heart. Had Ruby changed her mind since last night? Didn't she want to see him again, after all? Oh God, he prayed, please, *please*, not that . . . I don't think I could bear it.

After a while he wandered back into St George's Parade, hoping against hope she might have been delayed, scanning the tree-lined promenade from end to end for any sign of her, and starting up each time a solitary female figure came in view.

When the clock struck the quarter-hour Matthew ran out of excuses: plainly, Ruby wasn't going to keep their rendezvous. Right, if that's the way of it, he told himself, whatever the reason is I'm damn' well finding out. I've had enough of this.

Just as he was turning from the Parade into Bilston Street in the direction of the Old Still, a young lad came pelting helter-skelter round the corner, and colliding with him forcefully, went sprawling headlong.

"Here, watch where you're going–" Matthew exclaimed, helping the lad back to his feet. "You're in a mighty quick hurry for a Sunday morning."

"Sorry, mister, I've got a message to deliver and I'm flippin' late!"

The other moved away apologetically, and was on the point of dashing off again when Matthew reached out and grabbed him back.

"Hold hard a minute – don't I know your face? Didn't I notice you last evening in the Old Still pub?" he asked him.

"That's right. I work in the tap-room."

"This message – it in't by any chance from Ruby Dyson?"

"Blimey, how d'you know?"

"It'll be for me. I'm Ruby's husband."

The lad blew out his cheeks. "Thank cripes for that! Queenie was supposed to come and find you, but she's cried herself into such a right old state her face is all swelled up, and on top o' that she gi' me the flippin' wrong directions–"

"Never mind, you've found me now," the other cut him short impatiently "What is it you've got to tell me?"

"It's Ruby's brother Joe. He's been arrested and he's at the police station. Ruby says to go there as quick as you can, please."

Joe – *arrested*? Good God! "Which police station?" Matthew questioned urgently.

"Red Lion Street."

Shouting his thanks to the lad he spun on his heel and started running, his coat flying, arms windmilling as he swerved to avoid passers-by, down Bilston Street into Dudley Street and across Queen Square, dodging the horse-traffic, into Red Lion Street.

By a stroke of luck Ruby and Emma Tranter were only just leaving the station as he arrived; another few minutes and he might have missed them.

As soon as she saw him Ruby burst into tears of relief, and throwing herself into his arms buried her face against his labouring chest.

"Matthew – oh, Matthew – oh, thank the Lord you got my message! There's some'at dreadful happened."

He held her to him tightly, catching his breath, listening with growing incredulity as she and Emma between them poured out the story; and deep as his concern was, yet deeper still was his awareness of his precious wife, the scent of her hair, the touch of her skin, and his abiding love for her.

"This business about Joe's cap–" he said at length, when both were done and he'd asked them a number of questions, "there's some'at strikes me as odd about that. You say he kept on harping back to it, Ruby?"

"Aye, over and over again. He swears it should never have been in the place – says he'd left it back home to chuck out, and he only had his new 'un wi' him yesterday." Matthew longed to kiss the tear-stained troubled face she turned to him. "If he'd found the cap lying somewhere round the kitchen I could understand it better," she went on, "but what was it doing next to Mrs Finch on the parlour floor . . . and covered wi' blood?"

"Unless somebody else had dropped it there," said Emma Tranter.

Matthew nodded. "That's what *I* was wondering. And if it wasn't young Joe, then who? The old lady herself? Unlikely, I'd have thought. Maybe Martha, the niece?"

"But if it was the niece wouldn't she have told the police as much – I mean, as evidence?" suggested Emma, warming to him more and more.

"She might. If they'd asked her. But I doubt she would think of it herself, wi' all that shock and upset. Any case, it makes no sense her leaving Joe's cap untidying her auntie's parlour." Matthew stared thoughtfully across the police yard. "And how did it come to be so bloodstained. There's some'at – I don't know, there's some'at here I can't quite put my finger on."

"Shall I tell you what keeps going round my mind," said Ruby, hugging herself to him, comforted beyond words by the strength and safety of her husband's arms. "It might sound daft, but – what made Jack McShane go and gi' our Joe money to buy another cap when there's so much bad feeling between the pair o' them. Joe reckons it was a peace-offering to make up for the larruping he took off him. But I don't believe that."

Matthew looked down at her, searching her eyes. After a long moment he said, "No, it doesn't ring true o' McShane, you're right. The only thing he's ever give the lad is a belting and the rough edge of his tongue. Why treat him to some'at all of a sudden, unless–"

"Unless he had a purpose for it?" offered Ruby.

"Aye, my love . . . unless he had a purpose for it."

23

Jack's behaviour was beginning to get on Dorrie's nerves. Ever since yesterday morning, if he'd been into the parlour to the window once, he'd been in there a dozen times, peering through the curtain up and down the street as if he was expecting somebody. He couldn't sit still a minute. When he was in the kitchen he'd keep pacing back and forth, back and forth, picking things up and fiddling with them and putting them down; and the slightest sound of any voice out in the alley was enough to make him startle like a hare and strain his ears to listen who it was.

Another thing, he'd scarcely slept a wink these past two nights. Neither had Dorrie, which wasn't improving her temper. He kept tossing and turning, first one side then the other, and though the weather wasn't all that warm the sweat was running off him. He couldn't even manage to have sex with her – him, Jack McShane, who boasted he could satisfy a Sultan's bloomin' harem!

On Saturday night he'd come in late from work. He didn't want his dinner; he wanted to get drunk instead. So they'd gone to the Fox and Goose, and then the Swan, and then the Shakespeare, but for all the pints of ale he'd poured inside him it was wasted money: he stayed stone-cold sober. And for the first time since she'd known him he was sick as a perishin' dog coming home.

Then Sunday morning, instead of lying abed as they always did making love, he turned morose and irritable. And twitchy.

"For God's sake, Jack," she kept on asking, "what's got into you?"

"Nothing," he said. "I'm all right. Leave me alone."

Dorrie left him alone.

By Sunday night he was half-way to driving her doolally-tap.

"What d'you keep looking out the window for?"

"Nothing. Just leave me alone."

"Why don't you come and sit down and stop mooching about."

"I'm all right. Leave me alone."

Like a parrot.

She found herself almost wishing young Joe was in the house for somebody else she could talk to; but he'd gone off, she didn't know where, but she thought probably to that Matthew Dyson's lodgings in Gas Yard. He often stopped there lately.

It was a blessed relief on Monday morning when Jack had left for work. Dorrie took herself back to bed to get a decent bit of sleep, and it was nearly half past one when she woke up again. By the time she'd had a swill and dressed, the afternoon had brightened up, so fancying a walk to clear her head she went round to the Shakespeare and stayed there for an hour or so. One thing about Jack, he was generous with his money. She always had a couple of bob to treat herself to what she liked.

About four o'clock she came back to Minerva Lane, calling in at the corner shop for a bite of something for their dinner. The next-door neighbour from number 12, Mrs Evans, was in there. Dorrie's chief detractor.

"Oh," said Mrs Evans in a nasty, catty sort of way, "I think you ought to know there's been a policeman round your house this afternoon."

"Is that a fact? Maybe he wanted to ask the time," Dorrie answered her back, shoving past to get to the counter.

That raised a bit of a laugh in the shop.

"He was looking for Mr McShane, as it happens," said Mrs Evans, her face like a lemon. Nosey old bitch. Knowing her, she'd be out on her doorstep shaking her duster the minute she heard the knock. "I told him to try again later this evening."

"No doubt you made enquiry what it was about, an' all."

"Whatever the police can want wi' Mr McShane is none o' my business."

"None o' your business? Well, that makes a change, Mrs Evans." Give her half a chance and she'd want to know the ins and outs of Old Nick's backside, that one would. "Tell you what, I'll pop round later on after the copper's been again, shall I, and put you out o' your misery," Dorrie said cheekily.

She'd been pleased with herself, giving the old biddy one in the eye; but on the way home from the shop she started wondering what the Law could want with Jack. He'd never mentioned anything.

He was early coming in from work that night. The minute

he walked through the door she could tell by his expression there was something amiss with him: he looked frightened, she thought.

"Jack, a copper's been here asking for you."

He grabbed for the chair. His face turned the colour of putty.

"Christ, already," he said.

That was all; nothing else.

"Christ, already."

Dorrie was right. Jack McShane *was* frightened. He had never been so terrified in all his life. Like a rat in a trap trying to escape, his mind kept going round and round in a frantic search for bolt-holes, but every way he twisted and turned the nightmare sprang its jaws on him.

If only the old woman hadn't seen him ... if only he'd thought twice before he struck her down ... if only he'd made certain she was dead before he legged it. If only, God, if only ... ! He broke out in a muck sweat every time he thought about it. He'd been so bloody clever, hadn't he; so bloody clever making sure nobody saw him, making sure he had an alibi, making sure his plan was watertight.

Jack, it's too late now to wish you hadn't done it, but in hell's name what possessed you, man, to lose your head the way you did – not just your blasted head, your nerve an' all. And now the police have been here asking for you. Oh, dear Christ ...

The Monday early edition of the evening *Express & Star* had carried the story on its front page. Paper-sellers in the streets were shouting it, their raucous cries pursuing him like dogs on the scent of his guilt.

"Shocking assault! Elderly woman attacked! Read all about it!"

His guts had turned to jelly. It was what he'd feared the most: the old girl wasn't dead, she was in hospital, unconscious, but still alive to tell her tale. According to the news report; 'Mrs Finch's life was undoubtedly saved by the thickness of her plaits of hair which served to protect her head from the full force of the blows rained upon her by the assailant. We understand that an arrest has been made already, but police officers investigating this brutal assault state that further enquiries are still in progress.'

The sweat stood out in beads on Jack's forehead. Throwing the newspaper aside in the gutter, he'd made a bolt for Minerva Lane as if the Devil in person were at his heels.

He'd done it for Dorrie. He'd done it because of his love for her, because of his fear that she would leave him if ever she found out he'd had a bastard child by Ruby. Her own stepfather had interfered with her; he knew how much the experience had scarred her, and if she discovered he'd carried on the same . . . no, he couldn't take that chance, he couldn't risk Joe blabbing, that was why he'd done something so bloody stupid desperate.

"Jack – Jack, am you all right, love?" Dorrie exclaimed, staring at him across the kitchen table. "You've gone as pale as death. You ain't in trouble wi' the police, am you?"

He wiped the sweat from his face. His hands were shaking. "What time did they call round here?" he asked her urgently, avoiding the question.

"I don't know. I've been out this afternoon. It was her

next door–" she jerked her head "–who seen them come. They'll be back again later this evening, her said. Jack, what's all this about? I've got eyes, I ain't blind. Ever since Saturday night there's some'at been wrong wi' you, so don't you flippin' well keep telling me I'm imagining it."

He slumped down in the hearth-side chair, staring at the meagre fire in silence. Dorrie had put on a pan of potatoes to boil and a little wavering thread of steam curled about the water's surface.

"Did you hear me, Jack!" she persisted, almost angrily.

Should he try and bluff it out? Ah, the hell with everything, why not.

"All right, I'll tell you. It's that blasted Joe. *He's* the one that's got himself in trouble – thieving. Now am you satisfied."

"*Thieving*?" Dorrie's cheap little painted face seemed to sag in disbelief as she gaped at him. "God almighty, that's a turn-up for the books, ain't it? Who's he been pinching from – not the old woman?"

"Aye. The old woman."

"And the police cotched him doing it?"

"More or less." Jack stooped forward and began unfastening his leather gaiters so as not to meet her eye. "Dain't I tell you he'd kept bellyaching on about her being tight-fisted wi' his wages."

"You did, I remember it. But I never thought he'd go and help himself, the stupid barm-pot. Here – when did all this happen, then?"

"Saturday–" he began to say, then changed it hurriedly to, "last week some time or other. I don't know."

Blast it, Jack, you'll have to watch your mouth or you'll be giving the game away, he warned himself.

Dorrie stared after him, watching him get up to throw his gaiters at the back of the boot cupboard. Usually he would rub them first with saddle-soap to keep the leather supple, but her mind was too preoccupied to read any significance into his oversight; instead she said accusingly, "You knew last week, and yet it never occurred to mention anything to me? I have to live in this house an' all, you know, I think I've got a right to be told if I'm sharing the place wi' a perishin' thief—"

"I dain't want you worrying," Jack interrupted her harshly. "Now leave it will you, Dorrie. I'm fed up to the back teeth wi' the whole damn bloody business."

"*You* might be, but I ain't! I want to know just how and when you found this out 'cos I'll tell you for why – Joe was a-sitting here at this kitchen table Friday night behaving perfectly normal, and if he had a guilty face on him, all I can say is I never saw it – in fact, he seemed cheerful. Aye, he was whistling. So how d'you explain that?"

Jack's tension exploded into irritation. "For Christ's sake, Dorrie, *leave* it, I said! Hurry up wi' the dratted dinner, will you, I want to be out of here before the Law comes back."

"Want to be out? Why?" She set her fists on her hips in the prelude to an argument, still watching him intently, her expression full of narrow-eyed suspicion.

"Ain't it bloody obvious!" he started; and then catching the look, and realising he was going about this all the wrong way, he softened his manner and went across to her, pulling her into his arms.

313

"Come on now, sweetheart," he tried to coax her, "they'll only want to ask a lot o' blasted nosey questions and I don't want your name dragging into it. Tell you what – forget about cooking. We'll get us some'at to eat down the pie shop and I'll treat you to an evening in the Turk's Head. Would you like that, Dorrie sweetheart, eh?"

She could feel the heat from his body and smell the sweat and fear on his skin. His shirt was damp with it.

"I don't know as I feel like going out," she said.

He was about to urge her again when suddenly he gave a start and stared past her head towards the window. The dusk was too thick outside to see anyone moving in the yard, but he knew he'd just heard the sound of the gate latch and somebody's boots scraping on the flag-stones.

The double knock at the door when it came made him stiffen and look round him like a hunted animal.

"Don't answer it!" he said hoarsely as Dorrie went to move away. "Let 'em think we'm out."

She freed her arm. "Have you gone daft or some'at? What's got into you? The netting ain't drawn, they can see us through the window." And then in the next breath – "Hey, where'm you off to?" as he made a precipitant dash for the passage door.

"I'm legging it out of here–"

"Oh no, you'm not. My God, Jack, look at you – you'm shaking like a blinkin' leaf! You ain't *afraid*, am you?"

The knock at the yard door was repeated more impatiently; and with an angry, doubting glance at him she went into the scullery to answer it, expecting to find a policeman on the step.

Instead, she found Matthew Dyson.

The minute she opened the door Matthew thrust his way past, clearly in no mood for civility, and ignoring her exclamations went straight through to the kitchen.

The place was empty.

"McShane?" he shouted. "Come on, show yourself, I know you're about. Or are you too much of a coward to face me!"

"Here, you – what's going on, what d'you want?" Dorrie demanded, elbowing in front of him.

He pushed her aside. "McShane!"

There was a creaking noise of floorboards; then the brown chenille curtain covering the passage doorway was flung back on its brass rod and the other emerged.

Like all bullies, Jack McShane hid a craven streak beneath his braggart swagger. It was an injury to his self-esteem to be caught in the act of trying to flee, but what rubbed salt in the wound and threw him into a blustering fury was that the witness should be Matthew Dyson.

"Who the hell d'you think you'm calling coward!" he bellowed, advancing across the floor with his fists half-raised. "I'll teach you to come busting your way inside my house–"

"Shut up, McShane. You listen to what I've got to say," Matthew answered heatedly, standing his ground. "I've just come away from the General Hospital."

The other started rolling up his shirt-sleeves. "I'll bloody well put you back there an' all unless you shove off!"

"You'd do wiser to hear me first. Ellen Finch recovered consciousness an hour or so ago. Aye, Ellen Finch, from Brickhill Lane. Remember her?"

"What's he on about, Jack?" Dorrie burst in, shoving herself between them. "You never told me the old woman was in hospital?"

He didn't seem to hear her. The rage contorting his face slipped into a look which for a second revealed naked terror, and the dark blood that suffused it drained away, leaving his features glistening ashen in the gaslight.

Matthew smiled, grimly. "Oh, so he's mentioned some'at of the story, has he," he remarked. "Which half was that, I wonder?"

"He told me Joe's been done for thieving." Dorrie put her hand to her throat, mesmerised by Jack's expression.

"It's true, he has. But McShane hasn't given you the full account, I'll bet. Whoever robbed Mrs Finch, he'd tried to shut her mouth by almost killing her. It wasn't Joe."

"Has her said that? Has the old woman said that?" Jack cried out hysterically. "Has her said to the police who it was?"

Matthew eyed him up and down in contemptuous disgust, sickened by the stench of nervous sweat, an acrid musky sourness, that rolled off him. "Not yet, no. She's still confused. She's been unconscious for forty-eight hours. They're going to question her tomorrow."

"They wo' get any sense from her! Her's old, her's addled in her wits, her wo' remember!"

"Here–" Dorrie burst in again, looking at Matthew suspiciously, "what's that you just said? Her's been unconscious for *how* long?"

"Since the attack on her on Saturday."

"*This* Saturday?"

"Aye."

Her gaze swivelled back to Jack. "Saturday. An' *you* told me it had happened last week, as I recall." The suspicion in her voice hardened into accusation. "Seems a funny thing to me you couldn't say for certain."

"I said I didn't know!" he shouted at her. "That ain't a crime, is it? For God's sake, Dorrie, whose blasted side am you on?"

"I ain't taking sides. I want to keep my nose clean."

The potatoes on the hob were just coming to the boil, spitting drops of steaming water over the hissing coals. As she moved to shift the pan Jack lunged at her, catching her roughly by the arm to swing her back again.

"What d'you mean, you want to keep your nose clean? You don't want yourself mixed up wi' me in this business, is that what you'm saying?"

Dorrie tried to shove him off, but he held her fast, and giving her a little shake repeated hoarsely, "Is that what you'm saying – eh? Eh?" She was his love, his 'bit o' woman', as he thought of her, and his fear of being caught out for what he'd done was only matched by his fear of her deserting him. Whichever way, he'd boxed himself into a corner; and it made him desperate.

"'Course I don't want getting mixed up in any of it!" Dorrie said hotly. "It ain't nothing to do wi' me, I'm keeping out of it. But it strikes me as flippin' odd after the way you've been behaving this past couple o' days – I'm starting to wonder if maybe you don't know more about what's happened than you'm letting on."

"There's a lot he in't letting on," said Matthew. "In't that right, McShane. A man who's capable of molesting his own stepdaughter and getting her pregnant, then baldly denying he's ever been near her, is about capable of anything when it comes to lies and deception."

A sudden, terrible silence fell in the kitchen.

The circles of red rouge on Dorrie's cheeks stood out like doll-makers' paint as the colour fled from her face.

"Oh, didn't he tell you," he pressed on savagely, "it was him who fathered Ruby's child, the one she lost—"

That was as far as he got. With a roar of animal fury Jack McShane loosed Dorrie, and making a grab for the pan on the hob he flung its boiling contents straight at Matthew. Matthew jerked up his arm to try and protect his face, and as the scalding water caught him and Dorrie began screaming, Jack lashed out with the heavy iron pan, catching him a glancing blow that sent him reeling back against the kitchen table.

Stunned for a minute, Matthew slumped to his knees with his head singing and the skin of his forearm on fire from his soaking sleeve. In the nick of time he managed to recover his senses, scrambling out of the way as the pan was swung at him again with a murderous strength that would have cracked his skull if it had landed.

"Stop it! Stop it!" Dorrie screeched, punching and clawing at Jack. "Stop it for God's sake – you'll kill him!"

"I'll bloody kill him, all right. I'll knock his damn' teeth down his gabbing throat—"

Springing round the table in pursuit of Matthew he aimed another vicious swipe, then threw the pan aside and tried to grapple him. But Matthew's fist was already on its way towards Jack's chin, and the force of the punch jolted him back on his heels.

The next moment the kitchen exploded into stars for

Jack McShane as Dorrie, snatching at the pan, swung it round two-handed and smashed it with a sickening thud against his head. He staggered away, his legs going from under him, and then collapsed full-length across the hearth and lay unmoving.

A trickle of blood was running from Matthew's temple where Jack had clipped him, but the immediate, urgent thought was to tear off his jacket and let the air get to his badly scalded arm. Then he glanced across at Dorrie.

"Thanks," he said.

She tried to toughen it out with a shrug. "He had it coming to him, dain't he. Next time you see your Ruby, give her a message, eh – tell her from me, we'm even again. I've settled my debt. I don't owe her nothing now."

"Aye, I reckon that swipe's as good as an apology."

"I hope her accepts it that way." She paused, pushing back her frizzed dark hair; then – "Was it true what you said? About the little babby?"

Matthew nodded.

"You bastard, Jack McShane." She looked at the unconscious body of her lover, and a sudden revulsion for him seized her as she remembered the soiled innocence of her own childhood and the violations she had suffered from her stepfather.

"I'll wait till the coppers have come, then I'm packing my bags and I'm off out of here. I'm finished wi' you . . . aye, that's right, Jack, I'm *finished*."

24

The Wolverhampton and Staffordshire General Hospital where Mrs Finch was being treated was one of the several institutions which had benefited from the generous patronage of Jabez Reynolds. When Ruby arrived at the hospital early that Tuesday evening, Mr Reynolds had already been to visit the old lady and was coming away from the ward in conversation with her doctor and the Registrar.

As they passed each other in the vestibule their glances met, but apart from a slight inclination of the head Mr Reynolds gave no other sign of acknowledgment that he'd ever known her.

The encounter discomfited Ruby greatly. She was part of the jetsam of his past, as he was part of hers; but though their relationship was dead, it still remained unburied and was capable of causing mischief even yet. Loving Matthew as deeply and intensely as she did now, she was petrified of losing his respect: men put far greater weight upon the infidelity of women than upon their own. But the sense of self-worth and the honesty and truthfulness woven into Ruby's character insisted that she must make a full confession to her husband and ask for his forgiveness before her conscience would allow her any peace.

It had been both bliss and agony last night when he'd sought her at the Old Still to tell her what had happened earlier between him and Jack McShane and Dorrie Vickers. Bliss because they were with one another again, sitting in the Tranters' kitchen while she devotedly tended to his injuries; and agony because the charge against her brother had still to be resolved. There were so many vital questions demanding explanation, but none of them had been answered last night; by the time Jack came to his senses the police were at Minerva Lane putting their own to him.

Jack refused to co-operate. Swearing and blaspheming he kept asking them where Dorrie Vickers was. When she came downstairs with her things packed up and told him she was leaving him, he'd gone berserk. The two constables had had to send for reinforcements; but even then he'd acted like a madman and tried to fight them off to get at Dorrie, shouting at her, threatening, beseeching, weeping, almost incoherent.

In the finish he'd been cautioned and frogmarched down the station 'to lend assistance with enquiries', and all Minerva Lane turned out to stand, arms crossed, upon their doorsteps watching his departure.

Ruby didn't look back after Jabez Reynolds passed her, but with her chin held high continued on her way towards the main flight of stairs from the hospital's echoing vestibule. On the second landing she found the ward number she wanted, and turning in the direction indicated by a pointing hand-sign on the wall she went along a white-tiled corridor that was filled with golden evening sunlight streaming through the high, arched windows.

At the further end another hand directed her towards the visitors' day room.

"Oh, excuse me, please—" She looked round as a nursing orderly came up behind her pushing a trolley of bed-pans. "Can you tell me if it's possible to see a Mrs Finch? Mrs Ellen Finch? She's in this ward."

"You'll have to ask them in the matron's office, love," the orderly answered her briskly over his shoulder, leaving the trolley to open a swing door into the ward. "Through the day room and ring the bell at the window."

A nursing sister, equally brisk, dealt with Ruby's query in the office. No, very sorry, but they couldn't allow her to see the patient. Visits were restricted. In any case Mrs Finch's niece was with her at the moment.

"Aye, I know the niece," said Ruby. "Martha Becket. She's a friend o' mine. Will it be all right if I wait for her to come out, and have a word wi' her?"

The wait wasn't long. Mrs Finch still remained very ill and was easily exhausted. Martha came away from the bedside, walking with her hurried, fussy, hen-like gait, a brown paper parcel containing laundry under one arm, through the swing door out into the sun-filled corridor.

"My dear, I *thought* it was you!" she said by way of greeting the instant she saw Ruby. "I caught a fleeting glimpse of you a while ago from Auntie's bed."

"How is she, Martha? I was hoping to see her myself, but they wouldn't let me," Ruby said anxiously.

The other pressed her hand. "The doctors have re-assured me that she's almost out of danger, thank the Lord's mercy. But she's still very confused, which is only to be expected of course, after what she has suffered."

"Aye, o' course. Has she ... has she mentioned the attack to you at all? Has she said anything about our Joe?"

"I'm sincerely sorry about Joe. Look – let us sit over here to talk, shall we, my dear?" Martha indicated a bench between the windows opposite. "You must be concerned to know why your poor unfortunate brother was arrested. I can assure you, it was none of my doing."

"I didn't think it was. Oh, I know the case looks black against him, but he's innocent, Martha."

"That I believe, and I hope the evidence will show as much."

Ruby sat down and turned to look at her friend, her young face full of pleading desperation. "Tell me what happened on Saturday. *Everything*. The police are saying it was you as caught our Joe red-handed, but he swears he'd found your auntie hurt already when he come indoors to look for her. He's telling the truth, I know he is."

Laying the parcel of soiled laundry beside her on the bench, Martha answered in that carefully refined way she had of speaking, "I will tell you exactly what I told the Sergeant in the statement I gave on Saturday evening. I arrived at my aunt's a little after half past seven and went in by the front way as I always do. The cottage was in darkness, which seemed unusual – Aunt Ellen always lights the lamps at sunset, as you know yourself from when you lodged with us. I called to her. There was no reply. And then as I went past the parlour door, which was open, I heard this noise – oh, my dear, how it startled me!" Martha put her hand to her breast. "As if someone had uttered a terrible groan! I ran at once to the kitchen, found the lamp and put a match to it, came back to the parlour ... and there I found them both together."

"Where was our Joe?" Ruby questioned her eagerly.

"On the floor beside my poor, poor aunt. My immediate thought was that both had been attacked by an intruder. Aunt Ellen ... well, there was so much blood and broken glass ... and it was your brother making the noise which had alarmed me."

"He'd just had one of his turns. Din't you realise that?"

"It never occurred to me. I was far too shocked, my dear. There was no time to think of anything but seeking help as quickly as I could. I hastened down the path and called out to a passer-by to fetch assistance, then came inside again and did what I was able to make my aunt more comfortable. The state she was in, I feared she might be dying ... I can't tell you." Martha shut her eyes as if the memory still made her shudder.

"But you din't blame our Joe in any way," persisted Ruby.

"No, not at all. Why should I? We're very fond of him, we *trust* him, Aunt Ellen and I. In fact it crossed my mind that Joe had been struck down while he was trying to defend her. It's the sort of thing he'd do."

"Pity the police couldn't think that an' all, instead o' dragging him off and throwing him into a cell," Ruby said bitterly. "How long d'you reckon it's going to be before your auntie can describe what really happened?"

Martha gave a ladylike shrug. "Who can say? Dear, kind Mr Reynolds was here only a while ago enquiring after her – you may have seen him leave, perhaps – and I overheard the doctor telling him it might be days before her memory returns." Then seeing the disbelief in Ruby's eyes she added by way of giving her some reassurance, "But she has been asking after Tibb – you know, our cat. Which proves she must remember a little, doesn't it, my dear?"

Nothing very helpful though, thought Ruby.

She glanced down at her hands, twisting her cheap brass wedding-ring round and round in agitation. "I suppose . . . oh, I know this must sound daft, but I suppose you din't notice Joe's boots anywhere, did you, Martha? He was barefoot when they took him down the station in the police van. That Sergeant Darke reckons he'd removed 'em on a purpose so he could creep up behind your auntie, wi'out her being aware of it. I wonder . . . have the police mentioned this to you at all?"

"If they had, I would soon have pointed out to them their error. Joe's boots were by the kitchen door exactly where he always puts them when he comes inside. In fact – oh! . . . oh, now wait a moment!" Martha caught at Ruby's arm. "My dear, something's suddenly occurred to me. When I saw the boots and gave them to a constable, the mud on one of the heels was *wet* – it dirtied my cuff. Do you suppose that could be evidence?"

"What of?"

"Why, it shows that Joe cannot have been in the cottage above half an hour."

"Half an hour's more than long enough to do what the police are claiming he did."

"But don't you see? If the mud on your brother's boots was still fresh from the garden, the splashes of blood in the parlour would not have been dry." Martha's voice took on an edge of eagerness. "I noticed it especially because I

326

feared the stains would mark the wallpaper – you know how such silly thoughts pass through one's mind at moments of crisis. It's a shot in the dark perhaps, but details like this may help your brother to prove his innocence."

"Will you go and tell the police? I think they ought to know."

"I'll call at the station straight away before I catch the omnibus." Martha gathered her parcel and rose to her feet. Then with a sudden little exclamation of surprise – "Oh, my dear, look – isn't this your husband approaching?"

Ruby snatched a joyous glance across her shoulder. The golden sunset in the corridor outlined Matthew's strong figure as he strode along towards them, burnishing his skin with a glow of warmth which lit up the smile in his eyes when he saw it was his wife.

She sprang from the bench to run to meet him. Last night in the Old Still she'd said she would be visiting the hospital this evening, wondering whether they might go together; but Matthew had something else to do straight after work, he told her, and he wasn't sure what time he would be finished.

Martha had not been aware that the two had now become reconciled, although the way they greeted one another hardly left her in much doubt about their feelings. Yet beneath their affection she thought she sensed a curious reserve between them when they spoke, as if each were held by some restraint, some secret awkwardness which kept them from being entirely at ease with the other.

Whatever it was, she was both thankful and greatly relieved to learn that Matthew was doing everything he could to help Ruby clear her brother's name and trace the real culprit.

"That's clever thinking, Martha!" he said, looking at her appreciatively when Ruby told him quickly about the wet mud on Joe's boots. "The police ought to take careful note o' some'at like that, if they know what they're doing. And I've got some news of my own for you an' all—" He drew the two young women to the bench and sat himself between them. "I've been an hour or more knocking at doors up and down Brickhill Lane asking questions o' the neighbours, and d'you know what I've found out? The old lady living next to Mrs Finch, Miss Thorneycroft—"

"That's right, Miss Thorneycroft," said Martha.

"She tells me she saw young Joe working in the garden just gone half past six when she went to fill her kettle from the pump, and he was still out there at seven o'clock because she could hear him whistling. I asked her if she'd told this to the police and she said no, since they'd never thought to go and enquire of her."

"I suppose they couldn't be troubled. All they can see is the first thing that's under their noses," Ruby said heatedly. "Why should they bother looking further once they'd got a shorn lamb like our Joe to collar!"

Matthew put his good arm round her. The other was wadded and bandaged, and his forehead under the thick dark wave of hair bore a badly bruised cut from last night's assault by Jack McShane.

"Don't worry," he said, "by the time I've finished doing their police work there'll be more than enough evidence to prove to them Joe in't the one. I've got a description of the man I think they should be after."

"You know who it is?" Martha exclaimed.

"No – but I know what he looks like, I reckon. I've found two more o' your neighbours, a Mrs Bright and a Mrs Hickman – they were standing talking in Brickhill Lane about three o'clock and noticed this chap a bit further down, crossing the lane from your auntie's gate. Mind, they only got a back view of him–" Matthew paused to let a line of empty hospital trolleys pass the bench "– but he *was* a stranger, that they'd both swear to. He wasn't a tradesman. Neither could remember ever seeing him before."

"How did they describe him?" Ruby asked, her eyes not leaving his face for a second. She felt so humble, yet so proud of him, so much in love; what other man but her beloved Matt would have the wits and enterprise to do all this? She didn't deserve him.

"Well, there in't a lot to go on," he admitted. "They were some way off along the lane, but both say he was wearing leather gaiters, and a broad-brimmed hat pulled well down on his head, and his build looked fairly big and strong."

As she tried to picture this figure in her mind a sudden little shiver went through Ruby.

"Aye, I know," he added, looking at her. "It could be Jack McShane. Then again, it could be one of a thousand other men, we can't be certain. But I wouldn't put it past the wicked devil – I wish I'd had more chance last night to let him dig a pit for himself. He was frightened enough."

"And there's our Joe's cap, remember. We still haven't got to the bottom o' that business yet."

"What business is this?" enquired Martha anxiously.

Ruby told her.

"Why, yes . . . that's right! The cap was lying beneath one

of Aunt Ellen's silver candlesticks. I saw it there myself. A police constable picked it up and showed it to the Sergeant."

"Tell me – this is important – have you come across his other anywhere about the place," asked Matthew, "that new 'un he's just lately taken to wearing?"

She shook her head.

"Not in the scullery maybe?"

"No, I'm sure. Although . . . now wait a moment, he very often leaves his cap inside the garden shed. It may be there. I'll have a look this evening."

"Aye, if you will we'll be grateful, Ruby and me." Matthew glanced once more at his wife. The light from the windows touched the sweet, smooth contour of her face with a blushing rosy luminance shadowed by the pattern of the little lace half-veil decorating her Windsor hat. Each time he saw her she seemed to him even more adorably beautiful than the time before.

"Please do excuse my asking," Martha put in again, on a note of curiosity, "but if we are to suppose, or suspect, that Mr McShane might have a hand in this terrible affair, we ought to know a reason for it, surely? What motive could he possibly have to commit such violence? I mean, it makes no sense at all."

"It makes sense to *me*," Matthew said grimly. "Dorrie Vickers told me some'at last evening–" Briefly he explained the circumstances, since Ruby hadn't yet had opportunity to tell her friend about the confrontation. "The two o' them had been wanting young Joe to shift out o' the house, and he wouldn't, so they set about finding some way o' persuasion by making his life a blasted misery. Then all of a sudden McShane started changing his tune, according to Dorrie Vickers, and from half killing the lad he went to the other extreme and was buttering him up, gi'ing him money for the cap, asking him questions about his job wi' Mrs Finch and things like that."

"Joe was never taken in by it," said Ruby.

"No, but he went along wi' it. And being the sort o' lad he is, he maybe went along wi' it a bit more than he should because McShane knew all about those silver candlesticks at Brickhill Lane. Dorrie Vickers told me she and him had joked about it – if Joe was strapped for money he could always go and nick them. And as she said herself last night, that's the kind o' remark that could well put ideas in somebody's head, especially somebody looking for a way o' getting permanent shot o' the lad."

Martha's plain, pinched features took on a look of horrified disgust. "You mean ... *deliberately* contrive to make it appear as if poor Joe were the one responsible? Oh, but that's villainous!"

"Villainous or not, it convinced the police enough to lock him in a cell."

"I wonder what will become o' Dorrie now," said Ruby. "She's caused me such a lot of hurt and anger, and yet I can't find it in my heart to wish her ill. To tell the truth, I almost pity her. Did she say where she was going when she left the house last evening?"

Matthew slowly shook his head.

The last he'd seen of Dorrie Vickers she was walking away along Minerva Lane pushing a borrowed wooden handcart on which she'd loaded all her worldly goods. At the end of the lane she'd paused in the pool of yellow light beneath the gas-lamp, turning for a moment to look back towards the row of houses; and he saw her give a cheekily defiant thumb of the nose to Minerva Lane before she'd moved on again into the darkness.

"Something'll turn up for her," he answered Ruby. "Something always does for her sort."

25

For another two days Jack McShane tried to lie and bluster his way out of the mess in which his own wicked stupidity had plunged him. With a stubbornness born of fear and desperation he stuck to his story that he'd been in Gordon Street all afternoon last Saturday working in the stables giving the cart-horses their weekly drench, even though no one remembered seeing him there between half past one and four o'clock.

It had never been much of a solid alibi, and it was further holed when several witnesses came forward swearing they'd seen a man of Jack's description washing his hands in a horse trough close to Brickhill Lane about a quarter past three. One of them said they'd noticed him particularly because somebody very like him had shifted a load of furniture for them the previous month.

More damaging even than this was the testament the police had finally obtained from Mrs Finch. Despite being still extremely poorly, the old lady's wits were not so scattered that she couldn't tell them it had been some man, a stranger, who'd attacked her. Not Joe Gallimore; no, no, not Joe, of that she was quite positive.

All that was needed now was the evidence Matthew provided along with Martha Becket's deposition, to prove the case against young Joe couldn't possibly hold water. The lad was released from custody on the Thursday; and as he was being brought up from the cells in Red Lion Street he had the satisfaction of seeing his stepfather being taken down and locked up in his stead, all the snarling bombast and defiance punctured like a burst balloon, leaving Jack McShane a shambling, broken figure.

That night there was a celebration at the Old Still pub the like of which the place had rarely seen before except for family marriages and christenings, with Fred and Emma Tranter surpassing themselves in the generousness of their hospitality. No expense was spared to welcome Joe: it was open house for anyone who cared to come and raise a glass of Banks's best to him.

The first thing the lad did when he entered the saloon, his young face pale and hollow-eyed yet lit up with a grin from ear to ear, was to go across to Matthew and shake him most sincerely by the hand.

"I in't much cop wi' words," he told him awkwardly, "I wish I was so you'd know how beholden I feel to you, Matt. But since I in't, I hope you'll accept this as a thank-you for everything you've done to help – aye, an' that goes for all o' you," he added, glancing shyly round the crowded room.

Cheers and applause greeted this tribute, with cries of 'well done, young 'un!' when Matthew slapped him on the shoulder; and there were more cheers, with a few loud whistles, as little Queenie Tranter ran from behind the counter fiery-cheeked with happiness to throw her arms about his neck and kiss him.

"You don't have to feel beholden for anything, Joe," said Matthew, passing the lad a brimming pint of Banks's.

"I did no more for you than you'd do for me. Let's thank God there's folks like these and others who've gone out of their way to take your side–" and he looked at Fred and Emma Tranter, and at Ruby helping Queenie at the counter.

"No, praise where praise is due," Fred Tranter said. "I'm another as takes their hat off to your efforts, Mr Dyson. But I'll confess some'at now while I'm still three-parts sober – when Ruby come here first and the Missis and me were told about her circumstances, the opinion I had o' you then dain't amount to much. Oh aye, I admit it. Her's a bostin' wench, is Ruby. There ain't another 'un to touch her in the whole o' Wolverhampton, save my Missis here – and I have to say that, don't I!" as Emma aimed a swipe with her cloth at his balding head. "But I don't mind telling you, young man, it's beat me how a wench wi' a face as 'd make Lillie Langtry look like the back of a cart has to go out and fend for herself in the world when her's got a husband–"

"That's enough o' that, Fred," Emma interrupted, with a second, rather less playful swipe. "Sup your drink and mind your own business. Can't you see it's all been resolved between the pair o' them?"

"Aye maybe, but I think we should be told," he said, nonplussed, "is her stopping on wi' us or is her going to gi' us notice now her's patched things up wi' Mr Dyson."

"Matthew," said Matthew, taking no offence.

"Aye, wi' Matthew."

In spite of the joyful occasion, the landlord's question caused Ruby some discomfort. The last thing she wished was to put her employment here in any jeopardy, but she felt her life was in the melting-pot: what she desired most dearly was to start her marriage afresh from a better beginning, but until she'd been honest with Matthew about Jabez Reynolds there was no way of seeing ahead clearly enough to make any plans, least of all about the Old Still. Unless she made a completely clean breast of that relationship, she would always be looking back across her shoulder frightened that the past might leave its scars upon her future.

"I don't know about giving you notice," she answered hesitantly. "It in't a thought that's even crossed my mind. I love it working here, really I do, Mr Tranter, but . . . well, I suppose everything depends what Matthew thinks."

She looked at her husband. Perhaps she was being too sensitive, but it struck her he didn't seem entirely at ease as he replied, "Aye. There's a couple o' things need straightening out first, so I hope you'll bear wi' us. You never know, Mr Tranter, Ruby might not want to have me back again."

If that was meant as a joke, the way it came out sounded curiously serious; and instead of a smile to lighten the words Matthew drained his glass of beer and looked away across the room, avoiding her eyes.

For the rest of the evening he seemed very quiet. The others were too busy laughing and singing and drinking and making a grand fuss of Joe to notice anything amiss, but her husband's manner troubled Ruby. Something felt wrong. It was as if they'd come this far, and suddenly the shutters were down again between them; she didn't know why.

In between serving she tried to keep some sort of

conversation going, making a pretence of enjoying herself not to spoil the fun; but the smile on her face wasn't real. Then just gone closing-time, as she was coming away from the counter to make a start clearing the glasses from the tables, Matthew caught her by the arm and pulled her round towards him, almost roughly.

"I'm sorry," he said, "I haven't been much company. I'm angry wi' myself . . . and I wanted the evening to be so good for the two of us, an' all."

"But it *has* been good, Matthew!" she objected.

"It hasn't, my love. Not for me. There's some'at really serious I've got to say to you, and I've been scared to open my mouth in case it jumped out before I could stop it. Look . . . will you come for a walk wi' me? Now, when you're finished here? We can talk a lot better away from all this racket – and I need to be alone wi' you."

It was a perfect night outside. The soft May air still held some of the warmth of the lovely day just gone, and beyond the rooftops of King Street the sheen of a rising moon silvered the outlines of chimneys and factory stacks, lending them a graceful kind of symmetry. Wolverhampton's noises formed a background wash of sound, not loud but merged together and funnelled between high walls and alleyways and winding narrow streets to lose itself in the darkened spaces of parks and graveyards.

Matthew tucked Ruby's roughened little hand inside his elbow.

"Oh, it's beautiful, in't it," she said, falling into step with him and gazing at the velvet, moon-washed sky above their heads. "I love evenings like these, don't you, Matt?"

He didn't answer for a moment; and then he remarked as though incidentally, "D'you still hanker to live in the countryside ever? Or did Ivetsey Bank cure you o' that."

Her heart skipped a painful little beat. "Ivetsey Bank—?"

"Aye. You remember when we were just nippers at school you were always going on about how you'd one day have a cottage in the country, wi' nothing round but views o' fields and woods. I wondered, did you want it still, that's all."

She cast her mind back to her life a year ago. Ivetsey Bank had seemed a dream come true until its prettiness lost its enchantment, and its isolation turned to loneliness, and the smiling summer weather became dank and dripping autumn . . . and she fell in love with Matthew.

"No," she said quietly, "I've been cured o' the country. I'd rather stop in the town, it in't so forsaken-feeling."

"That's what I hoped you'd say." He squeezed her hand. "Aye, that's pleased me, that has. Because shall I tell you what I did today? I've been to see the landlord, Mr Hodgetts, about us taking over the tenancy o' number 11 and having Joe to live wi' us—"

Another young couple passed them on the corner arm in arm, wishing them a cheery goodnight. Ruby was so dazed she never even noticed them.

"—and if you're bothered about Jack McShane, he's out of it, he's had his notice. We could be in the house by the end o' this month if you wanted."

"If I *wanted*—!" She gave a little cry as if in protest; and thinking she objected, Matthew went on hastily, "I can understand you feeling you mightn't be too happy living there, not after Dorrie Vickers an' all, but look at it this

338

way – number 11 was never your stepfather's home, he only lodged there, aye even after he wed your Mam it was only a house to him, never a real proper home. But I'd make it different, Ruby! I'd try and clear out all those bad memories along wi' his garbage. I'd get rid o' the bed and buy us another, and put some new paper round the walls, and maybe get a few nice sticks o' furniture to make the place feel more our own. Now wouldn't you like that?"

"Aye, Matt, I'd like that," she said faintly, turning her head away. "Only..." and then her voice faltered again and she couldn't go on.

"Only there's some'at else. I know." He kicked a stone into the gutter. "I suppose you can guess what it is an' all. Well, I'm going to be honest wi' you, chick. I wish I knew an easier way to tell you, but there in't one. Any way, why should I make it easy for myself. You do believe I love you, don't you? You see that moon up there–? If I could reach it from the sky and gi' it you, I would."

She didn't answer. She felt like a child watching a bubble, a beautiful shining rainbow bubble, the kind her father used to blow when she was very small. Before this night was over she would have to confess her affair to Matthew; and that was her bubble, the dream he was offering ... the dream she must burst.

They crossed the street towards Queen Square.

"After you'd left me last year," he carried on awkwardly, "I went off the rails, I suppose. Or off my blasted head, I don't know which. I met a wench who fancied me and I started going round wi' her. Her name was–"

"I don't want to know her name," said Ruby. "Our Mam

told me you'd got yourself company. You don't have to explain."

"But I *do* – don't you see? She was more than just company, somebody to have a drink and a bit of a laugh with. She helped me to forget how much I was missing you, how much I needed you ... how much I wanted you back. Everything in my life that was precious to me had gone out the window, I thought, and I couldn't stand the loneliness o' living wi'out you, Ruby – coming home to an empty lodging at night, an empty bed. What I did wi' her wasn't right ... but it didn't feel wrong at the time. Is that any excuse?"

"Whatever you did, the fault was all mine. I should never have gone." Ruby stopped, turning to look him in the face, and the glimmer of a nearby street-lamp made her eyes seem to sparkle as they overflowed with sudden tears. "If I hadn't walked out on you you wouldn't have needed to turn to some other wench for your comfort. Don't blame yourself, Matt. I did far worse across you."

He didn't understand. His mind was too filled with his own guilt to realise what she was saying.

"Of course I blame myself! What sort o' married life did I offer you, for pity's sake–"

"You did the best you could on the little we had. It was *my* behaviour as drove us apart, not yours. If either of us acted in the wrong then it was me, by making you feel I din't want you any more."

"I've never stopped loving you, Ruby, that's the worst of it," he said, as though he still hadn't heard her. "I betrayed you, I betrayed our marriage vows to one another, and for what – pretending any other wench would do as well. I can never forgive myself for that, no, never, because it hurt us all – aye, every one of us. I'm bitterly ashamed, the way I carried on."

"But I did far worse across you," she repeated in a broken little voice, touching his face with her fingers. "Don't you understand what I'm trying to tell you?"

He caught her hand and pressed his mouth to its palm, then kissed away the tears from her eyes and cheeks.

"I understand, but I in't listening. Whatever *you've* done wouldn't make a ha'p'orth o' difference. Come on, let's find us a seat and sit down for a bit. There's one more thing I need to get off my chest to you, and after that the slate's wiped clean."

From somewhere a quotation came to Ruby as she let herself be led where he wanted to take her; 'Though your sins be as scarlet, they shall be as white as snow'. What was Matthew's sin compared with her own, she asked herself forlornly. She could forgive him ten thousand times for the little wrong he'd done, it seemed so trivial; she felt no jealousy at all now for the unknown wench who'd shared his arms and helped him bear his loneliness.

They went across Queen Square, busy with horse-traffic and people coming away from the Empire Music Hall, and into the quieter shadows of St Peter's terraced walk above the market-place. She remembered a July day two years ago, the day she'd first met Mr Reynolds to ask for a job on his stall, hanging about at this very spot while she'd plucked up the courage to see him.

It had been one of the crossroads of her life; and now she was at another, returned full circle to the selfsame place.

There was a bench – even the same bench, maybe – in a

patch of moonlight by the path. Sitting down, Ruby removed her boater hat and rested her head against Matthew's shoulder, feeling the warmth of his arms as he drew her against him.

"D'you recall that letter you wrote me at the New Year?" he began after a moment or two.

"Aye. I waited days before I gave up hope you'd answer it. Why din't you?"

"Pride wouldn't let me. And d'you know for why? I found out Jabez Reynolds was the landlord o' your lodgings and I couldn't stomach the thought you might be living off his blasted charity."

"Who told you that–? Who told you about him being my landlord?" Hearing the name from Matthew's lips made her jump.

"Somebody I asked. I went to the address you gave in Waterloo Road and catched sight o' the two o' you together in the doorway – here, what's the matter, chick?" He stopped. "You're trembling! You in't cold, are you?"

"No," she said in a low voice, "no, I in't cold. Go on . . ."

He held her closer, kissing her hair.

"I'm sorry now that I felt so angry finding him there. Maybe I could have been civil, but I'd been working myself up dreaming o' spending the evening alone wi' you, talking to you, *being* wi' you . . . and there was him poking his dratted nose in again, arranging when he'd call to see you next as if he owned you. I had to come away. I wasn't in the humour for a quarrel. No, hear me out–" he added as Ruby made to interrupt "–I haven't finished my piece. It wasn't the fact he was *there* as riled so much as the way you spoke to one another. So familiar. I half suspected . . . no, it doesn't matter, I won't say. But I felt bitter about it, if you want the truth. You know how I've always resented that man's interference. After what I've done myself, I had no right. I'm sorry. There, and now I've told you the lot."

He tilted her chin up to kiss her and seal his apology; but Ruby drew her head away, stiffening herself for the moment she'd been dreading.

"Matthew . . . Matthew, *listen* to me," she said on a little quiver of breath, "there was a good deal more to it than anything you saw or heard that evening. I don't know how to tell you. God help me, I'm afraid you'll turn against me and it'll mean the finish of us, but you've got to know. He wasn't just my landlord. He looked after me, Mr Reynolds did . . . he was good to me, and generous. I thought if I was to please him he'd be as good and generous to our Joe, so . . . so when he asked me, I went wi' him."

"You *went* wi' him−?"

She saw her husband's expression alter in the soft, betraying moonlight and for a moment, unable to continue, she could only mutely nod her head. Then gathering herself again, she choked through a fresh upwelling of tears, "Aye . . . like you went wi' that wench, I suppose. He took me to Ivetsey Bank . . . I made up the story about being in service there. I din't have to work. He kept me. I was his−"

"Don't say it. I don't want to hear."

But she had to: it was part of the self-punishment. "I was his plaything, Matt. His latest little fancy-piece."

"*I don't want to hear!*"

The sudden hurt of what deep down he'd guessed already, yet had always steadfastly refused to admit to himself, was too much to hold in check. He shook her violently; then cradled her back in his arms again and rocked her, struggling to control himself against the futility and waste of anger.

"You don't hate me, do you?" she asked piteously.

"Hate you–? God above, you're my life, don't you know that? I'd be dead before I could hate you!"

"Then can we put it all behind us? It's over now . . . hasn't it done us sufficient harm?"

"Aye," Matthew said bitterly, "it has."

Now that he'd been forced to face the truth of her relationship with Jabez Reynolds, that knowledge was something he would have to learn to come to terms with in his own time and in his own way. It was enough for him, though, that Ruby had been induced to act as she had by the selfless desire as always to help her brother.

"Even so," he went on, "a man of Reynolds's position – he *knew* your situation and yet he went and took advantage o' your trusting nature–"

"That was my own fault. It was me as caused the situation, turning my back on our marriage. As for my nature–" Ruby gave a wretched little laugh, "as for my nature, I should 've learnt my lesson after Jack McShane. I thought I was in love wi' *him* an' all. That's twice I've had my fingers burnt . . . once should 've been enough to teach me different."

A sudden intense compassion for all she had suffered overwhelmed him. "You mustn't keep blaming yourself, innocence in't a sin," he told her more gently. "And that's been your only crime, innocence."

"D'you forgive me?"

"D'you think you need forgiveness?"

"Aye," she whispered.

"Then of course I forgive you, from the bottom o' my heart . . . just as you've forgiven me, Ruby."

She turned her hot, wet face against his shoulder and was silent; then a shuddering sigh went through her and she said brokenly, "I love you so much, Matt. Maybe I've growed up at last . . . All this long time I've been hoping, longing, praying we could make it up and start our life again, because I can't live wi'out you now, I'm that far deep in love wi' you."

It was a creed she wanted to live the rest of her days by, and Matthew knew that and believed her.

With a groan he buried his face in the moonlit shining fragrance of her hair and let go of all the bitterness and pain within him. They'd been young and inexperienced, the two of them; they'd made their mistakes, and both done things which they regretted. But what was past was gone for ever now; old hurts, discarded memories, dispelled by the triumph of love over mistrust and jealousy. They had a life to make afresh together in Minerva Lane, and all the years of their future in which to know happiness.

"I love you that much an' all, my darling wife," he whispered, finding her lips and stilling their quiver with his kisses. "From this day on, whatever may betide us I'll never, ever let you go again."